ELEOS

A Book of Trials and Secrets

D. R. Bell

Also by D. R. BELL

The Metronome
The Great Game
The Outer Circle
Marshland

This novel is a work of fiction. The main characters and many of the events
portrayed in it are the work of the author's imagination. In such cases any similarity to
real persons, living or dead, events or entities is coincidental and not intended by the
author.
However, the backdrop for the story is formed by the events that took place
between 1915 and 1991 and people that lived during that time. The Commentary
section delineates which events and characters are real and which are entirely fictional.

The image on the cover is from the Auschwitz Album.

"The question of conscience is a matter for the head of the state."

Adolf
Eichmann

"Only the truth will make us free. The whole truth which is always awful."

Friedrich
Heer

CONTENTS

INTRODUCTION

The original premise for the book was a story of a German soldier saving a Jewish boy during the war and the two of them trying to make their way to safety. It was a tale of redemption – and who doesn't like stories of redemption, especially with a happy end? But as I was sketching the plot, other themes intruded. There was a personal angle: my late Armenian grandmother-in-law was the only member of her family to survive the slaughter of 1915 and I had felt for many years that there was a connection between the Armenian Genocide and the Holocaust. This led to a bigger question: how do people turn against others in a genocidal rage? Because throughout history the horror repeats time and again. My conclusion was that we choose to forget something important: even when we know "what" happened, we don't remember "how" it happened.

We view the past events as conflicts of good vs. evil. But the truth is much worse than that. Most of the perpetrators and enablers of genocides were not sadists or psychopaths but regular people. They had killed – or stood by – not out of pathological sickness but because of obedience to authority, false patriotism, career prospects, etc. The worst atrocities were committed under the guise of doing good, in the name of ideology, religion, or national status. That's why remembering the "how" is important: so we can recognize the patterns in the present. Without passing judgment on those who lived during such terrible times, we can – we must - learn from the choices they had made.

Because Eleos tries to address many difficult topics within its structure, it's designed kaleidoscopically, shifting the narrative between different characters with their viewpoints and objectives. I readily admit that the story is complex, and the subject matter is very challenging. I don't recommend it for someone who prefers a linear plot and/or is looking for a lighter read.

If you do decide to go ahead and read *Eleos*, there're two sections at the end designed to help you to understand the historical context and navigate amongst the many characters. The Commentary section delineates which events and characters are real, which are entirely fictional, and which are fictional but based on real events or people. The Characters section lists all the major characters in the story, together with a short description of each. Fair warning: the content in these two sections can end up being a "spoiler" by disclosing the connections or themes before they had a chance to emerge in the story.

DR

PROLOGUE

October 6, 1944

"Can you make the delivery to Oberscharführer Schawik tomorrow morning?"
Ezra asked.

"What if there is a transport?"

"We had no transports in weeks."

Ezra was right: transports stopped, and the great pyres no longer burned.

"Why won't you do it, as usual?"

"I can't. Hauptscharführer Möll told me to fix that oven where the bricks had gotten loose on the inside. You know how he is."

Yes, we all knew how Möll could fly into a rage at the smallest pretext. And one didn't want to be around then.

"But I don't have a pass."

"I have one for you. And here's the donation."

Inside the bag there was a gold ingot, a pair of gold cufflinks and gold earrings. The ingot bore "JK" initials, for Jacob Kurzher, one of the jewelers busy re-smelting gold fillings.

"Jacob made these cufflinks for Schawik," said Ezra. "A special gift. The earrings are for the guard. You'll be fine."

I inhaled the fruity aroma of slivovka, a plum vodka that Ezra "organized." It burned going down, chased away the autumn chill. We drank just outside our barracks: you were not allowed to be out at this time, but the discipline had gotten somewhat looser lately. Especially since bombardments began in August. Unfortunately, they bombed the IG Farben plant five kilometers away, not Birkenau. We were close enough to the door and the half-moon illuminated the path, so we could scramble inside if anyone was coming.

"I saw you whispering with Zalman and Yehuda this evening. Are you planning anything?"

"No, just organizing tomorrow's shift. David, what are you going to do when this is over?" he asked.

"I don't think about that. Nobody makes it out of here."

"But if you do?"

"Well, Ezra, if I do get out, I'll make them pay. Kill as many as I can."

"So, you want to be Raquel."

"Who?"

"Raquel, archangel of vengeance and justice." Ezra was religious and well-read. And when he drank, he became philosophical as well.

"Is that in the Bible?"

"No, the Book of Enoch. He is one of the seven angels. He takes vengeance on those who have transgressed God's laws."

"Well, he's been slacking on the job."

"But I was always more partial to his brother Ramiel, the angel of hope and compassion. He guides the souls of the faithful into heaven."

I'm afraid I snorted.

"Now, that one must have been working hard. But what a dull, wimpy name he has. Ra-mi-el." I giggled, the vodka spreading warmly through my body and my brain.

"You don't like Ramiel? How about Eleos?" I could almost see Ezra smile. "From Greek mythology. Eleos, the goddess of mercy and compassion."

"That's better."

"Why?"

"I don't know. I think of compassion, I think of a woman. And I like the sound: E-le-os. Rolls off the tongue."

"Very well," Ezra agreed. "Eleos if you prefer. You think you can change people with compassion?"

"Don't make me laugh, Ezra. All the compassionate people I've met here are dead. Next, you'll tell me about the merciful G-d that won't let innocents suffer. I've seen very little compassion lately."

"But what compassion you saw was that much more precious," Ezra said. "It was a German bricklayer that helped me to survive the first month. And you would not be alive if you had not met some compassion along the way."

"For each small act of compassion, there were hundreds of cruelties."

"You're right, David." Ezra poured us the rest of the slivovka. "But perhaps you think of compassion too narrowly. To save a life is an act of compassion. To punish a murderer is also an act of compassion, especially if it prevents another murder. We must remember those that helped. And those that killed. Anyway, don't forget to go see Schawik in the morning."

PART 1:
AVI

1

"Well, this is it," said Erik Babayan, after carefully leaning his surfboard against the fence. "Your late uncle's house." He was a solid-built man about fifty with sharp angular features, thin mouth, curly black wet hair with a bit of gray in it. An overweight version of Tom Petty in swimming shorts, a Hawaiian shirt and sandals. Normally, you would expect a lawyer to wear a suit, but Hermosa Beach was a very laid-back place. Babayan did carry a green folder under his left arm, giving a slight hint of being a professional.

"You've never been here?" He must have read the expression on my face.

"No."

"Hmmm, the man was your uncle."

"We were not close. I did not even know he was back in town, until the funeral notice."

"He was in jail in Europe. They let him go when they figured out he was dying and had a few weeks left. Didn't want to create a martyr, I guess."

"How did he find you?"

"It was his father who found me thirty years ago. Walked into my office and said: 'My name is Aram Arutiyan. You're the nearest Armenian lawyer and I want to make my will.' I had just opened my practice in the office on Pier Avenue, a five-minute walk from here."

"That was my grandfather."

"Yes."

"Did he leave everything to my uncle?"

"Not quite. Your father was the primary beneficiary. But there were conditions attached, and your father decided not to pursue his part. Your uncle had no heirs. He left everything to you, his closest living relative. Of course, 'everything' is this house and a few hundred dollars in the bank."

We were standing on a small street connecting Hermosa Avenue with The Strand on our left, where throngs of people were walking, rollerblading, bicycling. Beyond them was the beach and then the expanse of the Pacific Ocean. You could hear the breaking waves. Despite this being January, the day was sunny and warm, quite a contrast to the cold drizzle of Seattle.

The front of the house could not have been more than twenty-five feet wide, about a third of it taken by the garage and the rest by a small porch with a rusty beach chair. On the right side there was a similar small house, and then what looked like an apartment building. On the left the house abutted a narrow alley, followed by a two-story house that faced The Strand.

"It doesn't look like much, but it's only half a block from the beach. Some developer back in the fifties took regular-size plots, divided them in half and built small narrow houses shaped like wagons." Babayan shrugged. "Shall we go inside?"

The door opened right into a living room with a kitchen. The walls were plain off-white but with a tint of dirt. The wooden floor looked discolored with age and badly chipped, as it creaked under our steps. The furniture consisted of a couch, a table and three chairs, all from a different era. The kitchen was separated by a breakfast nook. I could see a big black spot over the stove and the two kitchen cabinets near it looked burned. There was another door on the right: I opened it and found myself in a dark one-car garage, which had no car but a lot of junk. The place gave out a stale smell of urine, ashes and motor oil.

"Well..." Babayan sniffed. "Your uncle was renting the place out while he was gone, and that did not always work out."

I shut the door and followed Babayan down a hallway. There was a bathroom on the left and two bedrooms, one on each side. One of the bedrooms had a single bed, a desk and a chair; the other was empty except for a mattress on the floor. Babayan opened the door at the end of the hallway, and we found ourselves in a tiny fenced backyard decorated with two dead plants and a chipped ceramic table with one chair. In the house across the alley the garage was open, and I could see a man standing by a Corvette. The lawyer waved to him.

"When did my grandfather buy this house?"

"Back in 1961. Sarkis inherited it in 1965."

"Grandfather was killed in Germany then. A robbery." I was not even four years old when it happened, but I remembered that year. Grandfather's not fully explained death changed the family, and not in a good way.

"And your uncle went to jail in France a few years later. Your family should avoid that part of the world," Babayan commented wryly. "Look, there is a bit of bad news. You see, the property taxes have not been paid in some time and the county wants to seize the house. You have a couple of months to come up with the payment."

"How much is owed?"

"Because of penalties, just under six thousand. It's all here." Babayan handed me the green folder.

"Can you help to reduce penalties?"

"You'll just waste your money trying. There is no mortgage, so when you fix up the house and sell it, you'll walk away with a quarter million at least."

He just assumed that I'd be going back to Seattle. Except that I had no good reason to go back.

I saw Babayan out and wandered through the house, trying to imagine myself living here. I grew up in West LA, spent the last eleven years in the Pacific Northwest. This was a different world from both. I went back to the courtyard and was about to open the folder that Babayan left, when someone called out to me.

"Hey." It was the man from across the alley. "Are you moving into this house?"

"I don't know yet. Just inherited it from my late uncle."

"I see." He came to the fence and offered his hand. "Jack Burns, your potential new neighbor."

Jack had a big, rhythmically moving gum-chomping jaw. Above the jaw there was a round big-nosed, full-lipped reddish face ringed by curly dark brown hair. The hand I shook was as meaty as the rest of him, except for the disproportionally small ears. He looked to be in his late thirties.

"Avi Arutiyan."

13

"Why don't you come over, Avi? Have a beer with me? We'll sit in the front, watch the girls go by on The Strand."

There were indeed tons of girls in bikinis walking, rollerblading, biking past the house. Jack seemed to know quite a few of them.

"How long have you lived here?" I asked.

"Almost ten years. Bought it in 1981. I came to the area a few years before that, when I took a job with TRW. It's a local aerospace company."

"I know. Are you an engineer?"

"Yes."

"Me too. I worked for Boeing in Seattle until recently. You could afford a place on the beach on an engineering salary?"

"Well, not quite." Jack laughed. "My dad left me some money. I always wanted to live on the beach. So, you are not sure that you'll keep the house?"

"I'll have to think about it. It all happened quickly. I lived in Seattle for eleven years, but things have changed."

"A woman?"

"Yeah."

"Got it. I stay away from complicated personal stuff." Jack nodded. "Been married once, that was enough. Listen, if you decide to sell, let me know. I'd love to buy it."

"Really?"

"To be honest, your house had been a bit of a problem. It was often vacant, so squatters moved in. Two years ago, they started a fire. Police would evict them, they would find a way to sneak back in. It was a pain in the butt."

"Hey, Jack!" Three bikinied girls stopped in front of us.

2

"Is it really over between you and Amy?" Mom avoided looking at me as she tried to pick up her take-out fried rice with chopsticks. "I heard you talking in your sleep last night."

"Yes, it's over."

"Perhaps you should try again? You've been together for twelve years …"

"Only ten, Mom, only ten."

Amy and I met in the summer of '79, the year that my family fell apart. In May, my older half-brother, Tigran, came back from Lebanon in a closed casket. Father aged quickly after that. In July, I ran into Amy at a party. She came down from Seattle to visit her friends. In September, instead of enrolling in UCLA, I packed a bag and moved to the Pacific Northwest. From then until our breakup in May of 1990, it was ten years and eight months. At least that was how I counted it.

Mother gave up and put the chopsticks aside. "In any case, it was a long time …"

"Mom, why are you digging?"

"Avi, I just worry about you," she said, her eyes getting moist. "I know it hurt you. Perhaps you two may want to try again."

That's what moms do to you. They worry, and it becomes your fault because you must fix whatever it is that worries them. Amy had given me a few of those "I'm OK, you're OK" or 'I'm OK, you're not OK" lectures about us being responsible for our own feelings, blah, blah, blah. I wondered at what point these talks were meant to prepare me for her departure.

"Mom, it's been eight months since we broke up. And she's pregnant. By another man."

I first asked Amy about having a baby five years ago, after I finally finished college and got a job at Boeing. She said we were too young; she was just getting going in her career at one of those giant department store chains. She was now engaged to their executive vice president. He came from the family that founded the chain and lived in a giant mansion on Bainbridge Island. I saw it when in one of those angst-filled days I took the ferry and parked my Datsun across the street. Until a cop car pulled up and started asking questions. Someone in the house must have called. Amy went from a wild skinny-dipping teenager to a trophy second wife, and I somehow missed the transition.

"So, are you coming back to LA?" Mom must have decided to stop with questions about Amy.

"Yes, I figure I am."

I'd thought about it for the last few nights. I needed a change, and there was nothing of substance keeping me in Seattle. The prospect of living by the beach sounded good. Especially next to a neighbor who knew a lot of local girls.

"I guess I won't be moving to New Jersey then." She smiled. She had a sister in one of those leafy New York commuter suburbs. "How are you doing on money?"

"I've got a bit of savings plus a severance package." Now that the Soviet Union had collapsed, the country was enjoying a "peace dividend." For some of us in the defense industries, this meant layoffs. Mine was two months ago, an accidentally good timing.

"Is Grandpa Aram's house a money pit?" I noticed she said "Grandpa Aram" instead of "Uncle Sarkis," even though Grandpa had been dead for over twenty-five years.

"It's not too bad. And I like the area. So different."

After all these years, my parents' old house no longer felt like home. I grew up in what Dad jokingly called the slums of Santa Monica, halfway between the UCLA campus where Mom worked and downtown Santa Monica where Dad worked. The area had a college feel to it because the north-south streets were named after famous universities: Princeton, Harvard, Yale, etc. Four blocks north of us, beyond Wilshire Boulevard, lived the really rich people. All quite different from the vibe of Hermosa Beach, the vibe I wanted now.

I flew back to Seattle, cleaned out the apartment. Anything that would not fit into my Datsun, I gave to the neighbors. Except for a few of Amy's things, which I mailed to her new place on Bainbridge Island. I ignored her voice mail and pointed the car south on Interstate 5. I did it all without slowing down to think, afraid that if I stopped, I'd lose my nerve. It was only after I crossed the Columbia River Interstate Bridge and found myself in Oregon that I pulled over. I sweated and had difficulty breathing, suddenly overcome with the fear of making a terrible mistake. I wanted to turn around and retrieve the box of pictures of Amy and me. I failed to include the box in the package of her things. Unable to decide whether to mail it or throw it away, I placed the box on the side of the stair landing and forgot it there. If I could only get that box, the last year could be rewound like a VHS tape. A knock on the window broke the spell: it was an Oregon state trooper asking if I was OK. I rolled down the window, assured him that I was indeed just fine, and drove the remaining nine hundred miles south to start a new life in the old place.

I emptied my IRA to pay the tax bill, did a quick cleanup, installed new locks, bought furniture —made it into a place that I could actually invite someone to. There were no outward signs of Amy in the place. I wondered sometimes what happened with the box of pictures that I left on the landing. Did the neighbor look through them with the guilty pleasure of spying on someone she knew? Or did the box go straight to a landfill, a part of life thrown away?

I had only four pictures left, the ones I took with me in 1979. One in color, taken in 1976: Tigran and I, taken by one of his girlfriends. I'm fifteen, he's thirty-three. We're leaning against his Ford F-250 truck parked in the driveway of the Wellesley Street house. We are in shorts and identical Hawaiian shirts that he bought, laughing, not a care in the world. Three others are older black-and-white photos. In one, my parents and I are in Disneyland for my fifth birthday. They both are smiling, but my father's smile already had sadness to it. The last two were taken on my third birthday on the bluffs in Santa Monica: my mother, her parents and I in one shot; my grandfather Aram, my dad, Tigran and I in the other. Mom had a photo of all of us taken that day, but I liked those two because I could see the faces much better. Of course, Mom had tons of pictures: an album of my baby pictures, a wedding album, an album of my school years, and more. But these four were the ones I chose.

17

I enjoyed the beach lifestyle of hanging out with Jack, dating local girls. Jack was careful with his money, but generous with things that didn't cost him anything: he let me park my car in his driveway, introduced me to his female friends. He didn't seem to have many male friends, so usually it was the two of us and the girls. There was a certain "beach culture" feel to the place: fun, leisurely, not too serious. I went to bed with one of the girls and it was nice. Yes, I saw Amy as I entered the girl and closed my eyes, but it didn't hit me nearly as hard as in prior months; it was more of a delicate sadness of a loss, a melancholy of something wonderful that was and is no more. The girl was pretty and bubbly and wanted to go out again, but I felt no real connection and politely declined.

Not quite ready to seriously look for a job, I methodically worked on the house instead: while not much of a handyman, I could do the basic stuff. My days didn't have a purpose save for completing a small mental to-do list that I compiled in the morning: make breakfast, sand kitchen cabinets, go for a walk, do some shopping, eat lunch, read, prime kitchen cabinets, and on and on. I'd been trying hard—and not very successfully—to not think about the future. By mid-March, the main unfinished item was cleaning out the garage. I had the bulkiest trash removed, but there was still a lot of stuff piled up against the walls. On a rare gloomy morning I bought a box of trash bags and rubber gloves, opened the garage door and went to work. I was not looking through things, just picking them up and throwing them into trash bags: moldy blankets and sleeping bags, cushions and pillows, ancient appliances.

Nested against the wall, I found a briefcase-sized blue valise made of hard plastic. I lifted it and was about to dump it into a bag, when the rusted clasp gave way and three yellowish notebooks tumbled out. I picked up and opened one of them. It was addressed to Aram Arutiyan, my grandfather. Careful handwriting opened with:

Frankfurt, 15 October 1964

Dear Aram,

In Carcassonne, six months ago, I told you "no, I am not a writer." And even if I was, how does one write about the events that I witnessed and took part in? …

I left the trash bags where they were, took the three notebooks inside, deposited them on the dining table and began to read. The man that wrote them was telling about his life, but it clearly intertwined with my grandfather's story right before grandfather's mysterious death.

PART 2:
DAVID

Frankfurt, 15 October 1964

Dear Aram,

In Carcassonne, six months ago, I told you "no, I am not a writer." And even if I was, how does one write about the events that I witnessed and took part in? And yet your request burned inside of me and I gave in to it. Perhaps somewhere, somehow it would help us—me—to find a meaning in these events. Because that's what I find the hardest: I can't fathom the meaning.

Nor can I claim that I am just presenting facts; my memory is far from perfect. From a distance, some memories are like Degas' paintings capturing the essence rather than its elements; others stand out in suspiciously bright detail. If not for the diary that I've kept—albeit without much discipline—my memory would have failed me completely. Once I began, I found it to be somewhat therapeutic. Cathartic, if you will. I chose English, your adopted language. It's not my best language, but it did seem the most appropriate here. I certainly couldn't—wouldn't—write in German. I hope you forgive the awkwardness of my prose. I am not accustomed to this. Some people's writing is like poetry. I don't have this gift. Like I didn't have Leah's gift of extracting beautiful music from a violin. I just wrote down what I remembered—events, conversations, dreams, thoughts. Frank and unfiltered: I am not a good man, I won't be a dishonest one on top of it.

I don't know yet how to answer the question that you posed when we were having dinner with your sons, Vrej and Sarkis: "What must we do now?" This question—and the debate between you and Ruben Matusian—keeps coming back to me as I attend the sessions of the Auschwitz trial taking place here in Frankfurt: What must we do with them? These now perfectly respectable men that twenty years ago ran the industrial death factory. Some people, especially here in Germany, say that we must forgive them. But so far, I found no forgiveness in my heart. Your friend Ruben argued that only the law can save us from recurrence of the horror. But the penalties that the law's been meting out are so unsuitable to the crime as to be laughable. You believe in biblical retribution—but where does that end? I'm torn.

Please forgive my skipping around. I tried to avoid unnecessary details and descriptions. You have my permission to edit this if you choose to publish the story in any shape or form. And if you think that this is not worth continuing, I trust you would honestly let me know. I don't want to waste your time with these amateurish scribblings.

With warmest wishes,

David Levy

P.S. Your associate Levon came to visit me from France. As we discussed, I will put him in touch with a friend of mine that's involved in the black market. I believe that he can help you procure the kind of military supplies that Levon is looking for. I didn't ask Levon how the equipment will be used, but I suspect you're planning on some measure of retribution for the wrongs committed against your people.

1

I remember exactly how I met Yosef Milman, on a typical rainy March afternoon in Jerusalem. I couldn't see the rain from my tiny windowless basement office, but blustery wind and heavy clouds in the morning left no doubt as to their intent to drench everyone who dared to go outside. Milman slowly opened the door after I responded to a gentle knock with an irritable, "Yes?" He carefully stepped inside and stood near the entrance. He was wet below the waist but mostly dry above, indicating that he had an umbrella, which he considerately did not bring into my office. A small puddle quickly formed around his soggy shoes. His face was composed into a guilty 'I'm sorry to trouble you' smile. He reminded me of Ori, the Labrador retriever dog that my neighbors had recently acquired.

"David Levy?"

"Yes." Normally I would have pointed out the stupidity of the question, since the door had a handwritten nameplate, but I had a decent five-hour sleep the night before and was in a relatively good mood.

"Yosef. Yosef Milman."

He looked to be in his early thirties, a bit on the tall side but not overly so, receding blond hair, thin fingers nervously fingering a checkered tweed cap. A comfortable paunch stretched a light blue shirt under an unbuttoned brown woolen jacket. Rather inconspicuous appearance except for a Kirk Douglas-like prominent cleft chin. There was an awkward silence, as he must have been waiting for me to say or ask something.

Then he offered, "The blond woman in the reception told me where to find you."

With that, my good disposition darkened. *Ruth.* I wasn't getting along with her after I declined her advances three months ago. I wasn't getting along with most of my co-workers, and that didn't bother me. But Ruth found a way to annoy me by directing most of the strange visitors to the museum to my office. And we had our share of strange visitors. Especially now, in 1961: they held on to their memories for sixteen years, but the upcoming Eichmann trial opened all sorts of mental floodgates.

"Why?"

"You work on stories about people that saved Jews during the Holocaust, right?"

"Not really." I wanted to get rid of him but figured he would go back to Ruth and she'd report on me and I didn't need that. There were complaints already about my lack of cooperation with the police on the Eichmann investigation. So, I grudgingly allowed, "Well, sometimes."

He was still standing by the door, the puddle by his feet growing larger.

"Sit down." I pointed to the simple wooden chair in front of my desk.

"Thank you." He gingerly pulled out the chair so as not to scrape its legs against the floor, delicately sat and looked at me. For a rather large man he moved cautiously and deliberately.

I opened my notebook and prepared to write.

"Who were the persons saved?"

"I was."

"And you were saved by whom?"

"A German soldier. An SS officer."

I gave him a more careful look. Because of the jacket, I couldn't see whether he had a number tattooed into his arm.

"Where and when did it happen?"

"August of 1942, in Rostov-on-Don." Yosef looked past me, into the corner of the room as if seeing something there, then added, "That's where it started."

"What do you mean started?"

"He brought me here."

"Here where?"

"Here, to Israel. Well, Palestine back then."

26

I paused writing and stared at him, looking for an outward sign of a joke. He just sat there calmly. We didn't get many jokesters, but we had our share of "confused" visitors. As my ex-boss pointed out to me once, traumatic experiences sometimes blurred the line between imagination and reality, between the past and the present. Then he—my ex-boss—caught himself.

I put down the pencil, leaned back in my chair.

"Mr. Milman, are you telling me that an SS officer saved you and then brought you to Palestine?"

He chewed on his lip. "Yes. Well, not quite. But almost."

"Do you know his name?"

"Arno. But his nickname was Prinz. That's what some people called him."

"What about his last name?"

Milman shrugged. "I don't know."

"Which town was he from? His military unit? Anything to help identify him?"

"Hmmm … He was in his early twenties, a scar on his left cheek. Oh, he had connections in Turkey."

"Connections in Turkey?"

"Yes. I mean, there were people there that knew him well."

I studied him some more. Probably made up the whole story as a defensive mechanism. He looked completely normal and calm, but that was what people did. The best course of action was to pretend that you believed them, and gently get them out of your office.

"Mr. Milman, I have a meeting in a few minutes. If you leave your contact information, we'll be in touch."

I pushed the notebook and a pencil to his side of the desk and watched him write, carefully scripting each letter with nicotine-stained fingers.

"I work for the Ministry of Posts, so I have a telephone," he said guiltily, as if apologizing for having this luxury. I figured he apologized a lot. He returned the notebook and got up to leave.

Just before disappearing, Milman turned back and said, "We should remember those who helped, right? Not just the murderers like Eichmann?"

Pretty much exactly what Ezra said to me over sixteen years ago.

We stared at each other for a moment.

Milman closed the door behind him as carefully as he opened it a few minutes before. I looked at the notebook. He was in Ir Ganim Aleph, a short walking distance from me.

I told Hannah about Milman two days later.

She sat up in bed, lit up a cigarette. Hannah was one of very few survivors whose identity number was tattooed over her left breast. Mine was more typically placed on the left arm. That was how we recognized each other, the ones from Auschwitz. The one and only *Lager* where they branded people with tattoos. Tattoos were reserved only for those sent to the right on the train platform. The majority, the ones sent to the left, didn't need tattoos—in a few hours they floated down from the sky as a bitter ash. People now call those places "camps." These were not camps. There are summer camps, fishing camps, sports camps. These places were *Konzentration Lagers*, in a rough, German language as it was practiced there.

"Do you think he is making this up?" She tipped ash into a small wooden ashtray I kept on my bedside table. The ashtray was for her. I don't smoke. I don't like the sight of smoke.

"I don't know. Sounds too fantastic. Hard to believe. But it's stuck in my head."

"Dovid, Dovid …" Hannah shook her head. Sometimes she used the Yiddish pronunciation of my name, even though I avoided speaking Yiddish now. "Have you learned nothing? Things that are impossible to believe, they are the ones that happened."

"The trial brings out all kinds of crazy stories."

"Ah, the trial. Everyone is worried about it. How will it go? Will there be international backlash? And on and on."

"They didn't give a damn about us during the war, they didn't give a damn for fifteen years after, but when we grab Eichmann, it's backlash-time. And you, are you worried?"

"No. What worse things could they do to us?"

She stamped out the cigarette, got up. Sixteen years after the *Lager*, she was still thin, bones protruding through the skin. After the war, I tended towards hefty women. Hannah was the only exception.

"Are you going to Ludwigsburg?"

28

Last time I saw her, we talked about what it would be like to go to Germany. Two years back the West Germans set up a commission for investigation of Nazi crimes. Like most official German things, it had a long and unpronounceable name, so we referred to it as a *ZS Commission*. Their central office was in Ludwigsburg, just north of Stuttgart. Recently we had a visit from Dietrich Zeug, a German investigator for the trial of SS officers and guards that served in the Chelmno extermination camp. I was asked to liaise with them and to personally deliver our report. *Because your German is so good*, I was told.

"I don't know yet. Probably in a couple of months if I agree." I didn't want to think about it now. "Why don't you stay? It's almost midnight."

"You know why. You've been asking this question for what—ten years now? You don't even mean it."

She was right, I didn't mean it. I didn't really want her to stay. Getting sleep was hard enough. I didn't want anyone next to me.

"Don't worry, I have only a few blocks to walk. Besides, you'll scream and wake me up if I stay," she added. Hannah swore she'd never again lose anyone close to her. One way to make sure of that was to not let anyone get close. Something that I could understand.

"But can I take a shower before I go? My apartment has had no hot water for two days."

She called out from the bathroom, "Do you have a new bar of olive soap? This one is almost gone."

"Yes, look in the cabinet. Second shelf."

Hannah wouldn't use any soap made with fat, so I kept a bar of olive soap just for her. It was a myth that Nazis made soap in Auschwitz, but it was so popular that *sabras*, the native Israelis called us survivors *sabon*, soap in Hebrew. It was an unkind, disrespectful term. You could recognize most of the *sabons* by a certain haunted look, as if always expecting a blow.

She took a quick shower, came out still drying herself off with a towel, didn't bother with the underwear, and pulled a dress right over her naked body.

"What's his name again?"

"Whose name?" I didn't immediately understand.

"The man who came to see you with that story of being saved by an SS officer."

"Yosef. Yosef Milman."

"Yosef," she repeated, eyes staring past me. She'd had a brother named Josef. They separated them on the platform. "And he lives here, in Jerusalem?"

"Yes, in Ir Ganim."

"OK, I'll look him up." She nodded.

Hannah worked in the Ministry of Foreign Affairs and she could find things about people.

"Why?"

"To help you. I mean, you're supposed to investigate these kinds of stories, right? You told me that."

She reached into her handbag. "I brought you something. A pass to the trial."

"I … I don't know …"

"It's up to you. You don't have to go. But these are hard to get."

I saw her to the door, then went to the bathroom. Somewhat prematurely, I'd reached the age where it was necessary to empty my bladder before going to sleep. When I complained to my doctor about this last year, he looked at me over his glasses and shrugged. "David, I know that nominally you are thirty-five, but each year in a *Lager* counts for at least five. So as far as I am concerned, you're pushing fifty. Don't complain." He also used *Lager* instead of "concentration camp," he was from Germany.

Ezra came later, sat on the edge of the bed.

"Can't sleep, David?"

"No."

"The roosters will go off soon."

"I know. My brain keeps going. You said we must remember the ones that helped. What did you mean?"

"Don't think about it right now. You need your sleep. I'll sing you a lullaby. *Fa la ninna, fa la nanna, nella braccia della mamma, fa la ninna bel bambin …*"

Despite being Italian, Ezra couldn't sing at all. But his scratchy voice did lull me into uneasy sleep, just enough to let my mind rest. I was no longer capable of deep sleep, always ready to jump up at any sound.

Hannah rang me up at work a few days later.

"A woman for you." Ruth the receptionist smirked as she handed me the phone.

"I had someone check the files on Yosef Milman." Hannah usually didn't not bother with "hello."

"And?"

"He came to Palestine from Lebanon in September of 1942. The British sent him to the Atlit detention camp, but he was released shortly as the camp was shut down …"

"Shut down? I was there in 1945!"

"The British reopened it after the war ended."

"So, if he somehow escaped from the Nazis when they occupied Rostov-on-Don in August …"

"Yes, the timing works." I could almost see Hannah nodding impatiently. "Assuming he managed to cover fifteen hundred miles in five weeks. But there is something else. The British made a note that he had Turkish papers, and that he claimed that there was a German officer with him who disappeared before reaching Palestine. They were concerned about the officer being a spy for Rommel."

"Anything else? Did they find the officer?"

"No, they didn't. Are you going to call him?"

"Who?"

"Milman."

"I was not planning to. Why do I need this headache?"

"*Tachat*," Hannah swore. "You're an ass. Why are you still at the museum if you stopped giving a damn? If your heart is not in it, move to a kibbutz, grow olives or whatever. Do something useful!"

I was still at the museum precisely because I did not want to go back to the kibbutz life. And that was how I ended up researching Yosef Milman's story.

I called Milman from Mah Zahl, a cafe in Kiryat Shmuel that I frequented, a hole in the wall with eight rough wooden tables and a small kitchen. Moshe, the owner, let us use his phone for local calls. Jerusalem was a city of cafes: Café Rehavia in the center of the city, Café Vienna on Jaffa Street, Café Europa on Yehuda Street, and others. Most of them quiet, refined, European. Mah Zahl was different, more like a noisy restaurant. Moshe put his own spin on

Mizrahi cuisine: vine leaves stuffed with minced lamb or beef, lentils, chickpeas, baklava. Moshe's food was good, and the place was usually full. Still, he always reserved one table for us, a small group of *sabons* like himself.

"Shalom?" a woman's voice answered questioningly. I could hear the noise of a loud discussion in the background.

"Shalom. I am calling for Yosef Milman."

"Who are you? Do you have to bother him with work late at night?"

"I am not calling about work. My name is David Levy. I am a researcher at Yad Vashem."

"Oh, you are the man he went to see." Her voice changed to a conciliatory tone. "Wait, I'll get him."

I heard her calling out "Yosik! Yosik! It's the Yad Vashem man!"

"David?" Yosef's voice came on. I figured *Yosik* was diminutive for Yosef. The background noise became muted; he must have put his palm over the receiver.

"Yes, it's me."

"I am sorry about the noise, we have people over. I didn't expect you to call."

"Why not?"

"I didn't think you believed me."

"Can we schedule a time to talk more?" I decided to avoid the matter of believing or not believing for now.

"All right." He hesitated for a moment, probably weighing whether it was best to meet at the museum. "Do you want to come on Sunday evening? It should be much quieter here."

We agreed on 5 p.m.

When I got back to the table, Izek and Max were discussing the upcoming Adolf Eichmann trial. Izek brought *The Jerusalem Post*.

"The trial starts next week, and the world is still not too happy about Eichmann's abduction. *The Washington Post* condemns our 'jungle law.' *The Christian Science Monitor* compares us to the Nazis. Somebody named William Buckley accuses us of 'refusal to forgive' and 'the fanning of the fire of anti-Germanism'."

"Fuck them all!" Max angrily retorted. "None of them gave a damn when the Germans were gassing us."

"Hey, I've heard something funny." Moshe returned from the

kitchen. "I guess they are trying to keep Eichmann entertained so they give him books to read. One was Nabokov's *Lolita*. He returned it after a couple of days, quite upset over 'this unwholesome book.' His sensibilities were offended!"

"Why shouldn't we gas him and publicly burn his body?" Max punctuated the words by slamming his fist against the table and sending a piece of falafel flying.

"Because we are not like them, Motke," Izek gently responded, causing Max to growl, "David, tell him he is an idiot!"

That was all everyone talked about then: the trial. I didn't feel like arguing over it, so I made a joke:

"Hey, do you know why the gypsies also ended up in Auschwitz?"

"Why?"

"Because they stole the Jews' train tickets."

I was rewarded with a push in the back from a man at the next table. "You're an asshole self-hating Jew! You don't talk about Auschwitz this way!"

Max stood up, ready to fight. "Shut up, you idiot! This man was in Auschwitz, he can make any joke he wants!"

"Fine, sorry," the man grumbled and sat down.

2

I had no problem finding Milman's house. It was close to my flat, a pleasant walk on the warm April evening: down Ringelblum Street to cross the valley between Kiryat Yovel and Ir Ganim, west on Janus Korczak Street, and it was almost immediately on the left once I turned onto Chile Street. It was the nicer part of Ir Ganim, where houses were closely bunched together, but had a bit of a land plot and a backyard.

Yosef opened the door almost immediately, as if he was standing there waiting for my knock.

"David, hello!"

Despite a cool night, he was dressed in white shorts and a green army undershirt.

"I am sorry, I was reading and lost the track of time." He nodded to a book he was holding in his hand.

A woman emerged from inside the house.

"Yosik, what's wrong with you? Why are you holding up our guest at the door? Please, come in."

Yosef smiled, embarrassed. "David, meet my wife, Rachel. But please do come in."

Rachel was a tiny, spry brunette, forming an "opposites attract" contrast to her tall and languid husband. She also looked to be in her early thirties and very pregnant, practically ready to burst. Her Hebrew was unaccented, telling me she grew up here. Her intense composure was betrayed ever so slightly by a hint of irony in her brown-grey eyes.

"Nice to meet you." Rachel simply extended her hand while she rested the other hand on Yosef's elbow for support.

"Congratulations!" I shook her hand. "Is this your first?"

"Thank you. Second. We have a five-year-old boy, Aron. He is one of the hooligans you probably met outside in the street."

Rachel looked up at her husband. "Yosik, I set up some drinks and snacks in the study."

"Thank you, I'd rather talk to David in the backyard."

"But it's noisy there and Yael is coming later," Rachel protested. "My sister, she dines with us on Sundays," she added for my benefit.

That was the first time I'd heard Yael's name.

"I'd rather be outside, it's a nice evening." Yosef smiled at his wife. "I'll go get drinks and snacks."

"Just go, I'll take care of it." Rachel irritably waddled away, murmuring 'stubborn like a mule' under her breath.

Yosef led me to a small backyard dominated by an old gnarled olive tree. Under the tree there was a plain wooden table with benches on both sides and a light bulb hanging overhead. Rachel was right, one could hear kids in the street playing.

We sat across from each other. I got out the notebook and two pencils from my bag.

"Is it true that Yad Vashem will soon start recognizing the righteous people that saved Jews during the Holocaust?" he asked.

"Yes. We're building the Avenue of the Righteous to open next year. Is that why you came in?"

"That, and the Eichmann trial. Not all Nazis were like him."

"Really?" I didn't try to hide my sarcasm.

His eyes wandered to my left forearm, but I was wearing a usual long-sleeved shirt and he didn't ask.

"Rachel doesn't want me to do this. She wants me to move on," he said quietly. "But whoever and whatever he was, he saved me. More than once. I wouldn't be here if not for him. After eighteen years, some memories are getting hazy and the longer I wait, the less I'll remember. It may not matter much to the world, but it matters to me …"

Guilt of surviving? I thought.

The light bulb over the table suddenly came alive. In a few seconds the back door opened, and Rachel came out, balancing a tray against her protruding belly.

"It'll be dark soon." She put down the tray crowded with a half-full bottle of vodka, a small pitcher of lemonade, four glasses and a plate of bread, figs and olives.

"Thank you, *neshama*." Yosef looked affectionately at Rachel's back as she walked away without saying a word.

He poured two glasses of vodka, but Rachel returned before we had a chance to drink them. With "it's going to get cold, you *meshuga*," she dropped off two blankets and left again.

"David, are you married?" asked Yosef.

"No. Never been married."

"They say it's like a lottery. You end up in heaven or in hell. I drew a lucky number. Let's drink to lucky numbers!"

We downed the vodka and sat quietly for a minute, in understanding that simply by being here we both drew very lucky numbers.

"All right, where shall we start?"

"How about you tell me where you were born and all that?" I got my notebook and a pencil ready.

"Sure. Iosif Aronovich Milman, born on July 16th of 1927 in Kiev, the only child of Aron and Sarah Milman. They were not devoted Communists, but they saw which way the winds were blowing and named me after our fearless leader Iosif Vissarionovich Stalin. I was unexpected; both my parents were in their thirties. The usual happy Soviet childhood and all that. My dad was a known doctor in Kiev, we lived well. He studied in Germany before the First World War, so German was a second language in the house."

Yosef paused, poured us another two fingers of vodka. I understood it'd be one of those conversations that couldn't be had sober.

"Germans killed your parents?" he half-asked, half-stated.

"Yes. Yours?"

"Stalin's NKVD. Let's drink to the parents."

He gulped the liquid, wiped his mouth with the back of his hand.

"They arrested them both in 1940. For, believe it or not, anti-German sentiments. Yes, anti-German sentiments! Stalin and Hitler were the best of friends then. Stalin's secret police, NKVD, was arresting people left and right on the slightest suspicion, and Dad used to correspond abroad in German. He knew NKVD was coming and didn't want me to end up in an orphanage, so he put me on a train to Rostov-on-Don to live with his cousin. He wanted my mother to go too, but she refused. Probably was afraid to put me in danger. I lived with my father's cousin and her two daughters until August of 1942. Germans came in November of '41 but were quickly driven away. In July of 1942 they returned. This time they rounded up the Jews and shot them in Zmievskaya Balka, a ravine on the edge of the city."

It was a story that I'd heard dozens of times now, only the names and the places differed. Zmievskaya Balka, Babiy Yar, Rumbula … the places where *Einsatzkommandos* murdered us. Except that Yosef was sitting here, alive.

"And how did you survive?"

"The Germans separated men from women and children. I was tall for my age and they took me with the men. Sabina, the relative that adopted me, shouted as I was led away 'You're Volksdeutsche from Crimea! Use your German!' You know, Rostov-on-Don is close to the Black Sea and there were thousands of Germans that lived in the area for over a hundred years."

Yosef paused again, his face blank and distant.

"They marched us to the edge of the ravine. Machine guns fired, and people screamed as they fell. I jumped out of line and called out: 'I am a German! Volksdeutsche from Crimea!' My German is good and I have blond hair from my father. That froze them for a moment. God forbid they'd shoot a Volksdeutsche by mistake. Spill precious Aryan blood. 'Are you really German?' asked one. 'Count to ten!' I began: 'Eins, zwei, drie, vier …' Another German interrupted: 'Cut it out! Drop your pants!' I understood what it meant, so I just continued counting: 'Funf, sechs, sieben …' The second soldier lifted his gun to shoot. 'Stop!' a commanding voice came from the side. 'What's going on?' The soldier lowered his gun and reported: 'This Jew is lying about being a Volksdeutsche.' The officer came closer. I stood there with my head down, trembling. I remember noticing how clean his boots were despite all the dirt and mud around us. 'Look at me!' he commanded sharply. I bit my lips and lifted my head, trying not to cry. I expected to see anger, hate … He stared at me for what seemed like an eternity. Even the soldiers had gone quiet."

Yosef reached out and grabbed my left hand, shocking me for a moment.

"Do you know what I saw in his face? Bewilderment. As if I were some exotic animal he never saw in his life … or an alien from another planet. Finally, he cleared his throat, said, 'I'll question him' and motioned for me to follow. 'Arno, why are you wasting your time? He's a Jew!' came a voice from the left. That's how I learned his name. 'He looks Aryan,' replied the officer."

Yosef let go of my left hand. I instinctively rubbed it, so hard was his squeeze.

"What happened?" I asked hoarsely.

"He walked me quite a distance away, around a mound of suitcases and clothes. I could see thousands of bodies piled down below, some moaning. I remember being completely, utterly terrified. Then he stopped and sharply grabbed my shoulder: 'The only thing that can save you now is the truth. Are you a Jew?' 'Yes,' I replied. I was too scared to lie. 'How come you speak German so well?' 'My father spoke German. He taught me.' 'Where is your father?' 'He was arrested before the war.' 'Here, in Rostov?' he asked hopefully. 'No, in Kiev.' That angered him. 'You're lying!' He slapped my face so hard, I cried out. 'No, it's the truth! My father sent me here to live with relatives just before they took him away.' 'What's your name?' 'Yosef.' 'Yosef what?' 'Yosef Milman.'

'Arno, what the hell is taking you so long?' came a voice from the other side of the mound.

The officer stepped back, got his gun out of its holster. I admit, I peed myself. And then he whispered, 'Get out of here!' I just stood there paralyzed, so he said again, 'Get out of here! Run! Run away!' I started running, heard a shot and looked back. He was staring at me while pointing his gun at the ravine."

Yosef stopped, exhausted.

I asked, "Had you seen that man … that officer … before?"

"No."

"Are you sure?"

"Yes. Absolutely, yes."

The backdoor swung open and Rachel came out with a tray of food. She was followed by a little boy carrying a large pitcher of water.

"Time for dinner!" announced Rachel as she put the food on the wooden table.

I looked at my watch, closed the notebook and got up to leave. I hadn't planned to stay that long. Perhaps the SS officer let Yosef go because he resembled a childhood friend. These bastards possessed a stunning mix of romantic sentimentality and unimaginable cruelty. I had much more humanely interesting stories to investigate: Wladislaw Kowalski, who saved dozens of Jewish lives in Poland; Mariya Babich, who sheltered a Jewish baby for four years; Anton Schmidt, a German soldier who was executed for helping hundreds of Jews. People that risked—and sometimes lost— their lives. It was close to seven o'clock, if I hurried up I would still make it to Café Europa, where a cute poetess was giving a reading today. I didn't care about her poetry, but I was getting close to having sex with her. We'd played our game of sexual innuendo and discussions of risqué literature for a while and last week she signaled her readiness by playfully placing her hand between my legs while discussing the injury to Jake Barnes in *The Sun Also Rises*.

"David, where are you going? You are staying for dinner!" Rachel demanded.

"No, thank you, I have ..."

Another woman came out of the house, also carrying a tray. I meant to lie, saying that I have plans, but words got stuck in my throat as I stared at that woman coming into the circle of flavescent light from the bulb. A feeling of recognition jarred me. Sometimes you have that instant attraction, that burst of desire that warms up the loins and makes hands tremble. She was a big girl, especially next to her sparrow-like sister. Her face, angular and pale-skinned, was framed by wavy dark hair. A narrow long nose contrasted with a small and delicate mouth, slender waist and broad hips. It was as if one of Modigliani's paintings came alive. You know, one of his late reclining nudes. An elegant, effortless, unconscious eroticism that just sets you on fire. She looked back at me, her eyes light grey and bottomless. The thought of the poetess vanished from my mind.

"Ummm ... David, this is my sister Yael," Rachel said in a gentle tone. "Yael, David works in Yad Vashem and he is researching Yosef's story."

Yael put down the tray she was carrying and offered me her hand.

"Nice to meet you, David."

Her fingers were long, handshake unexpectedly firm. Almost as tall as I, her body solid and yet supple. A green shirt unbuttoned just enough to outline her breasts. I lingered on them longer than appropriate and Yael cleared her throat.

"Nice to meet you, Yael," I finally managed to respond.

Of course, I ended up staying for dinner. Yael sat on my side of the table, with Yosef, Rachel and their boy, Aron, across from us. We were about a foot apart and I was careful to not stare at Yael or touch her. But even at a distance I felt the heat of her body.

I stole a few glances at her profile painted by the lonely light bulb: a slightly upturned nose, a delicate small ear, full breasts. A few times our hands collided when reaching for food and an electric shock went through me. I took a few long breaths to calm myself down and avoid a possible embarrassment. It's her eyes, I thought.

"David, what's the matter?" inquired Rachel. "You're not eating. Anything wrong?"

"Everything is wonderful, Rachel. I am just taking a little break."

Rachel's eyes narrowed and flipped from me to Yael and back.

We finished, and Rachel and Yael cleaned up the table and washed the dishes.

Yosef poured out the remains of the vodka into our glasses. He lit up a cigarette, offered one to me. I declined.

"Yosef, you said that he brought you to Palestine."

"Yes, he did."

"But how?"

Before Yosef had a chance to continue, Rachel and Yael came out of the house with coffee and strudel.

Yosef smiled. "I don't think they'll let us talk." And he was right.

"David, you can walk Yael home," Rachel said after we finished up the apple strudel.

"It's not necessary," Yael protested. "I am perfectly safe waking home. David and Yosef are talking!"

"That's OK. It's a long story and we won't finish it tonight. Right, David?" Yosef gave me a pass.

"I'll be happy to. Yosef is right, we'll need another meeting," I got up.

"It's settled, then." Rachel waddled back into the house, leaving Yael and me to look at each other uncomfortably.

As we walked to Yael's place, we traded the basics of our life stories. She was twenty-eight, a nurse in Shaare Zadek Medical Center nearby, recently divorced, no kids. Her parents lived in a kibbutz in Galilee.

We walked through Bostaniya Park. It was not much of a park then, a few shrubs in the desert. In the evening chill of Jerusalem, Yael wrapped her arms around herself to keep warm. I slowed down for a second, to see all of her. Her back made me think of violin's graceful curves. I wanted to put my arm about her shoulders but was afraid of scaring her off. I looked instead at her neck and delicate seashell-shaped earlobe, imagined myself gently circling them. I wondered how she would react if I kissed her. Would she keep her lips tightly closed or open them up and kiss me back and give out that deep-throated moan that women have when they desire you too?

Yael suddenly stopped, pulled on my shirtsleeve, faced me.

"David, Rachel told me you were in Auschwitz. What was it like there? How did you survive?"

I stood there looking at her, smitten by desire. Looking into her almond-shaped, light grey eyes. Could I have told her then? In sixteen years, I hadn't met a single *sabra* that understood.

"I was seventeen when they brought me there, but I was tall and strong for my age. During the selection, they sent me to one side; my parents and my sister were sent to the other. I never saw them again. I was lucky to mostly have jobs inside, cleaning, cooking. Then I pretended to be an electrician, I knew a bit from my father. I was lucky. There was no rhyme or reason or any kind of special meaning to it, just a random fate."

"David, I am sorry." Yael resumed walking. "I shouldn't have asked, I know it's difficult to talk about it. It's this Eichmann trial that's starting next week. When we heard that six million had been killed, we kept asking how could that happen? Why did people go to their slaughter? We here in Israel always wondered how the Nazis managed to kill so many."

Like lambs to the slaughter. That's how *sabras* viewed us.

"It was easy. You give people no food or water for days and then you tell them to take a shower and everything will be all right and there will be food and hot tea waiting for them. People want to believe that everything will be all right."

Only those that were there would get it. There is no point in telling the horrible truth, I can't change anything.

We walked in silence.

"You don't have to explain," she said finally. "Here's my place."

She lived on the northeast side of Ir Ganim. Her building was not a boring concrete monstrosity like mine but a graceful two-story house with an archway and a small garden with a fountain in the middle.

"It's pretty," I said.

"This is one of the first houses they built here." She nodded. "Before they started doing these larger apartment buildings."

Yael turned towards me again. "Why are you interested in Yosef's story?"

"We must remember the ones that saved just as we remember the murderers," I repeated, quoting Ezra's words.

That was no longer the real reason, but I had to give her an answer, and that was as good as any.

"I know it's important for Yosef," she said. "He's been talking about that officer a lot. Especially lately. Probably because of Eichmann."

"Is it important for you?"

She looked at me strangely.

"Yes, of course. I believe we all have a certain personal mission that we must satisfy so that we feel whole. I think that's what it is for Yosef. He won't be happy unless he does it. And that means that Rachel won't be happy either."

"And what if Yosef never finds out who the man was?"

"Well, at least he would have tried. Isn't it a shame to really want something and never reach for it? Isn't that the saddest thing?"

"Yes, it is."

I wanted to reach for her, embrace her, kiss her, breathe her in. Better yet, rip off her clothes, throw her on the ground, take her. Blood was pounding in my temples. But instead I shook her hand and wished her a good night. Before she disappeared into the darkness of the building's entrance, she looked back and waved. Like Leah. Just like Leah.

At night, I tossed and turned. At thirty-five, I thought I would be past such feelings, but physical desire for Yael was stronger than any I'd ever experienced for a woman.

Attirance immédiate! André would have exclaimed, my irrepressible rascal friend from the *Lager*. Being French, he thought of *amour* even amidst carnage. One of the guards shot André as he was returning from the women's barracks.

Neither asleep nor awake, I dreamt of kissing Yael as I unbuttoned her shirt and took her breasts in my hands. Removed all her clothing and put her on the bed. I stood up to take off my clothes. Suddenly, her body started turning blue before my eyes. I screamed and shook her "No!"

A loud knock on the wall woke me up completely. "Hey, we are trying to sleep here! Every fucking night it's the same crap! Go live where people can't hear you at night!"

The walls in Kiryat Yovel were thin.

I stood up, went into the bathroom, washed my face. I knew it'd be a while before I fell asleep now, so I sat at my desk, turned on the lamp. Years ago, a kind psychologist told me it would help to write about my experiences. I'd kept a rather scattered diary since. When I couldn't write, I read. That was my only indulgence, buying books. Books in Hebrew, in English, even in German.

3

In some way, I was not happy about The Trial. I was finally forgetting. Not forgetting but beginning to live here and not there. And now I'd have to go back. But I did have this desire to see Eichmann face-to-face. Thinking it would help me understand who he was and why they did it. I wondered—would this trial change something—anything—in the fabric of humankind? Like the other trial that took place here nineteen hundred and thirty years ago. Perhaps it was the fate of Jerusalem to be the center of the world. Here, on Mount Zion, David founded his kingdom. Next to it was the Al-Aqsa Mosque where Muhammad was transported from Mecca. It was built on top of Solomon's temple, of which only the Western Wall remains. Over there was the Temple Mount where Abraham bound Isaac and Muhammad ascended to heaven. And just to the east, was Golgotha and the Garden of Gethsemane. One could easily get caught up in the history of this place, but it felt like we were about to open a new chapter.

Café Europa was different from Mal Zahl, quiet, almost literary. Even though most patrons grew up in Europe, it didn't have the scent of *Lager* about it. People there hid the lost parts of their lives the best they could. They were nostalgic for their old countries, the countries that rejected them twenty years ago. Sometimes I would sit at a table in the back and just watch people, trying to guess which road they took to come to Jerusalem.

But this night the place was busy, no empty table in sight. The Eichmann trial was slated to begin tomorrow, April 11th. The holy city of Jerusalem was on edge.

"David!" Jacob Broder waved me over. He was an older German

Jew, originally from the same *Länder* as us, even met my father a few times. Jacob was still in love with the German culture, and spoke wistfully of Berlin of thirty years ago, before the Nazis. This at times irritated other conversationalists into suggesting that Jacob should move back there. Jacob would turn pale, pull back into his shell and become quiet. Tonight, he was sitting with his friend Maurice, a chessboard with an unfinished game and, uncharacteristically, a bottle of Gold vodka and two glasses between them.

"Did they ask you to testify at the trial?" Maurice asked me.

"Sort of."

"I've been asked to testify," Maurice said with a touch of pride. "I think they wanted someone from France, because Eichmann was involved in rounding up French Jews."

"What did you say?"

"I told them no. Why would I testify? So Halevi can crucify me on the stand and then some asshole will kill me like Kasztner, thinking he is taking revenge for his family?"

Kasztner was one of the leaders of Hungarian Jewry, who survived the Holocaust. In 1955, the judge called him a collaborator with the Nazis. Two years later, Kasztner was shot to death.

A sullen waiter slammed another glass on the table and walked away.

"Well, Kasztner did negotiate with Eichmann," Jacob pointed out. "You never even met Eichmann."

"Don't be stupid, Jacob!" Maurice became agitated. "Like Kasztner had any good choices! You know how in Russia they sent most of their people that survived Nazi camps to Siberia? Well, that's almost how it is for us. If you survived, you must have collaborated. They think we are all damaged, lousy human material. That's what they literally say about us."

His eyes lingered on me for a second and he looked away. Maurice was suspicious of anyone who made it out of *Lager*. He knew that one's soul was the price of survival.

Jacob poured what remained in the Gold vodka bottle in three glasses.

"Let it go, Maurice. We are damaged. We all died twenty years ago. It's our shadows that are here."

In the morning, I came to the *Beit Ha'am*, the House of the People. Soldiers and police surrounded the place. I wondered why, and then realized they were here to protect Eichmann. We had to keep him alive, so we could execute him properly. Almost a carnival atmosphere reigned outside. People waited in line for hours for entrance passes. Those who couldn't get in would listen to the trial carried live on the radio. My pass got me through the roadblock. A policeman searched me and let me inside the building. The courtroom looked like an auditorium in a university. Or a theater. Hundreds of journalists from fifty countries, official observers and invited guests, all crammed inside. How would one write about such a trial? What the prosecutor said, what the defense responded with, what the judges asked, how witnesses testified— that all would get captured. But this was not your usual trial.

I looked at the judges: Moshe Landau, Yitzhak Raveh, Benjamin Halevi. Yes, I remembered Halevi from the Kasztner trial. Sometimes I thought of him as just, sometimes as cruel. Perhaps he was both. But this was all about Eichmann. I was here to study him: perhaps a smile or a frown or a changed expression would betray what was on the inside. There was a hush as he came in, flanked by police officers, and took his place in a bulletproof glass booth. My seat was only about twenty meters away. People wrote about his "snake eyes," the look of a monster. Not so: by appearance, he could have been an accountant or a ticket collector or anyone. A balding, bespectacled man. I would have loved to pile on derogatory adjectives, but he didn't come across evil or cruel, just ordinary. A man that one would pass on the street without a second thought or look. I'd seen that before with the guards and *kapos* after the liberation: they looked completely different, pitiful and confused when they no longer had the power. For a moment, I thought that I recognized him from *Lager*: tall SS hat, shiny boots, square riding pants; haughty stare of a bloody barbarian god looking to sacrifice sub-humans. But I realized that I didn't know if I ever saw him.

The next day, Eichmann's headlines in the papers were replaced with the smiling face of Russian cosmonaut Yuri Gagarin, the first human to orbit the Earth. "We have no luck," my neighbor commented. "We threw a trial and one day in, it gets replaced by a Russian party."

Eichmann entered his pleas with a strong Austrian accent: "not guilty in the sense of the indictment." In what sense was he guilty then? Did he consider himself guilty of anything? His attorney was Robert Servatius, the man who called the Nuremberg trials "a regression to barbarism." I wondered if he ever referred to Auschwitz and Treblinka as "barbaric"?

Chief Prosecutor Hausner spoke of Pharaoh and Haman and Attila, expounded on Hitler, organization of the SS, cold-blooded extermination of millions. A horrible litany hour after hour. Words became sounds, vibrations of the air. Terrible numbers became statistics. We'd heard them before and nothing happened. The journalist next to me fell asleep.

Chaia, our research assistant, was waiting by my office.

"There is a new movie, *Spartacus*. Do you want to go this weekend? I'll make dinner."

"I am busy."

"Did I not please you the last time? Show me what to do." She began to sob.

Ordinarily I may have relented, but the urge for Yael was still too vivid, too real. Isn't it strange how a desire for one particular woman can make others unwanted? The sight of that fat cow, crying, only irritated me.

"Why did you do that?" she asked through tears. "I thought you liked me."

Yes, why did I? Because I wanted to. What's the big fucking deal? I just shrugged.

"I never told you that I love you or anything like that."

Which was true. I'm not a nice guy, but I don't lie to women in order to get them in bed. And I never tell them that I love them. That particular cruelty I don't possess.

"You should not have done this to me," she wept.

"What did I do to you? We went out, we had a good time, we had sex. You were not a virgin as far as I could tell." I was getting angry.

"There was only one before you. I was curious. This was different."

"That's enough, Chaia."

"Why are you so mean?"

"I am not a good person. Go find someone else."

Yosef called me during the week to see if I wanted to come on Sunday. I had plans already, so we arranged to meet in two weeks.

"Will Yael...?" I asked carefully.

"Yael what?"

"Be there."

"Oh. She usually comes on Sundays. But I can tell her not to."

"No, that's OK. Don't change anything because of me."

I couldn't very well tell him that his story interested me much less than Yael's body.

When I got back to my flat in a dusty squat two-story apartment building in Kiryat Yovel, I found Hannah sitting on the steps in front.

"What are you doing here?"

"Waiting for you." She always had a way of making me feel like an idiot at times.

"I was on a date. With the guy from the ministry that asked me out four times and I finally said yes."

"What happened? Was he mean to you?"

"No, not at all. He was a gentleman ... took me to a nice restaurant ..."

"Then why ..."

"Because I couldn't go through with it! He is a *sabra*, he was born here. This damn trial, it brought everything back ... He started asking me about the lager and I saw it in his eyes, that fucking '*how could you let them do this to you*' condescension..."

I sat down, put my arm around her shoulders. Hannah was about the only person in the world that I was still nice to.

"They don't know ... they can't possibly know. This country only respects dead heroes."

Hannah stood up, letting my arm drop.

"David, take me upstairs. Please."

To her, I couldn't possibly refuse.

In a cosmic joke, that year's *Yom HaAtzmaut*, the Independence Day, had fallen on April 20th — Hitler's birthday. A trick of the Hebrew calendar. Some bored journalists made a joke of it. There was a big parade with fireworks: the president's car, Prime Minister Ben Gurion, the marching army.

"It was a message to the world," I overheard Hausner's assistant saying in a café, his clenched fist raised. "We are armed now, our blood won't come cheaply."

"The whole trial thing is useless," replied a journalist wearily. "How could one man pay for six million deaths? Nine days in and everyone is tired. Perhaps having a trial at all was a mistake; most likely it will only start up a wave of anti-Semitism."

"No, no," protested the assistant. "Have patience. We've been silent since the war. If this brings out anti-Semites, so be it."

4

On a hot and humid Sunday, I took a smoke-belching Egged bus to see my old friend Hirsh. We descended the road to Tel Aviv: steep slopes, on the shoulder remnants of wrecked vehicles destroyed in 1948. They are monuments now. I was here then. At Lydda, I changed buses. The road bent to the north and soon we entered Samaria. The sweet smell of orange orchards mixed with the sweat of humanity. We drove jerkily from town to town, letting passengers on and off. People pushed and shouted in multiple languages, dragging old suitcases tied with ropes.

Hirsh met me at the bus station. Leon was there already, and we sat in the shade and waited for Abraham for a while.

"How's the oranges business?" Leon asked.

Hirsh and I fought in Lehi together. To the ruling Mapai party, that forever branded us as terrorists. After the war, Hirsh became one of the founders of the Kfar Tahpooz moshav. Kfar Tahpooz simply meant the Village of Oranges. Which was what they did, grew Jaffa oranges.

"Praise God, doing good." Hirsh nodded. "We have four hundred people."

"Whew." Leon whistled. "You must be way up in the pecking order now."

"I've been elected the head of the cooperative," Hirsh said proudly. "We would have been able to grow even more, but we need new markets. We must export our oranges to Europe. What do you think, David? We can use your language skills."

We had this conversation last year, and the year prior.

"I'm not much of a salesman," I answered. "I'm sure that amongst your four hundred members you have some that speak German or French or whatever."

"We do, but nobody that speaks multiple languages." Hirsh shook his head. "And not as well as you. I can't afford to send a bunch of people. I need one that can cover Germany and France and Spain."

"Selling oranges in Germany would make sense." Leon nodded. "The bastards have the money now. Back in the late forties, they were broke and hungry. I would be riding a tram and eating chocolate bars right in front of them, one after the other. Pissed them off."

"Nice, Leon. And how's the black-market business?" I changed the subject.

Leon and I were in the same displaced persons camp in northern Italy back in '45. But Leon didn't leave with me then. First, he wanted to kill more Germans and they were in Europe, not Palestine. Rumor had it that he hunted a few dozen SS. Meanwhile, he became big in the contraband business: the survival skills that Leon honed in Auschwitz suited him well there. Cigarettes, silk stockings, American cars—anything that the government tried to tax, Leon could get you cheaper. He knew how to read people, when to threaten and when to plead, when to attack and when to retreat. Leon had a place in Italy and a place in Tel Aviv and perhaps others, plus a woman or two in each of them. He was the ultimate survivor.

"Good, but getting more difficult," Leon said. "It used to be simple, you just had to have a few boats and people that could run them. Now, the patrol boats are faster and better equipped. If not for the Russians, I would have been in trouble."

"The Russians?"

"The Red Army in East Germany. They would sell their own mother for gold, hard currency, and American records."

"You mean military supplies?"

"Yes, handguns, machine guns, bullets, grenades. Heck, they would sell us the T-55 tanks if we could find a buyer. Their AK-47 assault rifles are very popular in Algeria. A solid, high-margin business. Look"—Leon turned to me—"perhaps you should start doing this oranges export thing. I need a better, legitimate business cover. You make money on oranges, and I'll give you a cut off the goods I'll bring back. What do you say?"

"I don't think so, Leon."

"Too bad. It's an opportunity." Leon shrugged. "Hey, here's a joke for you: What's the difference between a Jew and Santa Claus?"

"What?"

"Santa Claus goes down the chimney!"

Leon laughed so hard at his own joke, he doubled over.

"Very funny, Leon," Hirsh said. "Good thing Abraham isn't here yet."

"Yes, he's got no sense of humor."

Another blue-and-white Egged bus appeared out of a cloud of dust. A woman with live chickens dismounted, shouting angrily at the driver. Then Abraham materialized, calm, dressed in all black even on this hot day. In a way, Abraham never left the *Lager*. He worked for a burial society, saying prayers for those that died here in Israel, and for those that went up the chimney without a proper burial. I saw him once in Jerusalem, working after a bus exploded. Abraham collected pieces of torn-apart flesh as if there was nothing more important in the universe. I didn't call out to him.

There was no set date, but the four of us met once a year. All different, we were bearers of secrets that were supposed to die with us. We barely spoke. Just drank and remembered.

Dana, Hirsh's wife, came to talk to me at some point. She grew up in Warsaw and didn't like living on the moshav and dreamed of a private life in a big city, like New York, where she had relatives. She'd begged Hirsh to leave many times, but he could no longer trust any other country.

"Last year, after your meeting I found him in a closet with the door shut," Dana said accusingly. "He was on the floor, in a fetal position. Why can't he let it go already?"

I just nodded. What was I going to say? She wanted the impossible.

5

Rachel greeted me at the door. She didn't seem happy to see me. "Yosef is in the back."

"You didn't want me to come?"

She sighed. "I am sorry. Thank you for coming. I know he asked you. I just wonder where it's going. It's hard on him, he's drinking too much," she said protectively as she escorted me to the backyard.

Yosef was sitting by himself at the table, a bottle of vodka in front of him. Rachel sat next to her husband with "I want to listen too." She probably wanted to make sure he was OK.

"Do you ever go back? Like in your mind?" he asked me. "I wish I could forget the ravine. How do you just shoot women and children, reload and shoot again and again?"

I've seen worse. Much worse. I felt the wave of memory rising in the recesses of my mind, and I walled it off by focusing on my interviewee.

"Yosef, the last time we stopped with the officer by the name of Arno letting you escape from the killing ravine in Rostov-on-Don. Zmiyevskaya Balka, right?"

"Yes. After he let me go, I hid in a sunflower field. When it got dark, I ran to the woods about a kilometer away, found a hollow tree and spent the night there. In the morning, there was more shooting and screaming. I stayed in the woods until dusk. I was cold and hungry, so I decided to go hide with the family of my friend Vasya. But when I got to his street, I was spotted by a woman who was a known Soviet secret police informer. She screamed: 'A Jew! This boy is a Jew!' I turned to run, but a German patrol came around the corner. They took me to Friedrich Engels' street where the Germans set up their headquarters. There we came across a small group standing around a gray-uniformed officer, laughing and smoking. I tried to tell them that

I am a Volksdeutsche, but the officer waved it off."

"So you ended up back in the hands of the SS?"

"Yes. One of the soldiers took off his rifle, but the officer said: 'No, take him to the ravine and do it there.' 'But it's late and the ravine is far,' the soldier protested. 'Right,' the officer agreed, 'take the motorcycle.' They tied my hands, threw me into the sidecar, and the soldier drove us back to Zmiyevskaya Balka. There were very few people left when we got there, I could hear moans punctuated by an occasional shot. Through tears, I squeezed out 'There is an officer, his name is Arno. He knows that I'm a Volksdeutsche.' The soldier called out to a couple of Germans that were getting ready to leave 'Hey, is there anyone here by the name of Arno?' 'Yes, he's over there by the lorry,' one answered. 'But hurry up, we're almost done.' The soldier drove a bit farther.

The officer named Arno was watching workers that were gathering personal belongings left on the side and loading them into a truck. The soldier dragged me out of the sidecar and asked 'Are you Arno? This boy claims that you know him.' Arno stared at us for a moment, then answered, 'Yes, he's a Volksdeutsche.' 'No, he fooled you,' the soldier said. 'He's a Jew. *Obersturmbannfuhrer* instructed me to shoot him.' 'Fine, I'll take it from here, you can go,' Arno replied. But the soldier refused: 'My orders were to take care of it.' They argued for a minute, then Arno smiled and said, 'OK, you're doing your job. But you can't do it here, it's unsanitary. We must take him down into the ravine, there's a shovel and some lime there. I'll show you.' He turned to the workers: 'You can go. It's getting dark. We'll finish it up tomorrow; nobody will steal this old junk.' We went down into the ravine, the two of them behind me, the officer giving directions. It was dark already. Suddenly, the earth under our feet moved, I jumped to the side and fell. I heard soldier's laugh, then a muffled scream. I turned back and saw the officer behind the soldier, his palm clamped on soldier's mouth, knife in the other hand and the soldier's throat dark with blood."

"He killed that soldier?" I couldn't hold myself from exclaiming.

"Yes. Then dropped the body into the ravine, took a shovel and covered it with lime and soil."

I cleared my throat. "Did he tell you to run away again?"

"No. He just said, over and over: 'Damn you! Why couldn't you just disappear? Why did you leave me no choice?' Even in the dark, I could feel his hatred."

Yosef got up, went into the house, came back with a glass for me. He poured vodka for both of us and drank about half of his glass.

"We took the motorcycle and hid just outside of town for the night. Obviously, we couldn't stay there. He asked if I had anyone outside of Rostov that he could take me to. There was a marine captain in Gelendzhik, a resort town on the Black Sea. My family often went there on vacation. Years ago, my father saved the captain's life and he'd been our friend since. The officer studied a map and said 'It's over three hundred kilometers south. We can't go on foot'. He said 'WE' and that's when I realized that he was coming with me."

Yosef emptied his glass of vodka and stared into the distance.

"What happened then?"

"In the morning we drove towards Gelendzhik. Most of the area south of Rostov had already been occupied by the Germans, so he made up a story that I was a Volksdeutsche distantly related to someone important in Berlin, trying to re-unite with my parents near the town of Maykop. The few Germans we came across were quite happy to re-unite fellow Germans. But he kept the encounters short, probably afraid that I'd give us away. Of course, we avoided Russian soldiers too. The front lines were mixed up, with Maykop already in German hands, but Russian forces to the west holding Novorossiysk and Gelendzhik. There are forests in that area, and after three days we ditched the motorcycle and headed west on foot."

"Why didn't you run away from him and go to the Russians?"

"I was scared. Who could I trust? And why would Russian soldiers have cared about me as they retreated?"

"Did he say anything to you about himself?"

"No. Sometimes I caught him staring at me with hatred. But he asked a lot of questions about my father, for whatever reason that interested him. When we got to Gelendzhik, he hid in the woods outside. I went in, found our friend Mustafa and told him what happened in Rostov. Mustafa wanted to get rid of the officer, but the officer was ready with his own gun. They agreed to talk, with me being the interpreter. Mustafa offered to hide us, but the officer said it was too dangerous, the area would be occupied by the Wehrmacht soon and they might be looking for us already. He wanted to get to Trabzon on the Turkish coast. Mustafa asked why he was doing this, and the officer replied he was tired of the war. Mustafa explained that it's not possible to go from Gelendzhik straight to Trabzon; said we must go the smugglers' way: stay close to the shore, travel at night. He could take us to Sochi and arrange with fellow smugglers to then take us to Batumi and from there to Trabzon."

"*Bubele*, the dinner is in the kitchen. Can you put it on a tray and bring it over?" Rachel said, interrupting us.

When Yosef left the table, she told me, "I didn't know the details. He rarely talked about it. See, I tried to talk Yosik out of this."

"Out of what?"

"Telling the story. Trying to find that man."

"Why?"

"Just want to leave this behind us. Have a normal life. But he can't. This damn trial, it brought it back. He's suffering from nightmares now."

"I understand. It's hard."

She suddenly changed topic. "I know you like Yael. You don't have to answer. She has a boyfriend. You seem to be a nice man. I thought I should tell you. And she won't be coming today."

I cleared my throat. "Is she engaged to be married?"

"No."

"Then we won't be doing anything wrong if we ..."

Yosef came out of the house carrying a tray and I shut up. Rachel looked at me with what seemed to be a sorrowful kindness.

"Eat," she said. "You can eat and talk, can't you?"

"Where did I stop?" asked Yosef after we finished Rachel's lamb stew.

"You were in Gelendzhik with Mustafa," the two of us said in unison.

"Right. Mustafa hid us in his house and the next night we sailed from the bay in a small boat. Mustafa didn't want to use the engine, so we went on sail power. Before sunrise, we got to the port of Tuapse. We holed up with Mustafa's smuggling partner for the day, and the next night we continued to Sochi and hid there for a couple of days, while Mustafa negotiated for us a passage to Batumi, then Hopa and

Trabzon. He gave us food and some Russian and Turkish money. It was a dangerous run, but all smugglers knew Mustafa and were afraid to cross him. Until the last leg from Hopa to Trabzon, where they would have robbed us but for the officer's gun."

"Did you ever talk to Mustafa again?" asked Rachel.

"No. After the war he and his whole family were deported to Siberia." Yosef shook his head. "I tried to find them but to no avail. Ironically, the Germans never bothered to occupy Gelendzhik. But who knew at the time?"

"What happened when you got to Trabzon?"

"The officer forced the smugglers to take us to a man by the name of Ekrem Bey. Must have been an influential man in Trabzon, the smugglers knew exactly where he lived, in a large two-story house with an old hazelnut tree."

"Who was that man? 'Bey' is just a courtesy title."

"I don't know. That's what I remember him being called. He was connected to the Nazis: he spoke German, he immediately recognized the officer and called him Prinz."

"Prinz means 'Prince' in German."

"I asked later whether he was really a prince, a royalty of some kind, he said it was simply a nickname. The Turk's servant locked me in a second story room, but I crouched by the window and overheard Prinz and Ekrem talking. Something about metal ore that Ekrem supplied, that was valuable and appreciated in Berlin. Prinz told him that he was on a mission to Palestine, to connect with German Templers and set up a radio observation post to direct Rommel's troops, and asked Ekrem for assistance in getting there. I was supposedly a valuable hostage, a nephew of an important Jew. They also talked about a pro-German *jihad* that the Muslims in the Middle East would soon be called to by the Grand Mufti."

"What if your escape was a setup and he was using you to get to Palestine?"

"Perhaps…but why would he need me? Why would he kill a soldier?"

"For credibility?" I shrugged. "I don't know. Doesn't make a lot of sense either way. Sorry, please continue."

"Ekrem promised Prinz all the assistance he needs. And he asked

Prinz to send his best wishes to Prinz's uncle. That's what I remember clearly, this mention of the uncle: 'A big honor when your uncle and you came to visit', Ekrem said."

"But no name?"

"Not that I recall."

"How long were you in Trabzon?"

"Two days. Then one of Ekrem's men drove us to Erzerum where we took a train to the Syrian border. We got off just before the border, and the Ekrem's man took us to a Bedouin tribe."

"Probably to avoid the British border patrols."

"Yes. Bedouins had us change into Bedouin clothes and took us across Syria and Lebanon, all the way to Palestine."

"And how did this man—Arno, Prinz—behave towards you?"

"He barely spoke to me. Sometimes I caught him staring at me. But he came to talk to me on the last night."

"The last night?"

"Yes. We were near a Muslim village at the southern tip of Lebanon. Prinz sat next to me and said: 'tomorrow you'll be in Palestine'. He stopped me from responding and continued. 'I can't go with you. I've done terrible things, but I hope you'll remember me with kindness. I wish I could have met your father'."

"Your father?"

"Yes, that's what he said. I tried to ask him why, but he disappeared into the darkness."

"Did you see him again?"

"No. In the morning, the chief of the tribe took me a bit further and pointed to a British checkpoint in the distance. I asked him about the officer. The chief shook his head, made a shooting gesture to his temple and nodded at a distant wadi. I tried to run there but they wouldn't let me."

Yosef poured himself a glass of vodka. I did the same.

"To Prinz!" said Yosef. "Whatever else he did, if not for him I wouldn't be here. And neither would Aron or this new baby." He gently patted Rachel's belly. "Sometimes I think he's alive, somewhere here in Lebanon or Syria or Turkey. Or perhaps he went back to Germany after the war. Or South America. I hope he is alive."

"Arno, Aron … a bit similar—did you?"

"No." Yosef smiled. "My son is named after my father. I've been told that Arno is not an uncommon German name."

"That's true," I confirmed. "It means 'eagle'."

At night, I thought of Yael again. A boyfriend … *La Douleur Exquise* André would have said. The pain of wanting someone you can't have. But at least I was still here and could feel the pain. André couldn't; his ashes settled somewhere in the Polish countryside. What would André have done? Walked away? No, he would have pursued his passion against all odds. So should I. And Yosef's story turned out to be more interesting than I thought originally. I was not sure how much I believed, though.

I went to the balcony to read. Most people in our ugly typical Kiryat Yovel block apartment building converted their balconies into living spaces or tiny gardens with plants, chickens, what not. Not I. My two small rooms were quite enough for me. In the bedroom I had a single bed, a nightstand with a lamp, and a chair. The other room had a small kitchen with an icebox, a rough wooden table and two chairs, plus a second-hand sofa, a lamp and a bookcase. My best piece of furniture was the reading chair on the balcony. That's where I spent some of my late nights, covered with a blanket and reading by a lantern. Sometimes I was afraid to go to sleep, frightened of what I'd find there. I had a new book I'd picked from the library. *Lord of the Rings* by Tolkien. The local librarian saved new books in English and German for me. She was not positive I'd be interested, but I reassured her that escape into a fantasy was just what the doctor ordered. She smiled indulgently.

At some point I must have fallen asleep, as I often did. I had learned to sleep with a thin blanket in Poland's winter. Sleep is in your head. When I started coming about, the eastern sky was bloody red with the rising sun. I thought I saw the figures of Frodo and Sam carrying the ring into Mordor. And then it was Yosef Milman and the German officer plodding their way to a promised land, one in a crisp SS uniform, the other in tattered Auschwitz garb.

59

6

My boss, Dov Cohen, walked in and nodded at the papers spread on my desk. "Anything interesting that you're working on now?"

I was going through the notes I took at Milman's. A part of me wanted to find some glaring discrepancy in dates or names or places, but so far, I didn't.

I told Dov about Yosef. He listened carelessly, nodded.

"Intriguing. But David, why pursue this somewhat fantastic story when you already have a backlog of almost five years to investigate?"

"Aren't we planning to honor the righteous? You asked me to work on these cases."

"Yes, we're waiting for guidelines from the Supreme Court. But there are many stories of other rescuers, more realistic ones, correct?"

He was right, of course. I couldn't tell him about Yael. Or that it was the very fact that Yosef's rescuer was so improbable that I developed a certain curiosity about it. But Yael was more important.

I went to "the Trial" whenever I could escape. It proceeded chronologically, country by country. Killed with gas, shot with guns, burned alive, babies ripped apart, frozen to death, killed by injections, mountains of corpses, mountains of shoes, buckets of gold teeth.

Witness Wells: "We decided that a certain group of people must stay till the last minute and be killed, because they will be the cover for others. And they all accepted it very willingly ... The only idea was that one of us survives and tells the world what happened here."

Witness Berman: "Yes, I remember the orphanage of Janusz Korczak. He walked at the head of the procession, and next to him there were two small children. He was offered to go free. But he said that he didn't want to be separated from the children whom he had taught."

Witness Kovner: "Since October 1941, we were helped by Anton Schmid, a *Feldwebel* in the Wehrmacht. Schmid told me 'There is one dog called Eichmann, and he is organizing all this.' In March 1942, Schmid was arrested and executed by the Gestapo."

Witness Plodchlebnik: "I unloaded bodies of my wife and my two children off a gas van."

Witness Berman: "I came back to Treblinka in January 1945. A field of scattered skulls, bones, in tens of thousands, and very, very many shoes, amongst them tens of thousands of shoes of little children. I picked one pair." He carefully unwrapped and held a tiny pair of shoes for the whole courthouse to see. "All that's left from a child … from a million children."

A kerchiefed old woman began to weep silently. Behind me, like tree leaves in the wind, more women cried. I looked at the balding little man behind the bulletproof glass. He listened calmly via headphones, the index finger of his right hand pressed against his cheek, glasses slightly askew. When Berman raised the pair of shoes, the man tightened his mouth, blew his nose. Those of us who thought that just seeing Eichmann would provide answers were disappointed. And yet, his presence was essential: a locked door was being opened after many years. Things that happened had not been told. Thus, it was like they did not happen. Until now. The Holocaust was happening now, in this room.

I looked, and I looked, and I still couldn't find the key to who he was.

I felt guilty asking Hannah for help with fact-checking Milman's story.

She sensed it. "Why? How far are you going to take this?"

"I don't know yet. Maybe I'll just record the story and stop. We all want to find something good."

"Yes, perhaps so. Do you believe him?"

We both knew people whose stories of survival, for numbers of reasons, had taken on rather fantastic qualities. Before taking them seriously, one had to make sure that small details added up. That was where stories usually fell apart.

"He said they were aided by Nazi supporters in Turkey, something about metal ore. Doesn't quite make sense."

Hannah rubbed her forehead as she often did when thinking. "I'll try to set up a meeting with someone. He owes me a favor."

"How would he know these things?"

"He knows a lot about Nazis and their supporters. He was in Latin America last year …"

She let the words hang in the air until I comprehended.

"He was on the team that caught Eichmann?"

Hannah smiled, didn't say anything.

We met in Hannah's apartment. Benny Hadan was a short but sturdy man around forty, with a body of a weightlifter. He was almost entirely bald, but his eyebrows compensated by being rugged and bushy, merging together into a single dark line over a prominent nose. He reminded me of caricatures in *Der Stürmer.*

Benny's handshake left my right hand numb for a minute.

"So, Hannah tells me you're investigating a story of some good SS officer, yes?"

"Well, it's more complicated than that."

"Sit down, you two!" Hannah commanded as she poured us coffee and put a small plate of strudel on the table.

"What do you think of Hausner's handling of the trial?" I asked.

The whole country was glued to Kol Yisrael radio to listen to the proceedings.

"Meh, taking too long in my view." Benny shrugged. "I would have just called Eichmann a rabid dog that should be put to death."

"Yeah, that's why you are not a jurist," Hannah said.

Benny took a sip of the strong, bitter concoction that Hannah called coffee, waved his hand as if directing an orchestra.

"So, you tell me how complicated the story is, yes?"

I figured his folksy talk was an act.

"Well, there is a man, and an SS officer who saved his life in Rostov-on-Don …"

I opened my notebook and gave them a compressed version of Milman's story.

When I finished, Benny nodded and asked, "What was that officer's name again?"

"Arno. His nickname was Prinz."

Benny chuckled, then loudly sipped his coffee.

"I have a long list of senior and mid-level SS officers that took part in the Holocaust. I am sure I've never seen one with these names."

"Perhaps he was not senior enough. We know from the British records that the boy entered Palestine from Lebanon on September 22nd of 1942. He claimed that there was a German with him, but the German was never identified." Hannah tried to get past Benny's disbelief.

"What do you think about the part in Turkey?" I asked. "The officer telling the Turk that he is going to Palestine to connect with German Templers and set up a radio observation post to direct Rommel's troops."

Benny pulled out a crumpled handkerchief, loudly blew his nose. "Seems like something out of a spy novel, yes?"

"I don't know yet if I believe the story. Does it make sense to you?"

"Well, Rommel was coming, that much is true. And we had pro-Nazi German Templers here that the Brits arrested during the war. And there were Nazi spies and sympathizers all throughout Turkey and the Middle East. Being an SS officer, perhaps he was planning to rendezvous with Erich Rolff?"

"The gas vans' Rolff?" I asked.

"Yes, you know about him?"

"He's in the Chelmno report I'm working on for the German Nazi investigation office."

"The one in Ludwigsburg?" Benny's posture changed, he looked at me with curiosity.

"Yes. I was asked to be Yad Vashem's liaison to them. But I thought that from Poland Rolff was sent to Italy?"

"First he went to the Middle East. In the late summer of 1942, he was in Tunisia with Rommel. And he had an SS extermination unit with him, *Einsatzgruppen Tunis*. He was working with the Grand Mufti in Berlin, trying to get the Arabs to revolt. Mufti even had a couple of Muslim Waffen SS divisions organized. Had the British not defeated Rommel at El-Alamein in October of that year, *Standartenführer* Rolff would have come here with his lovely gas vans. Instead, he went to northern Italy as the head of Gestapo there. No gas vans at his disposal, just cattle cars to Auschwitz."

Benny lit up a stinky cigarette, blew out rancid smoke.

"Do you think that the officer was indeed on a secret mission?" Hannah asked.

"I don't know. The boy never saw the body, right? I'd say your officer knew about Rolff's plans and the Templers, so he was well informed. The secret mission theory makes little sense to me. But an SS officer suddenly deciding to take a Jewish boy to Palestine makes even less sense."

"Benny, if you wanted to find out who the officer was, how would you start?" I asked.

Benny stubbed out his cigarette, pointed at me. "It's hot but you're wearing a long-sleeve shirt. Hannah told me you were in Auschwitz. You don't want people to know, to see your tattoo?"

"No, just what I wanted to wear." But in truth, I'd been covering my tattoo for years.

"What did you do there?"

"Survived."

Benny stared at me. I was used to people looking at me with condolence or respect or fear. But I saw none of that in Benny's eyes. It was more of an appraisal. He slowly nodded.

"OK. To your question, I would go to West Germany. You don't have a lot of information, but you know where the officer was in August of 1942."

"Do you think it'll work?" Hannah asked.

"Perhaps something amazing will happen as it usually does in spy novels." Benny's sarcastic act was back on full display. "You'll run into his twin brother who'll tell you that Prinz joined the SS only to protect the Jews. Or you'll manage to get to Berlin, and Russkies will tell you that Prinz was a Russian spy."

"Seriously, Benny!" Hannah raised her voice impatiently.

"Well, it's worth a shot, OK?"

"Why Germany and not Turkey?"

"Germans are very meticulous people, good at keeping records. For them, order and documentation are the essence of civilization."

"David, you are planning to go to Ludwigsburg anyway, right?" Hannah turned to me.

"I have not decided yet."

"Germany's civil administration is full of former Nazis that will obstruct you, but Ludwigsburg is different," Benny said. "They have an extensive access to the SS files. But why would they help you?"

"Can you do anything?"

Benny chewed on his lip thoughtfully. "Perhaps. We don't have an official diplomatic mission in West Germany, but we have our representatives. Dealing with trade, compensation claims, stuff like that. One of them is a good friend of mine."

"Do you think this man, this Yosef Milman, is telling the truth?"

Benny shrugged "How would I know? You talked to him, not I."

"But what's your opinion?" Hannah asked.

"I sort of believe him."

"Why? The names he mentioned, they are known or not difficult to find."

"It's the ore ..."

"What do you mean?"

"The metal ore ... Turkey was supplying Nazis with chromite ore for steel production, at times openly, at times secretly. Not something one would know to make up."

I stayed a while after Benny left.

"Why would Benny want to help?"

Hannah shrugged.

"He likes me. We've been going out."

When I got to my flat, I opened the Chelmno file I brought from the office to work on. Benny didn't know that I had my personal interest in *Standartenführer* Rolff. After leafing through hundreds of pages of testimonials and documents, I found the one-page memo.

```
Secret Reich Business
Berlin, 5 June 1942
Changes for Special Vehicles now in Service at
Chelmno

Since December 1941, ninety-seven thousand have
been processed by the vehicles in service. In the
light of observations made so far, however, the
following technical changes are needed:
  1. The load space must be shortened. The operating
```

time can be considerably reduced if there is less empty void to be filled with carbon monoxide. The manufacturer is concerned that this would overload the front axle. In fact, the balance is automatically restored because the merchandise aboard naturally rushes to the rear doors in an attempt to escape and is mainly found lying there at the end of the operation. So the front axle is not overloaded.

2. The lamps must be enclosed in a steel grid to prevent their being damaged. It would be useful to light the lamp before and during the first moments of operation because the load rushes toward the light, making closing of the doors difficult. This would also reduce the amount of screaming.

3. For easy cleaning of the vehicle, there must be a sealed drain in the middle of the floor. The drainage hole's cover would be equipped with a slanting trap, so that fluid liquids can drain off during the operation. During cleaning, the drain can be used to evacuate excrement.

The aforementioned technical changes are to be made to vehicles in service only when they come in for repairs.

Submitted for decision to Gruppenleiter II D, by SS Obersturmbannführer Erich Rolff.

I wondered if this initiative had earned Rolff his next promotion. It came up in the Eichmann trial that Rolff had organized the deportation of Italian Jews in 1944.

That meant Ezra's family.

Ezra came again that night and sat on the side of the bed.

"David, you're getting close to my age. Soon you'll be older than I."

"You knew what was going to happen on October 7th?"

"Maybe I knew, maybe I didn't. What difference does it make now?"

"You should have told me!"

"Why? So you would throw yourself into the hail of bullets?"

"You made me live with this. I had the right to know!"

Ezra laughed softly, caressed my hair. "David, David, what does this have to do with 'right'? We were so far beyond all that. I did what I had to do. So, you're here now."

"Do you want me to avenge you and Lia?"

He got up without replying.

"Wait, please!"

But he backed away from the bed, eyes focused on me. And then he was gone.

7

It was almost mid-May when I gathered my courage and walked over to Shaare Zadek Medical Center. It wasn't too far and I walked everywhere anyway. Alas, I arrived dusty and smelling of gasoline fumes from Egged buses that passed me by. I walked into reception and saw my reflection in the glass: disheveled, white shirt stained with sweat. I would have turned around but for a friendly elderly woman who asked,

"What can we help you with?"

"Well ... I don't know ..."

"Young man, what's hurting?"

"Erhh ... Nothing. I was looking for a nurse. Her name is Yael."

"Which one?" The woman smiled. "We have two here."

"Erhh ..."

"The younger one is Yael Isenberg," she offered helpfully.

"Yes, yes, that's the one."

"Please wait, I will have her come down."

Yael was surprised to see me, but I couldn't tell if it was a pleasant or annoyed surprise. She looked good even in the nurse's uniform.

"David, what are you doing here?"

"I came to see you."

She looked around. Three women in the reception were busily shuffling papers, their ears no doubt tuned to us.

"Let's go outside."

Yael walked to a shaded area. I followed.

"David, I am working."

"I'm sorry. I didn't want to come knock on your apartment door, so I came here. It was a bad idea, I'll go."

"Wait." Yael's voice softened. "You're right, it would have been

68

creepy for you to show up at my door."

"You did not come to see Yosef and Rachel on Sunday. Was that because of me?"

"How did your conversation with Yosef go?" she said, avoiding the question.

"It's a fascinating story." I wasn't going to admit that my interest was largely due to her.

"Yosef is now obsessed. I think talking to you gave him the idea that he'll be able to find that German officer. I hope you can help him. If not, please discourage him."

"Is that important to you?"

"Yes, of course. It's my sister's family. Why do you ask?"

"I might be able to go to Germany and make some inquiries."

She raised her eyebrows. "Really? Oh, that would be so great of you!"

I did not say anything, just stared at her. Yael smiled. "So why are you here? To tell me you'll be traveling?"

"I came to ask you to go out with me this Saturday night."

"David..." She looked aside. "You're nice, but I've been seeing someone."

"I know. Your sister told me."

Yael looked at me with interest. "But you came to ask me nevertheless?"

"She didn't say that it's serious. Is it?"

Yael hesitated, then shrugged. "I don't know yet. I only got divorced recently. I'm not ready to get re-married or anything."

"Then go out with me. We eat, listen to music, see a movie."

"I don't know …"

I saw that she was going to say no if I kept pushing. "Yael, here's my office number. Just think about it." I gave her a piece of paper with my phone that I'd prepared beforehand.

"OK."

I watched her go, hoping she'd turn back and look at me before going inside. She did.

"I can't this Saturday night. But I will think about it."

I was planning to see Dov, but he showed up in my office first. He carried a small box that he put on my desk. I could see that the box was full of letters.

"You know what this is?" He nodded after sitting down.

"I can guess. It's because of the trial, isn't it?"

"Yes. People are sending us their stories. We must investigate. Here are the ones in German, English, Yiddish, and Polish. These are the languages you speak, right?"

"Yes. Also French, Czech and Spanish. But shouldn't these go to Tel-Aviv's department? They collect testimony of the witnesses."

"True, but they've been swamped and don't have enough linguists."

"We already have enough to investigate for the next few years."

"I gave you that junior researcher, Chaia."

"She's slow."

"There is no budget for additional researchers."

"And I can't make her work any faster!"

We stared at each other across the desk. We didn't like each other. I should have been promoted into his position, I was better qualified. But he had the connections. Party connections. He was Mapai and they ran the country. I belonged to Herut, and Lehi before. The Kasztner affair, the German reparations—we disagreed on everything. Dov's family came here before the war and he didn't like non-heroic survivors. To him, Yad Vashem was all about Jewish heroism, the Warsaw uprising and all that. Being shot and gassed without resisting was offensive to Dov Cohen.

"Look, I wanted to follow up on that deal with Ludwigsburg." Dov changed topics. I knew he would shy away from a confrontation. This *schlimazl* would not have survived a week in Auschwitz.

"What about it?"

"The Chelmno report should be finished by mid-July. I asked you to go, but you don't have to if you are too..." He paused, searching for an expression that would be insulting but not directly so.

"I am too what?"

"Well, you know … You don't have to go."

"I'm thinking of going. I'll let you know soon."

"You will?" Dov's eyebrows flew up in surprise and disappointment. He'd been looking for reasons to get rid of me. "OK.

70

Don't wait too long. They need the information soon. One of their lawyers, Fritz Jager, is here for the trial. You should meet him."

Dov got up, hesitated, sat back down looking at me.

"Come on, Dov, what's on your mind?"

He glanced aside, then back at me. "I did not think you would go to Ludwigsburg."

"I have not decided yet. Why?"

"Well..." His face reddened. "I ... I am not sure you like working here."

"What makes you say that?"

"The Eichmann prosecution team accused you of not helping ..."

"Rahel Auerbach has a team in Tel-Aviv. They're responsible for that." But I knew full well that Dov saw Rahel as a competitor and hated that she was getting a more prominent role at the trial.

"And your co-workers complain that you are rude and uncooperative. Chaia, that junior researcher, cried in my office. Your personal life is not my business ..."

Chaia, that little bitch.

"That's right, Dov, it's none of your business."

"OK, fine. But why can't you collaborate with your colleagues?"

"I do my job."

"You were more productive in previous years ..."

"And I was told to stop what I was doing, to focus on current issues!" I surprised him and myself by slapping my fist on the desk. "The directorate of the museum was opposed to the Holocaust research because it made us look weak. We didn't fit into the narrative. But you know that."

I stopped and stared at the wall. No point in giving him more ammunition.

"David, why didn't you want to testify? I know the prosecution asked you twice. You were in Auschwitz. You saw what happened."

"Yes, Dov. I was there. And I survived. You know that the best of us did not. And for some it makes me a suspect, as if I were a part of the same machine as Eichmann. The prosecution wanted witnesses that fought with partisans. Not those that just managed to survive."

Dov raised his palms. "David, these people didn't die in vain."

I lost control again and burst out laughing.

"Sorry, Dr. Cohen, but nobody cares. Nobody wants to hear about the dead. 'Forgive and forget', the world moved on. The Germans are paying us reparations for all that they stole from the Jews. What else can we ask for? They didn't die in vain? Then tell me, what's the meaning of their deaths? Do tell, Dr. Cohen!"

"OK, David." Dov looked at me with what seemed like sadness. That surprised me. But he couldn't fathom what it was like in Europe. "I also would like to think that there were some good Germans. You know, one of them, Father Grüber, will be testifying at the trial. I can get a pass for you."

He was doing me a favor; passes to Eichmann's trial were hard to get. It was a favor I didn't ask for, but I just nodded politely to show my appreciation.

"Thank you, I have one already."

Of course, if he did not take my job, I would have been the one distributing passes to the trial.

Pastor Heinrich Grüber, the only German to testify at the trial: "In 1938, I went to Switzerland to beg for more foreign visas for Jews. All the official institutions, embassies, they did not reveal any understanding or interest. Very often we came out of those places full of anger, not only full of shame at the lack of readiness to help; it would have been possible to save millions of souls." He went to plead with Eichmann: "I must say, having come here without any hatred or feelings of revenge, the impression I had of him was that he was a man who sat there like a block of ice, or a block of marble, and everything you tried to get through to him just bounced off him. The mercenary who, as he dons his uniform, doffs his conscience and his reason."

But Grüber would not tell the court the name of a compatriot, now living in Germany, who had *helped* Jews during the Nazi regime. "I could bring to the Court a whole file of threats and derision which I received, especially in connection with my trip to Israel.... To me these things do not mean much . . . but I would not like to cause this suffering to others."

Afterwards, I met Ludwigsburg's Fritz Jager in the bar of the King David Hotel. A young lawyer of around thirty, Fritz came here to observe the trial.

"He doesn't look like Attila or Tamerlane. He looks like a damn accountant." Jager emptied his glass of whisky and slammed it on the table. "Eichmann is here to take away German sins: 'He did it!' One monster out of the innocent multitude. And Grüber is to show the face of the other Germany. Except it does not add up."

We overheard a conversation behind us.

"Eichmann said he worked to help the victims by making their death easier," said a balding middle-aged man. "He was no anti-Semite, just a bureaucratic climber."

A woman that looked like his daughter said, "That makes it worse in my book: murdering people to get a promotion."

"The more I look at him, the more I believe he's not a monster but an imbecile," a woman with forceful, German-accent said. "He didn't really realize what he was doing. He's unable to think from the perspective of others."

"I don't know about that." Jager shrugged, smirking at me after overhearing them. "I do know he has an incredible memory about food. Heard it from Servatius's assistant. Eichmann remembers exactly what he ate, where and when: soup, entrée, dessert. But when asked about the number of Jews deported from a particular area, he says 'fifty thousand or a hundred and fifty thousand.' What's a hundred thousand murdered people between friends?"

"Did you read how that asshole Hausner attacked Moshe Beisky with 'Why didn't you revolt?'" Maurice was complaining angrily. "It's as if Beisky and not Eichmann is on trial!"

"Beisky gave him a good reply. And then there was that German priest, Heinrich Grüber," Jacob said, trying to re-direct the conversation.

"Yeah, well, I don't know why we even invited any Germans to testify," Maurice grumbled.

"I've met him," Jacob said. "I've met Grüber."

"Where?"

"In Dachau. The clergy were in a different camp from the Jews. But I saw him once in the building where the Nazi doctors conducted medical experiments. He and I were left waiting in the same room for a few minutes. He is a good man."

"He's still a German," Maurice spit out. "They used my wife for their skeletons collection. Fed her, killed her with gas, boiled her in a pot so they could send her bones to a museum. I hate them all."

That's when Yosef finally showed up. I took him aside.

"Let's go for a walk. Yosef, if you want to try to find out who Prinz was, we have to go to Germany."

"We? Germany?" Yosef stopped in his tracks, jaw dropped.

"Yes. Why did you come to me?"

"I want to know who he was ... I just ... I didn't expect I'd have to go ... there ... I thought you could research ... I thought you could find him."

"Sorry, I can't do much with what you gave me. And only you can recognize him. We have years and years of backlog to investigate. Your case would be at the bottom."

"I don't think I want to go," Yosef said firmly.

Perfect. I offered, he declined. I still look good before Yael, and I can tell Dov to send someone else.

"You said 'we'—why would you go?" Yosef asked.

"I might have a reason to go to Germany for work."

We walked in silence.

"I guess you're right." Yosef exhaled hard, as a man that's been deprived of choices.

"I must talk to Rachel. She is due any day now."

Rachel will surely kill the idea, I thought.

Yael called me in the office next week. Under Ruth's accusing gaze, we made plans to meet on Saturday evening.

I debated whether to wear my best and only suit, decided it would be too much in the heat of Jerusalem summer. But I put on a nice white shirt and polished my shoes. When I picked up Yael by her apartment, she wore a patriotic blue and white dress. It was light and close fitting. We took the Egged bus. It was full of people going downtown to party after *Shabbat*. On road curves Yael's body would press against mine. I began to perspire. She smiled, she enjoyed her power over me. We ate at a restaurant on Jaffa Road, where we had to buy tickets for our food, and walked in the shadow of a wall that blocked us off from the Jordanians. Then we went to see a movie in the old cinema in Geula. Everyone around us smoked and in the bluish haze Yul Brynner, Steve McQueen and other American actors defended Mexican villagers from bandits. Sound was drowned at times by people's conversations and bottles rolling down the aisles. Yael gently picked up my hand and held it in hers.

I took her back to Ir Ganim. We stood in front of Yael's apartment and I tried to draw her to me. She put her hands against my chest to keep a distance and kissed me with, "Thank you, David, I had a good time." I watched her disappear into the building.

At the trial, defense attorney Servatius: "Killing was a medical matter." Even Judge Halevi seemed stunned: "Was that a slip of the tongue?" Servatius persisted: "No, since the killing was done by gas, it was a medical matter."

The Trial's chronology reached 1944. Hungary. The place where Eichmann truly spread his wings. Everyone knew that the war was lost. Even Himmler told him to stop the extermination. But not Eichmann, no. He was the hands-on master of life and death. He worked hard to ship another four hundred thousand souls into our inferno.

Member of Budapest Jewish Council Pinhas Freudiger got on the stand. Back at Kasztner's trial, he testified that he bought the lives of his family and friends from the Nazis in late 1944. People in the audience screamed at him: 'You duped us, so you could save yourselves and your families. But our families were killed!' The man that protested most loudly was taken out of the courtroom. Here we were judging Eichmann, not the collaborators.

Joel Brand testified about Eichmann's proposal to release the Hungarian Jews in exchange for war supplies. One hundred people for one truck. Nobody would offer anything, and the British didn't want more Jews in Palestine anyway. The trains went to Auschwitz instead. I'd met Joel before. He just turned fifty-five; he looked seventy. For seventeen years now, he ate and slept and thought only of the hundreds of thousands that he could not save. Hausner submitted documents detailing what the Zionist leaders did to convince the British to enter into negotiations with the Nazis. Britain and the US were guilty, not us. But the heavy shadow of the Kasztner trial remained: did the leaders do everything they could?

Yosef brought me with him for moral support, which I was somewhat ambivalent to provide but figured it was better to come and keep quiet. Rachel was not happy. Actually, outright mad.

"Yosik, I know you want to find out who that man, that German was. But why do you have to go? Let him go!" she pointed at me. "That kind of stuff, that's his job!"

"But what if there are photos to look at? I am the only one who can recognize him!" Yosef protested.

"Yosik, you can't do this to me. You can't!" Rachel wrapped her hands around her bulging belly and started crying. We sat silently.

After a few minutes, she wiped off tears with her hand, sniffled, gathered herself up.

"Fine. Go. But at least two months after the child is born. And only for one week. And only if my mother can stay and help."

Walking back, I laughed out loud at the cosmic joke: I thought for sure that either Yosef or Rachel would have said no, and I would have come out smelling like a rose without actually having to do anything. But you know what they say about the best laid plans. To back out now meant losing Yael for sure, and I didn't want to lose her.

I walked into Dov's office the next morning. "Remember the case of Yosef Milman?"

He gave me a look of incomprehension.

"The boy that was saved by an SS officer?"

"Oh, right."

"Yes. I promised Yosef to go with him to Germany to try to find the officer's name."

Dov removed his glasses and squinted at me thoughtfully. I expected him to object but he instead nodded his head. "Very well. I presume you'll do it on your own time during your Ludwigsburg's trip."

"Yes. I wanted you to know that I'll go in August at the earliest."

He scrunched his face in disapproval. "The Chelmno report will be ready soon."

I didn't reply and turned around to go, when he stopped me.

"Are you following the trial?"

"Of course."

76

"Did you hear Kovner's testimony about Anton Schmid? The German officer that was executed by the Nazis for helping Jews?"

"Yes."

Dov put his glasses back on. "As you know, we plan to open the Avenue of the Righteous next year, for those that rescued Jews. Rescuers must be nominated. I want you to nominate some German rescuers."

"Really? You want me to nominate Germans? Me?"

Dov shrugged, rubbed his bald crown.

"Yes, why not?"

8

Witness: Eliahu Rosenberg, age 35. A young man who grew up in the death camp of Treblinka. There were thirteen separate gas chambers, and once, in thirty-five minutes, 10,000 people were killed in them. He had many jobs, this child, from cutting off women's hair for mattress stuffing to pulling out the gold teeth of corpses. From these teeth, eight to ten kilos of gold were collected each week and shipped in suitcases to Berlin. One day, Eliahu found his sister's corpse on the pile.

In the glass cage, the little man listened, unmoved. He didn't consider himself guilty. Not in the sense of indictment. You see a man alone, isolated and despised, and you want to pity that man. But not him. I could not understand him human-to-human; he was somehow from a different place. He had all the physical characteristics of a human being and yet he was different. What did the extermination even mean to him? He didn't remember where, when and how many he sent to their deaths. But he remembered nice dinners he had. From the Wannsee conference that planned a mass murder, he remembered having cognac by the fireplace. Here was Adolf Eichmann, in the dock, very ordinary, very harmless. But when he had the power... If they won the war, what would he have looked like?

That night I had another dream of dancing children. They wore school uniforms, the girls in white blouses and dark-blue skirts, the boys in white short-sleeves and black pants. Shirts and blouses were emblazed with a school logo of a tree being consumed by a fire. I couldn't see their faces in the darkness. The children took each other's hands and formed a large circle. All, but one boy that held a torch. The boy threw the torch into the middle and a great pyre lit up, hissing and crackling. I was outside of their circle and even there I felt the immense heat and took a step back. But the children didn't mind. The boy that had the torch joined the circle, and they began to dance: two steps counterclockwise, kicked off their left leg, then their right one, two more steps. They danced silently, with the roar of the pyre being the only terrible music. Their faces were lit up by the orange flames, but I still couldn't see their features. They went faster and faster. Soon they were dancing on their toes. And then they defied gravity and rose off the cold ground, first by a foot, then a yard, then the circle became a beautiful rotating blur that went up higher and higher, above the pyre, above the embers, into the dark sky.

I woke up in a cold sweat and remembered that we had school children visit the museum two days prior, and last night I walked by a building where they burned some old leaves.

Milman's little girl, Rivka, was born in late June. I was invited to the baby-naming ceremony at their synagogue the following Saturday. Afterwards, we came back to the Milmans' house to celebrate. That was how I met Yael's other boyfriend. They looked good together. Itzhak Rubin was a thirty-year old *sabra*, a major in the IDF decorated during the 1956 war. He shook my hand aggressively, his skin rough from sand and weapons.

"Ahhh, David Levy. Yael told me about you." Itzhak viewed me with jealousy. "You are going to Germany with Yosef to look for that Nazi that supposedly saved him."

"Well, according to Yosef it's not a supposition …"

"Why are you even looking to get help from the Germans?" he demanded.

"Itzhak!" Yael tried to stop him, but he just waved her off.

"Jews should not be asking Germans for any help! Not after what they've done!"

"If not for one of them, Yosef would have been killed," I protested without conviction. "This little girl Rivka wouldn't have been born."

"I have a joke for you." Itzhak smiled. "A Jewish village in Eastern Europe has been ransacked by pogroms. One of the villagers escaped to the neighboring town to tell them the story. The rabbi asked: 'And what did you do?' The man answered: 'We recited twice as many psalms and fasted.' The rabbi nodded: 'Good work, can't just sit around doing nothing'. Funny, eh?"

Itzhak slapped me on the back playfully, then bared his teeth.

"How could you Jews let that happen? Went to the slaughter without resisting!"

How do you explain to someone who wasn't there that everything that happened was incremental, leaving some hope for survival, a step at a time until you descend into an unimaginable hell?

"There was resistance, there were uprisings. Warsaw Ghetto, Sobibor, Treblinka, even Auschwitz."

"Yes, Auschwitz ... That's where you were?"

I nodded. There was a circle of silence around us.

"But you didn't revolt. You did whatever you had to do just so you could survive, right?"

Blood rushed to my face. "You don't know. You weren't there."

"No, I don't know. I'll never know. Because we'll never again be helpless, wait for someone to save us!"

I stood there looking at him, hating him.

"Itzhak, you stop it right now!" Yael begged.

Itzhak turned and walked away. Yael looked at me, then at him, stood glued to her spot for a moment. She walked over to me and whispered, "I am sorry. I must make sure he's OK. His parents were killed in the Scorpion Pass Massacre seven years ago. He just blows up sometimes." She turned to follow Itzhak.

"Yeah, because he's the chosen one!" I shouted at her back and left the ceremony.

Ten weeks into the trial, Eichmann finally took the stand. He looked different, grayish, afraid at last. In a low voice he told us the story of his misfortune. He was no anti-Semite. He was nobody important; he just happened to have taken up Jews as his specialty. He worked to help the Jews. He had always sought peaceful solutions, but like Pontius Pilate he had no choice. He never acted on his own initiative. Documents had been altered. Colleagues lied. He did not remember this, and he did not remember that. 115 skeletons for research? He did not remember. His name in the letter? OK, but he was not authorized. In Hungary, he was "marginally involved." He was simply an "observer." He was "unlucky." He was the victim. The *Washington Post* found "dignity" in Eichmann.

For two months in that courtroom, he was a puzzle, an enigma to me. I couldn't grasp the essence of his humanity. Until he opened his mouth and said that one sentence:

"The question of conscience is a matter for the head of the state."

And that's when I finally saw inside of him. Human beings have a conscience. Sometimes we blocked it in order to survive a bit longer, but it was always there. He did not have one, he gave his up voluntarily and permanently. He was a clever, malevolent non-human that feasted on power.

On July 2nd, Ernest Hemingway killed himself. The next evening, Café Europa was gloomy.

"Why? He had everything," Jacob pondered sadly. "His writing was full of vigor."

"His writing was all masculine potency: physical strength, hunting, sexual prowess," said a woman poetess. "Then he became impotent. I think he killed himself out of fear."

She looked at me as she said that. Back in April, I was supposed to attend her reading here and then take her to bed. We built up to it for a few weeks prior, talking about literature, flirting, kissing, touching. The main course was set—and I didn't show up for it. Because I agreed to take down Yosef's story that night, stayed a touch longer than I planned, and Yael walked in to have dinner with her sister's family. The poetess, having a sensitive and imaginative nature, had decided that I turned afraid of her female powers and used every possible occasion to subtly deride me. She emphasized the word "impotent" as she shot it in my direction. I smiled. The poetess spent the war years in the relative safety of Toronto and didn't have my appreciation of the power that chaotic randomness wields over our lives.

"Or it was his last masculine stand," Jacob disagreed with the poetess. "An assertion of making his own choices."

"Oh, I don't think so!" the poetess cut him off. "His female characters were either tramps, like Brett Ashley, or murderesses, like Margot Macomber. He was afraid of women and hated them. He was the ultimate Jake Barnes."

She continued to look at me and I remembered that our last intimate conversation was about *The Sun Also Rises*. The poetess saw herself as Lady Brett Ashley, with her mixture of sexual liberation and a romantic love for Jake Barnes. To her, I, David Levy, was a member of another war-damaged, emasculated lost generation, her Jake. Except not maimed, which she had verified by rubbing her hand against my groin and exclaiming: "Well, you're a better version of Jake!" She'd been symbolically taking back the exclamation since then.

I was sad over Hemingway's suicide; I liked reading him. And Jacob's words resonated with me. It didn't mean I agreed with Hemingway. But he lived his life by making his own choices to the end. Perhaps only those that were forced to exist in a place where all choices disappear would appreciate this defense of the last bit of freedom left to us: *how to leave*.

A couple of days later, we launched *Shavit 2*, the first Israeli rocket. This caused much excitement. "I think Itzhak had something to do with this," Yael confided proudly, then added "Sorry." A larger *Shavit 3* was launched a bit later. The rocket age had arrived in the Middle East, but we haven't quite appreciated its significance that day.

The Eichmann trial finally ended on August 14th. In a way, it was anti-climactic. It's not that I lost interest. It's just that he no longer seemed like such a riddle to me.

Yael and I went out a few more times during the summer. I knew that my plans with Yosef had a lot to do with it, and that she continued to see Itzhak. Strangely enough, I didn't even mind the largely platonic nature of our relationship. It wasn't that I didn't want to change it, but I was afraid to push for anything more than that, afraid that Yael would choose him over me. I had a feeling that the situation between Yael and Itzhak was similar. One time I was staring at a full moon from my balcony and thought of Yael as a beautiful moon caught in a gravitational pull between two planets, Itzhak's and mine. We were in a state of a delicate harmony that could be changed by the slightest of perturbations. And once the balance was broken in favor of one side, the pull from there would get stronger and stronger. Because that was how gravity worked. One gets strange thoughts when one's alone on a balcony at night.

That was how it went on, carefully, the passion simmering under the surface. This way, at least I had a connection and a chance. And dreams where Yael made love to me. I usually saw her on top, moaning my name and moving faster and faster, head thrown back, my hands kneading her breasts. Meanwhile, I got evening walks, movies, handholding and an occasional kiss. Once we went to see the American movie *Spartacus*. Kirk Douglas's chin reminded me of Yosef.

PART 3:
AVI

1

"Why do you want to know?" Mom was using a fork to torture her macadamia nut cheesecake. She avoided looking at me. I took her to lunch in The Cheesecake Factory in Marina Del Rey, by Mother's Beach. Mom liked coming here for their ice tea and desserts. I felt bad that I ambushed her like that, but I needed to know.

"I found some papers in the house. A correspondence to Grandpa from a man in Germany. Grandpa may have been planning something … something to do with military supplies."

"Yes, there was another man killed in the same robbery in 1965, and his name was Levon something. But, Avi, it's been almost twenty-six years. You can't bring them back."

"So what? This family's been full of secrets. I don't know who my grandfather was, or my father, or my uncle, or even my brother. They are all gone, and I don't have anyone to ask but you."

"You blamed your father for your brother's death and now you blame yourself for your father's," she said. "You shouldn't. You really shouldn't."

I didn't answer. Should, shouldn't—these were just words.

"It was all good until the summer of 1964." Mom drank the rest of her wine. "That's when your dad, your Grandpa Aram and your Uncle Sarkis all went to Europe for a week. Not sure what happened there, but something went wrong. I heard your dad arguing with them when they all returned, and these were angry arguments. And after your grandpa was killed in Germany the next year, your uncle and your brother stopped speaking with your dad. Cut him off completely. Some years later they left the country, first Sarkis, then Tigran. And Tigran came back from Lebanon in a closed coffin."

"You don't know what happened?"

"No, your father wouldn't talk about it." Mom shook her head. "I know you loved your brother. But your dad loved him too. Tigran's death broke him. He turned into a hermit afterwards."

My face grew hot. It was true. I was eighteen and I had to blame someone.

"What did Grandfather Aram do for a living?"

"He was an editor of an Armenian paper and he published a few books. I never had a chance to get to know him well. I was working, and you were a handful. You were not even four when—"

"Does the name Matusian mean anything to you?"

She thought about it, shook her head. "No, why?"

"It came up in the correspondence. I was thinking…who were these people at Dad's funeral? Many of them I've never met before."

Dad had passed away three years ago, at sixty-five. He was retired long enough that nobody from his bank had bothered to come, although the company did send a nice wreath. His parents were dead, so was his older son, his only brother was in jail in Europe. It was a small group besides Mom, Amy and I: a few neighbors, a couple of his war buddies. And a few Armenians that stood to the side and left without attending the reception.

"One was Anush, his first wife. The woman in the wheelchair was Maria, your grandpa's sister-in-law. Others, I don't know."

"Some of them were at my uncle's funeral. I think there were four of them, an older woman and three younger people."

"Yeah, the ones that I don't know. Anush died soon after your father, and the directory couldn't tell me where Maria is. The Fresno family … I think they blamed me for your father leaving Anush." Mom got the waiter's attention and ordered another glass of wine. "Even though he left her years before he met me. Perhaps they thought he'd come to his senses, but he asked for a divorce instead. Neither of our families was happy."

"What happened?"

"Well, back in 1960 I was already working in the Powell Library …"

"Just like the thirty years after that?" As I kid, I loved visiting Mom at work. I loved the campus, I loved the building with its Spanish and Italian influence, I enjoyed the quiet concentration inside.

"Yes, I like stability." Mom smiled through tears. "One day this striking-looking man, with an unruly jet-black mane of hair, showed up and asked to get a card, the kind that non-students need. He had an unusual name—Vrej. He explained that it means 'revenge' in Armenian. And that he just moved to the area because his son would be attending UCLA in the fall. Two days later he came back, checked out a few books and asked me to have a dinner with him."

"And you did?"

"Yes, of course. Ten months later you were born."

"Wow, you were not married yet!" It was hard for me to imagine my rather reserved parents acting like that. But then it's probably common for young people to not see their parents as lovers.

"You know, your dad actually made a habit of it!" Mom laughed. I think that wine loosened her tongue. "I understand that your brother, his older son, was also conceived before the vows had been exchanged. Anush and your dad were high school sweethearts. Tigran was born when they both were only nineteen."

"Why did they break up?"

"I don't know all the details. I think the Karayans, the family that your dad married into, was a known and powerful family in Fresno. And his father-in-law wanted Dad to work for him, and he was a man used to getting his way. Except that your dad was not the type to just go along. After the war, Dad went to college on the GI Bill and got a degree and started working in a bank. Put two stubborn men together and they'll keep butting heads. As the conflict escalated, at some point your father left Fresno and went to work for a bank in San Francisco. Dad loved your brother, and that kept things together for a bit. But when Tigran chose to go to UCLA, your dad just moved here. So you see, I did not break up their family. But that's what the Karayans thought, I was an *odar* that stole him."

"And what about your family?"

"Pfffft … They wanted me to marry a nice Jewish boy and instead I got pregnant by a *goy*. It was our version of *Fiddler on the Roof*. Years later, after seeing the movie, my late father started calling your dad *Perchik* and himself *Tevye*." She laughed. "Actually, my parents came to peace with this quickly. I was twenty-seven, kind of an old maid for that time, and none of the nice Jewish boys worked out. I think I was just attracted to older men. And they loved your father. My dad thought that Armenians are similar to the Jews. When I broke the news and my mother was wailing, he told her to stop because *he's a goy but at least he's an Armenian goy*. It helped when your dad agreed to name you Avram after my grandfather."

"They always called me Avi, not Avram."

"Well, Avi was a better name for a teenager in the seventies, don't you think? It was a matter of principle, knowing who you were named after."

"And what about my father's father?"

"Oh, surprisingly he accepted me without reservation. He did not like the Karayans either. He moved from Fresno to LA soon after, bought the house in Hermosa that's yours now. You may not remember, you were little, but he loved playing with you."

She was right, I did not remember much of him. Except for a scratchy beard and a smell of tobacco, wine and leather as he was kissing me.

"I know there was something different about Grandfather Aram," Mom said. "When we had parties, people treated him with great respect. He had many, many friends. When he died, it ripped the heart out of the family. There were no more parties. In one blow, your father lost his father, his brother and his older son. I know he reached out to Tigran many times, but Tigran never truly came back to him. And he was afraid of the influence they might get over you. After Tigran died, Father just went through the motions for the next nine years, waiting to die too. I tried to find something to … to wake him up, but I couldn't. I just stayed by his side, being his companion."

"Can I get you anything else?" the waiter asked in that annoyingly polite 'isn't it time to go?' tone.

"No, just the check," I snarled back, and he hurried away.

2

On the way back to Hermosa, I stopped by Erik Babayan's office on Pier Avenue. Next to an unmarked door, a surfboard was leaning against the wall and a wetsuit gently swung in the ocean breeze. The door was ajar and the first thing I saw inside were the lawyer's bare feet on the desk and the cover of a men's magazine. There was a distinct smell of pot in the air.

When I said, "Hello," the magazine came down and Babayan lowered his feet. He clearly hadn't bothered to shave in a couple of days.

"Avi, hello. I apologize. I didn't expect anyone. Walk-ins are rare."

"Sorry, I should have called."

"No problem. Everything OK? Do you need a recommendation for a real estate agent?"

"An agent? No, why?"

"Well, you are selling the house, right?"

"No, I fixed it up a bit and moved in."

Babayan's round face registered surprise. "Well, well, well … To be honest, I didn't expect that. Aren't you from Seattle?"

"I was. I moved there in '79 because of a girl. Decided to come home."

"Sorry, man. Women …" He reached into one of the drawers and got out a bottle of whisky and two glasses. "As that cliché goes, can't live with them, can't shoot them. Here, have a drink."

I sipped mine; he emptied his glass.

"So, what brings you over then?"

"Mr. Babayan, I remember you were at my uncle's funeral …"

"Call me Erik, please. Yes, I was. And your father's."

"There was a group of four or five people there. They seemed

Armenian. I don't know who they were. My mother does not know either. Do you?"

"Why?"

"Just trying to understand."

Babayan looked at me, chewed his lips. "Tell me more, Avi."

"Well, I found a correspondence in the garage. Addressed to my grandfather."

"What about?"

"The Eichmann trial and other things. It seemed like my grandfather was looking to publish a novel."

"So? He did some writing and publishing."

"There were other things. Do you know how he died?"

"I've been told it was a robbery gone bad in Germany. Why? Did you hear otherwise?" Babayan's voice was not very convincing.

"Well, from the correspondence it didn't sound like Grandfather was going there for a fun tourist trip."

"Then what was he there for?"

"I don't know yet."

"And what does that have to do with people at the funeral?"

"I want to understand who my grandfather was ... and my uncle and my brother. All I know is that in '79 we had the FBI come to our home, asking questions about Tigran. They said he was a terrorist who accidentally killed himself while wiring a bomb."

Babayan poured more whiskey.

"Avi, I don't have all the answers. As an attorney, one sometimes chooses not to know. It was whispered that your grandfather was not who he claimed to be. It was not a derogatory whispering but that of admiration. I know he was an editor and contributor to Armenian publications, such as *Asbarez*, *Hairenik* and *Aztag*. I believe your uncle and your brother were in The Armenian Secret Army or The Armenian Revolutionary Army. I don't think your father was. You know, in your grandfather's will he left the house to your father but with the condition that he would 'continue the struggle'."

"What did it mean?"

"I did not know. I can guess by what happened after. But your father knew. He refused the inheritance. And it passed to his younger brother, your uncle."

"Then why did you come to my father's funeral?"

"I was in touch with him over the years. Your uncle was arrested for an attack in France. The place had to be paid for, and your father took care of much of it."

"I thought the place was rented and paid for itself."

"Right … your uncle took a mortgage against the place. God only knows what he did with the money, must have financed whatever he was doing in Europe. Plus, there were taxes. And the renters would come and go. Your dad paid out the mortgage and took care of the taxes while he was alive. I guess in the end it worked out because it passed on to you."

Babayan poured himself another two fingers of whisky.

"From time to time, your dad would come here, and we'd have a drink and talk, just like you and I are doing now. He was a good man. But I know there were things that he didn't share with me, and I didn't ask."

He emptied the glass, stared at the ceiling.

"The people you were asking about … I don't know them, but I know who they are. Let me contact them and see if they agree to talk to you."

"Do you know the name Matusian?"

"I've heard it, but not in connection with your family. It's not uncommon."

"Erik, a couple more things. One, I'd like to talk to Maria, my grandfather's sister-in-law. If she's still alive."

"And?"

"The man who wrote the letters to my grandfather back in the sixties—I want to find him."

"Hmmm … There is a private investigator I worked with before. He's good at finding people," Babayan said. "His name is Collins, Paul Collins. Here's his number."

"How much does he charge? I've never hired a private investigator before."

"I'll call him." Babayan smiled. "He'll give you a good rate."

3

I passed Bakersfield and farms flew by on both sides of Highway 99. When was the last time I was here? I think it was summer of 1978, just before my senior year. Father took me camping on the Kern River, in the mountains northeast of here. Tigran was still alive, sending an occasional letter from Beirut. This time, I was driving to see Maria Sitasyan, my Grandfather Aram's sister-in-law. According to Paul and Gavin Collins, she was in assisted living near Fresno.

Paul Collins had an unusual family. Although perhaps it was normal since I'd never met any private investigators before. When I called, Paul answered. He was all business, speaking in clipped short sentences. Asked me a few questions about the people I was looking to find, suggested that I bring a copy of the letters I discovered in the garage, and told me to come over the next evening. The concept of regular business hours must have been unknown to him.

His home was a bit tricky to locate, even with the directions provided. After navigating the zigzagging Sunset Boulevard, I became lost in a tangle of small streets in the Palisades Riviera area. Thanks to a friendly man walking his dog, I finally found a spread-out one-story ranch house on Casale Road. The door opened even before I had a chance to knock, and I came face-to-face with a man around seventy. He looked like a welterweight boxer, lean and spry, with a nose mashed in against a smiling face haloed by light curly white hair that seemed to flow in the breeze.

"Paul?" I asked cautiously.

"Oh no." The man laughed, his voice a dulcet tenor. Definitely not the one I'd heard on the phone. "I'm Gavin, Paul's father. You must be Avi. Come on in."

Paul was waiting for us at a large dining table. He was short-ish, rather filled-out and bald. Reminded me of a singer with a similar name. Just like on the phone, Paul was very businesslike. He gave me Maria's address with "that was easy," and asked to see the correspondence between the man called David Levy and my grandfather. I visited Kinko's in the afternoon and made a copy of the notebooks. As Paul began looking through it, an older woman, probably Gavin's wife, appeared out of nowhere and the table got filled with two plates of cookies, lemonade and a wine carafe.

Gavin poured us the wine and said, "You know, Avi, I knew your grandfather. He and my father worked together back in the thirties."

"Really? In Fresno?"

"Oh no, here in LA. Your Grandfather Yakov."

"My mom's dad." Mom's parents passed away within six months of each other when I was still in school.

"Yes." Gavin sipped wine and nodded. "Your grandfather worked with Leon Lewis, as did my father, Doug, God rest his soul. Do you know anything about that?"

"No, nothing at all."

"Ah! Most of our work now is in insurance claims, missing persons and assisting jealous spouses, but we Collinses started our business with some real spying," he said proudly. "In the 1930s, we had thousands of Nazis in LA. They had their organizations, Friends of New Germany, German American Bund, and others. There was a Deutsches House with an Aryan Bookstore near downtown, a big park in La Crescenta that they called Hindenburg Park. German agents were all over the place. They spied on our Navy installations and airplane production, planned for the Nazis to take over. Hey, a five-minute walk from here there's Hitler's compound."

"What?" I kind of assumed at that point that the old guy had lost his marbles, but his son briefly lifted his head from reading and said, "That's true. There is an abandoned compound, a power plant, a water tank. Boy Scouts have a camp there now."

"You see"—Gavin clearly enjoyed talking about the old times— "rich Nazi followers built a ranch for Herr Hitler to stay as his West Coast headquarters. They had it all figured out. As a matter of fact, this house belonged to one of the supporters who took off in 1941 as the

FBI began sniffing around and the Immigration Board questioned his citizenship. My dad knew all that and picked up the house on the cheap, hehehe."

"And how was my grandfather involved?"

"He hired my father to join the German Bund. I was practically a member of *Hitler Jugend*," he said, and laughed. "See, my dad was decorated in the First World War. He was exactly the kind of a fighter that Nazis were trying to recruit. What they did not know is that we were spying on them. Father had to pretend to be a Protestant rather than a Catholic; they did not like Catholics. I was a teenager, so for a better cover he had me join their youth organization, attend summer camps, march and salute. Everyone was scared of the Communists, and there were many 'America First' leaders that sympathized with Hitler: Charles Lindberg, Henry Ford, Father Conklin. Only after they saw the pictures of the Nazi camps, had they realized what we were dealing with."

"OK, Dad, enough ancient history," Paul interrupted him. "Avi, what do you want to do with this material? Interesting stuff. It looks like your late grandfather solicited it as part of a publishing project. Erik Babayan told us that he was an editor and a publisher. But it was twenty-six years ago."

"Hey, we had a publisher client in 1986," Gavin said excitedly. "It was more of a personal affair, but still. We can introduce you …"

"Thank you, I'm not looking to publish anything." I politely waved him off. "These notebooks were written in 1964. A few months later my grandfather died, supposedly in a robbery in Germany. But it looks from the letter that he was trying to get some weapons or something like that. Perhaps this man, David Levy, knows what really happened."

"Right. And your family does have some terrorist ties, albeit a few years after."

"My grandfather was not a terrorist!"

"That we know of, Avi, that we know of. Anyway, it's a long shot."

"I don't have anything else to go on. If it doesn't pan out, so be it."

"All right." Paul handed me back the copy. "We'll make a few phone calls and let you know what we find."

4

I found Maria Sitasyan nodding off in a wheelchair in the backyard of the Mount Ararat Assisted Living house. Auntie Maria was the younger sister of my late grandmother, Anahit Arutiyan, nee Sitasyan. Anahit and my Grandfather Aram divorced about thirty years ago. The reasons were never made entirely clear to me, but in fairness I never tried to find out. Their parting coincided with my father's breakup with Anush Karayan, his first wife. Perhaps both father and son didn't want to stay in Fresno, and their wives didn't want to leave. I was largely cut off from the little that was left of the Fresno side of the family. The last time I saw Maria was at my father's funeral. When younger, she was a rotund, cheerful woman with a crown of jet-black hair, ready to laugh at any pretext. Even under a checkered beige blanket, I could see that her body shrank into nothingness. She must have stopped coloring and the hair turned wispy and white.

"Auntie Maria," I said cautiously. She opened her eyes. "Do you recognize me?"

"Of course, Avi. It's my legs that gave out, not my mind. Here, give me a kiss. What brings you here?"

"Wanted to talk about my grandfather and my father."

"I see … Why don't you roll me into that shady corner?" She raised her voice, adding, "No need for everyone to hear us!" I looked up and realized we were surrounded by gawking elderly denizens of Mount Ararat.

"Go away, mind your own business! Johnny Carson will be on tonight." She shooed them away as I pushed her into a spot under the tree. "We don't get many visitors here, so they are looking for entertainment."

"People don't come to see you, Auntie Maria?"

"What people? There's nobody here. My daughter-in-law remarried and moved to Florida years ago. My friends are all dead."

From the little family history that I knew, her husband was a Navy aviator who disappeared during the war in the Pacific, somewhere around the Solomon Islands. Her only son also became a Navy pilot and was shot down in Vietnam.

"Some families start like small saplings and grow into big tall trees," she said. "Others start big and wither. Ours was of the second kind. Are you still with that girl in Seattle?"

"No, Auntie. It didn't work out. I just moved back to LA."

"Well," she said sadly, "I guess it was not meant to be. But find someone else. Don't mope around for too long. Your mom must be happy to have you back."

"Auntie, you knew my grandfather when he just came to this country, right?" I tried to steer the conversation.

"Yes, 1922 it was. Yes, 1922. Almost seventy years ago."

"And? What was he like then?"

"There was an aura about him. Everyone knew he was a hero, but nobody would tell us who exactly he was, or his real name. That's so the Turks wouldn't find him. You see, my parents came to Fresno in 1896, right after the Hamidian massacres where the Turks killed hundreds of thousands of Armenians. Nobody knew that it was just a preview to what was to come, that twenty years later they would kill millions. My parents were part of two big families, but by the time the Great War was over, they were all alone. We were promised an Armenian homeland, the worst of the Turkish murderers were arrested. But nothing happened. The murderers were let go. Soviet Russia took over whatever was left of Armenia. People burned with anger. Some Armenians took matters into their own hands and executed a few prominent Turks."

"Was my grandfather one of them?"

She wrapped the blanket tighter around her dried-out frame.

"Perhaps. Now people call them terrorists, but back then they were heroes. Soghomon Tehlirian, the man that killed Talaat Pasha in Berlin, was put on trial and acquitted. When your grandfather Aram came to Fresno, he had his choice of girls. Everyone wanted him. He picked my sister Anahit and they had a child, your father, the very next year.

Named him Vrej, for 'revenge'. That's how people were thinking then: revenge. Some of your grandfather's aura reflected on your father. He married young, right after high school. Into a Dashnak family, like ours. But when your father came back from the war, he was different. It's like what he saw changed him."

"In what way?"

"He no longer desired war or violence. You see, of all the people in the family, he was the one that saw the war up close. My late husband, he was in the war, but he didn't come back. Vrej wanted no part of it. I remember talking to him and he said 'Maria, I want justice as much as the next guy, but vengeance is not the way to go'."

"Is that why my father left Fresno?"

Maria gave me a wistful smile. "How does a marriage fall apart? Many reasons. Vrej and Anush were high school sweethearts, but people grow up and change. Anush's father was a very strong-willed man who wanted to control everyone in his life, and Vrej was not going to put up with that. They kept fighting over many things, revenge for the massacres being one of them. I heard that his father-in-law called Vrej a coward, and that may have been the breaking point. But no one is left to tell. They all are gone."

"And my Uncle Sarkis?"

"Ahhh, your uncle. He always looked up to your father. Sarkis was too young to go to the big war. And he was in college during the Korean one, but never graduated. He was angry and thirsted for revenge." She shook her head sadly. "I felt it. Perhaps it didn't help that the woman he loved refused to marry him."

"How come?"

"Her family, they were made of a different cloth. They were repelled by the constant talk of revenge. Her mother said 'Over my dead body, I will not see my grandchildren die. An eye for an eye, the world goes blind.' They left Fresno rather than allow Sarkis to marry their daughter. Whatever anger Sarkis already had in him, that made it worse. There was one man he became friendly with: Yanikian was his name. In January of 1973, that man killed two Turkish diplomats not far from here, in Santa Barbara. After that, Sarkis declared an open war on the Turks and anyone he thought collaborated in denying justice to the Armenians. And he got your half-brother, Tigran, to follow. This must have been your father's worst nightmare."

She paused, her breathing became more labored. I thought I better hurry up with my questions.

"Auntie Maria, what happened between my father and Uncle Sarkis?"

"I heard that there was a falling out between the two brothers after your grandfather was killed, but I don't know why. They were no longer in Fresno by then."

"Does the name Matusian mean anything to you?"

"Hmmm ... Vahan was his name, I think. Had a small raisin farm. Why do you ask?"

"Oh, nothing, just checking. Must be a different person."

"Avi, sweetheart, can you bring me a glass of water?"

Auntie drank the water I fetched. She seemed tired from the conversation:

"That's pretty much all I know. I hear on TV that Armenia might finally get its independence, but there is another war going on between Armenia and Azerbaijan. More boys are dying. I don't know who was right, Vrej or Sarkis. When you deny people justice, their anger boils over and they want retribution. Our faith says not to seek revenge, but some crimes must not be forgiven. Otherwise, more crimes get committed. I remember Aram saying many years ago that because the Turks were not punished, another great massacre will take place, and another, and another. Soon after, they killed all the Jewish people in Europe. I read that they massacred millions in Cambodia not long ago. How do you stop this?"

"I don't know, Auntie."

"Thank you for coming to see me, Avi. But there is nothing for you here—this part of the family has withered away. You should break the spell. Don't let the old ghosts pull you back. Get married, have a lot of kids and don't send them to war."

I began to leave, then turned back. "Auntie, do you know those three Armenian people who were at my uncle's father's funeral? They were standing to the side, kept to themselves."

"No." She shook her head. "There were dozens of people from Fresno at your grandfather's funeral, but everyone moved on. None of them came when your father passed away. And the few that came, I didn't know."

5

Paul Collins met me a few days later at The Warehouse in the Marina del Rey. He must have gotten there early, because his beer mug was already half empty.

"Here's some information we got for you." He pushed an envelope across the table. "We could not locate David Levy, too popular of a name, and nobody who quite matches the description. Could not locate Yael Isenberg either. We did find a Yosef Milman who seems to be the right one. He's still in Jerusalem. Also, some of the Germans: Erika Jager and Gerhardt Shrumpf. Fritz Jager passed away two years ago."

"Thank you, Paul. How much do I owe you?"

"You can't afford us, Avi. Especially since you are not working."

"Why do you say that?"

"It's two in the afternoon."

"I'll be working soon. My neighbor is helping me with a local aerospace company."

"Well, when you get that job, you'll take me out for drinks." He motioned the waitress for another beer. "This project was on the house."

"It's nice of you, but ..."

"No 'buts,' Avi. My grandfather owed quite a bit to yours. See, it was the 1930s, the height of the Great Depression. Grandpa was without a job, with a wife and two kids. The work that your grandfather gave him, it didn't pay much but it paid enough to pull them through. And then it was your grandpa that helped to buy the house we live in. Loan on a handshake. Four thousand dollars was big money in 1940."

"How do you know all that?"

"I spent some time with Grandpa in the summer of 1967. I'd just finished my junior year and we rented a summer place by the lake. Just he and I, for the most part. It was right after the Six Day War, so Grandpa talked about the Holocaust a lot. He hated the Nazis. Perhaps because he had to go to their meetings and listen to their crap. And thirty years later, he was still ticked off that nobody wanted to pay attention back then. I understand that everyone was scared of the Reds and rightfully so, but it does not mean that one kind of hatred is better than the other."

He finished his second beer. I placed a bill on the table.

"No, no, no, it's on me," Paul said. "You buy when you get a job. Good luck with your investigation, remember the ten-hour time difference when you call Jerusalem. And if you need anything, anything at all ... it's a good karma to be able to repay a grandson for his grandfather's kindness."

Paul got up, then turned back:

"Avi, what exactly do you do? I mean, for work."

"Programming."

"With computers?"

"Yes." I smiled involuntarily.

"Don't laugh. We've been an old-fashioned phone-and-paper business all these years, but times they are a-changing. We have some big law and insurance companies as clients, and they now want to send documents by some kind of electronic mail. My two daughters got married and moved out of state, so they are no help. We need someone young to deal with this stuff."

"Paul, thank you, but ..."

He raised his hand palm up to stop me. "Don't say anything yet. Sleep on it. If you decide to, you can just try it out part-time. Until you get a regular job."

I called Milman's number early in the morning.

"Halow?" a guttural male voice answered.

"Hello. I'm calling for Yosef Milman."

There was a pause, then in an accented English: "Who is this?"

"My name is Avi Arutiyan. I am calling from Los Angeles."

"Why do you call?"

"Is this Yosef?"

"No, this is Aron."

"Oh, you are Yosef's son!"

There was another pause, then a suspicious, "How do you know?"

"Well, it's difficult to explain. You see, I have a letter from David Levy to my grandfather …"

"David Levy? You know him?"

"No, I don't. I just have this correspondence that he sent to my grandfather many years ago and he mentions Yosef and Rachel and Yael …"

"You know Yael?"

"No, I don't know any of them. I am just trying to learn about my grandfather."

There was a long pause, the man on the other end thinking. "Give me your number."

I did and hung up, feeling that I hit another dead end.

But I was wrong. I got a call that night.

"Hello, is this Avi Arutan?" A woman's voice. I didn't know why but I instantly liked that voice. It had a lower pitch than usual and a warm, slightly guttural hoarseness.

"Avi Arutiyan, yes."

"You called for Yosef Milman?"

"Yes."

"I am Rivka Milman."

"Oh my God, you are his daughter! You were born in June of 1961!"

"How do you know?" She sounded taken aback.

"It's all in the notebooks."

"Which notebooks?"

"From David Levy to Aram Arutiyan, my grandfather."

There was a long pause. She must have been wondering if I was crazy.

"Look," I rushed out, "don't hang up. You see, I inherited a house and I found these notebooks, three of them. It looks like David Levy and my grandfather were planning to do something in Germany in 1965. And my grandfather was killed in April of that year right there, in Bonn. And then my father and his brother … No, it's a long story.

Look, I'm just trying to find this David Levy. I can show you the notebooks. I can make copies."

"OK," she allowed. "Perhaps you can show them to me."

"Great. I need the address. Are you in Jerusalem?"

"No, I am in Los Angeles."

"In Los Angeles?" It was my turn to be flabbergasted.

"Yes. In Sherman Oaks. Just off the 101 Freeway."

I knew where Sherman Oaks was, I was just stunned.

"Well, I can mail them to you or I can bring them over."

"Fine, you can bring them over."

"When?"

"Tomorrow evening, at seven." She dictated the address.

6

"What do the inscriptions say?"

"Here lies Yakov, son of Avram. And the dates in the Jewish calendar: May 14, 1904 – September 17, 1978. Here lies Sarah, daughter of Yehuda. July 8, 1906 – March 5, 1979."

"And these letters?"

"An abbreviation for 'May his soul be bound in the bond of eternal life'."

"No epitaphs?"

"No. That's how they wanted it. Simple. They believed that we live on in what we leave behind, not in inscriptions."

"She outlived him only by six months," I said just to say something, to cover up my feeling of guilt. I'd been at the Mount Sinai cemetery only once since Grandma passed away twelve years ago. I left for Seattle that year and hadn't come back to LA much, until now.

"Yes, it was a hard year," Mom agreed. She reached into her purse and pulled out four grey pebbles, probably from her small garden. She gave two to me and placed one of each on the grave. I did the same.

"Why stones, why not flowers?"

"It's our tradition. Flowers are beautiful, but they wilt and die quickly. Stones endure, like our souls."

"I'm glad you got to know them," she said as we walked down to my car.

They were really the only grandparents that I'd known. Grandfather Aram died when I was not even four years old, and I had little contact with his ex-wife, my Grandmother Anahit. She died a long time ago too. Yakov and Sarah's other grandchildren lived in New Jersey, so they poured all their grandparently attention into me.

105

"I recently spoke with someone who knew your father. Gavin Collins."

"Hmmm, I don't recall the name." She shook her head.

"He said that Grandfather hired him to spy on the German Bund back in 1930s."

"Oh, OK. My father worked for a man called Leon Lewis and they were keeping an eye on the Nazis in Los Angeles. I was little, but I remember the threats we received, a brick thrown through the window. Only when the war had begun, the government had arrested or expelled those people. Why were you talking to that man Collins?"

"I was looking for Auntie Maria."

"Anahit's sister?"

"Yes. She's in assisted living near Fresno. I went to see her."

"Trying to find out more about your Grandfather Aram?"

"Yes. Do you mind?"

"No, not at all. You've been robbed. There was a whole side of your family that you didn't get to have. Some say that to know who you are, you must know your heritage. Your father would have wanted it, for you to learn about your grandfather. And your brother too. But I'm worried about you."

"Why?"

"The knowledge you seek, I suspect it'll be a heavy burden. Your father's family carried a lot. And they did it in the harshest way possible—silently."

My half-brother Tigran. For a while, for me he was a mixture of a brother and a friend and almost a substitute father. I was in my teens, my father in his fifties; we didn't have much to talk about. I listened to Led Zeppelin and The Beach Boys, Father to Miles Davis and Herbie Hancock. I wanted to go to the beach and surf, Father wanted to read. I went to all UCLA football games, Father didn't care one iota about football.

Now Tigran was another matter. Tall, good-looking, in his early thirties. I began attending the ninth grade of the University High School in 1975. It was a large public school about three-quarters of a mile from our house. Most of my friends from the middle school went elsewhere. Tigran was renting a tiny house squeezed between apartment buildings on Wellesley Street, between Texas and Rochester

Avenues. It was right on my way. I stopped by his place once, then again and again. Soon, I was there every weekday.

Tigran had an engineering degree, but he was a tinkerer that didn't fit into a corporate life. He must have been good, because he always did some projects for hire in his workshop in the garage. Tigran lived on his own schedule. A tough-looking Ford F-250 was parked in the driveway, a surfboard and a wet suit drying on the side of the house. Tigran bought me a surfboard as well and taught me to surf. He smoked Winstons, and to this day I like their aroma, even though I don't smoke. Tigran treated me as an equal and I loved him for that.

And then there were always girls. Tigran loved girls and they loved him back. Sometimes, I showed up in the late afternoon and found clothes strewn on the floor; Tigran would come out in his boxers, a giggling girl wearing a towel would follow. At times, they didn't bother with the towel. The girls were always young, in their late teens or twenties. I lost my virginity in that house. I was sixteen, she was nineteen.

My parents had mixed feelings about my hanging out at Tigran's so much. More than once, I overheard my dad grumbling about me being buddies with a grown-up man and my mom telling him to let it be, that it was good for me to have a real brother. And then they would switch to whispering. It was strange how Tigran lived less than a ten-minute walk away, but rarely came to our house. I guess that's how families can be at times. I passed on to him a few dinner invites, but he always declined, and we left it at that. Sarkis, my uncle, never came. From time to time, I did run into my uncle at the Tigran's place. He was always polite with me, but never mentioned my father. One day, I came in to find Tigran and Sarkis arguing. It had to do with whether to tell something to my dad. They stopped when they saw me.

A few days later Tigran told me he'd walk over with me. When mother saw him, she wanted to quickly set up a dinner table, but he asked her not to worry. Father and Tigran went into our small office and closed the door. Before long, we heard them shouting. Father didn't want Tigran to do something. Tigran stormed out. Just before leaving, he told me not to come over because he'd be going on a trip. Father stayed in the office with the door closed for the rest of the evening. That was the last time I saw Tigran alive.

7

For as long as I could remember, we on the LA Westside looked down on people from "the Valley." And they didn't much like us either. We'd only been to the Valley a few times, to visit some distant relatives of Mom's. Dad would joke on such occasions: "Do we need a passport?"

I carefully checked the Thomas Guide before leaving, fought the 405 traffic through Sepulveda Pass, turned right onto 101 East, got off at Van Nuys Boulevard and found the small street close to Ventura where the house was. I was early, so I walked by a couple of times. It looked like a typical one-story suburban house. The mailbox said "Goldfarb," which didn't tell me much. A woman walking a dog looked at me suspiciously and ignored my "I am safe" smile. Figuring she might call the police, I went through a low gate and rang the bell.

The door swung open and I was greeted with, "You're early."

It struck me how the owner of the greeting reminded me of Rachel's description in the letters: lithe, easy-moving brunette around thirty. Her eyes were spread a touch far apart for her narrow face and her chin had a noticeable cleft, giving her an exotic, slightly alien look. She seemed full of a nervous energy, slightly moving up and down on the balls of her feet as if ready to take off in flight.

"Well, since you are here, you might as well come in," she decided and stepped to the side.

"Hello." I was at a loss for words.

"You must be Avi. I am Rivka. And you should know that I served in the IDF and know *Krav Maga*," she declared.

"OK, I'll behave," I allowed.

"What's this?" She pointed to a large envelope I was carrying.

"A copy of the notebooks that I told you about."

"OK." She took the envelope from me and walked into what seemed to be the dining room, since it had a large mahogany table in the center. Another woman, tall, with a beautiful cascade of long blond hair, was standing by the other side, one hand on the back of a chair. She also had those slightly too-widely-spaced eyes.

"This is Iris," said Rivka. "And this is her mom's house. She also knows *Krav Maga*."

"Nice to meet you, Iris. Your last name must be Goldfarb."

"That it is," she confirmed. "And you are Avi Aru...Aruti ..."

"Arutiyan."

"Is that Armenian?"

"My father was Armenian, my mother is Jewish."

"So, you are Jewish," declared Rivka, a hint of satisfaction in her voice.

"I am half."

"In Jewish tradition, the lineage goes through the mother's side."

"And in Armenian, the father's side. I guess both tribes can claim me."

Rivka smiled, showing a row of small white teeth. "OK, fine. Now tell me, what are these notebooks?" She waved the envelope.

"Well, I inherited a house in Hermosa Beach from my uncle ... who inherited it from my grandfather, Aram. And as I was cleaning the garage, I found this correspondence from David Levy to him."

The chair that Iris was leaning against moved, its legs scraping against the floor, as Iris seemed to have lost her balance. "Iris!" Rivka rushed to help her, but the taller woman waved her off and sat down with, "Please, continue."

"You see, I am trying to find out more about my grandfather... I did not know much about him."

"Why don't you ask your father?"

"My father passed away."

"I'm sorry," they said in unison.

"Thank you. There is no one left who can tell me much. At least no one that I know."

"And you said that your grandfather was killed in 1965 in Germany?"

"Yes. In Bonn, on April 20th."

Iris exhaled hard and the girls exchanged glances.

"You see," I continued, "these notebooks…my grandfather was going to publish a book based on them. But what I find even more important—my grandfather was looking to get some military supplies—weapons—there, in Germany. And David Levy was helping him. So, I want to find that man."

"David Levy disappeared in 1965," Iris said tonelessly.

"Oh." It was a dead end, just as I was afraid. "Well …"

"My brother, Aron, said that you mentioned Yael …" Rivka prodded me.

"Yes, she was in the notebooks."

"What did they say?"

"She was a woman that he was very much in love with."

Iris covered her face in her hands.

"Yael is Iris's mother," Rivka said. "It's her house. She's away on a business trip."

"But … but in the letters her last name is Isenberg."

"She got married here, in America. To Jonathan Goldfarb. He passed away two years ago."

"Oh, I'm sorry about your father." I turned to Iris.

"Jonathan was not my biological father," she replied. "I'm David Levy's daughter."

8

Erik Babayan looked different this morning: clean-shaven, wearing a suit. No men's magazines lying around, no surfboard or wetsuit visible. He looked serious.

"The people you wanted to talk to … you know, the ones from your uncle's funeral?"

"Yeah?"

"Well, one of them is coming here to meet with you."

"Who is he?"

"It's a she. And I'll let her tell you herself, whatever she wants to say."

"Why?"

"It's complicated. Do you know who our governor was until this January?"

"Uhmm, I was in Seattle."

That's when the woman in her late fifties walked in. I could not see her face that well because of huge sunglasses and a head scarf. What struck me most was the elegance. My ex-girlfriend, Amy, had to dress for work and she liked it, so I was used to seeing nice women's clothing. But this was on a totally different level, simple and effortless. It was also in the way that she carried herself.

"Erik." She nodded to Babayan and turned to me.

"Ahhh, Avi. Avi Arutyian."

The woman extended her hand, her fingers long and smooth and well-groomed.

"Elena."

She did not offer her last name.

"Can I offer you some coffee?" Babayan pointed to a coffee pot in the corner. I had not seen it before.

"No, no, thank you." She sat down. "I can't stay long. But I wanted to meet you, Avi."

"You were at my uncle's funeral," I said.

"Yes. And at your father's and at your grandfather's. The men in your family die either violently or at a very old age. Your father was a sad exception. He died from a broken heart."

"My uncle was still young when he died."

"Your uncle had been wounded more than once and spent years in a French jail. They only released him because he was terminally ill, and they did not want him to die in their place and be blamed for it. This qualifies as a violent death in my book."

"You knew my grandfather?"

"He was a good man. I've met your father and your uncle too, but not since the mid-seventies."

"I've been told that Arutyian may not have been my grandfather's real name. Do you know who he was?"

Elena paused, lifted her hands and rubbed the temples. "Avi, I only knew him as Aram Arutyian. Look, I was not supposed to be at your uncle's funeral. I am not supposed to be here, but I didn't want to just send a message. Some conversations must be had in person."

"I'm sorry, I don't understand what this means."

"My mother came to America in 1914. She was sixteen and came from Turkey to be married to my father. Most of her family was killed the next year, except for the younger brother, my uncle. It's through my uncle's wife that we are connected. I heard a whisper once that back in Turkey your grandfather's name was different. But when I asked my mother, she told me to never raise this question again, that it would be dangerous for him. My mother is gone, my uncle is also gone, but his wife is still alive. You should visit her and ask."

"Of course! Where is she?"

"Beirut."

"Beirut?" This was ridiculous. "There is a war there!"

"There was, true, but it ended. Her name is Nouvart Matusian. She's very old, you don't have a lot of time. I'll call and leave a number with Mr. Babayan."

Elena got up to leave. Erik and I stood up as well.

"Wait," I asked. "Are you a Matusian?"

She smiled slightly.

"It was my mother's maiden name."

After she left, I stared at Babayan. "That was strange. And what were you saying about the governor?"

"For eight years our California governor was Governor Deukmejian. An Armenian."

"So?"

"Elena is part of a rich and powerful family with strong political ambitions. Our local Armenian royalty."

"Running for governor?"

"They are grooming the son. Perhaps at some point. Ronald Reagan showed us that it can be one step from the California governor office to the White House."

"I still don't understand why she had to be so secretive."

"Avi," Babayan said, shaking his head, "your uncle was a terrorist, on the FBI list. Same with your late brother. Not something one should have on a family resume when running for a high office."

"But she met them, she said so herself!"

"Not since the mid-seventies. It was 1973 when an Armenian killed two Turkish diplomats here, in Southern California. And it was 1975 when the terrorist group that your uncle and brother belonged to was organized. That's when Elena's family must have cut them off. You must understand: she had to protect her family's interests. She's already gone out on the limb for you."

"And what was that about Beirut? I thought all Armenians left Lebanon when the civil war broke out."

"No, not at all. Some left, some sent their children away. But many stayed. Beirut has been the financial center of the Middle East for a long time. You can move some of the assets but not the relationships, not the deal making, not the access to information. And money is power. Here, there, everywhere."

"But going to Beirut … this is crazy. My brother got killed there. Would you go if you were in my place?"

"Avi, I'm not in your place." He shrugged. "Your life, your family, your decisions."

9

I was pushing Mom's *gefilte* fish around the plate when I realized that Mom was staring at me.

"You don't like the fish? You can be honest; it won't upset me. After all, I didn't make it. It came from Izzy's Deli on Santa Monica Boulevard."

"No, the fish is OK."

"Then what's the matter? Your mind is a thousand miles away. Are you trying to become a writer, like your grandfather?"

"No." I smiled. "I'm not writing."

"Then what is it?" She leaned back in the chair, studied me some more. "A girl?"

"No, Mom, I'm just thinking."

"It's a girl then. Who is she?"

"Nobody."

"Avi, do you know the difference between a Jewish mother and a pit bull?"

"No, what is it?"

"Eventually, a pit bull will let go. You might as well make it easier on yourself and tell me."

"Fine." I laughed. In fairness, she didn't stick her nose into my relationship with Amy. She didn't have a chance, I just ran away. "I did meet someone I like. But I'm not rushing into anything. Really, not in a hurry at all."

Mom poured herself another glass of Chardonnay and drummed her fingers against the table, signaling that the questioning was not going to end here.

"Her name is Rivka. She's an Israeli."

"Yes?"

"She served in the IDF and knows *Krav Maga.*"

"Yes?"

"She is working on her PhD at UCLA."

"Kids?"

"Divorced, no kids."

"And?" Mom made a "keep it coming" gesture with her hand.

"She has unusual eyes. And a nice voice."

"Ahh, finally! Telling me all this stuff and not mentioning her looks."

"Is it really all about looks?"

"For you men, yes. Once your eyes are satisfied, you might look deeper." She nodded knowingly. "And how did you meet her?"

"You know these notebooks that I found in the grandfather's place? I've been looking for the man who wrote them. Rivka is a daughter of his friend."

"Did you find the man?"

"No, he disappeared in 1965."

"Hmmm, the same year that your grandfather was killed. So many bad things happened that year."

"And started too."

"What do you mean?" Mom looked puzzled.

"You told me that's when the estrangement between my father, my brother and my uncle began. Over what happened in Germany."

"Probably." Mom nodded. "But, Avi, sometimes you must let the past be the past."

"What do you mean?"

"I mean letting go. Forgiving. Leaving it behind. All families have difficulties with this, but your father's was especially so. Life is too short."

Yes, like me getting angry at my father and disappearing to Seattle for the last nine years of his life. How many times did I see him after that? Five? No, the fifth time was at the funeral. It was all about Amy. Amy this, Amy that, holidays with Amy's family. And now I have all these questions for him, but he's gone, and I must figure things out without him.

"Sorry, I didn't want to depress you." Mom looked at me with concern. "I'm glad you're starting to move on. I mean, from Amy. How are you going to see Rivka again?"

I had to give it to my ever-practical Mom—she said *how*, not *when* or *if*.

"Well, I am supposed to meet her Aunt Yael when she's back in town. You see, Yael was that man David Levy's girlfriend."

"OK, Avi, I want you to do two things." Mom was her organized self. "First, I want a copy of the notebooks. Seems like everyone has seen them but me."

"That's not true. Very few people have seen them …"

"And second," she interrupted, "since you are going to meet with them, invite them here."

"What?"

"It makes perfect sense. You kill two birds with one stone. First of all …"

"Mom, we already had one 'first'…"

"First of all, you are dealing with women and you have no idea how to do that. None of you men do. And secondly, I get to meet Rivka."

"There is nothing going on. Why do you have to meet Rivka?"

"Because you said that she has unusual eyes. I know you, Avi."

After I got done with Izzy's fish, I asked, "Mom, do you know if Dad had any relatives in Beirut?"

"Well, probably." She shrugged. "Armenians are like Jews, they've been diaspora'd all over the world. Twenty, twenty-five years ago we did socialize with Armenians here in LA. We even drove to Fresno a couple of times. But after 1965, your dad stopped. I was fine with that at the time. I kind of enjoyed having you and him all to myself. But looking back, it was bad for him. He lost something important."

"But you don't know of anyone specifically?"

"No, Avi. It was a long time ago."

So Dad never told her. Yes, that seemed like him. He always hid everything inside. He didn't cry when Tigran died, just calmly organized the funeral. I hated it at the time, thought him cold and unfeeling. Now, I figure he did what he knew: keep it together, keep it inside.

"You know…" Mom chewed her lower lip, as she did when she got nervous. "I am still planning to sell this house."

"Still?"

"I was going to sell it when I planned to move to New Jersey, to my sister. Now that you're back in LA, I won't move. But I decided to sell the place."

"Why? It's a good house."

"It is. Almost thirty years here, many memories. Avi, I don't want to become a prisoner of my memories."

I walked over to my neighbor Jack Burns to have a drink. He was by himself that evening, a bottle of Cab open. The front of his second story living room was all glass, the view from Palos Verdes to Santa Monica Bay. Jack poured me the wine, opened the glass doors, and we drank and watched people.

"No special lady in your life, Jack?"

"I have many special ladies, Avi." He laughed. "You've met some of them."

"That's not what I meant."

"I know what you meant. I've been married once already. Did not last."

"How come?"

Two pretty girls in bikinis rollerbladed by. One of them laughed and waved at us, her arm bracelet shimmering in the light. We followed them with our eyes until they disappeared in the direction of Redondo Beach.

"That's how come, Avi. What's gotten into you?"

"I met a girl. She has an amazing voice. You know how a voice can trigger something inside?"

"No, I don't." He laughed again. "I keep it simple. I need something else to trigger me. You're not falling in love, are you?"

"No." I waved it off. "It's just nice to feel that attraction. I'd been with Amy for over ten years, and except for the last few months, I really liked just being with her."

"Well, Avi, be careful. You get all cozy and comfortable and the next thing you know you've got a ring on and screaming babies to feed."

Could be not such a bad thing, I thought.

We sat in silence on Jack's balcony overlooking the Strand and watched the sun set. The street lamp in front of the house burned out, making for a better view. The distant sky was the color of the red wine we were drinking.

10

I got to Mom's house ten minutes early. To my surprise, Rivka opened the door.

"W-w-what are you ..." I stammered.

"Oh, just come in, we've been here for a while," she said and sauntered away.

Mom and another woman were at the table, an almost empty bottle of wine in front of them. Mom pulled in her head and looked to the side guiltily.

"Don't be angry at your mother." The woman stood up and extended her had. "I am Yael."

She was taller than Rivka and rather overweight. But she had similar eyes, widely spaced, almond shaped, lively and exotic. Just like David Levy described.

"It's good for women to talk sometimes without men," Yael said. "Your mom and I have a lot in common: born the same year, both widows, only one child."

"I called and asked them to come earlier," Mom admitted.

"But how did you find them?"

"Directory. 411." She shrugged.

"And where is Iris?" I asked.

"With her boyfriend," Yael explained. "He's been away for a few weeks. I wanted to give them the time. Also, there are things that I don't want to discuss in front of her."

I sat across from Yael and poured myself a glass of wine, intentionally ignoring Mom.

"Actually, Iris wanted to come, and I told her not to. I could not have her here today. She knew so little about her ... about David. And suddenly this torrent... I know they were not intended for me, but I read the notebooks," Yael said. "I am grateful to you for not throwing them away, but it's hard. This was a very painful episode in my life, but it also gave me Iris." She wiped off a tear.

"So what ..." I started but was interrupted by Mom's cough. When I looked at her, she gave me a *shut-up-and-listen* look.

"I'm sorry I was not there the night you met Iris and Rivka." Yael composed herself. "I run a cosmetics and personal products import business, so I have to travel sometimes. But I am glad I had a chance to read the letters before talking to you. I forgot how strongly David felt about me. His writing ... so explicit ..."

She stopped. Mom got up, brought her a glass of water and a handkerchief, sat next to her. I took a sip of wine and tapped my foot. I didn't like her.

"Thank you, Esther. When David and I broke up ... I did not know yet that I was pregnant with Iris. But I didn't want to have an abortion. When I began showing, my parents sent me to stay with relatives here in LA."

"Why?"

"Many reasons. Back then, it was embarrassing for an unmarried woman to have a child. My parents didn't like David; they thought him unstable. They didn't like my first husband either and they turned out to be right about that, and being still young ... You know how it goes, I didn't have much confidence in my decisions after the divorce. But more important, I didn't want David to feel that he had to marry me. I thought he did not want children."

"But ... but you were the one who broke up with him."

"Ahhh," she exhaled. "When Itzhak dropped that ... that bomb, I was so angry. Both for David not telling me himself, and for doing what he did. I mean, back then, almost thirty years ago, people thought about these things differently. And I was young and impulsive."

Yael stopped again. Mom caressed her arm, wiped a tear herself.

"I'm glad Iris is not here. There are things in the notebooks that were hard for her," Yael said. "I mean, they are written by her biological father whom she never met and who didn't even know she existed. In truth, when Iris was little, I wanted to reach out to David. Let him know. But I'd been told that he had a woman. A German woman, of all things. That was like twisting a dagger."

119

"And Itzhak?"

"Itzhak found me in 1964. Here, in LA. He wanted me and Iris to come back to Israel with him. But I could not. He was a brave man, very brave. But what he did to David, the way he did it ... I just could not forgive him. He was killed in the 1973 war. In some ways, David and Itzhak were similar."

"What do you mean?"

"They both burned with that most dangerous type of fury. The cold one. When the fury is hot, it cools off. But when it's cold, it's like a steel. Unforgiving. David was not quite that way when I met him, but from the letters ... he went there too."

"He thought you brought him back from the dead. Why did you tell him you couldn't be his salvation?"

"It was like he made me his reason for living. Love like this is a heavy burden. He had to find another reason."

"So you never saw David again?"

"No. In 1965, I married Jonathan Goldfarb. He was a good man. Much older, very kind. My parents really liked him. It was difficult to be a single mom and he kept proposing and I finally said yes. No regrets, he gave me a good life. We didn't have a great love, but he was calm and steady, unlike David or Itzhak. Jonathan was a good male role model for Iris. He just always had that distance from her. Sorry, you don't really need to know that."

"Did you ever hear about my grandfather Aram?" I asked.

"No, never. From their correspondence, it's clear David met your grandfather after he and I broke up. These writings ... I wish I'd seen them back then."

"Men are always like castles with bridges drawn up," Mom said.

"It was more than that. I mean, I judged him. We were ashamed of survivors. It was only later, when we began to understand how it happened, that one had to ask *what choice did they have?* And as I looked back, I said to myself 'He was brave. He fought in the War of Independence. He defended Yosef in Frankfurt. When he had a chance, he fought. But how do you fight when there is no chance and nothing to fight with?' I don't know. And I was angry with him that he was afraid to have children, but if I saw with my own eyes what he saw—would I have wanted to have any?"

120

We sat in silence for a few minutes. I wondered what David Levy saw in her. But it was many years ago.

"Aunt Yael." Rivka had been quiet until now. "Would you want to try to find David? There are some clues in the notebooks."

"I would want to know what happened to him," Yael said. "I would want nothing better than to find him living quietly with a wife and a bunch of kids, but I doubt that's what happened. It's more important for Iris. She always wanted to know her biological father. She's upset with me and I worry about her. About us. Even before all this… Iris is smart, good with numbers, but has some hard edges. She left a good job in a law firm, broke up with her fiancé, started dating this … this man Max. He's so not right for her, God knows what he even does for a living. For David's letters to come up after so many years, it's difficult. I'm afraid of what it'll do to Iris."

PART 4:
DAVID

19 November 1964

Dear Aram,

Thank you for sending me Hannah Arendt's book Eichmann in Jerusalem. What a fascinating and insightful take! Was Eichmann a monster as most of us thought, or a petty bureaucrat as Arendt found him? The "banality of evil"—did it come from a failure to think? Had Eichmann "never realized what he was doing," as Arendt found? I have no doubt that Eichmann had nothing approaching Arendt's intellect, very few people do. And yet, I believe that the "Cautious Bureaucrat" role that Eichmann played in Jerusalem was but a mask. He compared himself to Pontius Pilate. He was "unlucky." He was the victim. He established his line of defense and stuck to it until the end: "They gave me instructions; I was exclusively concerned with matters of pure transport; I did not have a choice." We were supposed to feel sorry for him—as some not-too-bright members of the press did. All they had to do, in order to see through the "pity me" smokescreen, was to comprehend that in his choice the alternative was a worse position and no promotion. And against that he placed innumerable lives of others. In Argentina, he was proud to be Adolf Eichmann. In his interviews, published in Life magazine in 1960, he said, "I regret nothing." "I was an idealist!" Eichmann insisted self-righteously at the trial. Was his motivation ideology or ambition of a petty bureaucrat? An ideological warrior or a mercenary or a seeker of power? But is there even a contradiction here? He was all of these things: a faithful follower of a murderous ideology, enjoying the privileges and the power of life and death. Cynical manipulator, proud of his lies and tricks. A smart, inventive machine without pity. That's what's terrifying: he turned into a machine while retaining his human brilliance. But one thing that he was not: someone who did not know what he was doing. He knew perfectly well. He appeared banal only because he was safely in a glass cage.

When I am in Frankfurt, which is rather often these days, I faithfully attend the "Mulka trial." The "Auschwitz Trial" as the press calls it, because the twenty-two defendants are being tried for their actions in Auschwitz. It's easy to attend, the gallery is always half-empty: the press cares about the proceedings, the public does not. It's my third such trial in as many years. Each one was different and yet similar. I sit, I listen to the witnesses, I get numb from the litany of horrors they describe. And I ask myself: what are we doing holding these trials? What is a trial when the crime is that of mass murder? The judges are supposed to right the wrong—but how can one do that? Something has to be done, and we humans want

125

a neat, simple solution—he did it! Two years ago, we hung Eichmann. No doubt he deserved it, but by doing so did we uncover the root of evil? Did we heal the world? Can we look at the countless victims and say: here, you cried out for justice and it has been done, it's been completed? We all know that the answer is bound to disappoint.

I tell myself that each such trial is just a small step we take in order to get to the core of that moral catastrophe, to extinguish the evil. But I despair of ever getting there. The public would repress this trial in Frankfurt just as it represses anything uncomfortable to it. Perhaps it's the embarrassment that someone of our species is capable of such unimaginable cruelties. Perhaps it's the guilty feeling of not being sure of what we ourselves are capable of. Our brain seems to have a self-protective mechanism of blocking the truths that it can't survive. And in a terrible display of Nietzschean eternal recurrence, the same self-protective mechanism enables the horror to return because we blocked the earlier one. Otherwise, how does one explain that only a quarter century after the Armenian genocide, an even greater catastrophe was allowed to unfold? It was preceded by others and, I am afraid, will be followed by more. Something must be done to stop this cycle, but what is that something? Because I'm not convinced that the trials are enough. The headlines will get forgotten as soon as they are replaced by new headlines.

With warmest wishes,

David Levy

1

We planned to leave in August but had to delay our trip after the Berlin Wall was erected overnight on August 13th. Right as the Eichmann's trial ended. The year 1961 turned out to be a very busy one.

It was September by the time Yosef and I left for Germany. His little girl Rivka was almost three months old by then. Rachel, being a travel agent, made the arrangements so at least we saved commissions. I carried a letter from Benny to our contact Shimon Bezor in Bonn. There were no official diplomatic relations between Germany and Israel. As Benny explained, Mr. Bezor was somewhat of a trade representative. He didn't specify what kind of trade.

On the flight, Yosef talked more about his officer, Prinz or Arno— I was not sure what to call him.

"He shielded me during shelling. Made sure I was safe."

"Did you ask why?"

"I was afraid to. Everyone I knew was gone. Dead. I was going to do whatever he told me."

I just wanted Yosef to shut up. Why didn't he or Rachel just say no? And me, a stupid fool in love—was Yael even worth it? I was terrified of where we were going. The night before, I didn't sleep well at all, so I tried to close my eyes and get some rest. I must have dozed off because the next I remembered was *Hauptscharführer* Möll pointing a gun and screaming at me, "An order is an order!"

"Are you OK?" The flight attendant startled me out of the dream. "I am sorry, you shouted and put up your hand," she apologized. "Would you like a pillow? That'll make you more comfortable."

"Yes, please, a pillow would be great."

But I figured I wouldn't be able to sleep. And my companion

127

seemed to be high with a nervous energy. He kept fidgeting in his seat and trying to talk.

"You know, after the war, I found out that my mother didn't survive the first winter in the Gulag. Which is not surprising. She was never in good health. My father was shot by NKVD in July of 1941. Which still bewilders me: the Nazis had already invaded, and someone executed my dad for anti-German propaganda. How was that possible?"

"I think that once set in motion, a bureaucracy moves forward under its own inertia," I said. "That NKVD executioner could have been an Auschwitz guard: he had his orders, he didn't see his victims as human."

"My parents didn't get along," Yosef suddenly confided. "Mother was moody, and she often accused Dad of having other women. She didn't like his correspondence abroad. There was some kind of an accident soon after they got married. They were both injured: he limped and she was badly scarred. I had a sense he stayed with her out of obligation, and she knew that. It was not a fun household. What about yours?"

I deliberated whether to answer. I still would have preferred for him to shut up, but clearly that was not going to happen. I didn't like talking about my family, not on a personal level. Partly out of guilt of barely remembering them: their faces faded after a few weeks in Auschwitz. I felt bad over seeing Ezra in my dreams more frequently than my parents. It may have been a self-protective effort of my subconscious to shut my family out of my dreams: even mentioning their names brought on a terrible, nauseous, painful feeling of loss. But Yosef was the brother-in-law of the woman I wanted badly and was going on this trip for. Who knows, he might become my brother-in-law, for the first time in my life I could not exclude the possibility. I had to be nice.

"I'd say I grew up in a happy family. My father was a newspaper editor and a translator. A quiet man. My mother, on the other hand, was very social; she liked parties, concerts, theater. They both had talent for languages, and I was fortunate to inherit some of it. One sibling: my older sister Leah. She limped after a childhood accident. Kind of like your father."

"Were you born in Czechoslovakia?"

"No, in Germany. Our family name is Levinsky, not Levy. I changed it when I came to Israel. We were all pressured to leave our Yiddish identities—and names—behind and take on the Hebrew ones. My father was not the most practical man, but he took the Nazis seriously. After they passed the Nuremberg laws, in 1936 he moved us all to Bratislava where my mother had a sister and a brother. He would have preferred to go farther, to Palestine or even America, but my mother wanted to stay close to her family. And when the Germans occupied Czechoslovakia, it was too late."

I didn't tell him the name of the small town in Westphalia where back in 1925, I, David Levinsky, came into this world screaming. The name of the town no longer mattered to me. From what I'd heard, it was totally *Judenrein* these days. One can never completely leave the past behind, but one can choose to not revisit it needlessly.

Some of my best memories were those of playing chess with my father. He did what he had to do to earn a living, but most of all he was a reader. Intellectual, calm, introverted. But when they shut the door of that horrible cattle car and the darkness descended, he was the one that didn't cry or pray. Instead, he entertained us with stories. He spent hours telling us the adventures of Edmond Dantes, *The Count of Monte Cristo*. He doesn't visit me often, but I miss him terribly.

"What happened?" Yosef asked.

"When the war began, we were herded into a ghetto. In 1942, they 'resettled' us to Auschwitz. My aunt's family was in the same boxcar."

"Anyone in your family survived?"

"Not that I know of, everyone was deported. There was my father's sister, she married into a well-to-do family in Berlin. We received a letter from them, I think it was in early 1942, saying that they are being helped with travel documents and hope to go on vacation in Switzerland. I presume they were trying to escape. I never found any trace of them, they disappeared like so many others."

I expected Yosef to ask the usual idiotic question of "what was it like in Auschwitz?" I can't tell you how many times I've heard this. Right after the war, I tried to answer honestly: *I was obsessed with the desire to survive; we all hoped to get out alive; only the present mattered. We were hoping that the world would find out and bomb Auschwitz to smithereens.* Until I realized that they didn't want the truth. Now I know that the world knew as early as 1942, but nobody tried to stop this. And I learned to give equally idiotic answers, like "It was pretty bad."

Instead, Yosef asked, "And after the war?"

"I spent a few months in a displaced persons camp in Italy, where I met a man from Irgun. I came to Palestine in late 1945. Lived on kibbutz for two years, but I did not like it. I was in the army from 1947 to 1949. Then studied languages at the Hebrew University and joined the museum. I think you pretty much know the rest. I don't want to overwhelm you with my memories."

"It's OK, David, I'm not overwhelmed," Yosef offered. But I thought I'd done the minimum necessary for a friendly discourse and closed my eyes again.

As we began to disembark, I stayed in my seat for an extra minute. A cold-looking drizzle streaked the window. For the first time since 1945, I was on the German soil. Back then, I vowed to never return.

2

Shimon Bezor met us at the Cologne-Bonn airport. He was about our age, just under medium height, well-dressed and intense, with dark unfriendly brown eyes and tightly curled black hair. Polite and businesslike, he seemed not thrilled with having to deal with us. "Benny is an old and close friend and I promised him to take a good care of you." We followed Shimon to a light-blue 220SE Mercedes Benz sedan. I'd never been in such a nice car, all chrome and leather inside.

Shimon saw Yosef and me admiring it and explained with a touch of pride, "Six cylinder, hundred and five horsepower, top speed hundred and sixty kilometers per hour."

I sat in front with Shimon. He smoothly guided the car on the highway with a blue '59' sign.

"*Flughafenautobahn*, the airport motorway. Germans make good roads. We'll be in Bonn in less than twenty minutes."

"How long have you been here?"

"A few years. I help with compensation claims for the victims of the Nazis." Shimon's tone did not encourage further details.

"Was there a lot of talk here about Eichmann's trial?" I asked after a few minutes, mostly to make a conversation.

"Yes. Then East Germans and Russkies built the Berlin Wall, and the trial came off the front pages. I know you were planning to come in August, but I asked Benny to wait. We have to visit the *Auswärtiges Amt*, West German Foreign Office, and there was no way to do it just after the Wall went up."

"Why do we have to go to the Foreign Office?"

"Courtesy visit. It's their country and we are dealing with sensitive subjects here. Especially just after the Eichmann trial: the hearings are

131

over, but the sentencing is still ahead. Have to follow their rules."

"What do people here think he'll be sentenced to?"

"Opinions split between death penalty and life sentence. I figure that most hope for the former."

"Why?"

"To get it over with. The Germans don't want to be reminded of their common Nazi past, just blame a few bad apples. After the Allies convicted about a hundred and fifty people in Nuremberg, the locals said: 'that's enough, they did it and everyone else was an innocent bystander.'"

The countryside gave way to suburbs. I remembered the country reduced to rubble by the war. Looking out the window, there were no signs of it now.

"Been in Germany before?" Shimon asked me.

"Briefly in 1945. It was bombed out by the Allies."

"Yes." He nodded with satisfaction. "The Americans and the Brits pounded them into the Middle Ages. But the Germans, they are an organized bunch. They rebuilt nicely. Although Bonn didn't suffer much during the war, there was nothing to bomb here."

"Germany looks a lot more prosperous than Israel," Yosef commented from the back seat. "Doesn't seem fair."

"The Federal Republic is now the great American ally against the Russkies, so they've gotten some nice treatment. The Marshall Plan, I'm sure you've heard of it. How's your German, by the way?"

"Passable," I answered.

"Mine is OK, learned when I was a kid," offered Yosef.

"Well, that makes things easier," Shimon said. "Although from what I understood, it's more than passable in David's case."

He declared that we would stay with him—"I have a big apartment on a quiet street"—and should cancel the hotel reservations that Rachel made. Must have been a part of his promise to Benny. Suited me fine; I didn't make much at the museum.

The cobbled, poplar-lined street was indeed quiet. Shimon exaggerated his apartment size; it was a modest two-bedroom. Yosef took the spare bedroom, and I got the couch in the living room.

Shimon had a cold-cuts dinner and a couple of bottles of vodka set on the table for us.

"Benny sent me a letter describing what you're looking for, but why don't you tell me the story in your own words," he said.

It took Yosef most of the dinner before Shimon nodded in satisfaction.

"That's pretty much what Benny told me. Not sure I approve of what you're doing, but Benny asked... So how long do you plan to stay?"

"A week at the most," Yosef replied.

"And I must visit Ludwigsburg for my job," I added. "I made the appointment for the day after tomorrow."

"I know about your Ludwigsburg business. I've made some arrangements to help you. But don't set your expectations too high. After the Nuremberg trials, Germans largely closed their ranks and shut the door on the Nazi past. Most of Bonn's bureaucrats used to faithfully serve Hitler, went through pro-forma *denazification* process, and now are so-called 'democrats'. But they won't air any of their dirty laundry. Plus, you don't even know the guy's name."

"We know where he was and when and that he was an SS officer. They should be able to narrow it down, then Yosef can recognize him," I protested. "And wouldn't they want to find someone who saved a Jew?"

"There were dozens of SS groups operating in Russia in 1942. He could have belonged to one of the infamous *Einsatzgruppen*, mobile SS squads that exterminated Jews and commissars. He could have been with the *Waffen SS*." Shimon shrugged. "As for saving a Jew...an officer that supposedly killed another German and then deserted... Nah, if he is alive and this becomes known, he would be a pariah here. Have you ever heard of Fritz Colbe?"

"No."

"Colbe was an anti-Nazi who worked in the Foreign Ministry during the war. He supplied the Allies with thousands of Nazi documents. Never took any money. To these people, he's a traitor. They brought back thousands of former Nazis, but the one guy that actually resisted—he has to live abroad, away from them."

"So, if they don't help us, that's it?" Yosef's voice went up an octave.

"Not necessarily. Do you know which killing squads operated in Rostov-on-Don in August of 1942?"

"Yes, *Einsatzgruppen D*," I replied. "Benny told me and then I confirmed in Nuremberg's documents."

"So, that's one clue. Perhaps we can find which other SS groups operated there. We can look for some of the members of these groups. Most of them live freely under their own names."

"We have only a few days, how can we do all this?" Yosef asked.

"Of course, you can't. I have a private investigator looking into this."

"We ... we don't have the money to pay him."

"Don't worry about that." Shimon magnanimously waved his hand. "He owes me. I directed a lot of work his way."

"How do you know he can be trusted?" I asked.

"Trusted?" Shimon laughed. "Trusted with what? It's not like you are here to spy for the Russkies. You're looking for a name of some SS guy that probably disappeared almost twenty years ago. Except for you, nobody cares."

"Then why should we check with the Foreign Office?"

"It's a formality. I told you, even though they may not care about this particular person, everything related to the Nazi past is a sensitive subject."

I had a sense there was something he was not telling us, but I had no idea what.

"And you think that private investigator can help?"

"He is the right guy for the job. Knows how to get information. Former SS himself."

"Former SS?" I spilled water from the glass I'd been holding.

Shimon eyed me carefully.

"I know what you think but not all SS are the same. Some didn't join voluntarily. Regular police officers were forcibly assigned an SS rank."

"I ... I can't shake hands with anyone who was in the SS."

"Don't be so delicate, David. Information is information. If you're looking to only deal with those Germans that didn't shout 'Heil Hitler!', come back in about forty years when they will all die out. Look, there are other people that we'll talk to, that are on our side. Like the Ludwigsburg justice office that investigates Nazi crimes. They have a lot of information about former Nazis. And they did file a class action suit against some of those that worked in Auschwitz."

My expression must have changed because Shimon's eyes narrowed again. "You were there, right?"

"Yes."

Shimon poured each of us a full glass of vodka, drained his. "David, did you want to kill all of them? All Germans?"

"Yes."

"Ever killed any?"

As Shimon's eyes bored into me, I emptied my glass and stared back at him.

"Yes."

Shimon's hard face changed. He was looking at me with a pleased curiosity.

"Tell me."

"In 1945, Germans marched us from Auschwitz to Bergen-Belsen. I survived the march. The British liberated us in April and moved us to a new displaced persons camp nearby. Some of the soldiers were so mad at what they found, they gave us weapons and told us to kill the SS guards and the *Kapos*. And we did."

"That's it?"

"No. Three of us snuck out one night in late April. We found a farm a couple of miles away. The owner had Hitler's portrait covered up but still hanging on the wall. We shot the farmer. But not before we had him show us where he hid his gold. And we did it the next night again."

"You killed them for their gold?!" Yosef exclaimed incredulously.

"We killed them because they were Germans!" I spat out. "Because of what they'd done to us."

I drank more, caught my breath. Yosef and Shimon stared at me.

"I used that money to get out of the camp, made it to the Italian coast. In three months I bought my way to Palestine. British caught me just as I landed in September and put me into Atlit internment camp. But *Palmach* stormed the camp and I escaped."

Shimon poured another glass.

"So, David, not counting the guards and kapos—how many did you kill?"

"Two."

"And you have nightmares about them? Feeling guilty, right?"

"Yes."

Shimon nodded. "In 1954, the Germans put Dr. Emanuel Schafer on trial for killing over six thousand Jewish women and children in gas vans in Serbia. He got six years in jail. That's about nine hours per murder. Or take *Standardenfuhrer* Willi Seibert, deputy commander of *Einsatzgruppen D*, the one that almost killed you." He pointed at Yosef. "Americans were planning to hang him, but then kind-hearted Germans got involved and in 1954 he walked out a free man. That's eight years for ninety thousand victims, about forty-seven minutes per murder. Yes, I calculated that many times before. You won't have to serve much, David. Using German justice, with your two dead Germans you should be out in a few hours."

"And what about you, Shimon? How many Germans did you kill?"

"A few."

We waited for him to continue, to tell us when and how, but he said nothing.

I tossed and turned most of the night. There were many things I didn't tell Shimon: raping the farmer's wife, killing a *Kapo* with a shovel, taking food from a dying prisoner in Bergen-Belsen, brutal contraband trafficking in Italy. And things much, much worse. I finally dozed off by early morning. I dreamt of Yael.

3

Shimon shook my shoulder "All right, time to get up!"

Judging by Yosef's tired look, he didn't get much sleep either.

Over coffee and breakfast, Shimon informed us that we would leave Bonn after our appointment at the Foreign Office later this morning. "We'll go to Frankfurt to meet Gerhardt."

"Who is Gerhardt?"

"He is the private investigator I told you about. He lives in Frankfurt."

"Why can't he come here to meet us?" Yosef asked.

"First, Yosef, unless you plan to spend your one week here talking to government bureaucrats, there is no reason for you to stay in Bonn." Shimon became agitated. "Secondly, we'll be going to Ludwigsburg to meet with the justice office there and Frankfurt happens to be on the way. Look, I promised Benny to help you, but I can't babysit you for days."

"OK, OK, Shimon, nobody's arguing." I tried to calm him down. "We really appreciate your help."

"Good," Shimon said. "We'll travel together, one big happy company. In my shiny new car."

I didn't feel any happiness over meeting a former member of the SS, but there seemed to be little choice in the matter. Shimon was in command.

Bonn looked to be an odd capital city for a major European country. We drove by a meadow where cows were grazing and by some quaint old villas.

"Do you know why they chose Bonn?" Shimon asked. He continued without waiting. "Adenauer had a country house in a nearby village. And nobody thought it'd be for long, expecting that Berlin would become the capital again. Of course, Berlin is behind the wall and off the table now, so they have thousands of politicians, bureaucrats, and diplomats stuck in the middle of nowhere."

The Foreign Office was in a basic ugly rectangular eight-story building. As we walked towards the entrance, Shimon warned us. "I don't know what kind of reception we'll get. More than half of the bureaucrats working here were members of the Nazi party. Keep your cool."

Once inside, Shimon asked for Wolfgang von Eckner. A severe-looking receptionist unhappily looked us over, wrinkled suits and all, took our names and told us to wait. After about a quarter of an hour, Shimon went back to the desk.

"How much longer is this going to be? We have an appointment."

"Mr. von Eckner is a busy man. You have to wait," the receptionist replied testily.

Ten minutes later, a good-looking tall young woman in a well-tailored dress came down to the reception and was pointed in our direction.

"Dr. Bezor?" she asked Yosef who was openly staring at her.

He froze and mumbled something incomprehensible.

"I am Shimon Bezor," Shimon announced. "And these are Mr. Levy and Mr. Milman."

She smiled like a woman that's used to making men speechless.

"I am Gisela, Mr. von Eckner's secretary. Please follow me."

We obediently shuffled behind Gisela, our eyes glued to her swaying bottom. As we were passing the desk, the receptionist muttered under her breath.

Shimon turned sharply. "Did you say something about 'our kind' being demanding?"

"I just cleared my throat," the receptionist said, trying to kill Shimon with her look.

"Gentlemen, please," Gisela pleaded.

Shimon stared at the receptionist for a long moment, then followed.

In the elevator, Gisela pressed '5' and stared forward, ignoring us but with a smile on her face.

"I wonder if he shtups her," Shimon said in Hebrew. "I would."

"Pardon me?" Gisela inquired.

"Oh, nothing, just commenting on the weather."

Wolfgang von Eckner had a nice office: solid mahogany desk with two carefully lined-up collections of papers, a pen holder with a few ballpoint pens and pencils; a Montblanc "writing instrument" in front of his right hand. Framed documents on the wall, a comfortable leather chair. Our chairs were not as ostentatious but still nice. He looked to be in his early forties, tall, blond, impeccably dressed. As if he came out of a Leni Riefenstahl movie, exuding Aryan racial superiority and all. I hated him on sight. After bringing in an extra chair and ascertaining that we were not in a need of coffee or tea, Gisela disappeared. Shimon sat in the middle directly across from von Eckner; Yosef and I flanked him.

Von Eckner glanced at a typewritten letter on his desk and skipped formalities.

"Thank you for coming. It is my understanding that while the official mission of Mr. Levy is to liaise with the Ludwigsburg office for investigation of the Nazi crimes, you're also looking for a member of the SS that was involved in repression of civilian population in Russia in 1942."

"Yes," Shimon agreed.

"Repression?" Despite Shimon's warning I could not help myself. "They were killing us!"

"There were atrocities on both sides, Mr. ..."

"Levy. David Levy. I studied enough war-time documents to know that Germans like to use a certain language obfuscation. Like 'resettlement' instead of 'extermination.' But let's call things what they are. Or were."

"We're trying to find the officer who saved Mr. Milman's life," Shimon pointed out. "This is a mission of gratitude."

"The museum plans to begin honoring people that risked their lives to save Jews during the Holocaust," I added. "Such as Anton Schmidt."

Von Eckner leaned back and thoughtfully intertwined fingers in front of his face. "But he was an SS officer. How do you plan to go about finding him?"

"Search the war records. Talk to some of the people that served in the area at the time."

"Dr. Bezor, this is a problematic subject right now," von Eckner said carefully. "The Cold War tensions intensified with the Berlin Wall. The trial of Adolf Eichmann fanned anti-German sentiments across Europe. The Russians and East Germans are accusing us of having high-level Nazis in sensitive positions."

Shimon smirked. "You mean such as Hans Globke, Director of the Federal Chancellery? The one that performed such an outstanding job for the Nazi's Office of Jewish Affairs, right? The anti-Jewish laws that Globke wrote were a stellar example of Nazi jurisprudence."

Von Eckner's face reddened. "West Germany left its Nazi past behind. The criminals have been punished. We've paid billions in reparations to Israel and, as you well know, we're providing some critical support to your country. It's not a good time to re-open these old wounds, no matter how well intentioned you might be. We don't want to play into the Russians' hands."

Shimon took a deep breath. "I have no love for the commies, but I'll give it to them, they don't tolerate Nazis in their midst. I wonder whether they have a file on your receptionist who didn't seem to get the memo that making anti-Semitic remarks is no longer the official policy."

"What about our receptionist? Wait, what are you doing?" exclaimed von Eckner as I stood up, removed my jacket and rolled up the left shirt sleeve. At least that was what Shimon and Yosef told me afterwards. I suffer from occasional blackouts. They come from the inside and I'm not sure how best to describe them: it's not darkness, more like separation, as if I suddenly exist outside of my physical body. I was looking at Wolfgang von Eckner, seeing his discomfort, smelling his fear. And from the ethereal, external me, I saw an invisible wall between us. Words bounced back off that wall, not reaching their destination. The sounds were heard, the meaning couldn't get through—unless I threw myself against the wall and shattered it.

"Do you see this? Do you know what this is?"

Von Eckner turned even more crimson and shrank into his chair.

"It's an Auschwitz tattoo," I explained.

"We Germans suffered greatly in the war too. Cities destroyed, scores of civilians killed. And the war criminals were tried in Nuremberg and punished," von Eckner protested without conviction. Perspiration broke out on his forehead.

Yosef gently guided me back into the chair.

"It's all perfectly understandable," Shimon said. "You were an occupied country after all."

"Well, I wasn't referring to the Americans or the British."

"Neither was I," Shimon snarled, polite rage in his voice now unmistakable. "I was talking about the Nazis. A few dozen of them took over the country and forced seventy-five million peace-loving Germans to start a war and exterminate millions of others. Outside of those few dozen, nobody else was guilty of anything. They all thought that their Jewish neighbors were just swell fellows. I am sure you didn't even belong to the National Socialist German Students League, right?"

"Well, I did, but so did most of the students." Von Eckner's face turned almost purple from embarrassment. "It's not fair to bring up this collective guilt thing. No matter what you say, I personally haven't persecuted anyone."

"And yet millions of our people were robbed and killed by those wearing German uniforms. The reparations are not a gift but a small portion of what's been stolen."

"Look, we can argue forever. I can instruct other ministries to not cooperate with your inquiries—"

"No, you look!" Shimon interrupted him. "This is a courtesy visit. We're not doing anything illegal. We're not asking for your help. We will not be making formal inquiries. We're trying to find the name of an SS officer who saved a life. I know you're worried that this will stand in contrast to all the others, but that's the truth. So, we will go and quietly do what we must do. We are just asking you to not interfere. And the current rather profitable arrangement will continue to flourish."

Von Eckner stared at us across the desk, drummed his fingers. After a long minute, he slowly nodded.

"Very well. I hope you know what you're doing."

On the way out, Shimon paused by Gisela's desk. "Fraulein, you were so helpful I would love to treat you to a nice dinner. I shall be back in Bonn in a couple of days." He handed over his card. Gisela took it with a smile.

"Do you think she'll call?" I asked after we left the building.

"Perhaps. The Nazi racial laws are no longer valid. Speaking from experience, some of the local ladies are curious what a circumcised cock looks like." Shimon laughed. "Not many of those around. But while I wait for lovely Gisela to call, let me treat the two of you to a hearty lunch. Even though you don't look nearly as good as she does."

"And what was that about the profitable arrangement with von Eckner?" I asked.

Shimon ignored my question with, "I hope you eat non-kosher food. Finding a kosher restaurant in these parts is a challenge."

After lunch, Shimon maneuvered his Mercedes on Autobahn 3 and we headed south. Traffic was heavy despite this being early afternoon. Then it started to rain, and we slowed down to a crawl. Shimon was swearing at other drivers and changing lanes every minute, ignoring angry horns. Yosef and I sat quietly, a bit scared of the maniac behind the wheel.

After a while, the traffic eased, and Shimon calmed down. "That von Eckner son-of-a-bitch pissed me off. I mean, what the hell? Except for a few people at the top no one's guilty? Like it was some force of nature, not a human deed."

"I wonder what he did in the war. He looked old enough," I said.

"Probably had some safe diplomatic job that his daddy arranged for him." Shimon shrugged. "You could smell an aristocrat even before we walked into his office."

"What was that about Globke?" Yosef asked.

"Hans Globke, co-author of the Nuremberg Laws and chief legal advisor in the Office for Jewish Affairs in the Ministry of Interior, the section headed by Adolf Eichmann. Now the national security advisor to the esteemed Chancellor Konrad Adenauer."

Yosef suddenly started laughing. We looked at him in puzzlement.

"It's just ... this von Eckner guy looked so perfectly Aryan."

"So what?"

"When I think of the Nazi leadership"—he broke down laughing again—"they are like the least likely example of that Aryan stock they worshipped. Hitler with his bizarre gestures looked like a bad copy of Charlie Chaplin. Short and club-footed Goebbels. Fat Goering. Rodent-looking failed chicken farmer Himmler in charge of racial purity. You look back and think—how did this band of nobodies unleash so much evil?"

"He called you Dr. Bezor?" I emphasized *Doctor*.

Shimon waved me off. "Yeah, I have a degree in psychiatry from the Hebrew University. Not practicing much right now. A few years ago, I was asked to help with medical claims."

"Is that what he referred to by a 'profitable arrangement'?" I tried again.

Shimon replied non-committedly, "In 1953, West Germany passed indemnification laws permitting survivors of the Nazi persecution to claim compensation for medical damages. They established special offices to review claims. *Entschädigungsämter*. Breaks your tongue, doesn't it? Anyway, some of my German colleagues don't believe that the Nazi death camps left any psychiatric damage behind. David, can I ask you something?"

"Would it matter if I say no?"

Shimon laughed.

"You seem to be well-adjusted, but would you say that your time in Auschwitz had a long-term effect?"

I closed my eyes. I was there, stoking the ovens of hell.

"You're the psychiatrist. What do you think?"

Shimon suddenly slammed the steering wheel, causing the car to swerve yet again.

"I think it's bullshit! I was not there, but I've had enough survivors as clients to know about their nightmares and fears."

I stared out the window, not answering. Heavy silence enveloped us. Lack of sleep caught up with me and I dozed off.

"David! Hey, David! Are you with us?"

I shook my head to return to the present.

"We are in Frankfurt," Shimon announced.

We turned east off the autobahn, crossed the Main River, fought our way through the industrial artery of Mainzer Landstraße with its factories and office buildings, and drove into the maze of smaller streets of Gallus. I was here once with my father, in a different life millions of years ago. The memories that I had buried hit with a vengeance. I closed my eyes trying to chase them away, push them back to the long-locked secret room.

4

Gerhardt Shrumpf's office was on the second floor of a rare older building that survived the bombings. Most structures around it had a distinctly newer, modern architecture. Shimon knocked and walked in without waiting for an answer. Shrumpf was in his late forties or early fifties, slight and short, dark hair with strands of gray, protruding ears and hooded eyes. A dark blue tweed suit and a white shirt with a necktie completed the picture. He looked like a hobbit from Tolkien's novel that I'd finished a few months earlier.

He awkwardly introduced himself as, "Gerhardt, Kripo on Alex." Seeing confusion on Yosef's face, he added, "Alex—that's what we called the place where I worked. Criminal police headquarters on Alexanderplatz in Berlin. *Kripo* on Alex for short."

Ever impatient, Shimon interrupted, "Let's do it quickly, it's almost five and the three of us have an early drive to Ludwigsburg."

"What do you mean 'three of us'?" Gerhardt protested. "You're not leaving me behind. I've met people from *ZS* before. Besides, as I will explain, you will need me. What time do you have to be in Ludwigsburg?"

"Eleven."

"We can leave at nine tomorrow morning. The three of you can stay in my apartment, it's only ten minutes from here. I can sleep on the office couch."

"Thank you, not necessary." Shimon waved him off. "We have a place. Now, give us what you've got."

"All right. I always look for bad in people. For a change, I am looking for someone because he did something good. It's a bit of a treat. Yosef—you are the one who was saved by the man we are looking for, right?"

144

Yosef nodded.

"And what is your role if I may ask?" Gerhardt turned to me.

"I am a researcher at Yad Vashem and a liaison to *ZS*. Yosef came to me with the story."

Gerhardt's face changed. "Shimon told me. You are the one from Auschwitz."

He walked to the cabinet on the side wall and got out a bottle of schnapps and four small glasses. He limped rather badly.

After pouring schnapps, Gerhardt said, "I joined the police as *Assistant Kriminal Kommissar* in 1938. When they placed detectives under the control of the SS, every detective automatically became a member of the SS. I became a second lieutenant, *SS-Untersturmführer*. In 1942 I was promoted to *Kriminal Kommissar*, which made me *SS-Obersturmführer*."

"Many detectives were sent to the occupied areas in the East," I said.

"Not me. I had been blessed: shot in the leg in 1941 while pursuing a criminal. I stayed in Berlin and worked on criminal cases until April 20th of 1945, our beloved *Führer's* birthday. The Red Army celebrated with massive shelling of the city. I am afraid I abandoned my post while there was still an escape route to the south, and made my way to Baden-Wurttemberg, where I've been properly *de-nazified* by the French. I wanted to tell you this." Gerhardt emptied his glass.

"So we don't think you killed Jews? You consider yourself innocent?"

"No." Gerhardt shook his head slowly. "I don't."

I liked him. I don't know why - I absolutely intended to hate his SS guts - but I liked him. There was something gentle and exposed about Gerhardt Shrumpf.

Shimon's patience ran out. "Look, for the second time—let's get to work!"

"OK, OK." Gerhardt raised his hands palms up. He walked back to the same safe and got out a file. "Here's how I understood the task. There was a German officer that saved Yosef from a mass shooting in Rostov-on-Don in August of 1942. He was named Arno. Also called Prinz, but that's a nickname. In the process of saving Yosef, the officer killed a German soldier. He had a connection in Turkey and possibly a well-known uncle. Yosef made it to Palestine, but the officer

145

disappeared before crossing the border. Is that a fair summary?"

"In a nutshell, yes."

"Very well." Gerhardt opened the file. "Please understand that, despite our German talent for documentation, it's not possible to assemble complete information. Many of the files were lost during the bombings. Many are in Allied or Russian hands and not available, at least not to me. Sixteen years after the war, we still have hundreds of thousands unaccounted for. And finding people in West Germany is not easy. We have no central population register. Each of our citizens must, by law, notify the local registry of his or her address. But if someone doesn't want to be found, they just don't do it. That's why it's important to have access to organizations that keep files on ... how shall I put it? ... the types of people that you are looking for."

"OK, Gerhardt, stop covering your ass."

"I like my ass. That's why I cover it," Gerhardt retorted. "This is the list of German military units that likely were in the area on those days. Just from the SS side: *Einsatzgruppen D* is the prime suspect in the *Zmievskaya Balka* shooting, but other SS and non-SS units could have taken part. Fifth SS Wiking Division, the one where Josef Mengele served before Auschwitz, was in the area. So were 1 SS Infantry Brigade and 2 SS Infantry Brigade. And non-SS was often drafted into *Aktions.*"

"Voluntarily, of course."

"Sadly, there was no shortage of volunteers." Gerhardt nodded. "Ideally, I would have found an SS officer that was declared missing around mid-August. But no such luck. Instead, I have a list of dozens of people that met some but not all of the criteria. In a few cases, I found pictures which I copied using my camera. Yosef, would you mind taking a look at them?"

Yosef studied a half-dozen pictures laid in front of him.

"No, none of these people."

Gerhardt crossed out names from one of the lists.

"Too bad, the only Arnos I found were amongst those. That leaves ... let's see ... fourteen possible candidates ...."

"Any of them had a powerful uncle?"

"Not as far as I can tell. None of the last names seem to be that of powerful Nazi families."

"What's next?"

"I have another list: people that might be able to help. Like Dr. Hans Vogel, SS *Obersturmbannführer*, officer of *Einsatzkommando* that operated in Rostov. And more veterans, relatives, and so on. Prinz is an unusual nickname. Someone might remember. Addresses are hard to get. People changed their names, they don't want to be found. The ZS lawyers in Ludwigsburg should be able to help. They have files, access to Allied's records."

"Have you done a lot of work with the ZS?"

"Yes, but I don't advertise it. It'd cost me my job like it did my friend Otto Busse."

"Otto Busse?" It was my turn to be surprised. "I've met him in Israel. We helped him to re-unite with some of his friends."

"Yes, during the war Otto saved a number of Jews. He lives not far from here, in Darmstadt. When his story was published earlier this year, he was denounced as a traitor and Jew-lover. Things got so bad, he had to quit his job. I heard he plans to leave the country."

"Are you taking risks by working with us?"

"It's not 1941, they won't throw me into a camp. But this won't make me popular."

Shimon got up. "Put all the names you want in one list, so we don't deal with multiple papers. Did you finish the other reports that I asked for?"

Gerhardt produced two thin files from the safe. Shimon looked through them without showing us, then nodded. "Good. We'll pick you up tomorrow at nine."

We went down a wooden staircase into a beer garden. The place was dark and smoky, smelling of sweat and beer. Laughter, drunken talk. I hadn't been in Germany, surrounded by Germans, in many years. The ones I remembered carried guns and barked out curt commands. Here, they were waiters, construction workers, salesgirls, clerks, doctors. Dressed in civilian clothes, discussing soccer matches. I imagined them in black uniforms, with black German shepherds. Which one was going to call the police about me? I brushed the picture aside.

Shimon tried to explain to Yosef regional differences between a wiener schnitzel and a pork schnitzel, when a man at the next table asked, "Excuse me, where are you from?"

"Israel."

"Oh." The man raised his beer mug. "Prost! We have no grudge against you people."

"Why would you have a grudge against us?" Shimon snarled.

"Well, it was a war. All the Jews were against us Germans. You won. We are paying reparations."

The man looked very sincere and rather confused over our hostility. We won? One more such victory and there will be none of us left in the world.

"My family is gone. How are you going to make reparations for that?" Shimon replied.

The man shrugged and turned away. He was tipsy.

Shimon shook his head. "They claim collective innocence."

After dinner, Shimon drove us to a place a few blocks away. It was another sparsely furnished two-bedroom apartment. Drapes were drawn, and we did not immediately notice that two Israelis were there, a man and a woman. Shimon was not happy to see them and barked in Hebrew, "I thought you were out doing interviews." Then he introduced them: "Nahum and Esther. They help me with compensation claims." The couple didn't say much and quietly left.

Yosef whispered to me, "Shimon seems to be very well connected. All these places."

"Feels too good to be true." I agreed. Something was off: this place, these people, Gerhardt's discomfort. I attributed the last to him being a Nazi amongst three Jews.

"Well, I am grateful for anything that makes this trip cheaper."

Yosef and I each took a bedroom; Shimon insisted on staying on the couch in the living room.

During the night, Nahum and Esther returned. I overheard a discussion in Hebrew. They were whispering, so I only got a few words: "Syria, Egypt, rockets."

Then I dreamt of Yael again.

In the morning, Gerhardt admired Shimon's Mercedes.

"Is this new? Very nice. And the back seat looks comfortable, the car can easily accommodate five people."

"Or a hundred and five Jews," Shimon said with a straight face. "Two in the front, three in the back, a hundred in the ashtray."

Gerhardt turned red. "Shimon, this is not necessary."

"Overheard at a party." Shimon shrugged. "I think it's funny. Come, Gerhardt, sit in front with me."

As we pulled onto a giant eight-lane *Bundesautobahn 5* in the morning, Gerhard announced,

"Welcome to the Führer's Autobahn!"

"What do you mean?"

"Construction for this section was started in 1933 by our then-beloved leader. Nazis called it 'Germany's first Autobahn'. Inconveniently, there was already a public autobahn between Cologne and Bonn. So, the Nazis downgraded it to a state highway. Anything for good propaganda."

"Politicians all over the world are like that," Shimon said. "Gerhard, can I ask you a theoretical question?"

"Of course."

"What if you were not shot in the leg in 1941? What if they sent you to Russia to run Gestapo services in Kiev or Minsk, like some of your police colleagues? Ordered you to round up and shoot Jews? What would you have done?"

It was a warm day, but it felt like the temperature inside the car instantly dropped by ten degrees. Gerhardt was in front with Shimon; I couldn't see his face. But he slumped, like a heavy weight had been lowered onto his shoulders.

After a long pause, Gerhardt replied haltingly, "I would like to believe that I would have refused. Back in Berlin, I avoided any work that involved looking for Jews, I avoided roundups in 1941 and 1942. But then ... you're right, I worked with some of the people that became mass murderers during the war. I would have never suspected that they had this capacity within them. Perhaps it's in all of us. Before 1941 was over, we'd heard about mass executions. Anybody who was not blind and deaf knew. Every day since I thanked the man who shot me."

"Did you thank him in person?"

"No, he was killed in the same shootout."

I tried to ask a question, but my throat constricted. We rode in silence for a few minutes until I finally squeezed it out, "Gerhardt, what if they threatened to shoot you if you didn't comply with the order?"

Gerhardt turned around to look at me, hesitated.

"I don't know how to answer. I don't think any of us knows ourselves that well. But it was established in Nuremberg and afterwards that no SS member had been prosecuted or seriously punished for refusing take part in the slaughter. Not a single case was ever found."

5

The Central Office of the Land Judicial Authorities for the Investigation of National Socialist Crimes (ZS) was established in December of 1958. It was housed in a typical modern building, just like a regular example of a bureaucratic German institution. Except that people inside dealt exclusively with industrial scale mass murders. After our long drive, I had to go to the toilet. Down the stairs, into the basement. Windowless, clean, meticulously plastered walls, low white ceiling, a dead light bulb was the only sign that not everything was in perfect order. The smell of disinfectant overpowered that of urine and excrement. I knew it was only my sick imagination, but I thought I heard the gas starting to hiss from under one of the stalls. I hurried out.

Four people joined us in a small conference room. Fritz Jager, a lawyer I'd met at the Eichmann trial, was one of them. Another older lawyer introduced himself as Phil Baier. I knew about him, he was the driving force behind the ZS. The other two were women, an older stenographer that curtly stated "Greta," and a woman in her late twenties that introduced herself as "Erika Jager, journalist with *Frankfurter Post.*"

"Are you?" Shimon looked from Erika to Fritz.

"Yes." Fritz nodded. "Hope you don't mind that my sister is here. Sometimes publicity helps us."

Shimon tried to flirt. "You live in Frankfurt? You could have come with us."

She nipped it in the bud. "Thank you. I took a train yesterday. I like trains."

"And Mr. Zeug?" I was surprised he was not there.

"Unfortunately, he couldn't join us today," Baier said apologetically.

"I'm here in his place. To be honest, we didn't expect a whole delegation. Mr. Schrumpf, I know we involved you in some of our investigations, but it's not appropriate to have you in this meeting. I apologize. There is a bar around the corner, if you like."

Gerhardt and Shimon exchanged glances. Shimon shrugged and Gerhardt left.

"Here's our report on Chelmno." I passed a thick file to Baier.

He grabbed it eagerly, began flipping through pages, caught himself.

"Thank you, I know this will be of great benefit. And we appreciate your help with the upcoming Auschwitz trial."

"What?" I was taken aback. "I thought this was only about Chelmno. I haven't been briefed about the other one."

"The Chelmno trial will begin next year in Bonn. But we are planning a much larger trial of those that served in Auschwitz."

"Dr. Cohen did not tell me about that. He only discussed Chelmno information and testimonials with me."

Fritz jumped in. "I am sorry, I was supposed to mention it, but got caught up in the Eichmann proceedings. Anyway, we are in the early stages. We need your assistance. Written testimonials. Witnesses to testify. It's my understanding that you were there. Don't you think it's important to punish these people?"

"The way you punished the Nazis to date?" Shimon retorted. "Not only did your country not put any Nazis in prison, you also released those that the Allies put away after the Nuremberg trial. How about Erwin Schultz? Walter Blume? Eugen Steimle? They were in charge of *Einsatzkommandos* that killed tens of thousands. Released after six, seven years."

"I know," Baier agreed. "This is not right. German churches started pushing for forgiveness, and the murderers were released after serving a few years. We can't change what already took place. And our judicial system limits what we can do. But we are working hard to bring more of them to justice. It's not easy. Most of our families are elsewhere, we see them only on the weekends. Locals hate us, we receive threatening letters. Especially with the Cold War heating up, we are being accused of playing into Soviet hands. Here, Mr. Jager's fiancée broke up with him because he's going after decent Germans that were just doing their duty during the war. That's the mentality we are fighting."

"Playing into Soviet hands by pursuing murderers?" Shimon's laughed sarcastically. He turned to Erika. "You don't go to a clinic in Baden-Baden by any chance? It's an hour west of here."

"No, why?"

Shimon threw a file on the desk, one of those that Gerhardt gave him.

"A good Dr. Aribert Heim works there, as a gynecologist. Very masterful. In the Mauthausen concentration camp he was known for deftly taking out internal organs of living patients without anesthesia. And for removing tattooed flesh from prisoners and using the skin to make seat coverings for the commandant. And for other things that earned him a warm nickname of 'Dr. Death.' Just imagine, Erika, all the pleasant *gnädiges Fräuleins* opening their legs to be examined by such an exquisitely skillful man. He is living under his own name. Is his gynecology clinic protecting him from the German law? There are a few others in the file. Living right here, under your very noses."

Erika turned pale, stood up with, "Excuse me," and left the room.

I wondered why Shimon was doing this. It seemed contrived and scripted.

Fritz looked down, took a deep breath. "Come on, Shimon, you've gone too far. My sister is on your side."

"We are all on your side," added Baier. "That's why we must put Auschwitz on trial. Not one person, the whole system. Please, think about it."

Erika returned and sat down without saying anything.

"*Fräulein* Jager, I'm sorry that I shocked you." Shimon lowered his head in apology.

"I've been shocked worse, Mr. Bezor," she said. "When two years ago we arrested Kurt Franz, a deputy commandant of Treblinka, we found his photo album of the death camp. He titled it *Beautiful Years*. That was the last time I've been truly shocked. It makes me mad that some of my compatriots literally got away with murder. At least so far. But I think the tendency to blindly follow orders in a most inhumane fashion is not limited to us."

"What are you referring to?"

"The murders of Kafr Kassim and the light sentences that perpetrators got away with. I thought that you, in Israel, would know better."

"There is a distinction between an isolated, regrettable incident and systematic acts," Shimon replied quietly.

"Let's get back to the main subject," Fritz offered after an awkward silence.

"Why don't you help us in the meantime?" Shimon asked in a conciliatory tone. "As you may have heard, we are planning an Avenue of the Righteous for those that saved our people during the catastrophe. Yosef here was saved by an SS officer. We are trying to find him."

"It's a wonderful story, but that's not what we are working on at ZS." Baier sounded surprised.

"But it's a good story," Shimon pointed out. "I think you want to show that there were others. To contrast the ones that will be on trial. The Foreign Office is in favor of this project. You can check with Wolfgang von Eckner; he personally approved it. Good publicity, right?"

So that's why we met with von Eckner. Shimon put on this show in order to twist their arms into assisting us?

Baier drummed his fingers on the table and asked, "David, you are going to help us with the trial, right?"

I nodded. What else could I do?

"What do you need?" Baier turned to Shimon.

"For starters, a few addresses." Shimon handed over a sheet of paper. "We kept it broad, because we don't have a whole lot to go on."

"That's a long list," Baier said suspiciously. "Like this name here, I know it. He was an engineer working on V-rockets, not a member of an *Einsatzkommando.*"

"Gerhardt would know, but you excluded him from the meeting." Shimon made a helpless gesture. "Perhaps the man was visiting the Eastern Front in the summer of '42. As I said, we kept it broad."

Baier shook his head, unconvinced. "We'll need time to consider your request."

Shimon said, "You are asking us for cooperation, we come to you, we ask for the same. Yosef and David are here for just a few more days. I'm afraid we don't have the time for bureaucratic games. You have the archives."

Baier considered, then nodded. "Fine, we'll check what we have in our files, but nothing more."

"Can't you get any additional information from the Soviets or the Allies?"

"Not possible. Soviets would cooperate sometimes over crimes in Russia, but they won't touch a story where an SS officer does something good."

"And the Americans or the British?"

"Only on request, in connection with an ongoing investigation. There was an *Einsatzkommando* trial in Nuremberg; they are no longer actively investigating. Some people we can't even go after because they now work for the CIA or MI6. Like Dr. Friedrich Burchard, a killer from *Einsatzgruppen B*."

"Protected by the CIA? With friends like this, who needs enemies."

Baier walked out briefly and returned with, "This'll take about an hour. I arranged for a simple lunch to be brought in. Should be done by the time we finish."

At the end of a rather quiet lunch, the assistant brought back the list with a few typed pages. Shimon grabbed them first, took a quick look and placed them into the folder without saying anything.

Baier got up with, "I apologize, but we have another meeting. I believe we are done. Mr. Levy, we'll be in touch regarding the Auschwitz trial."

6

As we were leaving the building, Erika asked, "Are you going back to Frankfurt?"

"Yes, we are." Shimon was again a perfect gentleman.

"If your offer of a ride still stands…"

Gerhardt selflessly offered her the front passenger seat, but to Shimon's visible disappointment Erika declined and squeezed in the back between Yosef and me. I finally realized how pretty she was, although not in the classic beauty way: short blond wavy hair, pale silky, almost translucent skin, pronounced cheekbones. Large blue eyes, narrow nose, surprisingly full lips not quite fitting the face. Long, elegant fingers. Slender, even skinny body with small boyish breasts. Blood rushed to my face and my groin involuntarily. No wonder Shimon flirted with her. I rolled down the window and focused on the road outside.

Shimon passed the typewritten pages that *ZS* gave us to Gerhardt, who read some of the names out loud: "Bremen, Frankfurt, Weiterstadt, Hamburg, Schweinfurt, Ettlingen…" His voice trailed off.

"I think you can cover them in the next three days. Although Bremen and Hamburg might be hard," Shimon said. "So, Ms. Jager, tell us a bit about yourself."

"What would you like to know?"

"Whatever you choose to tell us."

"I'm twenty-eight. Divorced, with a four-year-old daughter, Ingrid. My father died at Stalingrad, mother was killed in a British air raid on Berlin in December of 1943. Fritz and I were raised by grandparents."

"I'm sorry." Shimon sounded totally sincere. Perhaps under his prickly exterior was hiding an empathetic human being after all.

"The air is very clear here," Gerhardt stated in a clumsy attempt to change the subject.

"Yes, the air quality is excellent in these parts. They have a good chemist in charge. Dr. Gerhard Peters," Erika said.

"The inventor of Zyklon-B?"

"One of the inventors and suppliers of the gas to the SS. They all worked at a company called Degussa."

Shimon slowed down and looked back at me, his face scrunched into a worried expression. I smiled—probably grimaced—back at him and closed my eyes. I didn't like anyone looking at me like that.

"His colleague Bruno Tesch was executed by the British in 1946. But Dr. Peters somehow weaseled out. In '49 he was given a five-year sentence."

"Five years for a million corpses? Remember, David, what I told you about local justice?" Shimon's voice sounded strangled, squeezed out through clenched teeth.

"Except that he did not serve even that much," Erika corrected him. "More than two hundred of our scientists and public personas petitioned the court on his behalf. He was acquitted, and is now working at Degussa again, and serving on the federal air quality commission. See, Shimon, Dr. Heim might not be the worst murderer on the loose in our country."

Gerhardt, who listened in a depressed silence, suddenly spoke, "There was a man I met back in '45 who mentioned Dr. Peters. His name was Kurt Gerstein."

"Kurt Gerstein? Didn't he testify at Nuremberg?"

"Not in person. I met him in May of '45 in a little picturesque town of Rottweil. We both had given ourselves up to a local French commandant who treated us well. I spent about a week with Gerstein, then the French transferred him to a military prison. Gerstein was finishing his report when we met. He was a brave man. Opposed the Nazis in 1930s; they jailed him twice. He joined the SS in order to expose their crimes and became responsible for getting Zyklon B from Dr. Peters and delivering it to death camps. Gerstein witnessed gassings in Belzec and Treblinka and repeatedly reported this to Swedish and Swiss diplomats and to multiple representatives of the Vatican. But nothing happened. Nothing."

157

"You mean the Vatican knew?" Yosef sounded surprised.

"Of course they did. And so did the Evangelical Church. Gerstein told literally hundreds of people about the Holocaust as it was happening. But nobody spoke up until it was too late."

"And what about Gerstein?"

"He killed himself a few weeks later."

"I know his story," Erika said. "In 1950, the Tübingen Denazification Court had found him guilty. I helped to file an appeal last year. It's been rejected. We'll appeal again. Gerstein reminds me of King Oedipus. Oedipus committed a crime without meaning to, but when he found out, he deemed himself guilty and gouged out his eyes. Gerstein couldn't live with the crime that he tried to stop. Dr. Peters and others, they feel no guilt. We have millions like Peters and very few Gersteins."

"Do you mind if we make a short stop here?" Shimon pulled off the autobahn and guided the Mercedes across a picturesque bridge.

"What a pretty town!" Yosef was staring out the window. "Where are we?"

"Ettlingen. Beautiful, isn't it?" Erika smiled. "It goes back to Roman times. Used to be a trading crossroad, now a vacation place on the edge of *Schwarzwald,* the mystic Black Forest. The baroque palace over there was built in the sixteenth century."

"And they have some wonderful spas." Shimon stopped the car in front of a hotel across the palace. "Like in this *Erbprinz Hotel.*"

"And why are we here?"

"Ernst Ottsmann, *Unterscharführer* from the 2nd SS Infantry Brigade," Gerhardt replied. "He is on our list of 'Prinz' candidates. He was in the Rostov area and supposedly lightly wounded in action around mid-August. Not a great match, but easy to check out."

"And symbolically he works as a handyman in a 'Prinz' hotel," Shimon added, laughing. "I actually stayed here last year. Had no idea that an SS man was fixing toilets around this place. But of course, if one were to avoid all the German places where former SS members work, one would die of exposure and starvation. Anyway, no need for all five of us to go, it'll only scare the hotel people. But we do need Yosef to take a look at Herr Ottsmann."

They departed, leaving Erika and me outside. We got out of the car to stretch and walked around the plaza.

"I've been told that you were in Auschwitz. You must hate us all."

"Not all," I lied. "And how did you get involved in the *ZS* work?"

"We had an uncle named Karl. A quiet man, worked on a farm. Three years ago, he was arrested on a suspicion of being a war criminal. He hung himself in jail. Our family was in an uproar. Fritz went to Ludwigsburg to protest, only to find out that our quiet uncle had been in charge of an *Einsatzkommando 3a* that killed tens of thousands of men, women and children in Lithuania. Fritz quit his law firm and joined the ZS. He brought me to cover Kurt Franz's arrest for my newspaper later that year. That's when I saw that horrible Treblinka album."

"Why do you think he called it *Beautiful Years*?"

"The power. From what I read about him, he was a cook before the war and went back to being a cook after. A perfectly ordinary person, probably angry over his low position in life. In Treblinka, he became the master of life and death. What's the painful death of a few hundred thousand people compared to that feeling of covering the void inside with a cruel, god-like power?" Erika shrugged bitterly.

"Does your family agree with what you are doing?"

"No, they don't. They think that we are besmirching the memory of my father. Everyone glorifies the average German soldier, and blames any atrocity on a small clique of criminals. They say that everyone was all equally victims of the war. My ex-husband divorced me because I was jeopardizing his career in the CDU party."

Shimon, Gerhardt and Yosef came out of the spa.

"That didn't take long."

"Yosef took one look at him and knew that was the wrong guy. But it was hard to find Ottsmann. He hid. Afraid that Jews came to kill him." Shimon laughed.

"Any more stops today?"

"Yes, one. Let's visit Dr. Hans Vogel, former SS *Obersturmbannführer* of *Einsatzkommando 11b* that operated in the Rostov area. Being a commanding officer, he might know who had the Prinz nickname. Vogel now lives in Weiterstadt, about twenty-five kilometers south of Frankfurt."

"Was that the *Einsatzkommando* in Zmievskaya Balka?" asked Yosef.

"Possibly. *Einsatzgruppen D* had five *Einsatzkommandos*. Given the size of the *Aktion*, likely multiple *Einsatzkommandos* were involved," I explained. "Dr. Vogel was tried in the *Einsatzgruppen* Trial in 1948 and sentenced to life imprisonment. He was released in 1955."

Weiterstadt was a grim industrial suburb, nothing like Ettlingen. We had to stop for directions twice, until we found a small rundown house well off main streets.

"The man must like his privacy," Gerhardt commented drily. "Since we know he is not 'Prinz', let me question him."

Shimon and I went with Gerhardt, while Yosef and Erika stayed in the car.

Gerhardt rang the bell, then rang again. We were about to leave when we heard steps and the door opened just a bit, secured by a chain.

"What do you want?" All we could see was one suspicious angry eye, a grey-stubbled chin and half of a turned-down mouth with spittle running from the corner.

"We just have a few questions, Dr. Vogel," Gerhardt stated politely.

"*Doktor*," Vogel laughed. "I have not been called a *Doktor* in a long time."

"You no longer practice law?"

"Ha! The only job I could get is a night watchman at a local factory. You woke me up!"

"Tell it to twenty-seven thousand innocent people you killed in Rostov!" I spat out. Gerhardt shot me a disapproving look.

"Who are you? Are you Jews? You came to kill me? I have a gun!"

"Don't worry, Dr. Vogel." Gerhardt remained calm. "Nobody's here to harm you. We are trying to find a name of a man. Someone who may have served in your unit."

"Why are you looking for him? So you can kill him?"

"No, just the opposite. He did a noble thing and we'd like to acknowledge him, thank his family."

"Sounds fishy."

"Do you recall anyone who went by the name of Arno or nickname of Prinz?"

Even through the small slit we saw Vogel's eyebrows shoot up. He didn't reply.

"Well, it seems that you may know who I am talking about."

"Perhaps, perhaps not. Why should I help you?"

"Why not do a good thing just for the sake of it?"

Vogel cackled, then disappeared in a fit of coughing. He reappeared with, "Come back tomorrow at this time. With four hundred marks."

Shimon raised his fist. "Bastard! I'm going to choke the name out of you!"

"Leave before I call the police. And tomorrow you better bring the money." Vogel slammed the door shut.

"Well, the good news is that he knows something," Gerhardt announced as we got back in the car. "We'll have to buy the information."

"He might be just trying to shake us down."

"No, his first reaction when he heard the name was not calculated."

"Four hundred marks is a hundred dollars. Neither Yosef nor I have that kind of money on us." I shrugged helplessly.

"I'll take care of that," offered Shimon. "Benny will cover for me. Gerhardt is right: when there is information available, you buy it. It's cheaper in the long run."

In Frankfurt, Erika politely declined Shimon's offer to join us for dinner, but she left us her phone number.

As we dropped her off, Shimon turned to me. "She likes you."

"Nonsense."

"Hey, I know these things. She would look at you and touch her hair or her cheek. Here, you should call her."

"She's German!" I retorted without thinking. Then I realized what I just said and apologized to Gerhardt. He shook his head with, "I don't blame you."

7

The next morning, Shimon announced that there was no point driving to Hamburg or Bremen since we had a likely source of information in Dr. Vogel nearby. We did agree to visit Georg Wiesce, SS *Sturmbannführer* from *Einsatzkommando 10a* since he lived in Frankfurt. Wiesce was a portly red-faced man in his sixties. We found him working in a bakery, sweat pouring down his face. When we confronted him, he raised his palms in self-defense.

"I served my time, don't want to remember."

"You only served five years."

"I was in hell. It was very hard killing people. I still suffer from terrible nightmares. But I was a soldier, and I had my orders."

"Yeah, you poor thing," Shimon snarled. "That's why you Germans invented death factories like Treblinka and Auschwitz, so you don't have to endure looking at innocent people as you kill them."

"I aimed carefully so they didn't suffer. I never let anyone suffer needlessly. It was worse for them with others."

"You are all heart. You were a lesser evil, yeah?"

Turned out Wiesce was reassigned from the *Einsatzkommando 10a* in May of 1942 and sent to the occupied part of France, prior to the Rostov massacre. He claimed to not know anyone named Arno or Prinz. A hostile crowd gathered, and we left Wiesce to his baking.

After lunch, we visited a bank where Shimon got money for Vogel. He seemed impatient, and I had a sense that he just wanted to get rid of Yosef and me.

The four of us drove back to Weiterstadt. Shimon pounded on Vogel's door.

"Hey, *Herr Doktor*, we are here!"

This time the door did not open at all.

162

"What do you want?" Vogel asked from the inside.

"We have your money, Vogel."

"I don't know anything."

"What do you mean? You said you'd tell us who *Prinz* was for four hundred marks. Here, we have it!"

"I said I don't know anything! Go away!"

"Listen, Vogel, we are not going to talk to anyone." Gerhardt tried a softer tone. "Nobody will know about our meeting."

"Go away before I call the police!"

There seemed to be nothing else to do. We got in the car and drove back to Frankfurt.

"What the hell happened?" Shimon was visibly upset.

"Someone got to him," Gerhardt said.

"Who?"

"I don't know. Perhaps we were followed yesterday. As we are being followed now."

"What?"

"Don't look back!" Gerhardt raised his voice. "Grey Opel, two cars behind. They were parked across the street from Vogel."

"Police?" Shimon asked.

"I don't think so. Police wouldn't make such an easily noticeable U-turn on Vogel's street. Unless they want us to know that we are being followed."

"Well, whoever they are!" Shimon gunned the engine, got off at the next exit and made a few sharp, tire-screeching turns through the suburbs of Frankfurt.

"You lost them." Gerhardt's expression left no doubt that he was not happy with Shimon's maneuver. "Let's go have dinner."

Shimon drove us back to Gerhardt's neighborhood. We went to a beer hall near his office: large wooden tables, schnitzels, sausages, sauerkraut, waitresses in traditional costumes carrying huge beer mugs. A poster on the wall proclaimed: *Duty, Fatherland, Comradeship, Courage*.

"Does it look any different from 1930s?" I asked Gerhardt.

"No, not really."

"Gerhardt, would you be able to use your car tomorrow, take Yosef and David to see other potential contacts? You can bill us at your usual rate," Shimon said.

"You won't join us?"

"No, I am afraid I have to get back to my responsibilities."

I felt relieved at that point. Soon, I'd go home. My obligation with the *ZS* had been fulfilled. That Auschwitz trial they were planning, I wouldn't have any part of it. Nobody here wanted to deal with the past. They hung a few dozen in Nuremberg and that was that. I made it to Germany, I did not suffer a nervous breakdown, I did not try to kill anyone. Searching for "Prinz" was always a fool's errand. I only did it because of Yael. Perhaps she would take me into her bed now that I've done something for her brother-in-law.

As we were walking to Shimon's car, another Mercedes pulled alongside us. Five leather-jacketed men jumped out, armed with metal pipes.

"You dirty Jews, we're gonna finish the job!"

Then everything happened quickly. I saw Shimon taking on two attackers. I saw Yosef getting knocked down, a shaved-head punk swinging the pipe over his head. I rushed in towards Yosef, into a blinding pain in my arm and my side.

Another voice: "Horst, that's enough! Follow the orders!"

To me: "Stay out of Germany and don't ask questions."

And the lights went out.

8

When they came back on, I saw a white ceiling. I was in Block 20, the Auschwitz prisoners' infirmary. Joseph Klehr, the orderly, will come any moment, give me a phenol injection into the heart, and I will be no more. I must get out of here! I lifted myself up, but there were ropes around my wrists and a terrible pain in my chest. I tried to get the ropes off.

"Please, stop!" A woman's face above me. "Don't try to remove the IV!"

"I can still work!" I tried to explain to her, but she did not understand. "Is Klehr here?"

"Klehr? No, Doctor Werner is attending you."

"Werner? Is he new?"

"No, Dr. Werner has been in *Bürgerhospital* Frankfurt for at least ten years."

"Frankfurt?" I fell back into the bed and closed my eyes. There was a lot of commotion around.

"Herr Levy? Herr Levy?" another, male voice.

"Yes?" A man in his sixties was standing above me, studying my face.

"I am Dr. Paul Werner. You are in *Bürgerhospital* in Frankfurt.

"I thought I was somewhere else."

"I think I know where you thought you were." He grimaced. "I am very sorry."

"It's hard to breathe."

"That's because of a punctured lung. You also have a broken arm and three broken ribs. You took a couple of bad shots, my friend. But you are young, you will recover. You need good rest though. We are trying to keep you on oxygen and air tube. You will experience some cough and fatigue, that's normal. Nurse Monika will take a good care of you."

A woman's face, the one that I saw earlier, came into the view.

"A bit of bluish skin color becomes him. Doesn't it, nurse?" Dr. Werner tried to joke.

"What about my friends?"

"They are fine. Two of them needed a few stitches, but nothing major. You are the one that took the brunt of the attack."

"When can I go?"

The doctor stopped joking. "You must have complete, total rest for a couple of weeks. Then another month or so to get properly healed."

"I want to go home."

"That's highly inadvisable. You need rest. And definitely— absolutely—no air travel."

I was drifting in and out of a drug haze for the next two days, the fog occasionally parted by visitors.

Yael leaned over and kissed me on the lips. "Thank you!"

Shimon: "We are going to find these bastards."

Yosef: "That blow was intended for me."

I: "When did Yael get here?"

Yosef, confused: "Yael is not here."

Gerhardt: "I'm sorry, kiddo."

Erika brought a newspaper. "You have a headline: *A Survivor Brutally Attacked by Neo-Nazis.*"

On the third day things began to come into focus. I was surprised to discover Wolfgang von Eckner sitting by my bed.

"I didn't expect to see you."

"I thought about our conversation, and then I read about the attack here," he said, looking gravely serious. "I am very sorry. Please believe me that I was concerned about your safety. After you left, I checked the file of our receptionist. Turns out she was one of Odilo Globocnik's secretaries. You know who he was?"

"Yes, of course. The SS general. The chief exterminator in Poland."

"She typed up lists of Jewish deportees to Treblinka and lists of property confiscated from them. I confronted her about this, and she told me that she was just doing her job as one of many of 'Globocnik's women' and that I should mind my own business. I haven't slept well since. I keep seeing these proper ladies cheerfully taking dictation and typing up orders of murder and robbery. What I told you was just *Realpolitik*. I told you what I had to tell you."

"Yes, of course you had to. What do you want from me—an absolution? I am sure there is a church nearby."

"Please, don't base your view on a few thugs …"

"It's not about me, Herr von Eckner. It's about you, the Germans."

I exhausted the poor night nurse.

"Something makes you think of a fire, because it's the third time you screamed about it tonight. Ahh, I know!" she declared proudly. "It's the light on the monitor!"

"Why?" I asked.

"Because it's red. Red means fire. A subconscious association."

"Real fire is not red," I retorted.

"But of course it is." Judging by her look, she wondered if I had an undetected concussion.

"No, people only think it's red. The real fire, where it's the hottest, is white. Then yellow, then orange. Only at the very edges it's red."

"White? Fire is white?" she held up a towel and tried to joke. "You mean like the color of this towel?"

"No, like the color of hatred."

"OK," the nurse said carefully, as she placed the towel to cover the red light on the monitor. "Do you want something to help you sleep?"

Gerhardt came. "Are you able to talk about the attack? I went down quickly and didn't see much. Here, want to feel a bump on my head?"

"Nah, I have my own bumps. Still dangerous to be a Jew in Germany."

"I think it's dangerous to be asking questions about our brave *Einsatzkommandos*, the masters of shooting women and children. Or perhaps in your case it's both. Do you remember what they said?"

"Said they were going to finish the job."

"How about the car? Their appearance?"

"It was a Mercedes. Dark-colored, black or blue. I think they were in their late twenties or early thirties. Wearing leather jackets. The one that broke my arm was missing some teeth."

"That's interesting."

167

"Why?"

"Shimon also noticed that an attacker was missing teeth. And when you went down, one of the attackers shouted at the others to stop."

"Yes, I remember something about following orders. So?"

"Frankfurt is not known for neo-Nazis. And driving a Merc doesn't quite square with teeth-missing lumpen proletariat. Perhaps someone hired them to scare us but not injure too badly."

"Tell this to my arm. And my ribs. But who? And why?"

"That, I don't know."

"She had the sweetest voice," Ezra said. He sat on the edge of my bed, in a gray jacket and black paints with red stripes painted on them. His hands twiddled a checkered newsboy cap.

"Who?"

"Lia, of course. People would hear her sing and come and tell me 'Ezra, your daughter has the voice of an angel!' There was this man visiting from Rome and he wanted us to send Lia there for music lessons. He thought that with Lia's beautiful soprano and lovely face she would be an opera singer."

"Why didn't you send her?"

"Well, you know. The girl alone in a big city. Her mother would have none of that. I even told her 'Miriam, why don't you go with her?' But Miriam couldn't leave her parents. 'Families should stay together,' she said."

Ezra covered his mouth with the cap he'd been holding, and began to cry, quietly.

"I'm sorry, I don't want to disturb others. This looks like a fine hospital. I wish I had insisted, I wish I'd sent them to Rome. Most of the Jews there escaped the Nazis. They hid with the neighbors, in churches, in the Vatican. If I had only listened to that man, Lia and Miriam would be alive."

"You didn't know. Nobody knew."

"Oh, my baby, my baby... It was a cold December day when they took us to the train station. A crowd gathered, and our neighbor called out for Lia to come out. You see, Lia didn't look Jewish. Miriam pushed her 'Go, Lia, go!' But there was that officer on the platform. He saw us and barked out to the soldiers to stop Lia."

"What did he look like?"

"Like many of them did. A long black leather coat, a tall cap with a Deathhead emblem."

"Late thirties, protruding mouth, a long horse-like face?"

"Yes, yes."

"I know who he was, Ezra, I know who he was … Wait, where are you going?"

But just like he appeared, Ezra quietly vanished into the air.

Erika returned. The nurse Monika was puttering with the IV, perhaps not willing to leave us alone in case something untoward might take place.

"I am so sorry. But doctors say they expect you to fully recover."

I laughed and winced in pain. "Sorry, it's funny."

"I realize it sounds ridiculous. I know you want to leave as soon as possible, but please stay and recover. Not all of us are like that."

The nurse grunted. "I think we all have to stop digging. Close the door on that horrible war business and move on." And left the room.

I didn't know what to say, so I closed my eyes and ignored Erika. She left eventually.

Shimon came again.

"I want out of here. Shimon, please get me out."

"The doctors want you to wait."

"Screw German doctors! I have to get out!"

Shimon returned with Yosef in a couple of hours. "We are getting you out tomorrow, on your scheduled flight. A doctor will accompany you. Von Eckner made a stink, so the West German government will pay all expenses. They are trying to keep things quiet."

I flew back with Yosef, as Shimon promised. I am not proud of my childish insistence on being removed from Germany. People in the hospital were taking good, professional care of me. But sometimes healing is as much psychological as it is physical. I was suffering terrible nightmares in that hospital bed and I had to find a way to stop them. Shimon was on the plane as well, plus a doctor and a nurse. I had a whole row to myself and every effort was made to keep me comfortable, but Dr. Werner from the hospital was right—it was too early for me to fly. Internal bleeding re-opened on the plane and they had to whisk me to the hospital in an ambulance. Not sure who's doing it was to put me into Yael's hospital, but I was not going to complain about that. Especially since they gave me an individual room and Yael as my nurse.

9

I must say that being a minor celebrity, with an associated parade of visitors, became old after a week. Yosef and Rachel, Chaia, Shimon, Hanna, Benny, Maurice, Izek ... too many to recall, as I was still living in a haze. I do remember—or at least I think it was real and not a dream—how one night Yael was leaning over me to adjust the pillow, and with my one healthy arm I reached inside her uniform and touched her breast. And she didn't move away. Instead, she pressed herself against me, her lips finding mine and her hand reaching under the sheets.

In the morning, as I was waking up, I heard Benny and Shimon quietly talking by the window of my room.

Shimon's voice: "I don't understand the attack. It seemed staged."

"You poked that bush with a stick and snakes came out."

"Yeah, probably. But which particular name?"

"Or names. Shimon, who in Ludwigsburg saw the list?"

"I don't know, Baier gave it to his assistant, and who knows who was actually looking through their archives."

"There might be a leak in the ZS office."

"Possibly. But it could be not the ZS, but the Vogel connection."

"Anything's possible. I have to assume the worst. You could have been followed all the way from Ludwigsburg. Must check on Vogel though."

"Benny, I worry about David and Yosef. Especially David. Being attacked by the Nazis again."

"Shimon, stop being a psychiatrist."

"Well, I am one, and I know a depression when I see it."

A doctor walked in and their conversation stopped.

When doctor left, Benny was standing over my bed. "I guess my advice didn't work too well. I was torn between going to Germany and going to Turkey. I gave you a bad advice, I am sorry."

At the time, I did not give much thought to the conversation I overheard. I probably would have if not for the oppressive darkness that enveloped me. I was lying in that hospital bed, afraid to fall asleep because in my nightmares orderly Klehr continued to threaten me with a giant hypodermic needle.

Hannah came weekly.

"I am sorry I pushed you to go," she said on the third or fourth visit. "I didn't think working with Ludwigsburg would be dangerous."

"We don't know if that's why we were attacked. Could have been about Yosef Milman and his 'Prinz.' But Hannah, I was terrified to be there. I should close the door on the past. I mean, nobody cares. They don't want to remember."

"Then write about the righteous. Remember how Abraham begs for Sodom? *Will You indeed sweep away the righteous with the wicked? Suppose there are ten righteous found there?' And the Lord said, 'I will not destroy it on account of the ten.'* Only ten righteous to save the city."

"I guess they couldn't find ten. Everyone wants to forget, nobody wants to hear about the righteous. They are like a mirror we don't want to look into. Another ten years, and it will all be forgotten. Just like slaughtered Armenians of the previous war had been forgotten. People don't even intentionally forget. They block it out. So it can be done again and again."

"It's not black and white, David. Thousands of Jews betrayed their fellow Jews and worked with the Nazis. And thousands of Gentiles were killed for helping Jews."

I turned away, not wishing to talk.

"Not everyone wants to forget. Look at me, David. Look at me! Do you remember what Babiy Yar is?"

"Yes, of course."

"Tell me."

"Why? You know."

"Just tell me."

"A ravine in Kiev, where *Sonderkommando 4a* massacred thirty-four thousand Jews in two days. Germans were very proud that thanks to their clever organization the victims believed in their resettlement until the very moment of their execution."

"A Russian poet Yevgeniy Yevtushenko wrote a poem. It was published in *Literaturnaya Gazette* this month." She placed a folded newspaper on my chest. "*Maariv* printed the poem. Read it to me."

"Why?"

"Just read it. A poet risked his standing to write it. An editor risked his job to publish it. The least you can do is read it."

I picked up the paper. Small printed letters danced before my eyes.

I feel like I am Anna Frank
Translucent like an April leaf
I am in love and I need no words
Just to look into each other's eyes
How little do we see or smell
We have no leaves or sky
But we have so much in a gentle embrace in a dark room.
"They came!"
"Don't be afraid.
It's spring. It's coming.
Come here, give me your lips!"
"They are breaking the door!"
"No, no, it's ice on the river."

Wild grass ripples over Babiy Yar
The trees stand haunting like severe judges
Everything here screams soundlessly
I take off my hat and feel
My hair turning grey
And I myself am a silent scream
Over thousands and thousands of martyrs
I am each old man murdered here
I am each child murdered here
I will never forget!

"You only read the second half, below the fold."

"Hannah, it's hard for me to read. Can't focus."

"That's fine, that's fine. Just understand, this was published in the Soviet Union. And it was not popular with the Communist Party bosses. Because officially, in Babiy Yar the Nazis killed scores of Soviet citizens, not Jews. The poet, the publisher—they risked a lot in telling the truth. But they went ahead anyway. See, David, it does not have to be forgotten. So, stop feeling sorry for yourself. Get back to work to make sure that people remember."

10

Hannah's tough talk lifted away some of the darkness. The next day I forced myself to get up and walk. Two weeks later, I left the hospital. Yael moved in with me. Well, not moved in but stayed and started making herself at home. We didn't even discuss it. She was my nurse in the hospital, and we just changed the location. Except that now we slept in the same bed.

The first time that we properly made love ... She had beautiful, perfectly round red areolas. I circled them, traced my fingers down to her belly, felt her tighten under my touch. Ran fingertips along her inner thighs, from the lips covering the pink opening to the knees and back.

"David ..." she whispered.

"Yes?"

"I want you inside."

I parted her and slowly went in, pulled out all the way and entered again, slowly, cautiously. And again. Her warm hands on the back of my neck. Her head was up, but she was not looking at me, she was looking down, watching us connect. I was trying to hold my still-weak arms from buckling, her face just below mine, mouth open, breathing rapid. Afterwards, she lay with her eyes closed, arms stretched, tongue caressing her upper lip. That's how I still see Yael in my daydreams: eyes closed, one arm under her head, the other arm carelessly thrown to the side, pink tongue sliding over cherry-colored lips. A Modigliani nude.

As I woke up the next morning, Yael was quietly snoring next to me. I moved her hair and uncovered a small, delicate ear. I smelled her skin and shut my eyes from the wave of tenderness that spread through my body. I couldn't imagine my world without her.

This memory had been imprinted into my brain; it's as real today as it was three years ago. I'd had women before and after Yael, but I'd never had such an intense physical connection, never wanted anyone so badly. Yet Yael was not just a reflection of my physical wants, it was an emotionally savage link—I needed to possess her, she was mine. I usually refused to spend a night with a woman. I drew a mental distinction between the physical act and the intimate step of sleeping together. But I enjoyed sleeping with Yael, feeling her warm body next to mine. Sometimes I would touch it as she was asleep, to make sure it was there, that it was mine. What that was, I don't know. My irascible late friend André claimed it was all in the smell, but he was French.

Having Yael over brought back the memories of my family. A woman's things in the apartment: a brassiere drying in the bathroom, a dress in the closet, a hairbrush on the nightstand. She brought a radio and music broke the quiet. It was strange and scary. There were anxiety attacks, but I'd been training myself to let them pass over me.

I used the actual word: I told her that I loved her. I was happy, and that happiness remained embedded within and I could go back to it at any moment. Even Dov Cohen's usual complaints about this or that couldn't ruin my return to work. I asked him to let me focus on work about the righteous and he, surprisingly, did not object. I got a telephone installed courtesy of Yosef, and no longer had to take personal calls in the office. Everything was going my way. I even slept better.

"Who's Ezra?" Yael asked me in the middle of the night, her hands holding my face, trying to see inside. "You keep calling him in your sleep."

"My friend in Auschwitz. He told me that I was the son that he never had. Saved me during the uprising in October of 1944."

"What happened to him?"

"He died there."

On 15th of December 1961, Adolf Eichmann was sentenced to death by hanging. The judges of Israel had spoken:

"... For the dispatch of each train by the Accused to Auschwitz, or to any other extermination site, carrying one thousand human beings, meant that the Accused

was a direct accomplice in a thousand premeditated acts of murder, and the degree of his legal and moral responsibility for these acts of murder is not one iota less than the responsibility of the person who with his own hands pushed these human beings into the gas chambers.

Even if we had found that the Accused acted out of blind obedience, as he argued, we would still have said that a man who took part in crimes of such magnitude as these over years must pay the maximum penalty known to the law, and he cannot rely on any order even in mitigation of his punishment. But we have found that the Accused acted out of an inner identification with the orders that he was given and out of a fierce will to achieve the criminal objective ..."

One day, walking down Hillel Street towards Café Europa, I ran into Itzhak. I remember that it was the day after the American John Glenn orbited the Earth; that's what everyone was talking about.

He scowled at me. "David Levy. Or is it Levinsky?"

"It's Levy," I replied. I changed it in 1945, upon arrival in Israel. It had been over sixteen years since anyone used my old family name and I wondered how Itzhak got hold of it and why.

"Still looking for a few good Germans?"

"Actually, I've met a few."

"Ha! The only good German is a dead German."

"You have no doubts? Ever?"

"Not in this. My life belongs to this country. I will fight and die for my people."

"Our lives don't belong to countries and people without doubts scare me."

"Yes, yes, you research and doubt, you don't act ... You think too much, just a regular Jewish Hamlet. Don't you understand? They all knew. The Church, America, Britain—they all knew. They just had other priorities. I'm not going to wait for their justice or their help. For me, Israel is the only priority. There will be another war. And your good Germans are helping Arabs to wipe us out."

He walked away angrily.

Yael wanted children. After the *Lager*, I had decided that I would never have one. And yet, I began thinking about it.

177

She took me to meet her parents in Galilee. They were retired, although Herz, being a doctor, still saw some of his old patients that came to him. A typical *yekke*, a German-born Israeli, he looked down his nose on anyone not steeped in a high European culture, but somehow combined it with a passion for communal living, working the land, and so on. Yael's mother parroted her husband in everything. We did have something in common: both our families left Germany in 1936, after the Nuremberg Laws. But they went to Haifa and we went to Bratislava: a two-day travel, the difference between life and death.

Yael's father asked me:, "Auschwitz, what was it like?"

We were sitting in the garden, overlooking the Sea of Galilee, and he brought up the hell in a faraway Poland. I didn't answer. I couldn't. I saw from his expression that he thought me rude. Despite the similarities, we did not get along. Could have been my lack of respect for the culture that produced Goethe and Beethoven, because I couldn't forget the others that it produced. Could have been my dislike of the kibbutz that I lived in after the war, with its collectivist rules. Could have been my underlying resentment of them being alive, while my parents were gone. Could have been their view that nobody's good enough for their daughter: Yael told me that they didn't approve of her former husband either. I didn't know exactly what it was, but cracks of animosity appeared on our second day there and had gotten worse when Herz began to talk glowingly about Itzhak right in front of me. We left a day early and it was not a pleasant trip back.

"You could have made an effort," Yael said angrily.

I tried to make it up to her. On the way back, we climbed to King David's tomb and I took her in my arms as we watched the sun melt into the holy city.

I knew I should have made more effort with them for Yael's sake, but I had no experience in these matters: I'd never gotten to the "meet the parents" stage with any of the *sabras* I dated, and the ones that came from Europe usually had no relatives left. Yael forgave me—or so I thought—but it must have left a fissure in our still-fragile relationship.

11

One weekend in March, Yael and I came to have dinner with Yosef and Rachel.

As the women cooed over seven-months-old Rivka, Yosef and I remained at the backyard table under the old olive tree.

"How are you? All recovered?" Yosef asked.

"Yes, much better now. Why, are you looking to go back to Germany?"

"No, not Germany. Turkey, perhaps."

He paused, but I remained silent, so he continued.

"I met with Benny in November, and then again last week."

"I didn't realize you knew him."

"He was visiting you in the hospital when I came."

"What did he want?"

"He was asking me about Ekrem Bey. I gave him a description of the place in Trabzon."

"And?"

"Last week he asked me if I want to visit Trabzon."

"You are still looking for your Prinz?"

"I want to acknowledge the man, whoever he was. Our trip in September came to nothing. I've spoken with Gerhardt; he checked other names and came up empty."

He looked at me expectantly. I remained silent, figuring this'd be awkward.

"David, if I go—would you come with me? You've got the languages."

"I don't speak Turkish."

"You speak English, I hear you can get by with that. Look, it's not like going to Germany. A two-day trip, that's it."

"But why?"

"It's a simple thing and it bothers me that I haven't tried it. If I can find that Ekrem Bey and ask him, great. If not, I'll close the door on the whole thing with a clear conscience."

"I'm sorry, Yosef, I'm not interested."

But of course, things didn't end there. Later that month Benny, Yosef and I met in Café Vienna on Jaffa Street. I couldn't well say no to meeting for a drink.

"Yosef, you told me earlier about a mosque with ancient-looking walls, a newer, lighter stone round structure on top with a tall minaret, right?" Benny said.

"Yes, we walked from the boat for about ten minutes, came to a broad boulevard, turned right. After another ten-minute walk the mosque was uphill on the left."

"It's the *Yeni Cuma Mosque*, New Friday mosque built on top of an old Byzantine church. Easy to find, a tourist attraction."

"Benny, how do you know this?"

"I spoke with people that know Trabzon. Yosef's description matches the mosque very well. And it narrows Ekrem Bey's location quite a bit."

"Yes," Yosef said excitedly. "We walked toward the mosque, then turned left into a narrow street, then went up the stairs. I remember a tall, at least twenty-five meters spruce tree in front. Two-story reddish building surrounded by a stone wall. I can find it."

"Benny, why?" I asked.

"Why what?"

"Why are you still looking into this? What's your angle?"

"No angle." Benny shrugged, as he lit another cigarette. "You came to me, remember? You wanted to find the man."

"And the attack in Frankfurt?"

"I'm sorry about that. I think it was an unrelated neo-Nazi attack. The German police concluded as much. It's up to you. If you decide to go, I'll help you with logistics."

And that's how Benny cleverly dangled this before Yosef, and Yosef couldn't resist.

The next time that Yael and I visited them, Yosef announced that he decided to go to Trabzon. Judging by the reddish puffiness around Rachel's eyes, their domestic conversation took place already. Funny how Rachel was an obvious boss of that family, and yet Yosef showed this occasional stubbornness that she couldn't overcome.

Rachel sniffled and said, "We argued all night. David, would you do me a huge favor and go with him? Then we can put this whole stupid quest to bed for good."

Yael and I had our own argument just before that. She was twenty-nine, and conversations about having a child became frequent. I was coming to realize that my choices were "Yael with a child" and "no child, no Yael," and deep inside I already knew that I would choose the former. Still, I was not quite ready to say yes.

But at that moment, both Rachel and Yael were looking at me with that "You are not going to let him go by himself?" expression.

I nodded. "OK." Going with Yosef was my peace offering to Yael. I figured it'd be a short trip, like Benny said.

12

And so in April, armed with a Turkish dictionary and two backpacks, we flew to Ankara and then by a small commuter plane to Trabzon. Yosef asked the taxi driver to take us to the Yeni Cuma Mosque. The driver nodded and took off. The road shimmered from a recent rain and low dark clouds promised another one. We drove for about fifteen minutes with the Black Sea on our right when the driver turned onto a broad boulevard.

After a few minutes Yosef shouted excitedly in Hebrew, "Try this street!" The driver stopped and looked back. Yosef pointed to the left and we turned onto a narrow street, the mosque uphill straight ahead. After a minute, Yosef shook his head. "Stop. I don't think this is the right place." He got out of the car, looked around. "No, that's definitely not it." Between gestures, broken English and occasional Turkish words, we managed to get the driver to try two other streets, until Yosef said, "I think this is the place." It was all going surprisingly easy. We got out and asked the taxi driver to wait. He gave the universal two-fingers-rubbing gesture of "give me the money." We foolishly did, and he immediately took off.

Yosef walked up an even narrower street, up curving steps on the right. I followed him, until suddenly he stopped and excitedly pointed to a two-story white house surrounded by a low stone wall. "This is it!"

"It's white, not red. And where is the spruce tree?"

"Painted? I don't know. Look." Yosef pointed to a short stump. "The tree was there."

In front of the house was a semi-circular driveway, with a large American-made car parked there. Two men watched us suspiciously.

"Salaam Alaaikum," Yosef greeted them.

"Alaaikum Salaam," they responded without enthusiasm.

"Ekrem Bey?"

One of the men said something in Turkish. Yosef pulled out the dictionary, just as an older portly man came out of the house.

"Ekrem Bey!" Yosef shouted excitedly.

The man looked at us without recognition. Yosef in his agitation switched to German, "Remember me? I was here with Prinz in 1942!"

At that the man stepped back, as if he saw a snake. Yosef moved closer, but the two young men blocked the way.

The man screamed in German, "Go away! Get out!" then switched to Turkish.

Yosef tried to protest, also in German. "We came in peace. Ekrem Bey. I just want to know his name. You helped us in '42, I am very grateful."

The man shouted, "Murderer!"

One of the young men took out a gun. I grabbed Yosef's arm and pulled him back. The man pointed the gun at us, and we turned around and ran down the narrow street, turned right and continued until we got to the boulevard. We slowed down to a walk. There was a sign "Otel" and small café nearby that had a few people and a couple of open tables. We sat down at one.

"Why did he say I killed someone?" Yosef said. "I don't understand."

"He recognized you."

"Yes. It's him all right."

A waiter came out and we asked for coffee. It was early evening by now. Chilly, light rain began to fall.

"What do we do? Try again tomorrow?"

"Why? He did not want to talk to you. We can't force him. Came all the way and the man won't even see us. Yosef, we should go home. Enough!"

A police car pulled up just as the waiter brought our coffee. Two gendarmes came out, together with the taxi driver who pointed at us.

"*Bizimle gel!*" a gendarme commanded. His sour breath smelled like an ashtray.

"What?" I replied in English.

He gestured to come with them. A crowd began to gather.

"Why?"

The gendarme hit me with a stick. Onlookers cheered.

We got pushed into the police car and taken to the station, where they searched us, took away our backpacks, belts, passports, wallets, and threw us into a cell. It was dark, with a small wooden bench and a bucket in the corner which stank badly. I sat on the bench and leaned against the dank brick wall.

"Damn it." Yosef sat next to me. "What do they want with us?"

I stared at the dirty ceiling, hungry, angry at him, at Benny, at myself. We'd heard stories of people disappearing in Turkish prisons. Why in hell was I in this place? My stomach clenched, and I had to visit the bucket. It had not been emptied after whomever was in the cell before us.

"Rachel is probably putting Rivka to bed now," Yosef said wistfully. "I hope we make it out of here."

"We will, Yosef, we will. Just a misunderstanding," I reassured him, despite my lack of confidence.

"Yeah, I want to see my wife and kids again. I like having kids. David, I think you're going to like having kids too."

"What kids?"

"Come on, David, you know that Yael wants kids. A boy and a girl, like her sister. And when it comes to that, women get their way. You may as well accept it." Yosef smiled.

"Let's try to get out of here first."

"I'm sorry I listened to Benny and got us into this. He said it was going to be just a quick trip."

"Hmmm ... Yosef, exactly how did you meet Benny? You said it was in the hospital, right?"

"Yes. I just got done visiting you and literally bumped into him on my way out. He asked me if my name was Yosef Milman, and we talked for a while."

"And the next time, did he bump into you again?"

"No ... Well, kind of. I was sitting on a bench near my office, eating a *burek* that I bought from a street vendor, and Benny was walking by. Why?"

"Oh, nothing."

There was no point in getting Yosef more nervous than he was already. When it came to Benny Hadan, I doubted that the bumps were accidental.

Heavy rain fell during the night. I dozed off and woke up when I heard screaming. But it was quiet, the screams were in my head. Nobody talked to us or looked at us until the gray morning, when two gendarmes took us out of the cell and into a small room. A police detective sat behind the desk surrounded by files. Gendarmes pushed us into two wooden chairs across from him and left.

The detective studied our passports. He looked to be in his early forties, with a prominent hawkish nose and wavy black hair.

"Yosef Milman, David Levy. From Israel," he said in a heavily accented English. "I would offer you to shower but I'm afraid we don't have the time for niceties. You upset one of our distinguished citizens, Ekrem Celik Bey."

"Is that his full name? We did not do anything to him," I replied.

"He claimed that you barged into his house and tried to rob him."

"That's nonsense."

"His bodyguards confirm his version. But you don't look like robbers to me. Why would you come all the way from Israel?"

"It's a long story."

The detective called out and said something in Turkish to the gendarme that came in.

"I asked for coffee and breakfast. We are going to treat you to some *hamsi*. That's our famous anchovies. As long as you are here, you must try them. As for the story, I've got time. And you better tell me the truth. Exactly who you are and why you are here. And why you, David Levy, have a number tattooed on your arm. Because Ekrem Bey sure wants you gone. I've been told that if I carefully search your backpacks, I'll find heroin. And the penalty for that is a very long jail time. Which you most likely won't survive."

"This is crazy! We don't have any heroin!" Now I was really scared.

"This is Turkey."

I showed him my tattoo, and gave a condensed version of the story that brought us to Trabzon.

"Interesting. Very interesting." The detective leaned back in his chair. "I'm not sure I believe you."

"Why not?"

The detective opened a file and placed two photos in front of us with, "Who are these people?"

185

Yosef and I studied the pictures of two men, looked at each other and shrugged.

"Never saw them before."

The detective's eyes narrowed. "Don't lie to me."

"Really, don't know them."

He studied us carefully, then nodded, hopefully deciding that we were telling the truth.

"These people came here recently. Passports from England. Except that their English was not that great. Had them followed; they seemed to show a lot of interest in Yeni Cuma Mosque. Just kept walking around it. I was about to bring them in for questioning, when they disappeared. Left in the middle of the night. They were professionals. Unlike you."

There was a knock and a gendarme came in with a tray of food. He put plates and coffee in front of us and a coffee cup for the detective.

"You eat, I'll talk," the detective said. "My name is Arslan Demir. I am a *Komiser* here. Kind of like a Police Inspector in your country. You were followed from the moment you landed. As a matter of fact, I received a phone call that you were coming."

"From whom?"

"Anonymous. Someone else, besides Ekrem Bey, wanted you arrested. All that activity surrounding him made me curious. You see, Ekrem Bey came to Trabzon in 1937. Nobody knows for sure where he was before, but there were rumors that he ran away after the war to avoid prosecution."

"Prosecution for what?"

"Probably war crimes. He came with a lot of money for a small town like ours, bought an expensive house and quickly befriended the mayor and town's other prominent citizens. Very active in the forties. Multiple businesses: pharmaceuticals distribution, mining, shipping, smuggling. Had a small fleet back then. Secretive visitors from out of town. But for the past dozen years his family kept to itself, led quiet lives. So why suddenly all the interest? Why did he make so much noise about two tourists? You have no weapons, he's got armed bodyguards, you obviously are clueless amateurs. Seems that your presence is a threat to him for some reason."

"Perhaps he does not want his German connections to become known?"

"Being a Nazi sympathizer is not a crime. If anything, that was the predominant inclination here. Germans and Turks were allies in the first World War after all. Something else is going on."

He picked up the phone and spoke with someone in Turkish.

"In your backpacks there are tickets to fly back to Israel tomorrow. I just changed them to today. There was a bag of heroin in one backpack but it's no longer there. I think it would be best for all of us if you cut your sightseeing plans short. I need for you to disappear. You are too much of a liability to have around. And you should get out because I can't guarantee your safety."

"Why are you doing this?"

"Doing what?"

"Letting us go."

Arslan Demir looked at us, rubbed his chin, weighing how much to tell us.

"My mother is a *kes-kes*. Do you know what that means?"

"No."

"Fifty years ago, there were more people in Trabzon than there are now. Tens of thousands of Armenians lived here. In 1915, almost all of them were taken to the sea and drowned. Except for young girls that agreed to accept Islam—they were married into Turkish families. But some never forgot their Armenian roots. People like that are called *kes-kes*. And that house that Ekrem Bey lives in—it belonged to my Armenian grandfather."

"Shouldn't the house be in your family?"

"It should have been. But they made Armenians sign off their possessions to the state before being 'resettled.' First rob, then kill. Take your things, I will personally drive you to the airport."

"Thank you. You really don't like Ekrem Bey?" I asked.

"No, I don't. He's the kind of man that thinks he's above the law. And he buys protection to make sure of that. I know he paid to have heroin put into one of your backpacks, and I just don't care for that. I almost had him arrested once. Some years ago, he was accused of using counterfeit British pounds. He made up a story of how a Briton gave the money to him as a payment. I knew he was lying. But I couldn't prove it. And then a stack of pound bills had disappeared from the evidence room. All, but the one that was clipped to the file."

187

He showed us a twenty-pound note. "This one." He placed the note and Ekrem Bey's photo on the table in front of us and got up.

"I have to leave the room for a minute."

Yosef looked at me, then pocketed the note and the photo.

13

On the flight back from Ankara I asked Yosef, "You really don't know anything about the two people that were there before us, do you?"

"No, I swear."

"The detective seemed to think they were looking for Ekrem Bey too."

"Maybe they just wanted to see the mosque?"

"Or perhaps Benny sent them before us. And that anonymous call … We were being set up."

"Why would Benny try to set us up?"

"I have no idea. I did not say it was Benny."

I was a marionette that didn't even know who was pulling the strings.

Benny greeted us at the airport. "I was alerted that your names were on the passenger list. How come you are back early?"

"Here's Ekrem Bey's photo and a counterfeit bill that he tried to use some years ago." Yosef angrily pushed them into Benny's face. "I am out. Don't involve me in your dirty games anymore."

Benny raised his hands, pleading, "Wait, calm down, tell me what happened."

"Did you send anyone to Trabzon before us?" I asked.

"No." But he hesitated, and I knew that he was lying.

"Who knew about us going there?"

"Errr … very few people."

"Well, someone called to warn them!"

I stormed away from him, got into a taxi, went straight to Shaare Zadek Medical Center and found Yael.

"When does your shift end?"

"What? When did you get back?"

"We returned a day early."

"Is everything OK?"

"It is now. Come, I want to take you to a restaurant."

"But … but I can't. I traded with another nurse to take her night shift, so I could spend more time with you after your return. I won't be home until tomorrow."

"Oh. OK. We can go then."

"Did you come straight from the airport?"

"Yes."

She threw her arms around me and kissed me hard. "Thank you! I love you, baby."

"I love you too."

"David?" she called out as I was leaving.

"Yes."

"Itzhak phoned."

"What does he want?"

"He asked to meet with both of us."

"Why?"

"He didn't say. I told him you'd be back tomorrow."

I was lucky to escape Trabzon. I was going to tell Yael that we could have a child or two, if she married me. But I didn't want to do it in the hospital. There was not much to do but wait until the next day.

Yael, Itzhak and I met in Café Rehavia. Itzhak was waiting for us with a drink and three glasses.

"Yael, you look beautiful!"

"What do you want?" I cut him off.

"Sit down, David. Have a drink, cool off. It's a hot day."

"I don't care to drink with you. What do you want?"

"Fine, no drinks. Yael, how much do you know about your boyfriend here? Do you know what he did during the war?"

"He fought in *Palmach*."

"No, the one before that."

"He was in Auschwitz."

"And did he tell you what exactly he did in Auschwitz?"

I went numb inside.

"He worked in a synthetic rubber factory." Yael shrugged.

"Ha! That's a lie! He was in *Sonderkommando*. These were the people that ran the gas chambers and crematoria. He was telling his fellow Jews to undress. He escorted them to the gas chambers. Beat them up if they resisted. He took out their bodies and washed off the blood and shit from the chambers, so the next group wouldn't suspect that they were not going to take a shower, that they would be painfully murdered. He burned their bodies. He held still those that were condemned to be shot to make it easy for the Germans to kill them. He did all that, so he could save his own skin. He's a collaborator. No better than Eichmann. Worse, actually. Because he is a Jew."

I remember I had a ridiculous thought then: *Itzhak should have been an actor or a trial lawyer.* He rose up and delivered his accusation in a dramatically raised tone, stabbing the air with his finger so there would be no doubt who the beast was—me. A hush descended over the café. I felt dozens of eyes burning through my skin.

"Is this true?" Yael asked quietly.

I heard everything and nothing, the blood pounded so loud against my temples.

"Is this true?"

"Come on, David, say it." Itzhak sneered. "Enough lying, enough hiding. I'll make sure everyone knows who you really are. A murderer. A traitor."

"I am not a murderer or a traitor," I said quietly.

"I hate you both!" Yael got up and ran out of the cafe.

When I got home, Yael was crying and packing her things. I tried to embrace her. "Yael, I need you. Please."

She jumped away. "You've been lying to me. How could you do these things? We lived together for seven months, we made love hundreds of times, and I have no idea who you are. I want the past to be the past. You are looking for something I don't have. I can't be your salvation. I want to live normally!"

And with that, she walked out of my life.

PART 5:
AVI

1

"It's an unusually warm day for April," our host, Bruno Hüber, commented.

We—Bruno, Gerhardt Shrumpf, Iris, and I—were sitting in a café in Holzlar, a quaint suburb of Bonn. The café overlooked a manicured golf course, beyond which a watermill stood. A historic one, as the waiter proudly pointed out. Everything was clean and orderly.

Iris and I flew into Frankfurt three days prior, after speaking with Gerhardt by phone. Iris was looking for her long-lost father. I, for my real grandfather. We decided that finding out what happened in April of 1965 was as good a starting point as any. Gerhardt arranged this meeting with Bruno, a long-time police detective in Bonn.

"Bruno, what can you tell us about the death of Aram Arutiyan? You were a *Polizeikommissar* here, right?" Gerhardt asked.

"I was not a *Polizeikommissar* then." Bruno smiled. "Just a low ranking *inspektor.*"

"Bruno is now *Erster Polizeihauptkommissar*, the highest local police grade," Gerhardt explained to Iris and me. "It's very nice of him to give us this time."

"It's my pleasure, Gerhardt. I have learned a lot from you. But to your question: two people, Aram Arutiyan and Levon Bogosian, had been gunned down here in Bonn on April 20, 1965. When Gerhardt contacted me, I looked through the files to refresh my memory. After all, it's been twenty-six years."

"Where exactly did it happen?"

"In a park in Niederkassel, now it's the nature reserve Siegaue. First we thought of neo-Nazis because of the message found in the house they rented on the outskirts of Bergheim nearby."

"What kind of message?"

"A handwritten piece of paper with 'Turks, out of Germany!' Turkish workers had been invited to West Germany since 1962, and there were quite a few attacks on them. Plus, April 20th was Hitler's birthday. So neo-Nazis were the initial suspects."

"But you didn't believe it?"

"I was suspicious. Neo-Nazis were trash, but it seemed like someone tried to pin it on them. After all, even neo-Nazis would know the difference between Turks and Armenians. Why would these people go to a remote place? Must have been to meet someone they knew. Bogosian was shot in the chest with three 7.65 mm rounds, while Arutiyan was killed by one 9X18 mm shot in the back. From a Makarov pistol, not a typical neo-Nazi weapon. There was gunpowder residue on Levon's fingers, but no gun. There were drops of blood that did not belong to either one of the victims. They were not killed in an execution style; even eyes seemed respectfully closed by someone. And why would somebody go to their house and leave a message there? It also looked like the house was searched, things removed. Inside, we found 9X18 mm bullets and a residue of the Russian PVV-5A plastic explosives. The neighbors saw at least one other person in that house, but he—or they—were never found."

"So, what do you think happened?"

"Well, no one was ever apprehended," Bruno said. "But Aram Arutiyan was not exactly just another guy. His real name was Gor Grigorian."

"Excuse me?" I stopped him.

"Yes, Gor Grigorian. Back in 1921, he killed one of the former Turkish leaders here in Germany. Then he killed another in Turkey, in a brazen attack in the middle of Istanbul. After which he disappeared without a trace, until 1965. Turks had a reward on his head, they were looking hard for him."

"You didn't know any of that, Avi?" Gerhardt looked at me intently.

"No, I had no idea."

"Bruno, how did you figure out it was him?"

"Old files from 1921 had his picture. We Germans are good about file-keeping. Despite what Hitler said, we do remember Armenians. Like the one who killed Talaat Pasha here in Germany in 1921, and was acquitted by the jury."

196

"You could recognize Aram … I mean Gor Grigorian, after forty-four years?"

"Yes, it was him. More important, we had his fingerprints. Back in 1921, he was arrested, but released for lack of witnesses. It was right after the trial of the man that killed Talaat. Nobody wanted another trial. We had two theories back in '65. One, that the Russians were smuggling explosives from the East Germany, trying to stir up some terrorist activities. The other, that Armenians were planning something for April 24th, which they consider the anniversary of their genocide, the Turks found out and killed them."

"And what did you think?"

"I focused on the Turks. Wanted to bring some from the embassy for questioning. BND, the Federal Intelligence Service, got involved. Told us to drop it."

"Why?"

"Ever heard of Incirlik?"

"The air base in Turkey?"

"That's the one. Thousands of US soldiers, squadrons of US aircraft. It was too important to the Americans to irritate the Turks. It was the height of the Cold War, remember? Why are you interested in this old affair?"

"He was my grandfather," I replied as calmly as I could.

"Who?"

"Aram Arutiyan … Gor Grigorian. I only knew him as Aram."

"Whew!" Bruno whistled. "That's—how would you Americans say—pretty heavy, right?"

"Yeah, that's one way to put it."

"And you're sure there were Russian weapons involved?" Gerhardt asked.

"Yes. Russian-manufactured, to be precise."

"Then why have you decided it was not the Russians behind it? The KGB?"

"I could not see a good motive. And if they were behind it, they would not have used their own weapons or old Armenian terrorists. Also, how to phrase it … The KGB people were professionals. This looked like a purely amateurish affair. The mixture of weapons … It didn't make much sense."

"And that other man, Levon Bogosian, was that his real name?"

"Yes. Levon Bogosian from Marseille. We verified it with the French. He had some military training. And a psychiatric record."

"Are you OK?" Iris turned to me after Bruno left us.

"Well … in a way, I am not surprised. I already knew that my grandfather was not who he appeared to be. I didn't quite picture him to be an assassin though."

"Under extreme circumstances, people turn out different than we expect," Gerhardt said and quickly apologized. "I'm sorry, I didn't mean to give you a stupid cliché. It just came out."

Gerhardt still looked like an oversized hobbit, like David described him. And he still wore a tweed jacket and a necktie. But now in his seventies, his short hair was completely white. He'd met us at the airport and we had to almost literally fight off his insistence on hosting us.

"What now? Does it tell us anything about my father?" Iris asked.

"The fact that the Russian-made weapons were used doesn't prove his involvement, but certainly doesn't exclude it. Especially based on his connection with Leon Chorsky, a black marketeer and an arms dealer."

"What about that woman, Erika Jager?"

"I'm afraid we'll have to wait until Erika is back from Cambodia in two weeks," Gerhardt said apologetically.

"You told us she was going to be back this week."

"I'm sorry, I didn't mean to mislead you. That's what I'd been told by the newspaper staff, but they were wrong. The notebooks that you brought have some interesting leads that I am following. Sorry, it takes time. Remember, I've been retired for a while. My contacts are, well, rusty."

"I guess we should try changing our tickets to tomorrow," Iris said.

"Tickets?"

"We were planning to fly to Israel in three days," I explained. "To meet with people there. We thought that a week here would be enough."

"You can do some sightseeing instead of leaving earlier. Baden-Baden is less than two hours from Frankfurt, and …"

"I'm not interested in sightseeing," Iris interrupted him brusquely. "I just want to find out what I can about my father. I don't want to stay here any longer than absolutely necessary."

She struck me as pretty strung up even back in LA. She cut her hair short right before the trip, giving her a more masculine, stern look. Once we landed in Germany, Iris seemed to really fill up with intense animosity. I tiptoed carefully around her, regretting that I agreed we would travel together.

"I understand." Gerhardt lowered his eyes. "I don't blame you at all. I feel bad about the timing with Erika. I wish I could get in touch with her. Can I offer a suggestion?"

"Please."

"There is one person that both of you may want to talk to."

"Why?"

"He had a rather extensive knowledge of terrorist organizations. Sorry." Gerhardt saw my expression. "I didn't mean to imply that your grandfather belonged to one. I wouldn't say that he did. But your uncle and your brother… Look, you are here to find out what you can, right? Information is information."

"I guess it is."

"And what about me?" Iris asked.

"From the late 1940s through the mid-60s, the man I have in mind was involved with investigation of the Nazi criminals."

"He was in Ludwigsburg?"

"No. He was with the *Stasi*, the East German secret police."

"*Stasi*? Why would I want to talk to him?"

"Because it sounds like your father may have been in contact with them."

"Is he in Frankfurt?"

"He lives in Berlin."

"That's what? Six hours?"

"I'd say five. We can leave at seven, meet him for lunch, be back in the evening."

When we got back to Frankfurt, we found out that changing the flight at that point would more than double the price. We decided to stay and go with Gerhardt to Berlin.

2

"It's been only a year and a half since the Wall fell," Martin Möller said. "Still feels unreal."

Möller looked to be in his mid-seventies, like Gerhardt. The similarities ended there: Möller was tall and overweight, a short-sleeve polo shirt accentuating his heaviness, thick glasses constantly sliding off a fleshy nose. Even though the day was not hot, he sweated profusely and kept wiping his face with a greyish handkerchief.

"Is Berlin officially the capital again?" I asked.

"Yes. They are slowly moving the bureaucrats from Bonn. That will take a while."

We were in a small Italian *Ristorante* in the Kladow suburb of Berlin, just by the river.

"Gerhardt was lucky," Martin continued. "We worked together in Kripo and tried to leave Berlin at the same time. The guy could barely walk, and he managed to escape to the French zone. I got arrested by some stupid *Hitler Jugend* patrol and held up until the Russians arrived."

"I thought they shipped people like you to Siberia," Iris snarled.

"They sure did. Fortunately for me, they looked through the archives and figured out that I was never on the Eastern Front— thankfully, I am as blind as a bat—and that my skills could be of use in what became the East German Democratic Republic. They put me to work prosecuting Nazis. The Petri trial, the Globke trial, the Auschwitz trial ..."

"The Auschwitz trial?" I asked incredulously. "I thought it was in Frankfurt."

"Yeah, right." Martin chuckled. "Poles held a larger trial in December of 1947."

"Was that with Rudolf Höss?"

"No, Höss was tried by himself in March. They hung him in April in front of the crematorium. At the later trial, they had forty accused, starting with Arthur Liebehenschel, camp commandant for five months."

"They hung him also, right?" Gerhardt asked.

"Him, and twenty-two others. Whatever else you say about the Russians—and there is plenty bad to say—they really hated the Nazis. And you can't blame them. After what Wehrmacht did in their country, we were lucky they didn't burn Germany to the ground."

"So much of it was political,"

"In the sixties, true. But some well-deserved. Like Erna Petri's trial in '62. My skin still crawls when I think of her. She saw children crouching along the side of the road, they escaped from a transport taking them to the extermination camp. This sweet lady beckoned them, brought them home, gave them food. Then she killed them all. She got a life term, but I would have personally volunteered to hang her. If Erna Petri was in West Germany, she would probably not have been tried and slipped back into society as an ordinary *Hausfrau*."

"You don't know that, Martin."

"Yes, I do. And even if she had been tried, she would have received a much lighter sentence. Come on, Gerhardt, West Germany was crawling with Nazis back in the fifties and sixties. I am not talking about your run-of-the-mill order-following Germans, I'm talking about dyed-in-the-wool Nazis. You know, the Wannsee conference was right over there, across Havel." Martin pointed towards the river. "Fifteen educated, supposedly civilized men in an elegant villa drank cognac and planned mass murder. Do you know what happened with the participants?"

"Some, not all."

"Let's see. SS-General Hofmann—freed in 1954. SS-Oberführer Gerhardt Klopfer—a lawyer, died peacefully. Georg Leibbrandt—case dismissed. Erich Neumann—released, died peacefully. Friedrich Wilhelm Kritzinger—released, died peacefully. Dr. Wilhelm Stuckart—released in 1949, killed in 1953, likely by Mossad. I guess in his case Mossad drew the line."

"Look, Martin," Gerhardt said, exasperated, "we didn't drive here for five-plus hours to discuss the Nazi trials, or lack thereof."

"Right, you want to talk about David Levy and the Armenians. Was David Levy your father?" Martin looked at me.

"No. Mine," Iris replied.

"Sorry, miss. Yes, I met him twice. I think it was in early 1965. He brought us files on some former Nazis that were in high-level positions in West Germany. In banking, industry, foreign affairs."

"Why did he do that?"

"Unless you could prove with eyewitnesses that they personally pulled the trigger or poured in the gas, it was impossible to do anything about them in West Germany. Gerhardt, you may remember the Hans Globke trial *in absentia* that we conducted here in Berlin in 1963?"

"Yes, of course I remember." Gerhardt nodded. "In the West, we dismissed it as communist propaganda."

"Yeah, well, the guy pretty much wrote the racist Nuremberg Laws. And the trial must have been quite embarrassing, because four months later Globke had to resign."

"And David Levy wanted the same to be done to others?"

"Exactly."

"But it didn't happen, did it?"

"No." Martin shook his head. "We did the Horst Fischer trial in 1966, but that was pretty much it."

"So the information my father provided was not used?" Iris asked.

"Oh, it was used. Just not the way he intended. Instead of the trials, the Russians blackmailed them."

"My poor father, you betrayed him!" People in the restaurant turned to look at us.

"I'm sorry, child," Martin said gently. "For what it's worth, once I realized that there would be no trials, I told him. Not directly, but he understood. We never received anything from him again. And in the late sixties I began working on terrorist groups. Or freedom fighters, depending on the perspective. Sometimes we funded them, but I can't say that we liked terrorists too much. Double-edged sword, very volatile. In the case of the Armenians, we didn't support them. The Russians were just as threatened by this at the time as the Turks were. They didn't like the Armenian independence movement."

"Did you have anything on Aram Arutiyan? May also be under Gor Gregorian?" I asked.

"Yes, Gerhardt told me over the phone. I knew the name of your grandfather, of course. His murder in 1965. We did not supply him, at least not directly. There was a bit of a panic at the time— was it the Russians doing something behind our back? But ultimately, we felt they procured it on the black market. The border to West Germany was pretty porous; you could smuggle almost anything. The conclusion was that the Turks got wind of something being planned and killed him and his assistant. All that I can tell you for sure: unless it was a rogue operation, we had nothing to do with it."

"And what about my uncle and my brother? Do you know anything about them?"

"Well, there were at least four different Armenian terrorist groups: Justice Commandos of the Armenian Genocide; Armenian Revolutionary Army; Armenian Secret Army for the Liberation of Armenia, ASALA; and New Armenian Resistance Group. They didn't always get along, some were affiliated with the Dashnaks, while ASALA was more left-wing and PLO-aligned. I believe that your uncle and brother belonged to the ASALA group. The group was based in Lebanon in the seventies; they often trained in the PLO camps in Beirut. They were amateurish when handling explosives and there were at least half a dozen cases where bomb-makers accidentally blew themselves up. I'm afraid that's what happened to your brother. Your uncle had been implicated in at least four attacks in Europe until he was caught in France. I think you know the rest."

"Is there anybody I can talk to? Anybody who knew them at that time?"

"I wouldn't." Martin shook his head. "The ASALA group is still active, but barely so. The European attacks upset many people in the Armenian diaspora, and they withdrew their support. When Israel invaded Lebanon, ASALA lost PLO's support as well. Their founder, Hagop Hagopian, was assassinated three years ago. The Turks now have special killing squads to hunt the ASALA members. If you ask too many questions, they'll get interested in you. Especially with your family's history. My advice is, stay away. It's dangerous."

Iris and I dozed off on the way back, tired and still jet-lagged. Gerhardt remained silent, lost in his thoughts until we were minutes away from Frankfurt.

"I still remember the last free election before the war," he spoke suddenly. "Hitler got only one-third of the vote."

"And your point is?" Iris replied testily.

"The majority of the Germans didn't support him."

"Yeah, well, however you justify it …"

"Iris, I'm not justifying anything: we handed the power to a gang of criminals. And we—especially women and children—paid a heavy price for that. Not the terrible price that your father paid, but a harsh one nevertheless. You don't know what it was like to hate the evil regime and then carry the guilt for the horrors that it perpetrated in your name. Alas, the real murderers all too often died in their beds. And that's a shameful fact. Most of it is on us, but some of the fault lies with the victors."

"Whatever." Iris shrugged.

We drove the rest of the way in an uncomfortable silence.

3

"This is the same olive tree that David and I sat under, thirty years ago. Aron replaced the table and put in nicer lights."

Yosef Milman's English was heavily accented but understandable, as he pronounced words slowly and carefully. He groaned slightly as he lowered himself onto the bench. Except for the cleft chin, he looked different from David Levy's description: the blond hair receded all the way through the crown into a few thousand live follicles around the ears and in the back; a comfortable belly paunch expanded into a sizable spare tire.

"It's his house now. Rachel and I bought a place near the Sea of Galilee. We spend most of our time there."

Even with a closed door, we could hear laughter from the house where Iris, Yosef's wife Rachel, children Aron and Rivka, Aron's wife Sarah and their two kids remained. Yosef must have told them to leave us alone for a few minutes.

"Why did you want to talk to Iris and me separately?"

"Because I was sure the question of her mother, Yael, would come up, and that's a separate conversation with you vs. her. She's my niece after all."

"Were you surprised to hear about David Levy after such a long time?" I asked and immediately felt stupid.

"Yes, of course. I last saw him in August of 1965. I remember that it was right after the Frankfurt Auschwitz trial had ended. We followed it daily."

"Really? So, you reconciled after the ..." I searched for the right word but couldn't find it. "After what happened in 1962?"

"Ahhh! We never argued or anything. After that Trabzon trip, Rachel gave me an ultimatum. You must understand her—we had two

205

small kids, she did not want to become a widow. And the situation with Yael ..."

"But from the notebooks, it's Yael who broke them up."

"When two people break up, everyone has a different view. Yael is Rachel's sister, you know. And she was pregnant and did not want to tell David. Then David himself disappeared. Next year we heard he was living with a German woman in Germany of all places. Which at the time was not looked at kindly. So, it was uncomfortable. Very uncomfortable."

"Did it have anything to do with Itzhak exposing that David was in *Sonderkommando*?"

Yosef pulled a handkerchief out of his pocket and carefully wiped beads of sweat.

"It's complicated. Things were different at the time. Those that collaborated with the Nazis, we just saw them as traitors. So, yes ... Now, we know better. It actually started changing after the Eichmann trial, but it took years for people to realize that often the only difference between us and them was that we were here and they were there."

"How did you meet in 1965?"

"David called me. He came to Jerusalem. We met."

"In a café?"

"No, he did not want to go to a café. Probably didn't want to run into anyone he knew. We met at the Avenue of the Righteous at Yad Vashem, sat there and talked. I wanted to tell David about Iris, but Rachel asked me not to. Yael just got engaged to Jonathan Goldfarb, and Rachel thought it best to leave it alone. She wanted Yael to get some stability in her life, and David was anything but stable. Yael's parents were dead set against David. They wanted Yael to marry Jonathan. Whether this was the right thing to do, who's to say? I don't know. Iris doesn't feel this way. She thinks her father deserved to know. These come-out-of-nowhere notebooks, they drove a wedge between Iris and Yael. I hope Iris is not going to be too hard on her mother."

"The last time you saw David—what did you talk about?"

"He found the SS officer that saved me, showed me a picture of three boys, my officer being one. Hans Werner Arno Krentz was his name. I still have the picture, if you want to see it. But David couldn't find any living relatives. I guess they were all killed in the Russian offensive on Königsberg. David made inquiries in Russia, but the response was that those that survived repatriated to Germany."

"It didn't mean that they died."

"Not in those words, but you know how it was. Or perhaps you don't, you're young."

"Did David tell you anything of his plans?"

"No. David was different by then. He shared his time between Israel and Europe, where he was selling oranges. He said he was good at it, especially in Germany and Spain. He was making money."

"How was he different?"

Yosef pulled out the handkerchief again.

"Just the feeling. It's like he had a purpose. And he was angry. I mean, he was always angry, but now this anger was focused. I remember the two trees on the Avenue of the Righteous that he spent more time at: those of Ludwig Wörl and Oscar Schindler. Probably because they were Germans. And he said 'There are more Germans that we must honor and not forget. But I wish we had an Avenue of the Evil, where instead of trees we have ugly plaques where we list their crimes. And never forget those too. So for generations people will come and spit on them. That would be a small measure of justice.'"

Yosef dubbed the soaked handkerchief against his forehead.

"I said 'But the trials…like the one that just ended in Frankfurt…' And he became angry: 'This was not justice! These people will serve a bit of time and walk away and be respectable citizens again. Their crimes will be forgiven and forgotten.' 'But what would you have done?' I asked. 'Some crimes are such that to show compassion to these monsters is to invite more crimes on future generations.' There was something about the way he said it, I knew these were not just angry words. So I asked: 'David, are you planning something?' He didn't reply. I remember that conversation because it shook me up at the time."

"And you never saw him again?"

"No. I tried to find him, but he disappeared, this time for good. I was not too surprised. The way we parted that day… He was not an expressive man, he kept everything inside—but he gave me a big hug and thanked me, not sure what for. He was saying good-bye."

"You think he's dead?"

"Yes. And I have always felt guilty about that."

"Why?'

"It was me coming to see him in Yad Vashem that brought about the whole chain of events: Yael, Itzhak, everything that followed. If not for me, his life would have continued as it was."

"Who's to say?"

"Yes." He shrugged. "Who's to say? In a way, it was largely for nothing."

"What do you mean? You know the name of the officer now."

"But he's gone, his family is gone. I don't know why he did what he did."

"You still want to know?"

"Yes, of course. David used to say that there was no meaning to things that happened, no redemption of any kind. But I think that there might have been a meaning, at least in my case, and I wish I could find it."

"You have not tried to follow up with Benny or Shimon?"

"What for? They used us, especially David, for their own ends. Iris wanted to talk to them a few years ago, and I discouraged her. I was thinking that it'd be easier for her to leave these matters alone, to move on. How could I have known about David's notebooks?"

"All right, are you ready for dinner?" Aron and Rivka came out of the house carrying trays. It was the first time I saw Rivka wearing a dress and my eyes drifted down. When I lifted them, Aron was staring at me, a warning in his eyes. He was wearing a grey uniform of the officer of the Israeli Border Police.

After dinner, Aron called Iris and me aside. "I did a bit of checking around. Found Shimon Bezor, he lives in Tel Aviv. Hannah Shmulevitz died of cancer. Benny Hadan is alive and somewhere in Israel, but I couldn't get the contact information. I guess he doesn't want to be found. Hirsh Pozner is still growing oranges. I spoke with him and he last heard from David in the summer of 1965, doesn't know much beyond that. Leon Chorsky must have stepped on some wrong toes. He was assassinated in 1984. Arms dealing is a dangerous business."

"So basically, we just have Shimon Bezor to talk to?" Iris asked.

"I'm still hopeful about Benny Hadan, but for you, Iris, yes. Avi has some people in Beirut he wants to meet with." Aron turned to me. "I spoke with them, as you asked. It would take a bit of time to arrange."

PART 6:
DAVID

January 19, 1965

Dear Aram,

I have received the Journal of Psychology that you sent, describing Milgram's experiments. I found myself terribly unnerved by the results: the majority were willing to carry out the electric shocks to their conclusion??? I would have guessed at a much smaller number. After all the horrors, after the footage of concentration camps, so many are still willing to "just follow orders." And these were the people in a nice middle-class American town. Hannah Arendt's "banality of evil" might have been more perceptive than I gave her credit for. Perhaps "we are all potential Eichmanns." Evil need not be committed only by "idealists" like Eichmann but by regular people as well, as long as their deeds are sanctioned by what they perceive as an authority. Do we accept that rational explanations are not enough, that some— many—seemingly normal people have an inherent capacity for evil? That given permission, they will exempt themselves from normal moral and ethical considerations?

I have recently read Stanley Loomis' Paris in the Terror and came across this: "There is no crime, no murder, no massacre that cannot be justified, provide it be committed in the name of an Ideal." The same depressing sophistry: claim human well-being as the aim; the wicked enemies threaten it; harden your hearts and do what needs to be done in the name of revolutionary "morality." The essential difference between a mere crime and an evil one is ideology, the intellectual framework. The fact that someone did not have an emotional hatred does not mean that there was no ideological hatred, a much more dangerous one. Because emotion implies some measure of humanity while a cold rational hatred, the intellectual hatred, is robotic. Thus, evil is done in the name of good. It's not the opposite of good—as the German law would lead us to believe. If you have a small cadre of "idealists"—would the rest unthinkingly follow the authority? A terrifying prospect, but we've seen it happen. We need something that separates us from obedient automatons, instruments of pure force and will devoid of our common humanity. Otherwise, we are doomed.

You asked me to write about Auschwitz. Sorry, I don't have the voice to express what it was like. Words are just that: words. Vocabularies have not been created to describe these places. There are testimonies, there are numbers. There are—amazingly—photos. There is the Auschwitz album that's been presented here in Frankfurt, taken by someone from the SS. There is the Treblinka Beautiful Years photo album that was found in Kurt Franz's home. You want to feel what it was like? Study the pictures. Just like I am sure you've studied Armin Wegner's pictures of the destruction of your people. If you let the images inside of yourself, if you try to feel what they felt, they would tell you so much more than the words ever can. How many of those that had entered Auschwitz survived? One in ten? The weakest were killed within hours. The best of us, they did not survive either. In Israel, there is a stigma of surviving, the view that you've made it at the expense of others. To them, I am a traitor. Whenever I go back, I expect to be arrested and put on trial, like Hirsh Barenblatt. Lager shows you who you are and I, for one, had been found wanting. I am guilty. Guilty of surviving.

It's tempting to look for the meaning, for some redemption in the deaths of the innocents, as if they were soldiers on the battlefield. But there is none that I can think of. It won't stop people from trying to invent one. Once, with Yael, I went to see The Diary of Anne Frank. In the end, Anne's father opens her diary and reads, "In spite of everything, I still believe that people are really good at heart." The optimism, the meaning of it all, made people around me cry and feel good. Mine must have been the only dry pair of eyes in the theater — perhaps I was biased by the knowledge that in 1941 Otto Frank desperately tried to emigrate to the United States but was denied a visa. God bless Anne for writing this - but I can promise you that that is not what she was thinking as she was painfully dying from typhus, starved, covered in lice. The uplifting ending of the movie is just a part of the blocking mechanism we employ to not face the true monstrosity. So that we can go on believing that evil is an aberration. No, there is no meaning and no redemption in the horror. Not unless we recognize that there is some fundamental darkness in the human psyche and confront it head on.

I won't mail you my next "installment"—I know from Levon that you'll be here, in Germany, shortly and I'll give it to you in person. I look forward to seeing you again.

Warmest wishes,

David Levy

1

My memories of those weeks after Yael left are fragmented. Itzhak kept his promise. Israel is a small country, and within days everyone who knew me also knew that "David Levy survived Auschwitz by sending other Jews to gas chambers." People either avoided me, or openly called me names. Neighbors pointed fingers at me with contempt, spat at my feet. When I went to *Mal Zahl*, Max turned away and Moshe, the owner, demonstratively told me to get out.

Colleagues didn't want to talk to me. Dov Cohen walked into my office and said that if I wouldn't leave on my own, they'd find a reason to fire me. The Avenue of the Righteous was inaugurated on May 1st, 1962, but I was pointedly disinvited. The first eleven trees were planted. The next evening, I quietly went to pay my personal homage.

The morning after, I packed my bags, emptied my bank account, and took a *sherut* taxi to Eilat. As far as I could go without actually leaving Israel. There were two other passengers in the car, a man and a woman. Each of us paid ten pounds for a five-hour journey. It was a bargain fare. The man's name was Alazar. He came from Morocco last year and was going to Eilat to make money. Reina, the young woman, was going for adventure. I was looking for refuge. Eilat was our "Wild West," the final destination, the end of the world, a place to escape, whatever your reason. And so, we disappeared into the Negev, jolting down a one-lane asphalt road, until we came to the Red Sea. Jordan to the left, Egypt to the right, Saudi Arabia across the water. A place of contradictions: a village of six thousand people squeezed into a narrow strip of ten kilometers; no water here, but plenty of oil from the tankers; the soil is dead but the corals in the water are brilliantly alive.

I drank way too much. The *Eilati* style is tranquil and slow: you eat slowly, you sleep slowly, you make love slowly, you don't wear a watch.

You don't wear much clothing either, the heat is oppressive. Nobody gave a damn where I came from, or that I worked in a *Sonderkommando* eighteen years ago. I found a place in a not-too-run-down hotel. The first few days I would sunbathe on the beach and drink at the "End of the World" bar at night. I came across Reina and took her to bed. In the morning, when I woke up, she was gone. And so was most of my money—although she had the decency to leave me some. I came here to disappear, so money didn't matter much. I left the hotel and "roomed" with two oil terminal workers in a large tent on the beach. But they asked me to move because I screamed too much at night. "Look, David, I'm sorry, but I've got to get some sleep," one of them explained. "I'm tired of your shouting about Ezra, and children, and someone called Möll, and fire." I moved into my own small tent far away from others. I knew I wouldn't last very long this way, but I was fine with that.

One night, the police came and told me to clear off. I was drunk and tried to punch them. They arrested me. I fell asleep on a dirty bench in jail.

When I woke up, the bench was moving. My first thought was that *I am on a boat and they will throw me into Gulf of Aqaba, like they did with the Armenians in Trabzon.* As I painfully lifted myself, I realized that the bench was a back seat in a car, and we were not on water but on a dusty road in the middle of a desert. Two people were in front. The one in the passenger seat turned back to look at me, and I recognized Benny Hadan.

"Good afternoon, David."

The afternoon didn't feel good at all, my mouth felt rancid and my head was about to split open.

"What the hell is going on? Where am I?"

"You are in a car. Of the Carmel model, our own Israeli production."

"And what a piece of crap this car is," the driver commented to us. As he turned, he looked vaguely familiar. I forced my sluggish brain to focus and recognized him as one of the men from the photos that Turkish *Komiser* showed us.

"You were in Trabzon!" I accused him.

"This is Abe, short for Abraham. And yes, he was in Trabzon,"

216

Benny confirmed. "Look, before we get into the whole question-and-answer thing, have some coffee. You need it." He passed me a thermos. "You also badly need a shower, but that'll have to wait until we get to Jerusalem."

Strong coffee helped to lift cob-webs off my brain.

"I am sorry about you and Yael," Benny said as I was finishing the first cup.

"How did you find me?"

"We knew where you were all along. Hannah was worried sick, but we had to let you be. When you started getting into fights and ended up in jail, we came to collect you. Your duffel bag is in the trunk."

"How long was I in Eilat?"

"Almost five weeks."

"Did I miss anything?"

"They hung Eichmann a few days ago. Burned his body and scattered ashes in the Mediterranean Sea."

That seemed like an appropriate ending for him. Disperse his ashes the way that the ashes of those killed in Auschwitz had been dispersed, without a trace. And yet it felt anti-climactic and not satisfactory. No one was brought back. Nothing was redeemed.

"Benny, what was it about that list that we took to Ludwigsburg?"

"I'm sorry, I can't tell you yet. I will, in time."

"You fucking used us."

"I did. Didn't mean to jeopardize you. But then you were attacked. And soon thereafter Vogel, the man you talked to, was killed."

"What?"

"The factory that he was guarding at night had been robbed. Vogel died from a 'blunt trauma to his head' per German police. Some expensive scientific instruments had been stolen, so they treated this as a heist gone wrong. Shimon told me that Vogel didn't see the list, that Vogel was only asked about Prinz. True?"

"That's true. When did you know about Vogel?"

"A few days after you left Germany."

"And you kept it from us?"

Benny didn't answer.

"Because then I would have figured out that we were attacked in Frankfurt for asking questions about Prinz, not randomly by neo-

Nazis or because we went to Ludwigsburg." I was as bitter as the coffee in that thermos.

"We don't know why you were attacked, but that's a possibility. You also could have been followed from Ludwigsburg."

"It's more than a small possibility."

"We may have stumbled on something. After Vogel was gone, the man in Turkey with the Nazi connections was the only lead."

"But you never told us that asking questions about that SS officer could be dangerous. Did you send Abe to Trabzon?"

"Yes, I did. Abe and another agent. They realized that they were being watched, so they left before finding the house. We were on a short leash after Eichmann's abduction, had to stand down, avoid attracting attention. I wanted to send others but was told not to put resources on this."

"Why?"

"I don't know."

"What do you mean you don't know?"

"It means I don't!" Benny became irritated. "It means something is not *kosher* and I don't know what it is."

"Something is rotten in the state of Denmark," Abe said.

"What Denmark?" Benny snapped. "Oh, that's from one of your plays. You read too much."

"So, Benny, you talked Yosef and me into going. Two unsuspecting fools."

"Yosef came to me, he wanted to go. Nobody meant any harm. But we are definitely on to something here. That twenty-pound note you brought, it was made in Sachsenhausen. Nazis' counterfeiting Operation Bernhard."

"Someone called Trabzon police about us before we even landed. Who?"

"I don't know. I swear on the lives of my nieces, I don't know."

"Your nieces?"

"I would have sworn on my children, if I had any."

"How many people in Mossad knew about us going?"

"Not many. But you and Yosef did not exactly keep it a secret."

I stared out the window at the barren Negev desert stretching to the horizon. "Did Hannah know the whole story?"

"No. She was trying to help you and brought you to me. Look, I am sorry Itzhak attacked you like that. I don't know what I would have done had I been assigned to *Sonderkommando*. I asked Hannah why you'd become a Holocaust researcher, and she said to punish yourself."

I kept silent. Hannah was wrong. I took that job because I had certain illusions back then: supposedly, we survived to bear witness. But nobody cared. The truth was what politicians wanted it to be.

"David, can you talk to Hannah? I care about her. She's really upset over this."

"Benny, I think you are an ass. Yosef and I were not your agents. You had to tell us about Vogel and let us make our own decision."

"And if I did, would you have gone?"

"Of course not."

"You see the problem."

"It makes you an asshole nevertheless. And you still have not told me everything."

Pause.

"I told you as much as I can at this time."

We drove in silence for the next hour, passing Beersheba and Kiryat Gat. I imagined returning to Jerusalem. Would I really want to go back to Dov Cohen and the politics of the museum? I'm not wanted there. To the apartment and the streets that would remind me of Yael? Places you'd been to with someone you loved are never the same once they are gone. I went to Eilat to shut the door on the past, and that was what I must do.

As we approached Lydda, I asked Abe, "Do you know where Kfar Tahpooz is?"

"Yes." Abe's voice had a note of surprise. "It's past Netanya, about an hour north of here."

"Can you take me there? If not, let me off in Tel-Aviv and I'll take a bus."

Benny studied me, nodded his head.

"Very well, Kfar Tahpooz it is. Might be good for you to live close to the land for a while."

2

Hirsh Pozner was not surprised to see me. He already knew about me and Itzhak.

"I went to Jerusalem to look for you, but nobody had any idea where you went."

"We were worried sick," Dana added.

"I just took a bit of a vacation in Eilat."

"Must have been some vacation." She pointed to my left eye. I didn't realize I had a black eye, until I saw it in the car's rear-view mirror.

Later in the evening, Hirsh and I sat at the kitchen table with a bottle. We drank to Uri, another *Sonderkommando* survivor that we buried in 1948 alongside the road to Jerusalem. We wrapped him in a blanket, placed his body into the hard, arid soil, took off our tube sock hats and said a prayer.

"There are only four of us left that I know of," Hirsh said. "You, me, Abraham, Leon."

"I'm sure there are others. They are just laying low. The Germans were too busy running away from the Russians, and never fully eliminated the last *Sonderkommando*."

"Do you want to take me up on that offer to sell our oranges in Europe? Germany would be a perfect market for us."

"Why not?" I shrugged. *If I'm going to start over, might as well go all the way.*

Two nights later, I'd been introduced at the moshav's meeting. In front of what must have been two hundred people, Hirsh passionately argued that to prosper, they needed to find export markets. Because all the Europeans lusted for their famous Jaffa oranges and I, David Levy, with my linguistic skills, was just the man to make it happen. People didn't question the need to export, but many seemed to be unsure that I was indeed the man. And the harvest season was over, so they did not need any pickers just now.

"Can you repair radios and things?" someone asked.

Turned out that their repairman recently ran off to Tel-Aviv, to follow a girl. While oranges' export was of uncertain value, radio repair offered an immediate benefit.

"No, not really."

"Well, you speak English, right?" the same husky female voice persisted. It belonged to a large-framed woman in her late thirties. As I found out later, her name was Galit. She was a teacher and a librarian. Her name in Hebrew meant *stormy* and she lived up to it.

"I do."

"We have instructions, but they are mostly in English. You can read and learn."

Ultimately, the assembly agreed that I would teach foreign languages to the moshav's kids, and try my hand at radio repair, and in a couple of months there would be another discussion about the export stuff. In the meantime, I would get to have the apartment that the absconded repairman abandoned, and I would draw a small salary.

It was really one moment during the meeting that convinced me to stay: someone tried to bring up the *Sonderkommando* and was immediately shushed by the others. They all knew that that's where Hirsh was, and they accepted it. I think that was what I craved there and then: acceptance and a place to stop hiding for a while.

While most people ate at home, moshav had a small dining hall, which was very convenient for unattached people. I had my own room and a separate entry door, but I shared the kitchen with Elam Fishel and Ofer the mechanic. Nobody ever used Ofer's last name; he was only "the mechanic." Ofer worked on tractors and lorries; his hands were permanently black from oil and grease. He was fat, cheerful, and prone to laughing at his own bad jokes. Elam, on the other hand, was a thin, short man around fifty, whose face carried a permanently scared impression.

On the first day he greeted me with, "Brazil beat Czechoslovakia 3 to 1 in the World Cup final."

"Oh, you are a big football fan," I replied.

"No. Morocco banned Jewish emigration to Israel. Air France flight crashed in the West Indies, killing everyone."

Elam was a news junkie. He subscribed to three different newspapers and spent much of his free time listening to the radio. I had no idea how he got it, but he owned a top-of-the-line American Zenith Royal 500 radio set. When he did not read or listen, he tended to chickens. The moshav had a chicken coop and that was his job. Elam was more comfortable around chickens than around people. Before the war, he had a family in Poland, but he was the only one to make it out alive. He never talked about them.

My room had a few broken radios and other assorted devices that the previous occupant left. Galit brought in the manuals that were, for some reason, kept in the library. I tinkered and managed to fix a couple of radios, but I had no aptitude for electrical things. Still, I found it somewhat relaxing to do that.

I had never taught before and had no idea what to do when on the first day about forty kids and a dozen adults showed up. They ranged from six years old to over fifty and were irreconcilably split on the language that they wanted to learn. I was saved by Galit, who came and immediately took charge. It was agreed that only English would be taught, in two groups: the youngsters up to thirteen in the first group, everyone older in the other. Surprisingly, it was the second group that gave me headaches by generating a constant stream of visitors to my apartment. Young minds are much more open to new languages. A few students that were in their thirties and forties struggled; many of them dropped out soon. A more persistent group was that of four women in their early twenties. Some of them would have liked more than language instruction, and I did not want any complications with their parents or boyfriends.

Galit saved me again. One day she brought in some manuals and a bottle of sweet Carmel wine, and stayed the night. She was easy to get along with. It was the kind of relationship that we had in displaced persons camps right after the war, where you just want some human warmth. Galit's husband was killed in Suez in 1956, and her only son was in the army now. The arrangement seemed to satisfy everyone: my female students left me alone, and the women of the moshav knew that Galit was not sneaking out with their husbands.

She never invited me to her place. I asked her once. She said, "David, we have what we have. If one day it becomes more, I'll have you over." That was fine with me. Galit kept her distance and I was grateful for that. One day she looked at me carefully, "How did you deal with it? Death all around?" I thought about it. "There was nothing difficult about dying, it was the end of suffering. We stayed alive out of habit rather than instinct." She nodded and never brought it up again.

Some nights I sought out solitude. There was a tall cypress tree near our small building. I would go sit on the grass at its foot, watch the terra cotta moon shine down on us all. My days in the moshav were quiet and uneventful; they had followed one after the other like a procession of identical twins. After a storm, I put my anchor in a calm harbor. I admit that there were many—actually, most—nights when I lay there in dark despair over the loss of Yael, her images embedded in my mind. One dream kept recurring then: I saw my parents and my sister Leah on the train platform, about to march off into nothingness; Leah would turn back and wave to me, but she had Yael's face.

All through that time, I had a feeling of uncertainty, unreality, even falseness. Like I'd been temporarily given someone else's life, and my real one was going to come back with a vengeance.

It was a particularly hot day in July when Hannah came to see me. We sat in the shade. All I could offer her was a warm lemonade.

"This life in the moshav becomes you," she said. "You look slim, but well-nourished. And tan, very tan."

She seemed older and tired, her usually lively eyes fatigued and surrounded by dark circles.

"I teach languages and help in the orange grove. It's a simple life."

"You don't miss the city?"

"A bit. You knew about *Sonderkommando* all along, right?"

"I did, David."

"But you never said anything or tried to blame me."

"How could I? I was there, working for Boger in the Political Department. Typing 'died from a heart attack' lists of the ones he tortured and killed. We all did what we had to do to survive."

223

"Not all. There was a story going around *Sonderkommando's* about a transport from Corfu in Greece. Germans took four hundred men and assigned them to work in a *Sonderkommando*. They all refused. All, to a man."

"I've heard about it. They were all killed."

"But they refused."

"And their dying changed nothing. Don't be your own harshest judge."

I paused before asking, not sure whether I wanted to open that wound. "Is Yael marrying Itzhak?"

"Not as far as I know. I've heard that she left Jerusalem."

"So she moved on from both of us."

"You miss her?"

"Very much. I think that in a way she brought me back from the dead, gave me a connection to the past that I cut off. To my family. To Leah, my sister."

"David, you should go see a psychiatrist. Of all of us, you're the most fucked up."

"Yeah, a psychiatrist is probably not a bad idea."

Hannah studied her hand, as if seeing it for the first time. "You know, Benny asked me to marry him."

"Are you going to?"

"I'm not sure. Still angry with him over Yosef Milman's case. He had no right to jeopardize the two of you like this. But I also understand him. He is still at war, willing to sacrifice himself and his soldiers."

"We were not his soldiers."

"Everyone here is a soldier in his mind."

"Hannah, why did you want me to investigate that story?"

"There was something about it. Back in August of 1942, Germany was winning on all fronts. Stalingrad was about to fall, victory seemed at hand. Why would that officer not only spare Yosef, but abandon the winning side completely, risk his life to take the boy to safety—and disappear?"

"Yes, a strange story."

"David, I've been contacted about testifying in the Auschwitz trial they are preparing in Germany."

"What are you going to do?"

"I don't know. I get panic attacks when I think of being on the stand. Especially in Germany."

Hannah got up.

"I better go. Just wanted to see you."

She hugged and kissed me and left. I watched Hannah go. Of all the people that I'd met since Ezra, she asked the least of me. She was grateful to have me in her life, no conditions attached.

To Elam's credit, he was unbiased in his news coverage. Good news, bad news, any news—he was reporting it all. But that day in late July, Elam was unquestionably down.

"Egyptians successfully launched four surface-to-surface missiles."

For the next few days, a dozen men would gather around Elam's Zenith, the best radio in the moshav. We listened when the Egyptian President Gamal Abdel Nasser proudly declared in a broadcast from Cairo that they were now capable of hitting any point south of Beirut. To make sure we understood, the speech was repeated in Hebrew.

"They are going to finish Hitler's job," said Ofer. "I have a joke: Why did Hitler kill himself? He saw the gas bill."

Nobody laughed.

"I'm not going anywhere," replied Hirsh. "I have nowhere to go."

Even though the air was perfectly still, I felt a gentle breeze. Like a warning of a coming storm.

3

As if by request, the next week Benny was waiting for me by the moshav's public hall. I passed the Carmel auto that brought me here back in June. Abe the driver was smoking next to it. He silently nodded at me.

"The photo that you and Yosef brought has been identified," Benny said as an introduction.

"So?" I shrugged.

Benny wiped his bald dome with a handkerchief.

"It's hot. David, we are like fishermen. Throw the bait in the water, nothing bites. Then the line gets taut and you know there is something on the other end. There was not even bait here. Fortuity, kismet, whatever. But this line is taut. There is a lead on a network of Nazis working with Egypt and Syria."

"And why do I care? Go ask Itzhak. He wants to be the people's savior. Or Yosef. He was the one obsessed with finding his officer. I just wanted to sleep with his sister-in-law."

Benny extracted a photo from his front pocket. "The man had a safe deposit box in Beirut. This is one of the items."

I stared at the close-up of a gold ingot, suddenly unable to talk.

"There are initials there: JK. David, do you know what they mean?"

"Yes. JK, Jacob Kurzher. He smelted gold fillings into ingots."

I wondered if this was the same ingot that Ezra gave me on October 6th, to take to Schawik.

Benny carefully took the photo from my shaking hand.

"Right, a few kilograms each day. Then the SS would take the gold away. I've seen those before. Most of the gold from Auschwitz, Treblinka, Sobibor, Belzec was re-smelted into Reichsbank gold bars. The Nazis used it to pay the Swiss to buy war materials, or just hide in

226

secret accounts."

"But this ingot is directly from Auschwitz."

"They probably did not have a chance to process them towards the end, as the Great Reich was collapsing. And the SS stole left-and-right, figuring they'll need gold for after-the-war."

"Damn you, Benny! Why do you keep dragging me into this?" I swept my arm through the expanse of the orange grove. "This is my life now. I am trying to shut the door on Auschwitz, and you keep bringing it back to me."

"I'm sorry, David." Benny put his hands palms together, apologizing. "I don't think this here is your life. But if you want me to just leave, I'll do that and never trouble you again. I promise."

"Why do you need me?"

"You speak multiple languages. You easily fit in Germany. You know things that very few people do. Shimon thought that you are a natural, you have the nerve and the composure. And most important, it's personal for you."

"I'm an orange salesman now."

"I know. You'll be selling Jaffa oranges in Europe. A perfect cover."

"Cover for what?"

"For whatever needs to be done."

"Does anyone else know about this?"

"Just me and Abe. And now, you. Officially, I've been told to stay off this case."

I didn't reply, just stared into the distance.

Benny wiped his forehead once more, got up, placed a folded piece of paper on the table.

"Abe and I will be going to Beirut next Saturday. This is the Middle East, important things must be discussed face-to-face. It'll take a day, four hours there, meet, four hours back. You can come with us, then you decide for yourself. I swear I won't twist your arm. Here's my direct number. Let me know before the week is out. And don't tell anyone."

Benny and Abe showed up exactly at 8 a.m., as Benny told me.

"What is this car?" I expected the Carmel again.

227

"It's a 1960 Ford Falcon. American. Lebanese like American cars. You don't expect us to drive an Israeli car in Lebanon? Might as well sign our death warrant. Hurry up, we must cross the border at ten and cross it going back no later than six. It's a two-hour drive to the border and another two hours to Beirut. If everything goes smoothly, we'll have perhaps three hours for a meeting."

I understood why when we got to the border crossing at Kfar Rosh. We parked on the Israeli side and waited until a few minutes past ten.

There was a tense moment as one of the guards trained his carbine on us, but an officer came out and told him to stand down. He leaned into the car and said in French, "There are checkpoints in Tyre and Sidon; I'll phone ahead and they'll wave you through, but you must clear Sidon by five o'clock on the way back. Five, not six, remember."

"Thank you, Emile," Abe replied in French as he got out of the car to change our license plates.

"Emile's a Maronite Christian," Benny explained as we drove off. "They are informally aligned with us. The Middle East makes for strange partners."

Strange partners? I was staring out the window at the sparkling Mediterranean. *Strange* was a good word to describe my life since that afternoon when Yosef Milman knocked on my office door. Then again, the last twenty years had been a bonus. How many people out of that cattle car were still alive? I bet I was the only one.

"Ruben Matusian," Benny said.

"Who?"

"The man we are going to meet. Ruben Matusian. He is one of the key people in the Armenian Revolutionary Federation, popularly called Dashnaks. A well-known lawyer and a member of the parliament. After I was told to drop the Ekrem Bey investigation, I asked him for help. An enemy of my enemy, you know."

"And this is not a sanctioned trip?"

"Not exactly."

"You have many enemies, Benny."

"A lot of politics going on for a small country like ours. Especially after the Mapai government fell following the Kasztner trial, and then again after the Lavon affair. Menachem Begin from Herut is gaining strength. People don't agree on taking "blood money" from the

Germans. You know that, you are a Herut man yourself. Abe here is a Libralit voter, he's aligned with you."

"People put their party above the state," Abe grumbled in one of those rare moments when he opened his mouth. "Jews arguing between themselves, while Arabs are preparing to wipe us out."

"Well, at least we are not killing each other now. Back in 1948, I was in one of the Haganah units that fought Irgun on the Tel Aviv beach."

"I was on the other side, Benny."

"I know, David. It's a good thing we had not met that day. Anyway, let's get back to the matter at hand. Most Armenians moved to Lebanon starting 1915. There are probably over a hundred and fifty thousand now. They lived relatively peacefully until 1958, when the American marines had to land in Beirut to stop the civil war from spreading. These days Lebanon's politics are even more convoluted than ours. The Armenians are split: the Dashnaks are pro-Western and largely allied with the Maronites, while other, smaller factions are sympathetic to the Soviets and to the Muslim opposition. The Maronite Christians and Muslims are killing each other. And now Hitler's buddy, Haj Amin Al-Husseini moved there."

"The former Grand Mufti of Jerusalem?"

"Yes, the one that in 1941 fled to Nazi Germany and helped to raise two Muslim Waffen-SS divisions. After the war, he was arrested by the French. Yugoslavia wanted to put him on trial and would have executed him, but the French allowed him to escape. The Mufti went to Palestine, then to Egypt. Wherever he goes, he stirs up trouble. He is now in Beirut, and the people we are going to meet are concerned about his influence. So, for multiple reasons we are cooperating in some areas. As I said, an enemy of my enemy ..."

"And what does this have to do with Ekrem Bey?"

"Everything points to Ekrem Celik being not just a Nazi sympathizer, but an active agent. It's no longer the matter of the past. There are hundreds of Germans working with the Arabs on military training and technology right now, as we speak."

We passed the airport and drove through the center of Beirut. Abe knew his way around, must not have been the first trip for him. After empty Saturday roads in Israel, Beirut was a madhouse. A maddeningly hot madhouse, but Abe prohibited us from opening windows.

"Americans were here four years ago. There is still some tension in the air."

We drove through what looked like a shanty town and pulled up to a high-walled compound. Two guards with machine guns waited at the gate. Benny rolled down his window, the guard looked inside, recognized Benny with "Shalom." The gate slowly swung open, Abe pulled the Falcon to the entrance. We were quickly escorted inside into a large formal dining room where ceiling fans hummed, and mountains of food and drinks invited visitors to the table.

Four people waited for us there: three older ones, two men and a woman; and a man in his thirties. The oldest-looking man walked to Benny, embraced and kissed him three times on alternate cheeks. Then he shook hands with Abe and me.

"I am Ruben Matusian." He introduced the woman and the younger man. "My wife Nouvart, my son Van." Then turned to the older man. "Aram Arutiyan, a family friend."

I remembered his face. "Didn't I see you in Jerusalem, during Eichmann's trial?"

"Yes, both Ruben and I were there. I think we came to different conclusions …"

"Aram, now is not the time," Matusian said, a hint of tension in his voice. "Welcome to Bourj Hammoud. You know, this place was founded by survivors of our genocide. When those who had survived the death marches in Deir ez-Zor arrived in Beirut after the war, they were allowed to construct shacks on the eastern banks of the Beirut River. At the time it was swamps and marshy lands. They were then allowed to erect houses and buildings. Like you, we know how to start over and rebuild."

"How are things after '58?" Benny asked.

"Calmed down a bit. Christians against Muslims, Armenians fighting Armenians, not good. I had to double my guard. But I am afraid it's only a temporary respite. Lebanon is fractured now, irreparably so."

"What are you going to do?"

"The same thing that your ancestors did when pogroms were getting worse: start sending family members to America. Some of our relatives are already there."

"And you?"

230

"We have too many interests here. Beirut is the financial center of the Middle East. I don't like it that Sheik Amin al-Husseini moved in. He now barricaded himself in his villa in west Beirut and barely ventures out. Probably afraid you'll grab him, like you did with his friend Eichmann."

"We were planning to eliminate him back in '45, but Ben-Gurion cancelled the mission. Too bad." Benny shook his head. "We were just talking about him. Do you think al-Husseini is a part of this network?"

"Yes. But you had a long drive. Let us relax and enjoy some food and drink, then we'll move to another room for a business discussion."

"Ruben, my friend, we must be south of Sidon before five. I'm sorry, but let's attend to business first," Benny apologized.

"Of course. Please follow me." Ruben Matusian led us to the second floor, down a corridor and into a medium-sized circular room, with a round table and chairs in the middle, additional chairs against one wall and file cabinets against others. The walls were covered with photos, many of which had a black ribbon around them. There was a thick file on the table.

"Usually this office is locked," Matusian said. "Please sit down. This is a special room dedicated to our revenge."

"Operation Nemesis?" Benny asked. "You may want to explain for David's sake."

"Yes. This is what we call it, the 'Nemesis Room.' After a million-and-a-half of our people had been killed under the cover of the war, there were trials and dozens of Turkish war criminals were sentenced to death. But none of them served more than four years. The world didn't care about the extermination of Armenians then, just like it doesn't care about the extermination of the Jews now. I wish we had our own state, so we could do what you did with Eichmann. But it was not possible. Instead, the Armenian Revolutionary Federation, ARF, met in Yerevan in 1919 and drew the "black list" of those we, *Dashnaks*, deemed responsible for organizing genocide against our people. Being young and romantic, we named our plans for revenge after the Greek goddess of divine retribution. Forty years ago, we carried out some very public operations."

Ruben went around the room, pointing. "Said Halim Pasha in Rome in 1921; Talaat Pasha, Behaeddin Shakir and Cemal Azmi in

Berlin in 1922 ..."

"Talaat Pasha was in 1921," Aram corrected him.

"That's right, my mistake." Ruben smiled. "Behbud Javanshir in Istanbul in 1921, Djemal Pasha in Tiflis in 1922 ..."

"While it was a long time ago," Aram added, "Operation Nemesis never ended; we just stopped being overt about it."

I followed Ruben around the room, looking at the photos. Seemingly normal people, secure in the knowledge of their own importance.

Ruben pointed to another section of the wall. "But this part, it's dedicated to those that helped. These men defied the orders and protected the Armenians: Celal Bey, the governor of Konya; Faik Ozansoy Bey, the governor of Kutahya; Reshit Pasha, the governor of Kastamonu; and others. They were eventually either killed or removed from their posts. And this is a German soldier, Armin Wegner, with the photos he took to show the world what was being done to our people."

Ruben sat down, opened the file, spread a few photos, and pushed forward an old yellowish photo showing an officer in full regalia.

"Now this man: Ahmet Yavuz, the butcher of Erzerum. Number 17 on the original list. Also known as Ekrem Celik that you found in Trabzon. This photo is from 1920, his dashing young officer appearance changed quite a bit. But that's him. Born in 1890, studied in the Turkish Military Academy as a cavalry officer. Through family connections he was close to the Young Turks that took power in 1908. When the orders to eliminate Armenians came in 1915, Yavuz took charge of a specially formed brigade of irregulars, so-called *Hamidiye*. They were the original *Einsatzengruppen*."

Benny pointed to one photo. "Is this what I think it is?"

It was a picture of six men posing for the camera. Human skulls were scattered all over the earth in front of them.

"Yes. The skulls are those of slaughtered Armenians. These three are Turkish officers in their tall, soft hats. Ahmet Yavuz is one of them. This one, to the side, is a Kurd," Ruben explained. "But the two other men are Germans, dressed in the military flat caps, belts and tunics of the Imperial German Army of World War I. Looks like pictures from Treblinka or Auschwitz. David, you seem surprised?"

"Yes, I am."

"In 1904 in their African colony, the Germans drove the Herero tribe into the desert, where a hundred thousand starved to death. The Turks had learned from them: a few years later they drove our people into a Syrian desert to die." Ruben said. "Our tragedy has been forgotten, just like the Hereros'. But not by us. Ahmet Yavuz is responsible for tens of thousands of deaths, the Armenians either being killed outright or starved on death marches into Syrian deserts. He was arrested after the war but released from jail in 1921. We had no reliable leads since—until you contacted us. We assumed that he escaped to South America. Turns out he came back to Turkey under a different name, as Ekrem Celik. His cover was pharmaceuticals distribution, but under different companies' names he bought four chromite ore mines in Diyarbakir and Malatya regions. As you suspected."

Benny nodded. "Close to Trabzon, far away from the Allies."

"Exactly. Bring the ore by railway to Trabzon, ship it to Constanta in Romania, Germany's ally. By being far away from Istanbul and using small ships, they kept the operation undetected."

"Did you get him?"

"Our team got there quickly, but he was gone. Left not just Trabzon but the country. We don't know yet where he went. Searched both of his houses, the one in Trabzon and the one in Istanbul, but he was thorough in leaving no clues."

"Ruben, you must have something, if you asked us to come."

"Yes, Benny, we have something. A man doesn't live in the same place for twenty-four years without leaving traces. We lucked out at the post office in the neighboring town. The postmaster worked there since 1934, started as a letter sorter. A nosy fellow, curious about who his neighbors communicate with, what went into post office boxes. A generous donation boosted his memory. Ekrem Celik Bey used to receive a lot of mail from Berlin and from the Turkish branch of Deutsche Bank. Yes, there was one until 1945. When the Nazis lost the war, the branch was closed, and letters stopped."

"Well, that doesn't give us much."

"Don't be impatient, my friend. About eight years ago the postmaster noticed that Mr. Celik— under a different name—started

233

getting letters from Société Générale's branch right here in Beirut."

"He needed an international bank with presence in the Middle East?"

"Looks this way. Especially since Société Générale only returned to Lebanon in 1953, so he jumped at the opportunity."

"Let me guess ... you have connections at the bank."

Ruben laughed.

"We have some. The account belongs to a dental supplies company which is a subsidiary of another company, and so on."

"A new address?"

"Not yet, only instructions to hold the correspondence. But we got eight years' worth of transactions for the account. I think you'll find them quite interesting." Ruben handed the envelope to Benny. "Donations to certain organizations that your government accuses of terrorism. Checks cashed by Haj Amin Al-Husseini, first in Cairo, now right here in Beirut. Some other interesting names. Nazis that escaped to Egypt and Syria. Still a lot of money left in the account. Millions of dollars."

Benny whistled. "Where did the money come from?"

"A private Turkish bank."

"And before that? I am sure you've looked into it."

"I did. Originally, the money came from the Swiss National Bank. That's as far as I could get. Even my connections can't get past the Swiss secrecy."

"Anything else?"

"A safe deposit box. We sent you some pictures of what's inside. Blank passports, American dollars, British pounds, gold bars stamped Reichsbank, gold ingots ... there are more photos in the envelope. And for now, that's all I have for you, my friends."

"What are you going to do about Ahmet Yavuz?" Benny asked.

"Wait and watch the money. Eventually, there will be a lead. Someone will try to take it."

"You won't let it go after forty-plus years?"

"Never! No statute of limitations for this. Can we count on your cooperation?"

"Yes, Ruben. Can we count on yours?"

"Yes. We have good reasons to cooperate. And now, I hope we still have time for a quick lunch."

"Ruben, one more thing. Do you know which German officers or diplomats Ahmet Yavuz was friendly with during World War I?"

"Hmmm … It might be worthwhile to look into that." Ruben turned to his son. "Van, please get the Erzurum file from the cabinet and copy the names of the Germans that were in Erzurum during 1915-16."

I sat next to Nouvart as we ate.

"I understand you survived Auschwitz?" she asked.

I nodded.

"I saw men bludgeoned in front of their families. I saw hills of corpses. These horrible movies of Bergen-Belsen and Dachau after liberation, we saw them thirty years earlier. But there were no cameras."

As we were leaving, she took my hand and said, "Retribution and gratitude, don't stop in either."

On the way back, Benny studied Ruben's papers, angrily mumbling to himself.

"Hmmm … checks to Carl Debouche aka Hans Eisele … SS doctor that murdered hundreds in Buchenwald, Natzweiler and Dachau. Sentenced to death in Nuremberg, kindly released in 1952, escaped to Egypt. Georg Fisher, aka Alois Brunner. Adolf Eichmann's assistant. Fled West Germany for Syria in 1954. Wilhelm Beisner, the SS *Sturmbannführer* that worked in *Einsatzkommandos* in Serbia and Tunisia—now supplying arms to Middle East terror groups and paying Erich Rolff for 'services to the BND.' Johannes 'Omar Amin' von Leers, a specialist on the 'Jewish Question' in Josef Goebbels' propaganda department. Now a great friend of the Grand Mufti and the head of Egyptian Anti-Israeli bureau …"

He turned to me. "Your trip to Trabzon brought some interesting results."

"Are you surprised?"

"Yes. I'd like to claim that I had an intuition, but no, not at all. It has not been officially disclosed yet: the rockets that the Egyptians launched have been developed by Nazi scientists. That's right, some of Hitler's most senior engineers, men who'd worked during the war at the research base at Peenemünde where the Third Reich's most advanced weaponry was developed, are now in Egypt. And more scientists and military and security experts are coming. There are clandestine networks financing and protecting them. Ahmet Yavuz was using the Nazi money to finance Nazis and terrorists. The ultimate insult: they took the gold from dead Jews, literally ripped it out of their mouths, and now use it to pay people that want to finish Hitler's job."

"Are you going to look for Yavuz?"

"We'll let Ruben lead, follow the money. I can't put internal resources on this, until I know where the leak came from."

"How about the Germans that Yavuz may have met back then? Remember the mention of the uncle?"

"Right. That's why I asked for the list. We don't know if Yavuz met that mysterious uncle in Erzurum, but it's a lead."

He read the notes that Van copied for us: "Carl von Feurath, attached to the 4th Turkish Army, followed operations against the Armenians. Oscar Werner von der Mulenburg, German consult in Erzurum 1915-16. Peter Klopher, Vice-Consul in Erzurum, 1915-16. Oh look, a familiar name: Rudolph Höss, German cavalry regiment."

"Höss? The commandant of Auschwitz?"

"The one and only. He must have learned a few extermination techniques in Turkey."

There must have been something in my face because his expression changed.

"David, Eichmann was only the beginning. I know it's been seventeen years since the war and we have barely started, but we will settle all accounts."

4

"Marilyn Monroe died," announced Elam. He looked even sadder than usual.

"Such a woman, such a woman," moaned Ofer the mechanic.

"Tipesh!" Galit swore. "Idiots! There are real live women here in Kfar Tahpooz that can use some love. And you are weeping over an American actress."

"Oh, but what an actress! So sexy! Why did she do that?" the usually cheerful Ofer seemed on the edge of tears.

Galit walked away in frustration.

Moshav's people largely gave up on my ability to fix radios, but I continued to teach English. I also worked in the orange grove. Working outside in the fresh air felt good.

October was a busy month for Elam.

"The Second Vatican Council began in Rome," he announced one day.

"And why is that important to us?" Ofer shrugged.

"The radio reported that they will address Christian – Jewish relations."

"We've already seen what kind of relations they want with us."

"The rumor is that they may no longer hold us responsible for the death of Christ."

"Pffttt … I'll believe it when I see it. But after two thousand years of beatings, that would be nice."

Soon, the Vatican Council was overshadowed by the Cuban missile crisis. For two weeks, we— together with the rest of the world—had been glued to radios and TVs, as the American and the Russian ships steamed towards each other on a collision course. Nuclear war seemed inevitable, until the Russian ships turned around.

"The world may end tomorrow, but oranges must be harvested," Hirsh reminded us.

During that time, I received a letter from Fritz Jager. It contained two newspaper articles. One was about twelve defendants in the Chelmno trial that opened in Bonn. The other article discussed the disappearance of a German scientist Heinz Krigger, implying possible Israeli involvement. There was a handwritten note with two sentences: "Thank you for your help with the trial. I hope we'll put them away for a long time. The name of the scientist should be familiar, he was on the list that you brought to Ludwigsburg."

Jacob Broder, my friend from Jerusalem, came to visit me soon thereafter. I was working in the grove when I got the message, and found Jacob sitting on the bench with a glass and a pitcher of orange juice. And a thin file.

"*Shalom*, David. Good orange juice."

"*Shalom*, Jacob. Orange juice is something we have plenty of. It's good to see you. Many of my old friends no longer want to know me."

"They'll come around. Nothing would have changed, no one would have profited from your death. You look good. Very tanned."

"What's this?" I pointed at the file.

"I submitted a claim for damages to Germany, but it was denied. I thought that perhaps you could help. Do you know much about medical experiments in Dachau?"

"I've heard some names, like Hans Eisele."

"Yes, he was there. What did you hear?"

"He served a few years after the war, denied the allegations and represented himself as a devout Christian and a compassionate physician. Worked as a doctor in Munich until another Nazi ferreted him out, so he ran off to Egypt."

Jacob laughed bitterly:

"A compassionate physician! They were doing hypothermia and high-altitude experiments. They would strip us naked, insert a rectum probe, force us in the vat of cold water and measure when we would lose consciousness and, in most cases, die. Or suck the oxygen out of the room and see what happens. Here ..."

He picked out a page from the file and handed them to me.

238

To Reichsführer-SS Himmler, 11 May 1942:

Highly esteemed Reich Leader,

Enclosed I am forwarding a short summary on the principle experiments conducted up to date. For the following experiments Jewish criminals who had committed race pollution were used. The question of the formation of embolism was investigated in 10 cases. Some of the experimental subjects died during a continued high-altitude experiment; for instance, after one-half hour at the height of 12 Km. After the skull had been opened under water an ample amount of air embolism was found in the brain vessels and, in part, free air in the brain ventricles.

To find out whether the severe psychic and physical effects are due to the formation of embolism, the following was done: After relative recuperation, however, before regaining consciousness, some experimental subjects were kept under water until they died. When the skull and the cavities of the breast and of the abdomen had been opened under water, an enormous amount of air embolism was found in the vessels of the brain, the coronary vessels, and vessels of the liver and the intestines, etc.

SS-Untersturmführer Sigmund Rascher

"They killed thousands like that," Jacob said when I put down the paper. "I was one of those that polluted the Aryan race, I dated a German woman. Luckily, I was in the test group where they wanted to see how far they could go and still resuscitate. Not all of the doctors were the SS—some were academics from universities, researchers from IG Farben and Bayer. When the Americans liberated Dachau, corpses were lying all around the camp, in the railway boxcars nearby … The Americans went berserk when they saw it. They lined up some of the guards and machine-gunned them. When the Dachau Trial was going on in Nuremberg, when the Americans hung commandant Martin Weiss and the chief medical tormenter Claus Schilling, I thought 'here it is, the justice'! And then it all stopped. I wish we'd killed them all right there and then."

"Why was your claim denied?"

"They replied that the damage was only psychological."

I burst out laughing. "Brilliant! If your damage was more than psychological, you would have been dead. This way, they never have to pay."

"I've been told that if I go to Germany and argue the case in person, I'll be more likely to get a compensation."

"Why won't you?"

"My roots are there. I still love it, you know… Despite everything, I've never really left. That's why I can't go back. Nostalgia or nightmares would kill me. David, do you like it here? Did you find your home?" Jacob swept his arm to indicate the moshav's land.

"Yes. I like it. It's not home but it's nice. Calm."

Jacob nodded. "I'm here because I lost my home. It's hard to find a new one."

"There is someone I know in Germany who works on these cases. I'll ask him to intercede in yours. His name is Shimon Bezor."

"Thank you, David. Are you going back to Germany?"

"Yes, I'll have to do it for work. To sell oranges."

"Are you going to be OK?"

"Yes, I think so."

5

Jaffa oranges are harvested beginning in November, with the marketing season starting before that. We were late already. The fault was with the moshav's finance committee—they had difficulty spending money. Eventually, Hirsh pounded the table with, "If you don't want to grow the moshav, I'm out!" The committee ended up agreeing to pay for the trip, but with my compensation based strictly on sales. They ended up regretting the arrangement, but that's another story.

I flew to Frankfurt, the *de facto* business center of West Germany. There, I had discovered that most import-export outfits already had deals in place, so I started visiting headquarters of supermarket chains. I quickly realized that I would need at least a month to get anything done, but the money that the finance committee gave me would not last that long, even after I moved into a cheaper boarding house with a free breakfast. I remembered the couch in Gerhardt's office, and as much as I didn't want to re-open the past, I went to see him.

"Good to have you back, David," Gerhardt greeted me at the door. "How's the oranges business?"

"You don't seem to be surprised to see me."

"Not really. Shimon called me two days ago and asked me to look for you."

"Oh. A friend needs help with his damages case. Shimon didn't return my call."

"He did, but you moved out of the hotel. I was there yesterday, and they didn't know where you went. But then you called."

"Yes, I needed a cheaper place. I'll have to be here longer than planned. Even the place I'm in now is too much."

"You're welcome to move in with me."

"Thank you, Gerhardt. I'm busy during the day, but if I can stay the night on the couch here in the office, I would really appreciate it."

"David, I guarantee you that the couch in my living room is more comfortable. But whichever one you like."

"Was it Shimon who told you about the oranges?"

"Yes. He also sent me names of some Germans that were in Erzurum during the first World War."

"Really? Why?"

"He didn't explain. Do you still want to find who that man was? The one they called Prinz?"

"I don't know." I shrugged. "It was such a strange story. I was doing it because of Yosef. I was in love with his sister-in-law. But that's over."

I threw it out there calmly, but my face must have betrayed me, because Gerhardt lowered his eyes.

"I'm sorry. You never know, life is full of twists and turns. But I thought that you yourself were interested in those that saved during the war. You call them the Righteous, right?"

"Yes. But I no longer work for the museum."

"Many changes in your life."

I pulled out of my pocket the scientist disappearance article, the one that Fritz sent to me.

"Gerhardt—why was he on the list we took to Ludwigsburg?"

Gerhardt stared at the ceiling, drummed his fingers against the table.

"Did Shimon tell you to add names of some of the German rocket scientists?" I pressed.

"Yes. The ones that were working with Egypt and we couldn't find on our own."

"What happened to him? Is he alive?"

"I don't know. Look, of course we were in the wrong." Gerhardt shifted uncomfortably. "But there is a legal wrong and there is a moral wrong, and morally we were in a grey area. This man was a member of the SS. After all that happened … he had no business building weapons for Nasser, the man that threatens to finish Hitler's work. If you become a mercenary, you risk being treated like one."

"But you lied to Yosef and me."

242

"I apologize, David. I didn't like doing that."

As I was leaving, he cleared his throat. "David … I didn't know about the *Sonderkommando*. I'm sorry."

"I'm a collaborator to many people at home."

"Those that were not there, they shouldn't judge."

The next morning, I was having breakfast in the common room, when the landlady came in with, "You have visitors." Behind her were Fritz and Erika Jager, and a man I had not met before.

"We apologize for such an early intrusion," Erika started, "but we wanted to get you before you leave on your errands. Gerhardt told us where to find you."

The landlady offered them to sit down and have coffee, then discreetly disappeared. Fritz and the other man sat across from me, Erika next to me.

"Fritz"—I cleared my throat—"I swear I didn't know about the scientist. I'm very sorry."

"I understand. You'd been played."

"What can I do for you? I don't mean to rush you, but I do have a business meeting. Must go sell oranges."

"Mr. Levy," the other man spoke up, "my name is Karl Sassen. I am a prosecutor here in Frankfurt, working on the case against Robert Mulka and others."

"Excuse me?"

"It's the Auschwitz case," Fritz explained. "We are planning to put the people that worked there on trial. Remember, we spoke about this a year ago."

I figured they were going to ask me to testify, and I prepared myself to say no.

"We need your help," Sassen continued. "We still don't know enough about the operations in the gassing chambers and crematoriums. Our likely witnesses are either those that worked in the prisoners' hospital or secretaries from the political department. You are one of very few living witnesses we have that saw the actual..." He hesitated. "The actual process. Even if you don't testify, the knowledge will help us to construct the picture and to evaluate the testimony of the others. After seventeen years, people's memories differ."

243

"Who are you even going to try?" I asked. "There were over seven thousand SS working there. The Poles took care of thirty or so. Some are in East Germany, some in South America, some are dead. That still leaves at least five thousand here, in West Germany. How many of them are you taking to court?"

"Twenty or so."

I started to laugh. I didn't mean to, but the number seemed so ridiculously low.

"David, I understand how it sounds." Erika put her hand on mine. "It's not a matter of how many. People here don't know. They think that Auschwitz was a regular labor camp. They will be outraged when they hear what went on there."

"That's right!" Sassen jumped back in. "The people we are going after did horrible things. Boger, Mulka, Kaduk, Hoffman, Stark, Schawik …"

"Schawik?" I interrupted involuntarily. My body must have jerked, because Erika quickly removed her hand.

"Yes, Hans Schawik. You know him?"

"I thought he disappeared."

I looked for Schawik after the war but found no trace of him.

"He's been living under a false name," Fritz explained. "We found his new identity by accident, when searching Aribert Heim's home."

"Did you get Heim?"

"No, Heim escaped. We were coming to arrest him literally a few days after your friend Shimon brought it up. Someone warned him, and he ran off."

"Yes, likely someone in your own police. And Schawik?"

"We are finishing the paperwork and will arrest him soon."

I deliberated for a long moment. They stared at me anxiously.

"Very well. I'll give you the interview, but on one condition: after you arrest Schawik, I want a private meeting. Just he and I."

Sassen spread his hands helplessly. "What if he won't talk to you? We can't force him."

"That would be my problem. You just get me into the room with him. One on one."

That night, I went to a bar around the corner from my boarding house. The bartender poured me a whisky and brought a plate of salted almonds. I downed the drink and asked for another.

It was October 7, 1944.

Ezra Klaudia came to *Sonderkommando* in December of 1943 and was assigned the bed next to mine. He was from Turin in Italy, an affable and friendly man in his forties, more than twice my age. His wife was gassed upon arrival, but he and his older daughter Lia passed the selection. As a dentist, Ezra was put on gold extraction and processing. He was the one that established a connection with SS-*Oberscharführer* Hans Schawik. Once a week, Ezra and I would "organize" an ounce of gold or similar for Schawik. In return, Schawik protected us and let Ezra visit his daughter. Once, he had us reassigned just before *Sonderkommando* liquidation, and then put us into the new command. In May, Ezra was stopped by a new guard while carrying Schawik's *donation*. He was taken to the political department and severely beaten but didn't give away our names. Schawik managed to get him out.

The night of October 6th Ezra asked me, "Can you make the delivery to *Oberscharführer* Schawik tomorrow?"

"Why?"

"I can't. *Hauptscharführer* Möll told me to fix that oven where the bricks had gotten loose on the inside. You know how he is."

Yes, we all knew how Möll could fly into a rage at the smallest pretext.

"But I don't have a pass."

"I have one for you. And here's the *donation*."

Inside the bag there was a gold ingot, a pair of gold cufflinks and gold earrings. The ingot bore "JK" initials, for Jacob Kurzher, one of the jewelers busy re-smelting gold fillings torn from mouths of the gassed Jews.

"Jacob made these cufflinks for Schawik," said Ezra. "A special gift. The earrings are for the guard. You'll be fine."

I was a bit nervous the next morning, but Ezra was right: the sentry inspected the pass with the earrings wrapped inside, gave it back to me minus the earrings, and waved me through.

Schawik looked agitated. "What took you so long?"

His demeanor changed when he saw the cufflinks. He rolled them in his fingers, clearly pleased, then quickly pocketed the ingot.

"*Gut, zehr gut.* OK, let's go, we have a bit of a walk to Block 24."

Schawik took off, I obediently trudged after him.

"Remember, you have fifteen minutes, so hurry it up!"

"Fifteen minutes for what?"

Schawik stopped, turned around, looked at me and burst out laughing. "Ezra didn't tell you!"

"Tell me what?"

"Youngster, I am taking you to a brothel!"

And that's when the explosions and gunfire started.

"Hey, don't crush the glass." The bartender was standing in front of me. "You're squeezing it so hard. I wouldn't want you to injure yourself."

I looked down. I was bathed in sweat and my right hand clenched the empty glass as if it were a person I was trying to choke.

"Seems like you need another drink," the bartender said affably. "Here, this one is on the house."

He was about fifty, and his left hand was missing three fingers. He noticed me staring.

"El Alamein, November 5, 1942," he said proudly. "The British shot my fingers clean off. You can say I was lucky. What about you? Probably too young to have served."

"I'm from Israel."

His expression changed.

"Your German is very good."

"Grew up here. We left when I was twelve."

"I'm sorry for what happened," the bartender said. "I was a soldier doing my duty. I only fired at other soldiers."

He poured himself a drink and offered to clink my glass.

What was I going to tell him? That he may have fired at soldiers, but Erich Rolff was following him with gas vans? There were millions like him, that personally had done nothing wrong except pave the way for the murderers. Do I forgive and forget? But if everyone forgets, what's to prevent it from happening again?

"Prost!" I drank with him.

246

6

I gave my interview to Karl Sassen in the basement of Frankfurt's courthouse. Erika Jager and a stenographer were there.

I told them how I was assigned to *Sonderkommando* in October of 1943, one year after we arrived in Auschwitz. I was separated from my parents and sister on the train platform and never saw them again. I ended up at the Monowitz camp that was just being constructed to produce synthetic rubber. In September of 1943, a new foreman disliked me and reassigned me to the quarry work. After a month of working outside, I figured I wouldn't last much longer and I looked to transfer to a different work command. The SS asked for volunteers to do plumbing, and I stepped forward. It was a trick—all volunteers ended up in the Birkenau sub-camp, in a *Sonderkommando*." The Nazis killed the *Sonderkommando* workers after about four months, but I survived by blind luck and my good German. There was no rhyme or reason or any kind of special meaning to it, just random fate. I didn't tell them about Ezra. Or *Oberscharführer* Schawik. I reviewed the Pery Broad report for them. I had seen it before. It was quite accurate.

On October 7, 1944 *Sonderkommandos* staged a rebellion. One crematorium was destroyed, two others damaged. Hundreds broke out, but they all were hunted down and killed. I didn't take part, I didn't know about it until after it began. I was sent on an errand and was not in the area at the time. Gassings largely ceased after that. As the Red Army came closer, on January 18, 1945 they evacuated the camp and led all the prisoners on a forced death march. I ended up at Bergen-Belsen.

After the interview, I felt the blackout starting, got up and left with, "I am sorry, I must go."

Somehow, I made my way out of that basement. I wandered down the street, sat down on the sidewalk. People walked around me. *Betrunkenes Schwein, drunken pig*, someone said in disgust.

Suddenly, there were Erika's arms around me.

"There were those that refused," I said. "I did not. They turned us into animals. I was a beast. How do I make up for it? You're going to put them on trial, but I'm a murderer just like them."

"No, you're not," Erika said. "They had a choice. You did not. You are a victim. Come with me, please."

She brought me to her apartment, undressed me, put me to bed.

We became lovers that night. Instead of Gerhardt's place, I ended up staying at Erika's.

I came to see Schawik in the police headquarters at Friedrich Ebert Anlage, literally hours after he was arrested. The police officer said, "You have fifteen minutes. I'll be on the other side of the door," and let me into a windowless room with a table and two chairs. Schawik already sat in one of them. He didn't seem surprised to see me.

"So, we meet again. You survived. I'm glad to see that. Changed your name, erhh? They told me that David Levy will come to see me, and I said, 'I don't know anyone by that name.' But it's old David Levinsky. I forgot your number though."

"We don't use numbers anymore. Only names. You changed yours too. And your appearance as well."

In the *Lager*, Schawik's nickname around the inmates was *Rennpferd*, a racehorse, because he moved fast and had a long horse-like face with a bulbous nose. Now his face was more rounded, and his nose greatly narrowed.

"I had my reasons, as you know. That damn Aribert! I was just doing some business with him, I don't know why he had to write my old name down. Anyway, our roles have been reversed a bit. To what do I owe this visit?"

"Do you remember the day that the *Sonderkommando* rebelled?"

"Of course, how could I forget?"

"Why did you send me to the whorehouse?"

"Because that's where Ezra always went when he had a pass."

"No, that's impossible!"

"Yes, absolutely, that's what the old lecher did." Schawik laughed.

"He had his favorite girl, a beautiful Italian brunette of about twenty. I'm not sure he even fucked her. People heard them whispering. She caught syphilis from some soldier or Kapo and they treated her with a bullet, like they did to sick whores."

"No, no, he was going to see his daughter …" That's when I understood. I guess he did too, because his face dropped.

"*Scheisse* … I didn't know. They were not supposed to have Jewesses there; it was against the race laws. But they did, as long as the girl didn't look Jewish."

"Did you …" I lost my voice. "Did you see Ezra after?"

"I saw his body."

I stood up to leave.

"Wait, please," Schawik asked. "Can you help me?"

"How?"

"Can you testify on my behalf? I gave you cigarettes a few times. I saved your life, after all."

"Ezra saved my life, not you."

"Come on, David, I just followed orders. Like you."

"But you didn't have to. Do you think I don't remember you laughing and saying 'the water must be really hot' when people screamed in terror in those gas chambers?"

"I was only trying to get along with others. I was just a doctor. I had to be present, to tell them when it was safe to open the chamber. It was all about regulations. I was doing my job. I didn't kill anyone."

Despite everything, they would not acknowledge it for what it was.

"I'm done here!" I called out to the police officer outside the door.

7

By the time I returned to the moshav, it was almost the end of December. Business-wise, the trip was a big success: I signed deals for almost a fifth of the current crop. Hirsh was ecstatic; the finance committee less so, because of the commissions. They called me in, berated me for my greediness, and requested to change the agreement to a flat fee with a lower commission.

"A deal is a deal!" Hirsh argued on my behalf. "You were the ones that asked for it. Besides, that's just stupid—David is just starting, he can do a lot more sales for you. Would you rather have him go to our competitors? They'll be happy to have him."

The finance committee grudgingly agreed, but my relationships with people in the moshav became strained. Also, someone reported that I stayed with a German woman while in Frankfurt. I don't know how they found out, but it did not help. Galit pointedly shut the door in my face when I showed up at school. No one would join my table in the dining hall. Except for Hirsh, Ofer and Elam, I had nobody to talk to. When people celebrated the new 1963 year, I was in my room, drinking and talking to Ezra.

In early January, I sat down with Hirsh and told him it would be best for everyone if my relationship with the moshav was to be strictly that of sales business. I offered to cut my commission in half. He was visibly relieved; I'm sure the situation was difficult for him too.

I didn't go back to Jerusalem. Before Yael, I'd been in the same job and the same place for seven years. Ever since I met her, my life had become unanchored. It moved off its foundation, first slowly, then faster and faster, until it went completely off the rails. I was very grateful to Hirsh; the five months that I'd spent in Kfar Tahpooz stabilized it. But there was no road back to the way things were. And selling oranges suited me fine; it was just a way to make a living without engaging me emotionally. Now, I had things to do.

I had to find the man that deported Ezra Klaudia's family to Auschwitz.

I chose Tel-Aviv. Psychologically, it seemed halfway between Eilat and Jerusalem. It was easy to disappear in the city of four hundred thousand people. I was not running into old acquaintances. And the place had even more cafes than Jerusalem.

Leon had a place in Tel-Aviv. I called him for help.

"So, you are an international businessman like me now," he said, when we met at the Bograshov Beach.

"I only sell oranges."

"Well, if you decide to diversify, let me know. The arms business is good. Things calmed down in Algeria, but they are just warming up in the Portuguese colonies."

"Thanks, Leon, I'll take it into account."

"All right. I heard you are fucking a German bitch. Be careful, they might arrest you for polluting their precious Aryan blood."

"It's not like that, Leon."

"Whatever. I have a joke for you: A child plays with a bar of soap. Grandma says 'Stop, keep your hands off Aunt Etzel.' What do you think?"

"I think it's not funny."

"Of course you do. You're too damn serious, David. I, on the other hand, am a cynical shit. What can I do for you?"

"I need a place here in Tel Aviv. Something not too expensive because I'll only be here a part of the time."

Leon found me a cheap hotel near Tomer Square, an easy walk from parks and beaches. The proprietor seemed anxious to do a favor for Leon. He offered me a nice weekly rate and said that I could leave my things in his place when I travel. It was a perfect arrangement.

Hirsh forwarded me a letter from Germany: Fritz and Erika were coming here to interview potential witnesses. I went to see them, stayed with Jacob for a few days. Jacob's damages claim was approved, thanks to Shimon's help.

Jacob and I took Fritz and Erika to Café Europa to meet with

251

Maurice. I decided to ignore a few pointed remarks as we walked in. Maurice waited for us at the table in the back.

Maurice's family were caught in the Vel' d'Hiv roundup in Paris in July of 1942. Taken to Drancy afterwards. Maurice was deported first, he pulled out a floor board, jumped off the train, got caught, ended up in Natzweiler-Struthof. A year later, he met his wife in the same camp. She came from Auschwitz, didn't know where their children were; they had been deported separately. Maurice's wife disappeared after two weeks. In 1944, Maurice was also transferred to Auschwitz, that's where I met him.

Later, as I was researching Nuremberg documents, I found out that his wife was a part of the Jewish skeleton collection. German doctors and scientists decided to create a "racial inferiority" display. They took 115 Jewish inmates from Auschwitz, shipped most of them to Natzweiler-Struthof, fed them well, then gassed them. When the Allies arrived at the Anatomical Institute, they found the corpses, some complete and some beheaded, preserved by formalin.

Maurice's kids were killed in Auschwitz upon arrival, like most children.

"Have you gone back to France?" Erika asked.

"No. It was not the Germans that rounded us up; it was the French police. There were only fifteen hundred Germans in the whole country. Germans didn't even want the children, but Pierre Laval, the French head of the government, said to take them away."

"I'm very sorry. We want to get some measure of justice for your family. That's why we want you to testify," Fritz said.

"Justice?" Maurice laughed. "Kurt Lischka, the chief of Gestapo in Paris, served three years in prison and is now a judge in Germany. The French policeman Jean Leguay, the one that managed the roundups and deportations, is president of a big pharmaceutical company in Paris. What justice are you talking about?"

I met Hannah outside of the King David Hotel, where Fritz and Erika were staying.

"I gave an interview to your friends," she said. "They mostly wanted to know about Wilhelm Boger."

"That's to be expected. He was the captain in the Political

Department, and you worked for him. Are you going to testify in person?"

"I don't know yet. Talking brings it back. And just the thought of some lawyer questioning everything after twenty years …"

"You don't have to put yourself through this."

"You know what was the worst? As I was talking to them, I noticed that I imitate Boger's gestures, and I hated myself for it."

"We all identified with them at some point. In order to survive not only physically but psychologically. There is no equivalence."

"I don't know if I have it in me to testify."

8

Benny found me in a café in the old Tel Aviv port. He just plopped himself in the opposite chair, as if we'd parted last night. He must have walked some distance, because the armpits of his light blue shirt looked drenched.

"How did you know I was back here?"

Benny just shrugged. "You've got a few trees on that Righteous Avenue of yours."

"It's Avenue of the Righteous, Benny. And it's not mine. I am no longer with Yad Vashem, remember? What do you want?"

"I just stopped by for a few minutes."

I grunted in disbelief.

"I don't want Hannah to testify. She's not been herself after the interview with the Frankfurt people. It's not good for her."

"I agree, Benny, but she'll do what she wants. That's Hannah."

"True that. But if you have a chance, tell her not to do it, OK?"

"OK."

"I hear that you're going back to Germany, to sell more oranges."

"Yeah. You want me to bring anything back?"

"I wouldn't mind a few scalps. But you're not the type to ask. You know Gerhardt, that detective in Frankfurt, is doing a bit of research into Germans that were in Erzurum back in 1915, right?"

"Yes, so? You and Shimon are the ones paying him to do that."

"So, we asked him partly because of that Yavuz fellow, partly to see if we find anything on that 'righteous' German officer that saved your friend Yosef."

"Is that your way of making amends?"

Benny stopped, pulled out a grayish handkerchief from his back pocket, wiped his brow.

"David, do you think it matters? That whole Righteous Avenue thing. Millions died. We're not going to bring them back."

I took my time to answer.

"I know that millions died. I saw them. They were not human beings. They were not even numbers. Germans only tattooed numbers on those that they kept alive for a while. They were just flesh and bone and hair and teeth, to be robbed of everything and disposed of."

"And?"

"And I don't want to see millions anymore. I want to see people, you know? Individual, unique people—not a mass—one at a time. Good and evil and somewhere in-between. Germans, too. Otherwise, how am I different from Eichmann? That SS officer ... he betrayed his tribe to save someone he was supposed to hate. He saved a life. Whatever else he did, he saved a life. Which is more than what I did."

"Hmmm..." Benny rubbed his bald pate. "I can think of a few ways that you're different from Eichmann. For one, at your age he was better looking. So, you still want to remember those that saved?"

"And those that killed too."

"Acknowledgment to the former, revenge to the latter?"

"Something like that."

"That's good, that's good. I myself am more on the revenge side."

"Benny, why are you here?"

"Because I have something for you. Remember the bank account that Ruben was watching?"

"Yes, of course."

"A substantial check was cashed in Rome earlier this year. We recognized the name. Alfonse Hulda."

"Who is he?"

"Bishop Hulda, known in the CIA and Mossad as the 'Brown Bishop' because of his love for the Nazis. An Austrian, like Hitler. When the Führer rose to power, Hulda vowed to be his 'servant and herald abroad.' After the war, Hulda organized a major 'ratline', an escape network for the Nazi war criminals. He ran a seminary in Rome, where many Nazis were hiding while waiting for their tickets and visas to Latin America and other places. He processed sometimes a hundred Germans a day. Hulda organized the escape of Adolf Eichmann, Josef Mengele ..."

"The 'Doctor Death' from Auschwitz?"

"Yes. I know you've met him. You have not met Franz Stangl, commandant of Treblinka. Or Gustav Wagner, commanding officer of Sobibor. Or Alois Brunner, Eichmann's right hand, now helping the Syrians. Or Erich Rolff, who committed war crimes in Poland, Tunisia and Italy. You asked me about Rolff before. These, and many others, were helped by the kind bishop."

"How was that possible?"

"His work was sanctioned by the Vatican as a part of an organization called the Vatican Relief Commission. Hulda wrote letters of recommendation for thousands of Nazis."

"And this Hulda is helping Yavuz now?"

"Possibly. Ruben will be sending his team to find out. If, as they suspect, Hulda helped Yavuz escape, I wouldn't want to be in his shoes."

"Are you going to go with them?"

"Yes. I wanted to talk to Hulda for many years. To see if he has records on Mengele and others. I would have done it earlier, much earlier. But we were told 'hands off the churchmen'. Even the ones that were Nazis through-and-through. But Dashnaks, they don't worry about that. This will likely be my last and only chance to talk to the good bishop."

Benny stood up. "I'll let you know what I find out."

"Wait," I called out as Benny opened the door to leave. "Are you sure he helped Erich Rolff?"

"We believe so."

"I want to meet with him too."

"David, I appreciate your help in the past and I may call on you again, but we don't need you in this particular business. I was just letting you know because I owed you."

"With the German scientists, you owe me more than one favor."

"Why do you want to meet him?"

"I want to ask him myself. A man of God protecting Stangl and Eichmann? At the time when people already knew about Treblinka and Auschwitz? I want to understand."

And I want to find the man that deported Ezra's family.

"OK, I'll tell Ruben," Benny said. "If not for your craziness, we would not have found that bank account." He smiled. "It's my job to read people. You have a detective in you. And an avenger. Be careful, this stuff is addictive."

After Benny left, I went for a short walk. Was he right about me? Was I still a marionette in his hands? Did it matter?

9

"I'm afraid I don't have much for you," Gerhardt apologized. "I checked the names of the Germans that were in the Erzurum area in 1915-16."

He pushed a thin file across the desk.

"Carl von Feurath, attached to the 4th Turkish Army, died in 1956. No relatives that fit the man we are looking for. Oscar Werner von der Mulenburg, German consult in Erzurum back then, no nephews, only nieces. Peter Klopher, Vice-Consul in Erzurum, 1915-16: a friendly reply, denies knowing anyone like that. I hit a wall."

"Well," Shimon said, "thank you for trying. By the way, the Chelmno trial in Bonn ended a few days ago."

He read from a newspaper:

"Two people received terms of fifteen years, one was given a thirteen-year term. Others got eight, seven, three-and-a-half-years. The jury court president also announced that while the remaining six defendants were found guilty of complicity in the mass murders, the court did not impose any sentences on them, in accordance with a provision of West German penal law."

Shimon threw the paper in the wastebasket. "Meanwhile, in the Soviet Union they tried eleven Ukrainian guards who served at Sobibór. Ten were found guilty and executed, one was sentenced to fifteen years in prison. Which justice do you like better? David, come, have a beer with me."

"I thought you were avoiding me back in November," I said as we were walking to a beer hall.

"No, just busy. I helped your friend Jacob."

"Yes, thank you for that."

The place was half empty. We got our beers and found a quiet table in the corner.

"I've never met anyone from a *Sonderkommando*."

"Well, I am glad to be an interesting psychological case."

Shimon laughed. "Sorry, that came out wrong. You see, I've lived here in Germany for some years now. I go to meetings and dinners with people. And whenever I meet someone in his forties or older, I wonder if he killed my relatives. I mean, between *Einsatzgruppen* and Police Battalions and guards in death camps, hundreds of thousands were in the extermination machine. I figure that one in twenty is a killer that got away with murder."

"Who did you lose?"

"We were from Konin, a town of about twenty thousand on the Warta River, halfway between Warsaw and Poznan. A synagogue, a school, the Jewish quarter with a square in the middle. My family left in 1934. I was only ten, so I don't remember much. My two aunts with their families stayed behind. An uncle lived in Zagorow, about ten miles down the river from us."

Shimon drank his beer. The features of his face suddenly looked very sharp.

"In November of 1941, the SS rounded them up and marched them to a forest just north of Konin. They forced the people to strip and jump into a pit, into which the Germans dumped quicklime. The pit was deep enough so once you got in, you could not climb out. And once the pit was full, the Germans turned on a pump and started pouring water into it."

"What does that mean?"

"When you add water to quicklime, it turns into calcium hydroxide. Concentrated bleach. If you drop a bit of a regular bleach on your skin, it'll sting. Concentrated bleach will literally burn you alive. And dissolve your body. Killing and disposal, all in one step. Very efficient."

"How do you know this?"

"A Polish veterinarian, Mieczyslaw Sekiewicz, told the story. He was forced to collect clothing and shoes from the victims. That's how my extended family was wiped out. Twenty-three people disappeared, burned alive by chemically skillful people. Technically competent barbarians. I've tried to find which German unit actually did this, have not been able to. Every German of a certain age I meet, I wonder:

259

Were you in the Kazimierz Forest in November of '41?"

"And what will you do if you find one of them?"

"I will kill him."

"No forgiveness?"

"Not for this. But when all is said and done, I still don't understand why. What did my uncle Shmuel do to them? He was a tailor. He met some Germans during World War I. He thought they were educated and cultured compared to the Russians. I am a psychiatrist. I am supposed to understand people's motivations. But I don't get this."

Erika and I went to see *The Deputy* in the local theater. It was the most widely talked about play of the year, contrasting Kurt Gerstein's attempts to convince Pope Pius XII to openly condemn the Holocaust and the Pope's unwillingness to do so. We stopped at a bar afterwards. Erika lit up a cigarette. She had dressed up for the play: grey silk gown with silver leaf motifs accentuated her pale face and blue, gold-speckled eyes.

"Do you have other women? Like when you go back?" she asked.

"No." Which was true. She was enough.

"Is there a future for us? As in you and me 'us'?"

"What do you mean?"

"Would you ever be able to move on? Put the past behind? Not erase, that's not possible, but close the door on it? Just a little bit?"

"I don't know how."

"It's horrible beyond comprehension, but it's been almost twenty years. It will not happen again. The world has learned its lesson."

"Erika, how do you know that? Twenty-five years before our catastrophe, it happened to the Armenians. Before that, to others. In a few years, it may well happen to some other people. The true horror is not that it happened once, but that it keeps happening. The lessons get forgotten."

Bobby Vinton's "Blue Velvet" streamed out of the jukebox. Erika closed her eyes, swayed to the music. When the song ended, she said with her eyes still closed, "A friend of my father was wounded and evacuated back to Germany. He brought father's diary. Father hated the war. He hated what it had done to him, to the men under his command. Not a day has gone by that I didn't think of him."

She opened her eyes, focused on me in the darkness of the bar.

"I hope that one day you'll be able to forget that I'm German. I hope that I'll become just Erika, a woman that you make love to."

I didn't answer. She was right, of course. In some parallel universe where these things didn't happen ... but they happened in this one. I really liked Erika. It was a different connection than with Yael: calm, strangely serene, emotionally peaceful. Yael was like slivovka, burning and intoxicating; Erika like a drink from a cold mountain spring—one's always glad to go back to it. I was surprisingly comfortable sleeping with her. I didn't feel the need to possess her completely, and except for the first, violent time, our lovemaking was gentle and enjoyable. I think the shared loss of both of us being orphans was a part of the rubric that united us. But I couldn't tell her that every time I saw the tiny shoes of her daughter Ingrid, I thought of the pair of tiny shoes that witness Berman raised in the Jerusalem courthouse two years ago. I felt a measure of guilt, as it was not her fault by any possible stretch of imagination, and yet I couldn't fully overcome it.

We walked back in silence and I was somewhat relieved to find a "call immediately" telegram from Shimon waiting for me.

"Benny instructed me to take you to Italy where your Armenian friends are planning to question a certain old Catholic bishop." Shimon sounded grumpy. "If you want to, of course."

"Yes, Shimon, I want to."

"OK," he said reluctantly. "I already arranged for travel papers. I will come to Frankfurt to pick you up tomorrow at eleven."

<u>10</u>

A few minutes to eleven the next morning, the familiar Mercedes pulled up.

"You're not too happy about this." I stated the obvious as I climbed into the passenger's seat.

"No. I think Benny's taking unnecessary risks by running an off-the-books operation and involving you. I know he's in a tough spot, unable to trust people on the inside. Ironically, you're one of the few he can count on."

"Why didn't he come himself?"

"He'll meet us in Italy. Benny can't step his foot on the West German soil. A few years ago, one of the Wannsee Conference participants died in a car accident. The police wanted to question Benny."

"Did he ... ?"

"Perhaps if the Germans had the decency to put Dr. Wilhelm Stuckart—one of the legal experts behind the 'Final Solution'—in jail for a few years, the good doctor would have still been alive. But they just fined him five hundred marks."

We didn't get too far. Two blocks after we left the apartment, a police car blocked our way.

"What's the problem, officers?" Shimon protested. "We didn't break any rules."

"Shimon, just come quietly," a man in his mid-thirties approached from behind.

Shimon shook his head in frustration. "I see. David, meet Raul Scifres of the *Bundesnachrichtendienst*, the Federal Intelligence Service, or BND for short."

"Good morning, Mr. Levy. I am afraid we need both of you to come with us."

"What's going on, Raul?"

"Just a friendly talk. We won't cuff you or anything."

"You need a police escort for a friendly talk?"

"Let's not make a scene, Shimon. Leave your keys in the car, one of my associates will drive it."

Scifres pointed us to the BMW 1500 stopped behind us. There being no choice, we got into the back seat.

The man in the passenger's seat turned around. "I am John Smith."

"John Smith, eh?" Shimon laughed. "BND and CIA, working hand in hand."

Neither Scifres nor Smith bothered to reply. We crossed the river and drove through Frankfurt in an angry silence, until we arrived at a large modern villa in the northern end of Bornheim.

"A new place. So that's where you've made your nest," Shimon smirked. "How appropriate, *Das lustige Dorf, The merry village.*"

"What?" The man that introduced himself as John Smith scrunched his face uncomprehendingly.

"It used to be the red-light district, until about fifty years ago," Scifres explained.

"Picked this location because of proximity to the American consulate, eh?" Shimon continued. "Don't have to go far from the formal office to the...well, less formal one."

A bored-looking guard opened the gate, and let the BMW and Shimon's Mercedes in.

We were led to a large windowless room with a polished oak table in the middle. Raul Scifres and "John Smith" sat across from us.

"It's a big table. Expecting company?" Shimon quipped.

"No. Stop clowning." Scifres showed no inkling of humor. "Just us."

He waited for us to say anything, but Shimon just sat there, smiling vaguely.

Scifres gave in. "We understand that you're heading to Italy."

"Yes, it's beautiful there this time of year."

"Enough of that!" Smith's accent was heavy and nasal. "We know what you're doing, and we prohibit you from going."

"You prohibit us? And what will happen if we don't listen?"

"You may not leave this building," Smith snarled.

"Wow, wow, Larry!" Scifres raised his palm.

"Larry? Hmmm, next thing you'll tell us his real name is not Smith," Shimon mocked.

"Shimon, we've known each other for what—eight years?"

"Yes, Raul. From back when you worked for the Gehlen Organization. 'The Org' as you called it before it became the BND. But Reinhard Gehlen stills runs it, so not much has changed."

Shimon turned to me. "I like Raul. He is one of few non-Nazis in the German Federal Intelligence Service. Unlike, say, Rolff or Beisner, that smoothly transitioned from the SS to BND."

"There is no need to go there, Shimon." Scifres waved his fingers as in *let bygones be bygones*. "We no longer have anything to do with Rolff. As for Beisner, he's down to one leg after his car mysteriously blew up two years ago ..."

"We had nothing ..." Shimon started, but Scifres cut him off.

"Shimon, we are not actively pursuing the investigation. As for Bishop Hulda, I know that he had certain pro-Nazi sympathies, and helped a few of them get away. I know he helped Eichmann escape to Argentina back in 1950. That's bad. But the man is past seventy, his ratline days are far behind him. Let it go."

Shimon thoughtfully stared at both of them, then said with fake sympathy. "Your superiors must have been really shitting themselves during Eichmann's trial. I mean, what if little Adolf sang something new about Hans Globke? Or about Gehlen's propensity to recruit his old Nazi friends? Such as Otto von Bolschwing, who had worked with Eichmann in the Jewish affairs department and was later Himmler's representative in Romania?"

Shimon turned to Smith.

"Although, Bolschwing is now on your CIA payroll, right? You moved him to New York City almost nine years ago. But you waited until 1956 to bring a certain Aleksandras Lileikis to America. He was only guilty of killing sixty thousand Jews in Vilna, not something terrible enough to disqualify him from working for you."

Smith's face turned so red, I was afraid he was about to have a stroke.

"How do you know this?"

Shimon leaned back. "Guess what? Eichmann did sing like a bird.

But we decided to keep it quiet. We are allies, after all."

"Shimon, we don't need any complications," Scifres almost pleaded.

"Raul, you're barking up the wrong tree." Shimon shrugged. "Bishop Hulda would have been completely safe, had he stayed out of the ratline business. But he did not. Perhaps he needed the money for his comfortable lifestyle, publishing his memoirs, who knows? Last year he ratlined a certain Turkish gentleman wanted by the ARF for the 1915 genocide. Dashnaks have long memories."

"Who the fuck are they?" Smith asked.

"Armenians," Scifres cut him off. "Shimon, if this is an Armenian operation, why are you involved? And why Mr. Levy?"

"Mr. Levy is on a business trip; he's looking to export more of our famous Jaffa oranges to your country. Sometimes he plays a humanitarian, searching for a few good Nazis. Which in a rather crazy fashion involves the said Turkish gentleman. I ... well, I do have a few questions of my own as Bishop Hulda seemed to be plugged into a certain Middle East terror network. If it were up to me, I would have offed him right after the war, before he shipped thousands of SS murderers to South America and the like. Better late than never, one might say. Look at it this way: it's in your interests to not only let us go, but to make sure we get to Rome safely."

"Why's that?" Smith asked gruffly.

"Because we'll at least make sure that the morning after, Bishop Hulda would be discovered to have peacefully died in his sleep. Instead of a gruesome revenge scene that our Dashnak friends are sometimes fond of."

"Please stay here." Scifres motioned to Smith to leave the room with him.

"Our flight is leaving in fifty minutes!" Shimon shouted at their backs.

Scifres returned by himself.

"My American colleague would have liked to throw you in jail, but I convinced him it's less trouble to let you go. Just remember, keep it clean and quiet. We'll have you taken to the airport in a police car and call the airline to hold the flight."

"What about my car?"

"We'll park it by Erika Jager's place and leave the keys with her."

"How did they know about me and Erika?" I asked Shimon in the police car in Hebrew.

"Don't be naïve, David." He just shrugged. "You've been asking questions in a country that's still full of Nazis. They are keeping an eye on you. I am not happy they found out about Hulda."

"Why did they let us go?"

"Pfffft ... it was just a good cop – bad cop show that they put on for us. They are anxious to start tying up some of the loose ends. After the war, it was not only the Arabs and South Americans that hired the Nazis by the pound. The Americans and the British did too. I'm not talking about the rocket scientists—the anti-communist specialists were in high demand and there were few questions asked. And now, with all these trials the Nazis are back on the front pages and things are getting potentially embarrassing. Dear Bishop Hulda is a liability for them now. He knows too much. They don't care to save him; they just want things quiet."

It was getting dark by the time we got to the address in Rome.

Benny was there already. "You are late!"

"We got delayed. They had to hold the flight because of us."

"Problems?"

"The BND and the CIA are concerned about possible publicity. Raul Scifres picked us up for questioning. How did they know?"

Benny rubbed his bald head. "Damn! I didn't tell anyone but Abe and the two of you. Probably someone in Ruben's organization is playing it both ways. Well, we don't want the publicity either. And neither does Ruben."

"What if the word gets home?"

"It won't be good," Benny said. "But I don't see Raul going to Jerusalem with this. He always worked through you. Take some rest. We'll get picked up at half past midnight."

"Why are they doing it now?"

"Hulda's beginning to attract attention. The rumor has it that he provided the materials for that popular new play, *The Deputy*. Trying to embarrass the Catholic Church for his own reasons, while Russians are doing it for theirs. Now, I suspect that the Dashnaks got an assurance of a benign neglect for the operation, perhaps for a promise to share what they find. Plus, it's a moonless night."

266

Grottaferrata was a charming small town about twenty kilometers south of Rome. It had grown up around the Abbey of Santa Maria, founded many years ago. That was all I vaguely remembered from passing through it once in 1945, as the fires of war were dying down. Back then, I saw the abbey in the bright light of the Italian sun. Now, we passed it the dark. The three of us: Benny, Shimon, and I squeezed in the back seat of a Fiat 600. Van Matusian was in the passenger seat in front, giving instructions to the driver.

He handed us foam galoshes. "Here, put these on."

We turned off the lights, slowly coasted to a two-story building at the end of a small street and parked behind another, slightly larger Fiat. Van put a finger to his lips as we quietly climbed out of the uncomfortable car. The tall iron gate was slightly open, and we followed Van into the house.

A man with his gun ready waited just inside. "He's on the second floor, being questioned."

"And the secretary?"

"Sleeping like a baby in his lower bedroom." The man motioned behind him. "Their dinner was laced with Amytal."

"Amytal is a sleep medicine and a 'truth serum' drug," Shimon whispered to us.

We followed Van up the stairs.

Another armed guard stopped us. "We need a few more minutes, still questioning him. His files are in the office next door. You can go look through them."

In the office, the heavy curtains were carefully drawn, and a man was looking through the files spread on the floor. A lamp was carefully positioned to shine on the papers.

"We should have brought more people," the man whispered angrily. "Not enough time."

"Which ones are recent?" Benny asked.

"These." The man nodded to a small stack on the left, then to a few large stacks on the right. "He was a lot more active in the forties and early fifties."

"Did you find where Yavuz went?"

"Yes, to Barranco Blanco in Spain, under an assumed name of Isa Mansur."

Van poked his head in. "You can go see him now."

"You go." Benny pulled out a small camera from his pocket. "I'm going to take some photos and join you."

"There is someone I'm interested in," I said. "Erich Rolff."

"Right, you mentioned him before. I'll see if his file is here."

Bishop Hulda was sitting up in bed, his eyes glassy and unfocused. The curtains were drawn here as well and the only light in the room was shining into his face.

"He's in a bit of a hypnotic state," the man sitting by the bedside explained.

I stared at the old bishop. He looked pitiful and harmless.

"Why did you help them?" I asked.

He made an effort to concentrate on me, the unseen source of the sound. "Who are you?"

"My name is David Levy. I was in Auschwitz."

"Ahhh, a Jew." He nodded. "You and your 'an eye for an eye' revenge."

"You don't believe in it?"

"No." Hulda suddenly raised his voice. "I believe in justice, a true Christian justice!"

"You believe it was justice to help the war criminals escape their punishment?"

"So-called 'war criminals' … I thank God that He opened my eyes and allowed me to visit and comfort many victims in their prisons and concentration camps and to help them escape the lynchings that the victors prepared for them."

"They were murderers. They killed millions of innocent people. They deserved to face trial."

"They were fighting godless Bolshevism, defending the eternal Church. The Bolsheviks had to be defeated. This was more important than some of the war casualties."

Hulda fell back, exhausted, closed his eyes and appeared to be asleep.

"He has a lot of Amytal in his system," the man by the bedside said. "Do you want to kill him?"

I didn't immediately realize that the question was addressed to me.

"What?"

"Do you want to kill him? For Auschwitz? I'm offering this to you as a privilege."

The man extended his hand to me, palm open. In it lay a needle with a clear liquid.

"Would you in my place?"

"Yes," he answered without hesitation. "I'm a doctor. I heal. And yet, after hearing what I've heard, I wouldn't hesitate. His passing would be a lot more peaceful than for those he dismissed as 'war casualties'. More peaceful than he deserves. In the morning, it'll be assumed that he died from a heart attack in his sleep. Which will be pretty close to the truth."

"He still believes in his righteousness."

"That's what makes it so much worse." He kept the needle extended towards me. But I shook my head and stepped away.

"We must start wrapping up," Van said. "It's well past two and we must leave while it's still dark."

As I was leaving the room, Benny said, "I would have taken the needle."

Van and his driver took us back.

"So, Yavuz is in Barranco Blanco," Van said. "I've never heard of it."

"I'm afraid we did," Benny replied. "It's a valley about twenty miles southwest of Malaga. During the war, Franco, Hitler and Mussolini met there. Now it's a little remaining slice of the Third Reich."

"Why Spain?"

"When the Nazis ran, many of them ran to Spain. They called it Das Trampolin, because from there they were sprung across to South American friendlies. But many stayed and settled there, feeling quite safe. Generalissimo Franco protects them. After all, it was Herr Hitler's planes, tanks and guns that he used to win the Spanish Civil War."

"Can you help us in Spain?" Van asked.

"Perhaps," Benny allowed. "I'll talk to your father."

After Van and his chauffer drove off, Shimon asked, "Anything of interest?"

"Yes," Benny said. "Most of the data is dated, and it's possible that some of these Nazis changed their assumed names. Especially after we kidnapped Eichmann. Still, there are good leads to follow. With what we have, we can start shutting down the Mufti's network. And inform the CIA and BND of some of the double agents on their payrolls. By the way, David, the man you asked about—Erich Rolff—also went to Spain in 1952. Hulda issued him the Vatican Relief Commission documents under the name Wolen. What are you planning to do?"

"I was just curious." I didn't feel like explaining.

11

It was in late August that Erika invited me to a dinner at her grandparents. I declined previous family invitations. I still had a bad aftertaste of the visit to Yael's parents. One reason that Erika and I got along was due to both of us being orphans. With her, I didn't feel the same jealousy and sadness that I did with Yael: our sorrow was shared. In general, I avoided social events in Germany, unless it was necessary for business. The awkwardness would begin once other guests found out about my background. But this was a big deal of their grandfather's seventy-fifth birthday, it seemed important to Erika and I reluctantly agreed to go.

Fritz looked tense when he picked us up. We drove in silence to Bad Homburg, an affluent suburb about twenty minutes north of downtown Frankfurt. Their grandparents had a large two-story house, surrounded by wooded grounds, with a private driveway leading to a colonnaded entrance. The maid awaited us at the door and took our hats. We went through a hall with portraits on the walls and arrived in a large dining room. Perhaps a dozen people were there already, congregating in small groups. Music floated through the air, Mozart's Violin Concerto No. 3. Leah's second favorite. I looked around expecting to see a small orchestra, but it must have come from a record player.

"Grandmother, this is David," Erika introduced me to a tall, slim handsome woman with silver hair pulled tightly back.

"I can see where Erika got her good looks." I bowed slightly.

"Pleased to meet you. I am Ursula." Grandmother extended her hand coldly, eyes skirting over me without lingering. "Werner, come here!"

Werner, the grandfather, was shorter than his wife, but he made up for it in girth and sunny disposition. "How nice to have finally met you, David."

In a rapid succession I was introduced to Ursula's brother Gustav who carried himself as if he were still in the military; his daughter Helga who apologized that her husband Heinz was running late; Inge, widow of Werner's late brother Karl; and two Catholic priests, young Father Ulrich from the church that Werner and Ursula attended, and much older Father Theodor who christened Fritz and Erika.

"Father Theodor has retired and lives in Baden-Baden," explained Werner. "He came just for the party. His visit is a wonderful treat for us all."

I was introduced to other people as well, but my memory did not retain their names.

"We will wait for Heinz just a bit longer," announced Grandfather Werner. "Please help yourself to drinks in the meantime."

They did have nice cognac and I gratefully poured myself a good-sized helping and tried to hide in the corner. Conversations at German parties invariably took one of two directions: the moment people realized that I was Jewish, they would either turn apologetic or start with "how horrible, but we Germans suffered terribly as well." I was not sure which one I disliked more.

Alas, Father Ulrich just waited to join me.

"I've heard about the upcoming trial. You know, Robert Mulka and the others. The Auschwitz trial."

"Ahhh, yes, I know about it."

"Erika told me you were in Auschwitz."

"Yes, I was." I didn't feel like having this conversation, so I attempted to shock him. "I survived by helping to murder other Jews."

"Your survival is a miracle," Father Ulrich pronounced. "Things happen for a reason."

"No, this cognac—that's a miracle. There was no reason for my survival. Just an accident. Blind luck."

"I pray that you see a way to forgive us."

I drank the remainder of the cognac, so I would have an excuse to leave. Unfortunately, the other priest, Father Theodor, took a beeline towards us and cut off my escape route. I was cornered. Ironically, he wanted to speak with Father Ulrich. I was just an innocent bystander.

272

"Father Ulrich, did you see *The Deputy*?" Father Theodor's voice was filled with indignation.

"Yes."

"What a terrible display of anti-Catholic propaganda! Putting late Pius XII on trial like that. I heard that the Soviets are behind it."

"And I've heard that the late Bishop Hulda provided the materials," I couldn't resist chiming in.

"It's a vicious rumor," Father Theodor retorted. "Bishop Hulda was an honorable cleric. He helped many of those that suffered after the war."

"Yes, like Eichmann and Mengele and ..."

"A few bad apples!" Father Theodor interrupted me.

His raised voice attracted other guests, and they began to converge on us, diminishing my already slim chances of escape.

"I saw the play," Father Ulrich said calmly. "Unfortunately, it can no longer be denied that the Vatican knew about the Holocaust back in 1942. Too many witnesses, too many documents, including the Gerstein's report."

"His Holiness Pius XII valiantly spoke about it in the Christmas 1942 address!" Father Theodor shouted.

The younger priest remained composed. "He made an oblique mention of people being put to death due to their nationality or descent. I would not call this a courageous public stand. Especially since the Allies had already made a public joint declaration specifically condemning mass extermination of Jews."

I chuckled. In truth, it had nothing to do with what was said; I just thought of the ridiculousness of myself being caught between two arguing priests. But Father Theodor must have misunderstood, because he shot me a venomous look.

"The Catholic Church had many things to fear from the Nazis; he could not speak openly. He had to make compromises."

"Ahhh, the 'lesser evil' argument," Fritz joined the fray. "The most dangerous argument in the world. Especially for a man of God."

"And the Lord said to Cain, 'Where is your brother Abel?' 'I don't know,' he replied. 'Am I my brother's keeper?'" Father Ulrich's tone was mild, but his face was anything but.

"There were thousands of Jews saved by priests during the war," Father Theodor countered.

"No question, there were countless acts of individual courage by the priests during the war," Fritz said. "But millions perished, while Pius XII remained mum. And after the war … Let's face it, after the war Pius XII and some of his bishops and cardinals showed a lot more compassion for the Nazi criminals than for their victims."

"We must learn to forgive!" Father Theodor's face turned so red, I worried he'd have a heart attack. Then he looked at me. "I know you suffered during the war, but won't you forgive for the sake of peace? 'Love your enemies' as Mathew the Apostle begged of us."

I was so surprised at being asked, I undiplomatically blurted out, "The people that robbed and killed my parents and my sister? I would love nothing better than for them to choke on poison gas and die in their own excrement."

Everyone paused. Then Father Theodor addressed me with, "It's the *Christian* way to forgive. *Christian* love." He emphasized *Christian*.

"Yes, of course. The love." Now I really wished that I hadn't come. I covered my anger with heavy sarcasm. "When the Church burned heretics, it was always done out of love, to save their souls. Sorry, Father, my love extends only so far. Some crimes don't deserve forgiveness."

The loud quarrel finally attracted Werner's attention, and he came to us to announce, "Please, no arguments on my birthday! I'm sure that's because everyone is hungry. Even though Heinz is not here yet, we shall begin. Please take your place at the table."

Unfortunately for him, the tone for the evening had been set, and it was only going to get worse from there.

I rushed to refill on that rather excellent cognac, then took my place between Erika and Fritz.

We ate and drank toasts to Werner and Ursula and all was well until Helga's husband Heinz finally arrived and made a noisy entrance.

"My sincere apologies. It's less than an hour from Mainz to Frankfurt, but I was delayed by lawyers. Our company was doing really well, until this unpleasant business with a book."

"What book?" Father Theodor asked politely.

"Some troublemaker published a book accusing poor Heinz and his father of collaborating with the SS," Helga explained. "Even though the company was only founded in 1951. That's six years after the war!

Some of our clients went to competitors. And then the state prosecutors in Frankfurt kept dragging Heinz into proceedings."

"Sadly, Topf and Sons had to declare bankruptcy two months ago," Gustav commiserated. "That's why Heinz is dealing with the lawyers. Such a sad business when you can be ruined by vile accusations."

"I'm sorry, what did you say the name of your company was?" I asked.

"Topf and Sons."

The rest here is partly from what Fritz and Erika told me afterwards. I suffered one of those blackouts that sometimes happened to me. According to them, I dropped my glass and said, "I remember the name. I met someone from a company named Topf. Kurt Prüfer. He inspected crematoriums and helped to optimize how they work. That's what he called it, optimize. I remember that the best temperature was 1470 degrees Fahrenheit, 799 degrees Celsius. You had to arrange bodies a certain way, so they burn better. Bodies of freshly arrived women had more fat and you were supposed to place them with a body of a child or a starved inmate ..."

There was a horrified silence, broken by Fritz with a sarcastic, "L'chaim! Poor Heinz and his father."

"My father was innocent!" Heinz snarled.

"Yes, he was just an accessory to murdering a million people," Erika shot back. "Think about it, a million! That's more than Frankfurt's population."

"Stop it, Erika." Werner raised his palm. "Business is business. They were asked to deliver the crematoria installations. What else could they have done?"

But Erika didn't stop. I suspect it was something that'd been building inside of her and Fritz for a long time and found the occasion to erupt.

She stood up. "Right, the business. I researched, Grandfather. You didn't have this big house before the war. We weren't rich, until you purchased a textile factory for a song in 1941 from an old Jewish man. He 'bought' a home in Theresienstadt and starved to death there, together with his wife."

"We paid the market price in a fair sale! We've been running it for over twenty years now."

"Fair price? From a man who was forced to sell?"

"His children never tried to claim it back."

"That's because they were shipped to Auschwitz."

"We had Jewish friends. We did nothing illegal. We obeyed the laws of the country."

"Grandfather, in 1944 was your factory getting shipments of human hair to make mattresses with? Or did you use them to make slippers for U-boat crews? Or felt stockings for the railroad workers? So many good uses for human hair," Fritz said grimly. "You don't have to answer, I saw Reichbahn's invoices. Transports from Poland directly to the factory. Have you ever wondered where the hair came from?"

There was no answer, so Fritz continued. "It was from murdered women. Hundreds of thousands of them. First gassed, then shaved. Their hair washed in ammonium chloride and hung out to dry before they shipped it to you. A Reichsmark for two kilograms of hair. I look at this beautiful chandelier and I think: how many mattresses did you sell to pay for it?"

"I didn't know." Werner turned red.

"You chose not to know. You were so anxious to belong, you did it voluntarily. Closed your eyes and thought it made you innocent."

"Don't be holier than thou," Heinz uttered angrily. "You are no better than the rest of us."

"The picture of Uncle Karl." Fritz pointed to a picture on the wall. "You refused to take it down. Do you know what he did? The Russians sent us the report. The Jager report."

"It's a fake!" Inge shrieked. "My husband was a soldier and a war hero! The Russians besmirched his name!"

"I wish it were a fake, Aunt Inge. But the evidence is in. Your husband's report is a tally sheet of actions by *Einsatzkommando 3* written in his hand. Running total of the murders of 137,346 people, from 2 July 1941 to 25 November 1941. Line them up and shoot them. Day after day. Ninety thousand women and children. Such a great hero."

"It was war!"

"Their deaths had nothing to do with the war!"

Fritz turned to his grandfather. "The Jager name will now live in posterity. You always wanted that, didn't you?"

"Get out of my house! I'm writing you out of my will!" Werner shouted.

"Gladly. We don't want any part of your bloody money."

"Who are you to judge?"

"I judge because I am not like you! I would kill myself rather than become like you."

"What's done is done!" Ursula screamed. "What do you want?"

"I want my parents back!" Erika slammed her fist on the table.

"Russians killed your father and the British killed your mother, blame them!"

"Russians didn't ask my father to come to Stalingrad. British didn't invite us to bomb London in 1940. They didn't attack us. You all marched, and watched books burn, and shouted *Sieg Heil*, and took pride in your 'master race' superiority crap and followed your beloved *Führer* into the war until nothing was left standing!" Erika slumped at the table and began to cry. So did Ursula.

There was sort of a terrible silence surrounding their sobbing.

Then Fritz stood up wearily, "Erika, David, let's go."

In the car on the way back, he said, "This generation is too entangled in what happened. The hope lies with the children."

12

We met in a nondescript bar on HaMered Street right behind the Italian Embassy. Benny thought it best to meet in Tel Aviv.

"So, Van, what went wrong?" he asked.

"We tried sending our people to Barranco Blanco, the 'White Valley'." Van shrugged, embarrassed. "Two of them went looking for it. They drove down a dirt and gravel road into the thickly wooded valley, saw a guard tower, behind it houses flying the swastika flags and what looked like military barracks. Armed guards appeared, our people pretended to be lost French tourists, the guards escorted them out with a warning."

"That's it?"

"No. They went to Mijas, the nearest town. Started asking questions. Three days later their hotel rooms were completely ransacked, with a message to get out."

"Amateurs," Benny said under his breath.

"We can't storm the place. We need to draw him out. Can you help us?"

"I can try. You know our conditions, right?"

"Yes. You get to question Yavuz and we cover all the expenses."

"Now, about the expenses: David will go to sell oranges along the Spanish Mediterranean coast. From Malaga to Marbella. He'll need money for the trip, a new passport—we are not going to send him under his own name—and a sizable sales contract upon return. Even if you must buy those oranges for yourself."

"OK. But why David?" Van looked at me doubtfully. "Why not send one of your experienced people? Or work with one of ours. No offense, David."

"Van, you know the saying—don't look a gift horse in the mouth."

After Van left, Benny explained, "Look, kiddo, I'm sorry. I need Abe here and I can't send anyone else. This is strictly off the books. Remember, I was told to keep my hands off Yavuz."

"So why not let one of Ruben's people handle it?"

"No way am I going to introduce them to our contact. You must be careful. There are tons of Nazis in that area, but as long as you follow instructions and don't go around asking questions, you'll be OK."

"Benny, why is this still 'off the books'? You still haven't found the leak?"

"No. If you don't want to go to Spain, I'll figure something out."

But I did want to go to Spain.

Benny got up to leave, I motioned him down.

"Benny, back there, in Grottaferrata … why would you have taken the needle?"

He sat back in his chair.

"He helped Eichmann escape … and Stangl, and Brunner, and Rolff, and others … millions of murders between them. I know that at some point the numbers become almost meaningless, but that's millions of human beings that used to live, and breathe, and laugh, and love … By then, he knew what they did and yet he shielded them from justice."

"But he didn't personally kill anyone."

"Neither did Eichmann. There were people that thought that Nazis had something, then they saw the camps and screamed in horror. But not him, not Hulda. He knew it all and still …"

Benny pulled out his grayish handkerchief, rubbed his forehead.

"Look, I know I'm not explaining it well. I'm not a lawyer, I'm not talking in a legal, procedural sense. At some point, you must look at the dimension of the crime. *Thou shalt not kill*—that's the essence of everything. And these people turned it around and said: *Thou shalt kill*. And that's not the same as me being Mapai and you being Herut—we disagree, we argue, yet we can live together—but with the *Thou shalt kill* crowd, there's no way to share the same planet with them. And by what he did, he made himself a part of that, a co-conspirator in this savage abomination. That's why I would have taken the needle."

Benny stared at his soaked handkerchief, said quietly, "The better question is—why didn't you take the needle?"

I'd puzzled over this ever since we left Grottaferrata. When there, in the room, I just knew that I could not do it. Did I associate a needle with Klehr killing Auschwitz inmates? Was it an aversion to taking a life? Perhaps, although I'd done it before—but killing a kapo in Bergen Belsen was not the same. It was not cold-blooded. Not a calm execution. Did Hulda not deserve to die? I thought he did. Then why didn't I do it? The best I could come up with was that I didn't want to be an executioner. And yet it was entirely unsatisfactory.

13

Frankfurt am Main, December 20, 1963. Light snow fell, Christmas being only five days away. The American president had been assassinated less than a month ago, but that was off the front pages now. Germany doing well, people were laughing, congratulating each other, rushing to buy Christmas presents. A small choir caroled. The mood outside was that of joy and celebration.

I was standing across from the Frankfurt City Council Chambers, where a trial was about to get underway. Close to where a former Nazi slave camp once was. A sizable crowd gathered to watch the defendants arrive.

A TV commentator excitedly spoke into a microphone. "The trial will serve as an attempt to penetrate the wall that has kept us so safely away from all this horror. A majority of Germans are against this trial. Many feel apprehensive because we'll be connected to this. Many wish for the curtain to be finally dropped. But it's only just beginning to rise."

Agitated arguments were breaking out all over the place.

A beefy man in his fifties: "Why is it always the Germans? What about other atrocities: Gulag, Dresden, Hiroshima? Nobody's going on trial for that!"

"The dirt of others can never be the soap to clean ourselves with."

"But what purpose does this trial truly serve? The dead can't be revived."

"But we Germans must cleanse ourselves. How was Auschwitz possible?"

"Jews better stop talking about their misery, enough is enough. I have my own problems. We know already."

"You don't know shit!" from a young student.

281

"Speaking of shit: A Turk and a Jew fall from a house. Who falls faster? The Turk. The Turk is shit, the Jew is ashes."

"You go to Cairo today, the hotel porter will greet you with a radiant 'Heil Hitler!' if he recognizes the German in you."

"How many of these disgusting show trials are we going to have?"

"We must know the truth, enough cover-up!"

"They were soldiers doing their duty. No country has ever charged its own soldiers."

"Nobody wants to talk about it, but we have murderers in our midst."

"We are only singled out because we lost the war. Everyone had these camps. The Americans, the Russians."

"Auschwitz was just a protective custody camp."

"By the end of this trial, everyone will know what Auschwitz really was."

"You are a communist agitator!"

"And you all became anti-Nazi after 1945."

"These people were acting under orders. We all must love and serve our country. That's the meaning of honor."

"All for one and one for all? Honor? What honor is there in murdering others?"

An ambulance arrived, one of the defendants not feeling well. It was by Red Cross ambulances that the gas was delivered to crematoria.

German juries in criminal trials consist of nine members—the three judges plus six jurors—and verdicts must be arrived at by a two-thirds majority.

Twenty-two defendants. Auschwitz would have not been possible without them, and thousands of others. Here they were: Boger, Stark, Baretzki, Schlage, Mulka, Kaduk, Capesius. Respectable German citizens. Murderers. Do I even share a common humanity with these people? They obliterated the idea.

They were not being tried for the mass murder of innocent people. An SS man who had beaten one inmate to death on his own initiative could be convicted of murder, because he had not been following orders. A SS man who killed hundreds of thousands while operating the gas chambers could only be found guilty of being an accomplice, because he had been following orders.

"How does that even come close to explaining Auschwitz?" I asked Fritz Jager. "Why are they not tried for crimes against humanity?"

"The trial will be conducted under ordinary statutory law. We don't have crimes against humanity laws in Germany."

"So individual unauthorized acts of cruelty are punishable but 'non-cruel' mass murder is OK?"

"We must render justice for the crimes of Auschwitz within the limits of the law and regulations that were in force at the time. I know it's a sad paradox: the prosecution has to rely on Nazi regulations to demonstrate that the defendants had exceeded them."

"You asked for our help in order to serve justice. This is not justice!"

"I understand it's upsetting," Fritz said apologetically. "But the reconstruction of the general legal consciousness is most important for us. We must reintroduce natural law into Germany. Trials are not history lessons."

"You speak as a lawyer."

"I am a lawyer. It is about establishing guilt within the penal code. David, please give it a chance. You don't know what we had to go through to get here. I realize this is not enough, but it's an achievement to have been able to charge these men. Our institutions are full of Nazis, and they had nothing to fear until now. We are admitting that our fathers were murderers. I know this is only twenty-two out of more than seven thousand that served there. But at least it's bringing Auschwitz from a faraway unknown place in Poland right here, into the middle of Germany."

In that, he was right. Sounds and images from 1944 fused with those of 1963. The Lager and the Courtroom. The chaotic pastiche that's within me. At times, I could no longer tell where my recollection ended and testimonies of others began. It all coalesced together.

Just like in Jerusalem, I don't know how to describe the trial. Who wanted to wade through volumes of documents and testimonies?

I stared at the accused. They seemed quite normal, bland. They lived the past eighteen or so years as wholesome German citizens. They did not appear ashamed of what they did. I was the one ashamed for them. They were so different in the *Lager*, full of themselves, enjoying their power over life and death. And now I saw them again as agreeable peaceful middle-aged men, the kind that I saw playing chess in a neighborhood park. They were not even tried for the hell-on-earth they created, but for going above and beyond the hell that'd been sanctioned. As if getting an order relieved one from having a conscience. If it was within these innocuous, even banal people to do this, could it be in all of us?

Robert Mulka, commandant's adjutant. The de-Nazification court in Hamburg essentially exonerated him despite Mulka admitting that he served in Auschwitz. Nobody's ever guilty in a giant bureaucracy.

The very first witness was Dr. Otto Wolken, the SS physician.

"One inmate, 180 cm tall, weighed 43 kg. Another, 175 cm tall weighed 39 kg. Another, 180 cm tall, 36 kg."

"Well now," Judge Hofmeyer cut him off, "we don't want to read the entire list."

"Yes," agreed Wolken, looked at his notes, added, "Here's one more, he weighed 28 kg."

"Twenty-eight kilograms," repeated a stunned Hofmeyer. An adult male weighting the same as a nine-year old child.

A huge mass of journalists, photographers and camera people from all over the world and half-empty seats in the visitors' gallery. Auschwitz could not compete with a new British group called the Beatles. Or with Richard Burton and Elizabeth Taylor getting married.

14

Spring was beautiful on the Spanish Mediterranean coast. I sat in the car in a residential area near Marbella, hidden behind two palm trees. In my hand there was a photo from 1952, taken from Vatican-issued travel documents. He'd be older now, by twelve more years. Recognition could be difficult.

There were stories of tall, lean German men growing old on Andalucian beaches. Stories of all-German communities sheltered in locations away from the coast. Many of them had the tattoos on their inner arm or, more often, a mark where it had been removed. A give-away sign of the SS.

I waited for an hour. The man I followed was slowly drinking a beer, staring at the ocean.

He stood up, illuminated by the sun. No, he was not Erich Rolff.

As instructed, I drove north-east to Malaga and waited in the designated bar. I came here with a fake passport issued to Alexander Krause from Stuttgart. An old man in Haifa took my picture and made the document while I was waiting. He was recommended by Leon.

"Is it good?" I asked as he handed me the passport.

"Pfftt." The man shrugged. His eyes looked tired from the effort. "It'll get you across the border in most places. People get caught because they do stupid things, like forget what name is on the passport. Not because some underpaid customs officer suddenly becomes a world expert in forgery."

"Which *Lager*?"

The man looked at me more carefully. "That obvious? Sachsenhausen. We were forging British pounds. A valuable work, that's how I survived. You're wearing a long sleeve, must have been Auschwitz."

"Is making passports a good business?"

"I'm not complaining, good passports are not cheap. But for your friend Leon, you get a better rate. If you ever decide to get another one, I'll give you a *sabon* discount," he cackled.

The man was right, I had no problems with the passport. And here I was, drinking a bottle of *Estrella* in the back of a small bar on Calle Echeverria, trying not to look anxious.

"*Herr Krause?*" a beefy man in his mid-fifties stood by my table, a beer in his left hand. I'd seen the photos of most of the Nazis that the Allies tried at Nuremberg. This face was hard to forget. "Do you mind if I sit down?"

He did so without waiting for my reply. My instinct was to run, as my cover had obviously been blown. The man gently but firmly placed his hand on mine, anchoring me in place.

"It seems like you have recognized me." He smiled. "Then just call me Anton, please."

I still had not responded, so he continued. "I presume your speaking ability will return at some point, but for now just listen and nod. I can't stay long. You need a man called Isa Mansur who's hiding in Barranco Blanco. It's not possible to get him there, but the next month there will celebrations in local towns."

"What kinds of celebrations?" I realized that he was not there to kill or arrest me. And I understood why Benny wouldn't send Ruben's people to this meeting.

"Why, our beloved *Führer* was born in April, seventy-five years ago. I will organize a party in Fuengirola, the nearest town to Barranco Blanco with a decent harbor. I'll make sure that Isa Mansur gets invited. There will be security, but after a few drinks and singing of *Deutschland über alles* and *Horst Wessel Lied*, people won't be alert. You must grab him, get him on a boat, and out of the country. No port on this coast of Spain is safe for you."

"How would we know the exact date?"

"I'll try to give a few days' notice of where and when. You must have a team on standby for a week or so around the April 20th. You got it all, right?" He rapped a finger against his forehead.

"Yes. I have a question though. Erich Rolff—do you know him?"

The man looked at me through narrowed eyes.

"That was not a part of the deal. I helped you with the German scientists working for Egypt, I personally delivered Dr. Krigger. This Mansur deal is just a favor. Now you want Rolff?"

"It's personal," I said. Then I carefully rolled up my sleeve, showed him the tattoo, and covered it again.

"Just for the record…" His face darkened. "I know what he did, and I never approved of that gas vans business that Rolff was in. I'm a soldier, not a murderer. But why? He was not in that *Lager*."

"He deported someone there. I'll pay you to bring him out, like Mansur."

"I don't want your money and I can't bring you Rolff," he said. "But if I were looking for him, I would go to Costa Blanca, between Valencia and Alicante. I met him at a large dinner in Gandia once, he must be somewhere in the area. You're on your own there. Your German is good, but I would be very careful. Don't use the same passport you registered in the hotel, and after Mr. Mansur's kidnapping your name would be known. And I would most definitely not call the police. What are you going to do if you find him?"

I shrugged.

"I see. I guess you won't be bringing him to court. Well, if you need to find me, leave a message with the bartender: Herr Krause looking for Anton."

"Why are you helping me?" I was genuinely curious.

"I'm just living out my life. You know, the first time I heard the *Führer* speak back in the thirties ... I was a young man then. It was a rapture. We were going to become great again, to transcend the state of corruption and nihilism. I was a part of that glorious force, much larger than myself. Oh, it's an amazing feeling! To transcend our human limitations, to live forever. It all turned out to be a pack of crazy lies. And the murderers like Rolff, they stained us for generations."

In the Belzec trial in Munich, the District Court released seven out of eight defendants because at the time of the crime they were under a putative claimed threat from the Nazi authorities. Even though in Nuremberg not a single case would be found in which an SS member

287

had suffered a substantial punishment for refusing to take part.

Fritz Jager sighed guiltily. "We'll try to get them in the Sobibor trial."

We sat for a minute in an uncomfortable silence. I broke it up with, "I read in the paper that Hans Globke is out of the government for good."

Fritz nodded. "Yes, I guess the show trial that the East Germans did made it too embarrassing to keep the writer of racist laws around."

"Perhaps we should help the East Germans to stage a few more of such trials."

"David, I know that look." Erika interjected. "What are you thinking?"

15

Van Matusian called in mid-May.

"David, can you be ready to go in two days?"

"Go where?"

"We picked up Yavuz four weeks ago. We are putting him on trial in France. You're welcome to join as our guest."

Why did I agree? Because I never had a chance to sit across a table from one of them and ask him directly.

Van and I flew to Marseille. Van directed me to a particular passport check officer.

"*Barev*, Raffi."

"*Barev*, Van."

The Armenian officer checked us through without looking.

From there, we took a small private plane to Carcassonne, where a car picked us up. We turned off on a dirt road fifteen minutes after passing Limoux. It led to a large gated château in the middle of nowhere. Armed guards checked us at the gate.

"Do they usually have such an army?" I asked.

"No. Special circumstances. We are less than two-hundred kilometers from the Spanish border. We rushed to put this together. You can't keep these things secret for long."

A guard escorted us into a room in the basement. Three judges in black robes were behind a long table: Ruben in the middle, I didn't know the other two. Ahmet Yavuz sat at a small table in front of them. There was another table with a chair to the side of him. About three dozen people faced the podium, all Armenian-looking. Except for Benny, who turned and waved to me.

Ruben stood up and pointed. "We have a new guest; he's been instrumental in making this happen. David, we thank you. You are welcome to be a witness to our court."

"I don't recognize your court of Armenians and Jews." Yavuz turned and looked at me with pure hatred.

"Nevertheless, the court recognizes you and will proceed." Ruben sat down. "We are going to call the next witness."

"You will be given a private meeting with Yavuz to ask your question," someone whispered in my ear. I recognized Nouvart.

An old dignified-looking man in his late seventies, dressed in a dark suit, white shirt, a tie and a fez, took a seat at the small table to the side of Yavuz.

"Please state your name and where you are from," Ruben asked.

"I am Faiz El-Usein, a sheik and a lawyer from the Hauran in Syria."

"How did you come to be in Turkey in 1915?"

"The Turkish government accused me of trying to obtain independence for the Arab people. They arrested me and put me on trial. Even though I was acquitted, they exiled me to the Erzurum area where I stayed until my escape in 1916."

"You should be ashamed of yourself!" Yavuz shouted. "Here you are, a Muslim, testifying for these unbelievers!"

"Why are you testifying?" Ruben ignored the outburst.

"What this man and others did was in direct contradiction of the laws of Islam, as I know those laws. It is incumbent on true Muslims to hold them responsible," El-Usein replied.

"Do you recognize this man?"

"Yes. His name is Ahmet Yavuz. I'd come across him twice in 1915, in August and in September. I understand he was an officer in charge of the Hamidiye regiment that expelled and exterminated the Armenians."

"Can you explain what Hamidiye regiment is? We have some young people that were not even born then."

"These were irregular formations modeled after the Russian Cossacks. I understand that some of them were released from jails with the express purpose of killing Armenians."

"And where did you see the accused?"

"The first time I came across him near Bingöl, about forty miles southwest of Erzurum. I was traveling with a local doctor. We came across mounted Hamidiye, who stopped us. We asked them what was going on and they said that just ahead a caravan of Armenians was being executed. My companion asked to see the operation. We received the permission to proceed. After a quarter of a mile in a ravine on the side of the road, we found four butchers, each with a long knife. The *Hamidiye* gendarmes divided the Armenians into parties of ten and sent them up to the butchers one by one. We were amazed at their steadfastness in presence of death, not saying a word, or showing any sign of fear."

"And where was the accused?"

"He was on the horse on the edge of the ravine, commanding the execution."

"And the second time?"

"That was near town of Elazig. I was with an official of Diarbekir, where I was staying. Even though technically I was in exile, he sometimes used me when he did not want to pay a local lawyer. We saw smoke rising ahead. A mile down the road a barn was burning, with people screaming from the inside. More people were being pushed into another barn with straw piled up on all sides. Gendarmes searched these poor souls one by one, taking any money they might find, and stripping them of their clothing. If someone had gold teeth, the gendarmes pulled them out. A band of Kurds was waiting on the side. They were buying young women and boys for a few liras each. I asked one of the Kurds what would happen to these people and he said they would be sold as slaves or used and killed. Then he complained that they were not allowed to purchase the whole caravan like before, when he and his companions bought a thousand Armenians for five hundred liras, killed them all and found at least twenty times as much on the bodies. I had turned to my companion who was a member of the Young Turks party and asked: 'Have you no fear of God? What right do we have to take life in defiance of God's law?' He replied: 'It was the Sultan's order; the Sultan's order is the order of God, and its fulfillment is a duty'."

"And where was the accused?"

"He was on the same white horse, near the spot where the Kurds were waiting. He would point left or right with his whip whether the person was to be sent to be burned or sold to the Kurds."

Ruben turned to Yavuz.

"Does the accused have anything to say to this?"

"This is a kangaroo court. It's all lies. This man is too old to recognize anybody."

The next witness was a woman around sixty. She slowly walked with a cane and took her place at the witness table.

"Have you met the accused before?"

"Yes, in August of 1915 in Erzurum. Early one morning Turkish gendarmes forced us out of our houses."

"Us who?"

"It was only my mother, my older sister and me. Our father was taken away into a labor battalion two weeks earlier. Later I found out that he was killed almost immediately."

"What happened?"

"We were brought to a square, hundreds and hundreds of women, children and old men. Mounted Hamidiye soldiers surrounded us, their sabers ready. This man"—she pointed at Yavuz— "was in charge, prancing on his white horse."

"It's been almost fifty years, how do you recognize him?"

"Oh, I do. He changed, but I remember those eyes. And that cruel mouth. He announced that we will all be resettled. Our priest stepped forward to protest, but this man cut him down. People started shrieking in terror. Then he gave a command and his soldiers pulled out four young women from the crowd."

She took a sip of water.

"They were looking for girls with long hair. Soldiers took my sister and three others, none of them older than fifteen, tied their hands and then hung them by the hair off the porch of the courthouse. Then this man rode away, turned around and galloped towards the girls with the saber on the ready. The saber sliced through their necks and the bodies had fallen on the ground, leaving only their heads hanging."

The silence in the room was interrupted by angry shouts.

"We'll have quiet!" Ruben banged his gavel. "What happened after?"

"They marched us out of town going south. The next day we

reached the hills on the border of the Erzurum province. There they bound most of our people and threw them all off a great height. That's how my mother died, amongst a heap of shattered bodies on the ground below."

"What about you?"

"A Turkish man, Kudret Osman, pulled me away. He was from the town of Tekman nearby and knew my father. He told me later that he offered to save my mother, but she did not want to live after seeing her older daughter murdered this way; she asked him to save me. I was only eleven at the time. He brought me to his family and I stayed with them for five years, until I could leave for France."

"Does the accused have anything to say to this?"

Yavuz didn't try to deny the testimony. "It was a war and the Armenians supported our enemies, the Russians. I had my orders. I followed my duty."

"Your first duty is to be a human being!" someone shouted.

"I am an old harmless man. And in any case, you have no right to judge me."

"If we had a state of our own, we would have put you on a proper trial. But as it is, we do our best."

"These events took place almost fifty years ago." Yavuz sounded resigned.

"In this court, there is no time limit on murder."

"We'll reconvene tomorrow," Ruben said.

16

Benny and I were taken to a small room. Yavuz was there already.

"We want to know about your funding of Nazis and of terror groups. We are ..." Benny began but Yavuz interrupted.

"I know who you are. Why should I provide you with any information? They are going to kill me anyway. If not for him"—Yavuz pointed at me—"none of this would have happened."

"But what does it cost you? And you still have a family out there."

"You are threatening my family? And sitting here in judgment? The Armenians promised me that they won't touch my family."

"But we are not Armenians. We didn't promise anything. Your call, Ahmet." Benny shrugged.

"How do I know you won't touch my family even if I talk to you?"

"We prefer not to inflict unnecessary pain or punish the innocent. Talk to us, and we'll leave them alone."

Yavuz thought about it, shook his head affirmatively.

Benny looked at me. "Go ahead, David, you deserve the first question."

"I just want to know why."

"Why what?"

"Why did you do it? How did you justify these ... these acts to yourself?"

"I was a soldier. We received orders; it's not for a soldier to question the orders. Soldiers must carry them out. It was war. We are all guilty. Including you."

"But women and children?"

"Women give birth to children. Children grow up to become avengers."

"You're an educated man. You must have questioned the purpose

294

of killing defenseless people?"

Yavuz looked at me uncomprehendingly. "We were trying to create a greater country. A country where our Turanian people could prosper. There was a higher purpose. We had to put our people first and act after the decay and disintegration of pre-war years. The immortality of the nation required it."

It was like in von Eckner's office three years ago: an invisible wall between us; words bounced off that wall; the meaning didn't get through. And yet, there was a pattern.

"David, are you done?" Benny asked.

"One more question. Two years ago, I saw you in Trabzon. The man that came with me was looking for the German officer that took him through Turkey in 1942. They stayed in your house. How did you know that officer?"

"He was Otto Klopher's nephew."

"Otto?" I was puzzled. That was not what I saw in Gerhardt's file. "Wait, do you mean Peter Klopher? He was a Vice Consul in Erzurum in 1915."

"I meant Otto. That's how I met the family, through Peter. They were very helpful to me during my years in Germany. Peter Klopher went into business, while Otto rose up high in the Nazi government. He was the one who came with the boy in 1938 to check on me."

"But Otto Klopher's only nephew is Artur, Peter's son."

"I know Artur, I'm not talking about Artur. I saw the boy at Klopher's during 1930s, he was like a member of the family. He called Klopher 'Uncle Otto.' Everyone called him Prinz because he was so good looking. I don't know exactly how they were related."

"Do you remember when they came to you in 1942?"

"Of course. With a Jewish boy. Prinz told me a story how he was being sent to Palestine. I helped them. We thought Rommel was about to defeat the British. We were planning to begin an Arab uprising, with the Mufti's help. A few weeks later I had a visitor from the Gestapo asking questions. For Germans to send someone from the Gestapo to Trabzon in 1942, it must have been serious."

"When did you go to Germany?" Benny asked.

"In 1921. I was one of the accused in the Constantinople court-martials in 1919, but they did not convict me. The British arrested me and sixty others and took us to Malta to face an international tribunal.

But they never did anything, and in 1921 the British exchanged us for twenty-two of their hostages taken by Mustafa Atatürk. The Armenians started killing the Turkish leaders. When they killed Behbud Javanshir in July of 1921, right in the middle of Istanbul, I decided to go into hiding."

"And you contacted Peter Klopher?"

"Yes, we had a profitable business relationship by then."

"Funded by gold taken from murdered Armenians?" Benny's mouth curled in disgust. "You don't have to answer. Why did you go back to Trabzon?"

"I was sent back to Turkey in 1937. We picked Trabzon because of its location and the port. Germany had to secure a supply of chromium. It is a strategic metal mined in only a few countries. They were concerned that Britain would cut it off. Which is partly what happened. In 1939, Germany bought over a hundred tons of chromium ore from Turkey, but in 1940-1942 there were no official sales. However, we were moving tens of tons a year over the Black Sea to Constanta in Romania. In 1942 and 1943, we even had German submarine escorts."

"Must have been expensive."

"It was. I had to pay off a lot of people. But the Germans needed that ore."

"How did they pay?"

"In gold. Nobody would take the Reichsmarks. Later, they tried to give me British pounds, but I found out that those were counterfeit, dangerous to use."

"Did you know where the gold came from?"

"It was stamped either with Reichsbank or with the Swiss National Bank's emblem."

"What about this?" Benny produced a picture of the gold ingot.

"Oh, yes, a few of these came later in the war. Things changed by then."

"How's that?"

"In 1944, it was no longer possible to ship. Romania changed sides, the U-boats were scuttled. I was operating out of Istanbul that year. The assets were coming in all shapes and sizes: gold, diamonds, currency, even paintings."

"What were you doing?"

"In March of 1944, the Germans invaded their ally Hungary. I was working with the SS office in Budapest."

"With Eichmann?"

"Mostly with Kurt Becker. The Klophers introduced us before the war. Wealthy families, they hung out together."

"Did you travel to Budapest?"

"Yes, and to Berlin too. To meet with Otto Klopher. Everyone figured that the war had been lost, and people scrambled to get alibis, to store some money abroad."

"Like the alibi that Kasztner gave to Becker by writing him a letter of recommendation after the war?"

"Yes."

"Was that about Becker selling seats on the Kasztner train that took sixteen-hundred Jews to Switzerland?" I asked.

"Not only that. Some people left Hungary by other means."

"Like what?"

"Like being taken to Istanbul and then to the British territory. Without the risk of the train, that went to Bergen-Belsen first. I helped with that."

"Who?"

Yavuz named a few names.

"That must have cost a lot of money?"

"It did. People paid a lot to save their relatives."

"And now, after the war?" Benny looked at his watch.

"I've been helping certain people to leave Germany and settle in Arab countries."

"There was no substantial ratline through Turkey?"

"No. There were better routes, using the Vatican's documents. It was all financial help."

"With the gold accumulated during the war?"

"Yes, and quite a bit was transferred towards the end."

"But you were funding others too. Like the Mufti, the terror groups."

"Yes. The Mufti was a supporter during the war."

"Why didn't you stop? Just take the money and get out of business?"

"It was their money as far as they were concerned. They would have killed me in an instant. And my family too."

"OK." Benny tapped his fingers against the table. "Here's paper and pencil. Write down all you can about who the money went to."

"You promise not to harm my family?"

"I promise."

After Yavuz's interrogation, Benny said, "Now I understand why I've been blocked from going after Yavuz. The names that he gave us … to make them public would bring down the government."

"What Turanian people was he talking about?"

"Oh, they have this myth of a great Turanian race that populated Atlantis and from which they descended. The immortality hunger, anything to feel themselves superior. He's still full of hubris."

We were taken to a room where a dinner table had been set up. Six people were there already, arguing loudly.

Ruben pointed to two empty chairs. "Please, Benny and David, join us. You know Aram, Nouvart, and Van. These two young men, sitting next to Aram, are his sons, Vrej and Sarkis. We have a bit of an argument underway."

"About what?"

"I think that my friend Ruben is wasting time and money on this trial," Aram said. "We know what that man Yavuz did. We should have executed him and left his body on the *Champs-Élysées* or another place where everyone will know. With a big sign explaining who he was and why he was executed."

"I disagree," Ruben said. "The rule of law is the only guarantor of a free society. One day we'll have our own country and we must teach our young people this lesson. This is what this trial is: a lesson to the next generation."

"How much did the law do for us? They sold us for oil, and any justice we got, we had to get ourselves!" Aram slammed his fist on the table.

"That's because the law was wrong then. I wish we could do it publicly, like Eichmann's trial."

"Eichmann's trial, yes," Aram said. "But the ones in Germany, what do they accomplish?"

"I believe the trials will change the future. As long as the memory is alive, future Eichmanns will know that they will be held responsible. If

298

the perpetrators of the genocide against us faced proper justice, perhaps Hitler would not have said 'Who now remembers the Armenians?'"

"Justice?" Aram laughed bitterly, pointed at us. "They will get no justice in Germany. Remember the trials of war criminals that Germans conducted in Leipzig in 1921? Everyone walked away free or with slap on the wrist. And now? I follow their trials. The Chelmno trials: a hundred and eighty thousand dead, most either acquitted or received minor sentences. The Ulm *Einsatzkommando* trial: ten people convicted of massacres of thousands, most got three to five years. Do you think this kind of justice would defer anyone?"

"I agree that the punishments have been ridiculously light so far," Ruben conceded. "But the trials are taking place."

"And what good are trials without punishment? What do they teach: that you can kill and get away with it? It's been almost fifty years and, we, the Armenians, are still waiting for justice."

"You executed the leaders," Benny offered.

"We took revenge on some of those at the very top. But that's not enough. People sitting behind their desks giving orders, they have no power unless they have the underlings that follow up. The retribution must reach them. So next time, there will not be enough followers. Meanwhile, in Turkey it is perfectly acceptable to name neighborhoods, streets, and schools after Talaat Pasha and other 'heroes' that exterminated our people. We are still very far from getting justice, and this trial of ours is not getting us there."

"And what would you do, Aram?" Benny asked.

"I will continue hitting them, until everyone remembers the Armenians. Until civilized countries have remembrance days for the genocide against us, like the Holocaust remembrance day in your—he pointed at Benny and me—country. If you want justice, you must do it yourself!"

"Terror is not the way," Ruben replied quietly.

"And what other avenues of justice are open to us? What shall we do now?"

After dinner, I asked Ruben, "What are you going to do to Yavuz's family?"

"Nothing." He shrugged. "We won't touch them. Nor his other family. He fathered two children with another woman. Kept her in a nice house in Istanbul. Why, did he ask you?"

"He seemed worried about them."

"Eichmann was also a doting father and a loving husband," Benny added. "And had numerous mistresses, at least during the war. They are like masters of the universe, take what they want. They doted on their own, they just didn't care a bit about children of others."

Aram Arutiyan came to see us off in the morning.

"I didn't realize you were leaving so soon," he said. "I was really hoping to talk to you."

"Sorry, we just came to get some answers. This trial is an Armenian affair," Benny replied.

"Oh no, it's not. Just like your catastrophe is not only yours."

"Well, I'm afraid we have to go catch our flight." There was a note of impatience in Benny's voice.

Aram turned to me. "David, can I speak with you privately?"

I looked at Benny, who shrugged. "You have five minutes."

I followed Aram for a few steps.

"David, after my experiences, I turned to writing. I edited, I wrote articles, I wrote books …"

"Aram, what are you saying?"

"It was good for me. It took some of the anger, some of the madness, and channeled it into words. What you saw, very few people saw and lived to tell about."

"Why not leave the dead alone? They are gone. Ashes to ashes, dust to dust."

"It's not for the dead. It's for the living that …"

"Aram, I already gave my testimony in Frankfurt," I interrupted. "The mechanics of the operation are well known by now. To anyone who's interested."

"I'm not talking about the mechanics, David. Bearing witness is not only about the details. I know you speak many languages—is Russian one of them?"

"No, why?"

"I do. I volunteered with the Russian Army back in 2016, in order to return to Turkey and I learned the language. There was that poet, Alexander Pushkin."

"Yes, I've heard of him."

"He wrote a poem called *The Prophet*. It says:

An angel opened my chest, took out my heart,
replaced it with a burning coal,
and the Voice told me
'go and burn with your word the human hearts'.

"Don't you understand what it means?" Aram grabbed my arm. "David, you were meant to bear witness."

"But what will I say? I'm not a writer."

"Just write to me. It's not the facts that get through to people, it's getting to their humanity. Give me your words and we'll burn people's hearts with them."

PART 7:
IRIS

1

"When was the last time we saw each other, Iris?"

"Two years ago, at Jonathan's funeral."

"Right, in LA. And here, in Jerusalem?"

"Five years ago, Uncle, when Aron and Sarah's son was born. Were you the one that suggested calling him David?"

"Yes." Uncle Yosef studied his hands that he placed on the wooden table. He sat across from me. The rest of the group—Aunt Rachel, Rivka, Aron, Sarah, the kids and Avi Arutiyan, their overwhelmed guest and my traveling partner—were in the house. I wished Max was here, he is good at managing his anger.

"I thought so. I liked that."

"You cut your beautiful hair," he said regretfully. "Why?"

"After I read the notebooks. My way to mourn him."

My uncle's head shrank into his shoulders. I could smell his discomfort, but I was not going to let him off easy.

"You don't know for sure. He may have found a new life under a different name."

"Why didn't you tell me the whole truth about him?"

"Iris, everything that we told you was true."

"Hah!" I laughed angrily. "You told me a sliver of the truth. That my parents separated, and my father left the country to live with another woman. That's the kind of truth that's almost a lie."

He folded his hands, then unfolded them again, without looking at me.

"I told you what Yael ... your mother ... wanted us to tell you."

"When was the last time you saw him?"

"August of 1965."

"I was two years old already..."

I let the weight of unspoken accusation hang in the air.

"Rachel … and your mother … they didn't want to tell him."

"And you? What did you want? What did you think was the right thing to do?"

"Iris, please," he pleaded. I didn't feel sorry for him whatsoever. "We did what we thought was best at the time."

"Uncle, you keep saying 'we'—what about you? He was your friend! You were the one who got him involved in this whole thing! Was it because he was in *Sonderkommando*? Were you ashamed of him?"

"I was not ashamed … but there was a stigma back then … and the German woman …"

"It seems to me that that 'German woman' was the one that actually stood by him. And her name is Erika Jager, not some 'German woman'."

"Iris, I'm sorry. He deserved to know about you."

"You just don't get it!" I slammed a fist on the table. Aunt Rachel's worried face appeared in the door. "Not only him … I … I deserved for him to know! All these years I thought that he knew about me and still walked away … and I hated him for it. Turns out he never even knew! And had he known, he probably would have come to me. He would have had a reason. You, all of you, took him away from me!"

I pushed myself up, off the bench, and walked over to the side to the fence. I didn't want them to see me like this. I knew I was not being fair. I saw a movement out of the side of my eye. It was Aunt Rachel. I extended my hand, palm up, and she went away.

After I composed myself, I came back to the table. Uncle Yosef still studied his hands.

"Do you think there is a chance that my father is still alive?"

"There is always a chance," he said without raising his head. "He could have disappeared, if he wanted to. He certainly had his reasons."

"But you don't think so …"

"I doubt it. But I don't know." He shrugged. "I really don't."

2

"I'm afraid I was not there for David back in 1965."

Shimon Bezor didn't sound very sincere. He sipped bitter Turkish coffee, while his eyes followed women strolling down Dizengoff Street. His curls turned mostly white, but he still seemed full of wiry, crackling, even aggressive energy. "After the arms deal got splashed all over the German papers in late '64, I became entangled in negotiations."

"That was your main job, the arms deal?" I asked. I disliked him immediately. He must have chosen the busiest nightlife street in Tel Aviv. We sat outside, surrounded by a din of hundreds of loud pedestrians, a dozen restaurants on the short block, and the noise of endless scooters.

"One of my main jobs," he corrected me with a half-smile. "I went there in 1957, just after Shimon Peres and Josef Strauss—they were the respective defense ministers then—met. It took three years to get it going, until Ben-Gurion convinced the Germans to loan us the money to buy weapons from them. We got the NATO surplus: aircraft, tanks, artillery, antitank missiles, boats, French helicopters, British submarines. The Germans even trained our pilots and officers. Had to keep it quiet; many people in Israel didn't want anything to do with Germany. They just didn't understand how desperately we needed to re-arm—and we had little of our own defense industry then. After the story broke, West Germany announced that it would terminate the arrangement. Especially since we had no diplomatic relations. We were in a panic. Thankfully, the Arabs came to our aid."

"The Arabs?"

"Unwittingly, of course. Nasser thought to punish West Germany and invited East Germany's Ulbricht to Egypt. West Germans figured they had nothing to lose and offered to establish diplomatic relations with Israel. So, it worked out well for us. But it was touch-and-go for a while."

Shimon said something in Hebrew to a young woman passing by our table. They chatted for a minute, the woman wrote down something on a piece of paper that Shimon pocketed. I dug my nails into my arm to keep myself from screaming at him.

"I love this city," he said. "So, yes, 1965 was a busy year. I think the last thing I did for David was contacting that German diplomat, von Eckner, about two women that disappeared after the war. Von Eckner tried with the Russians; they just blew him off. David left me a message at some point, but I didn't immediately get back to him. And then I received a call from—erhhh, what was her name?"

"Erika Jager?" Avi offered.

"Right, Erika. She was looking for him. First, we thought he went back to moshav, but they didn't know where he was either. Erika reported it to the police, but they came up empty-handed. He disappeared without a trace."

"Have you heard anything about him since? Anything at all?"

Shimon thought for a long moment.

"Not directly, no. A few years ago I spent a day with his friend Maurice. David's name came up. Maurice and I went to Koenigstein to see Bruno Beger. It's kind of off-topic, but also kind of not. Beger was tried for preparing people for the skeletons collection, got away with a probation. Maurice wanted to see one of the men that murdered his wife. I was curious in a psychological sense: here was a philosopher, a friend of Dalai Lama, who had no problems killing people for an anthropological 'collection.' We pretended that it was about Beger's Tibetan expedition in the 1930s. He still believed in his old racial theories, showed no regrets. Baffled why he was even tried in court. Fascinating. To be honest, until you called, that must have been the last time I thought about David. I just imagined myself in his shoes, so to speak. He survived against all odds, seemingly to bear a witness— but nobody wanted to hear. And then he came to West Germany, and it's permeated by former Nazis. That's how it was."

Shimon's eyes strayed back to the street, and I realized that we were losing his attention. An old disappearance did not interest him much. I just couldn't take it anymore.

"Look, Mr. Bezor, we came a long way to talk to you about my father. The man that, as far as I'm concerned, you used and betrayed. So at least have the fucking decency to look at me as we speak!"

Shimon's whole body swung in my direction, a flash of anger in his narrowed eyes, hands rolled into fists. The café's noise quieted down. I felt many pairs of eyes burning into my back.

"How dare you …"

Shimon stopped, looked down, took a deep breath. His face muscles relaxed, fists unclenched. When he raised his eyes, they were no longer angry.

"You're right, Iris. I apologize. I've grown cynical in my old age. You deserve better. Your father deserved better. I wasn't there for him. After his disappearance, Erika told me that he was just not himself that summer. Whatever 'being himself' meant in David's case. Please understand that I'm not saying it in a judgmental way. I don't dare to judge. Adaptations to the pathological existence in places like Auschwitz had life-long consequences. In order to physically and mentally survive, people had to dissociate, create a different meaning of that reality. You adapt to a normal life afterwards, but the guilt, the numbing, the rage—they lie dormant, waiting. I know, I'm speaking as a psychiatrist. I figured that your father had internalized the damage, pushed it inside. He wore a mask, so to speak. And just as he began to develop a relationship, let someone—your mother—get close to him, that other man stripped off David's mask and took it all away. The stored anger erupted. I think he first channeled it into seeking justice in the trials, but that was not enough, he wanted more. Erika also told me that during the Frankfurt trial he went with her to Auschwitz, and that's what triggered a further change. Which is not entirely surprising."

"Have you dealt with many cases?" Avi asked.

"Which cases?"

"I mean survivors. You see, my grandfather survived the Armenian genocide …"

Shimon nodded.

"When I returned to private practice, I saw a number of people that came out of the Nazi camps. There were even two former *Sonderkommandos*. Turns out dozens of them made it out. All our moral preconceptions are based on a certain reality, where hope and dignity exist and are celebrated. Auschwitz was entirely different. We don't have the language to speak of it. The words have a different meaning in our world. We are not qualified to use them."

"What do you mean?"

"What do I mean?" Shimon covered his eyes with his hand, slowly moved it down. He no longer paid attention to strolling beauties.

"Judith Newman, a survivor, wrote an account of a child being born in their block. A girl, a clerk from the Political Department—could have been Hannah—took the child away and drowned him. Newman wanted to scream "Murderess!" but the clerk turned to her and said: 'This way we can save the mother; otherwise both would have gone to the gas chamber.' So, you tell me how to judge that clerk girl. Can one speak of morality in this case? Moral behavior was fatal there."

"But why did the people here"—Avi made a semi-circular arm gesture—"why did they dislike the survivors?"

"I'd say it was guilt and embarrassment," Shimon replied. "Guilt, because we didn't do enough to save them. Embarrassment, because we instinctively wanted to separate ourselves from the 'weak Jews' who died without a fight. We were supposed to be like the heroes of the Bible, different from the shameful diaspora. Until Eichmann's trial, we refused to listen."

"Mr. Bezor ..." I started.

"Shimon, please."

"OK, Shimon. My parents met because of the search for the SS officer that saved my uncle, Yosef Milman. I understand that Father did it to impress my mother—but why did he continue after they broke up?"

"Redemption, I think. He didn't see anything redeemable in the fires of the Holocaust, but probably still believed—wanted to believe—in a personal redemption. It was not just the fact of it happening, he wanted to understand why, what made the SS officer do that. It's so easy to get lost in the body count statistics, that we forget that behind the numbers there are individual people. I was surprised that the story checked out. I thought it was just an illusion on your uncle's part. Not an intentional lie, but a traumatic event combined with an imagination of a teenage boy. But it turned out to be true."

I clenched my teeth, anger flaring up again.

"So, you thought it was an illusion, but you still went through with the whole Ludwigsburg trip to get leads on the German rocket scientists. Was my father just a statistic to you, to be used to get what you needed?"

Shimon sighed.

"No, he was not a statistic. Yes, we used him. It was not easy to find people in Germany, especially if they didn't want to be found. We had German scientists helping the Egyptians. And that was not only the question of the missiles, the Egyptians had access to specialists in biological warfare, in dirty nuclear bombs. At least that's what we believed at the time, and we were desperate to stop it. The Ludwigsburg office had an extensive file system on the Nazi party members, not only the worst of the SS. Between David's work trip to Ludwigsburg and Milman's open-ended search, Benny saw the opportunity."

"We'd like to talk to Benny, but nobody knows how to reach him."

"Benny retired to a small kibbutz and does not accept visitors."

"Can you help?" Avi asked.

Shimon thought about it, chewed his lower lip.

"OK, I'll talk to him."

"Dr. Bezor … Shimon … what do you think happened to my father?"

"You are asking me to speculate … I think you should re-phrase it from 'what happened to David' to 'what David caused to happen' or something along these lines."

"Why do you keep saying 'David' and not refer to him as my father?"

Shimon shrugged. "I'm sorry, Iris. A few days ago, you called and told me you wanted to speak about 'David Levy, my father'. But I only knew him as David. Many things happened to him … to your father … and—I believe—he wanted to actively make something happen instead."

"I'm not sure I follow."

"How do I explain?" Shimon shook his head. "It's not only about survivors and not only about Auschwitz. Hiroshima, killing plains of Anatolia, Treblinka, Stalin's Gulag: they are like childhood traumas that we humans try to suppress. Auschwitz is a symbol, a singularity of

311

concentrated evil. A Rorschach test for mankind, if you will: people find their reflections in it. You can see in these places the need for God, or the proof that God is dead. You can see the imperative for questioning, or the imperative for a certain absolute truth. You can blame technology, or you can blame people. We marvel at human progress and technological miracles, but deep in our psyche we know how quickly and brutally others can turn it against us. It does not matter who you are, because there are always 'others,' someone who is not like you, someone you can blame or be blamed by. We can never fully grasp the horror, so we suppress these traumas as a defense mechanism. But the very act of suppression leads to repetition."

"Don't you think these were aberrations, horrible episodes of insanity?" Avi stared at Shimon, eyebrows raised. *What an idiot*, I thought. As if he hadn't read my father's notebooks.

"Avi, I was in the Frankfurt courtroom, watching the accused. I am a psychiatrist, and I can assure you that these people were not insane. They revealed the possibilities in human nature that we thought we left behind. Education, progress, learning, law—all turned out to be not only not barriers but enablers, the instruments of aggression. Response to a genocide—and genocides themselves—have always been driven by politics and power, not morality. The answers seemed more obvious when I was young, but now I know there are no easy answers. If we want to change the future, it's not enough to remember these episodes as historical facts. We must internalize them, feel them in our very souls. Otherwise, 'never again' is just a statement without any meaning."

I grew impatient with their exchange.

"What does this have to do with my father?"

"As I said, I've counseled many camp survivors, the people that lived through a terrible, degrading experience, where they had no control over anything, including their own life and death. Many of them became fatalistic, no longer believing in the 'fairness hypothesis' of life and just accepting it. But some went in the opposite direction: while still believing that life is not fair, they aggressively tried to change it, to regain control. Even if it was only a choice of how to die. They spanned a gamut, from criminals to successful—often ruthless—business executives to avengers. I think your father was a bit of a lifeless fatalist when we met, but he changed in the time I knew him. Could have been the love for your mother, or the search for the SS officer, or something else. I remember he took interest in Eichmann. Trying to understand what made the man tick: was he a bureaucrat, an anti-Semite, a sociopath?"

"And what do you think—who was Eichmann? Was my father right in thinking that Eichmann was like a malevolent machine?"

Shimon rubbed his face, his expression that of a man being asked an impossible question.

"Trials are not a good place to study someone's personality. In Nuremberg, some psychiatrists concluded that most of the Nazi leaders were depressed psychopaths. Maybe, maybe not. As a group they had very high IQ's—so intelligence is not a barrier to monstrosity. Hausner, the prosecutor in Jerusalem, thought Eichmann to be an incomparable monster, a Nazi-produced personality type. Yet genocide is not unique to the Nazis. Arendt, the philosopher, found him to be an unthinking bureaucrat, a buffoon if you will. To me, both views seem to be dangerous oversimplifications. Eichmann was not stupid or ordinary. The real enemy is not some unique Nazi makeup. It's the ideology of hating 'the other' combined with obedience to authority and groupthink. Propaganda can appeal directly to the psychological defense mechanisms of our psyche and turn the world upside down, where murder of defenseless people becomes a cause for celebration. Perhaps that's why human progress resulted in more rather than less bloodshed: powerful states have much greater ability to shape the narrative and force compliance. We need independent thinking, the courage to go against the prevailing current, to resist the urge to feel righteous through aggression."

Shimon paused, the emotional monologue visibly tired him out. He took a deep breath, continued in a subdued tone.

"As for your father, he wanted to figure out how to stop future Eichmanns. My guess is, he turned to revenge. It's dangerous to come so close to what Joseph Conrad called "the heart of darkness." The rage and despair might just consume you. David was neither the first, nor the last in that. You should be careful too. People resent being reminded of what they are capable of."

They don't want to be reminded? Well, we'll see about that, I thought.

313

3

Shimon kept his word. He arranged for Avi and me to meet Benny Hadan, who now lived in a small kibbutz on the north shore of the Dead Sea.

We were met by a robust honey-skinned girl in a sleeveless low-cut sundress. When she figured out that we were looking for Benny Hadan rather than the nearby Qumran Caves, she took us to a stone bench in a small grassy shaded area under a juniper tree. The Dead Sea blazed ahead of us like a slab of blue and gold marble, locked in by barren tangerine and copper hills. We could see people floating and splashing in the water, but their sounds didn't carry over. Avi and I sat quietly. I savored the respite, breathing in air heavy with heat and history.

The honeyed girl returned with a pitcher of cold water and three glasses, followed by a tired old man in khaki trousers and a short-sleeved beige shirt with reading glasses sticking out of the breast pocket. He was thin, almost corpse-like, not looking like a weightlifter at all. Sizable nose and ears contrasted the gaunt face.

"Fighting cancer," Benny said. His breathing was noisy, and his speech had a wheezing quality to it. Laboring, he paused after each sentence. "And losing. It's eating me alive. I don't want people to see me like this. Shimon asked, I made an exception for you. So, you are Iris and Avi... Asking questions about David Levy. Why? It's been a very long time."

"I'm his daughter," I replied.

Benny looked at me with interest. "Shimon, that shyster, he didn't say anything about that. Just mentioned a surprise. With that German woman? What was her name?"

"Erika Jager. But no, I'm Yael Isenberg's daughter."

"Oh, I did not know." Benny seemed embarrassed.

314

"David did not know either."

"Sad. How strange," he sighed.

"Some new information came to light. Letters from my father to Avi's grandfather."

"Ah, yes." Benny turned to Avi. "You are Aram's grandson, that much Shimon had told me. David and Aram ... they both carried a burden of needing to do something to justify their improbable survival."

"Did you know my grandfather well?" Avi leaned in anxiously.

"I can't say so. I think I only met him twice. He seemed like a good man."

"Did you know who he really was?"

"Not until after his death."

"How did you find out? It was not publicized."

"From the West German police. We were interested in what happened. Understandably, they kept it quiet."

"What did happen in Bonn?"

"Sorry, not sure. It didn't seem like a robbery, but this was Armenian business, and we had plenty of our own at the time. They and us, it was a relationship of mutual benefit ... We helped them to catch and try a Turkish war criminal, and we got good information from that man, turned some people into double agents. We had common interests in Lebanon afterwards, but we kept it low."

Benny poured himself a glass of water, drank it noisily.

"What happened to my father?" I used the pause to jump in.

"He disappeared." Benny shrugged. "Sometimes people do that."

"You encouraged him to go to Germany when he came to you. Was it because of the rocket scientists?"

"More complicated than that. It was Hannah who brought him to me. I wanted to help. I loved Hannah." Benny paused again to take a deeper breath. "But when I found out that David was going to Ludwigsburg, I saw an opportunity. We were very concerned about the Egyptian weapons development. Appeals through diplomatic channels did not help. We decided to intimidate the scientists working for the Egyptians, sent a team to Germany. But we could not find some of the people that we really wanted."

"So, you used my father?"

315

"You can say that. I paid for it. Hannah never forgave me. She died of cancer two years ago. I'll follow her soon."

"And the Trabzon trip?"

Benny looked up.

"I'm trying to remember. Something happened on that trip to Ludwigsburg."

"They were attacked."

"Right, and the man that they were questioning was killed. Looked suspicious to me, and did not seem to be directly connected to the scientists ... Just in case, I sent a couple of people to Trabzon. I still recall a big blowback that resulted. I'd been told to stand down. So, I offered to help Yosef to go, and your dad wanted to join in. Much later, after we questioned that Turk, I realized why they wouldn't let me pursue it ..."

A sprinkler suddenly went off behind us, Avi jumped. Benny Hadan took a breather.

"One of the highly placed people, very close to the prime minister, paid out the Nazis, Becker and Wislisceny, to have his relatives secretly taken out of Hungary in 1944. That counterfeit British pounds bill was a giveaway, but I missed it. You see, the fake notes were a part of the Nazi's Operation Bernhard. They forged British pounds in the Sachsenhausen concentration camp, then used them—amongst other things—to pay their Turkish agents."

"Fine, the Nazis paid that Turk, Yavuz, in counterfeit bills, so what?"

"It was not the Nazis. There was an agent in Budapest, Jaac Van Harten. His real name was Jacob Levy, no relation to David. He was in Abwehr's employ and a wholesale distributor of the counterfeit currency. Some of which he used to pay off Becker and Wislisceny. I think it was a part of his payout that ended up with Yavuz."

"Why was that a problem?"

"Oh, but you must understand what kind of time it was. Right after Eichmann's trial, where people were screaming how the leadership saved their relatives and left the rest to die. And a few years before, we had Kasztner's trial. The government had fallen in 1957 over this very issue. We had plenty of unsavory characters of our own, but for that to come up would have brought down the government again. We just

316

couldn't afford it with the war brewing."

"What happened?"

"I briefed the prime minister. To avoid a scandal, the man was quietly pushed out after the 1965 election."

"Basically, you protected the collaborators?"

Benny got out a handkerchief, wiped the rivulets of sweat from his bald head, crumpled it between his bony fingers.

"It's always hot here … You know, I don't think there are many that got through the war without feeling some measure of guilt afterwards. Of surviving, of not helping … It's not fair to blame people for wanting to live, to save their family. We tend to judge in hindsight, knowing what happened. But they didn't know as they lived through it."

"Really? Are you saying that in the summer of 1944 people like Kasztner didn't know about Auschwitz?"

"Perhaps he did. I was not there. Once you start going down the rabbit hole … Do you think that having a few bad apples is enough to wipe out a whole people? Nah, it takes millions. The ones at the top offered everyone a piece of the action. Robbing and killing Armenians was a good business. Robbing and killing Jews was an even better business. The Nazis made sure that everyone had something to gain. They literally catalogued everything they took and distributed. Would you like a bigger flat and a new dresser? Sure, your Jewish—or Armenian—neighbors have just been deported. Are you a doctor wanting to expand your practice? No problem, the party just barred the Jews from the profession … And business is business: IBM, Ford, GM, they all had subsidiaries working for the Nazis. The tattoo on your father's arm was probably the number on the IBM Hollerith card in the Auschwitz Labor Assignment Office. As I said, it's a rabbit hole into hell that you should think carefully about going down into."

The honey-skinned girl appeared with another pitcher of water. She leaned over Avi as she placed it on the table, and Avi turned crimson. Benny smiled, but I didn't think it was funny.

"Why did you look for my father after Trabzon? You went to Eilat, you brought him with you to Beirut. You could have continued to investigate on your own."

"Was all that in these … erhhh … diaries?"

"Yes."

"Hmmm." Benny used the crumpled handkerchief again. "I'm sorry, it's been some years. It was a combination of things, I'd say. I felt bad about what that other man—what was his name?"

"Itzhak?"

"Right, what Itzhak did to him. I wanted to redeem myself with Hannah. And I truly believed that David could be of help to us. Especially his language skills. I encouraged him to go to Germany. This business … was it olives?"

"Oranges."

"Yes, oranges. It was a great cover. The Soviets armed the Egyptians to the teeth. The two most important things at the time were the weapons for the army and stopping the missile program. John Kennedy was our friend, the first US president to sell us arms back in '62. But after he was killed, we desperately needed the West German arms deal to continue. David really helped: he dug up information on a certain high-ranking German official. Incriminating information that made that official change his position on the arms deal, and it went on."

"Father mentioned in his letters some man called Anton that you set him up with in Spain, but he didn't put down the real name."

Benny laughed, although it was more of a cackle that turned into a fit of coughing.

"Oh, that was a good one. Did he say anything about a scar?"

"No."

"Good. David learned to protect sources. The man had a deep scar running from the left ear to the corner of his mouth. His name was Otto Skorzeny. Anton was his father's name."

"The Otto Skorzeny?" Avi exclaimed.

"Yes, the one and only. He died way back in the seventies, so now it can be told. After the war, he moved to Spain. In 1953, he went to Egypt as a military advisor and recruited a staff made up of former SS and Wehrmacht officers to train the Egyptian army. He had also trained Arab terrorists in commando tactics against us. When we found out about the Egyptian rocket program and his participation, we sent people to kill him. In exchange for his life, he agreed to work with us. He helped to eliminate some of the German rocket scientists."

"What a strange story," Avi said.

"Yes, indeed. I have quite a few strange stories."

"When was the last time you saw my father?" I asked.

"I think it was in 1964, in France ...." Benny paused, suddenly unsure. "Wait, David came to see me once after that."

"Was it in late August of 1965?"

"Yes, something like that. How did you know?"

"He was saying good-byes."

"Oh ... Sorry ... I did not realize that at the time."

"What did he say?"

"I'm sorry, I don't remember the exact words." Benny shrugged. "He wanted us to pursue other Nazis. There was one that he was particularly interested in—what was his name?"

"My father was looking for Erich Rolff."

"Yes, I recall David asking questions about Rolff. I don't know why that particular Nazi. Rolff operated in Chelmno, not Auschwitz."

"Rolff was in Italy later in the war, and he was responsible for sending to Auschwitz the family of my father's friend."

Benny nodded. "I see. We all had our personal reasons. You know, before the war there was a rumor that Rolff was assassinated in Spain."

"Which war?"

"The one in '67."

"Do you think it's true?" Avi wondered. "I saw Rolff's name in the notebooks and tried to check, but he just disappeared."

"I believe it's true. The people for whom the message was intended, they got it. A bunch of these rats got up and left for South America or Egypt."

"Why did you offer Hulda and Yavuz to my father?" I wanted to know.

Benny smiled. "In our business, you have to figure out what a person is willing to risk everything for. Some people work for money, some for the country, some for an idea. In your father's case, it was revenge. I watched him in Beirut, in the Nemesis room, and I knew that that's what he wanted."

"Didn't you want to get other Nazis, after Eichmann?"

"Of course, I did. But we just had other, more urgent things to do. After Eichmann, we shut down the Nazi hunting for some time. I couldn't directly help your father."

I closed my eyes and sucked in the hot, burning, salty air. "They exterminated us as if we were not human, and you had other things to do? At least Avi's grandfather did something!"

Avi placed a hand on my arm. I pulled it away. It became so quiet, we heard people splashing in the water.

Benny looked around helplessly, must have realized he wouldn't get any assistance, pulled reading glasses out of his pocket, put them on, spoke quietly and slowly. "Did Shimon tell you how we met?"

"No."

"We were both in the Jewish Brigade of the British Army. There were about five hundred of us. We fought our way into Germany through Italy. And when we got there ... we would go out at night, look for Germans that were Nazis. Or just Germans. It's not like they distinguished between Jews. All Jews had to be killed, so as far as we were concerned, any German was fair game. We gave them a mock trial, which is more than they gave us. Then we executed them."

Benny drank a glass of water, his eyes far away. "We planned to poison the German water supply. Six million of their lives for six million of ours. We didn't go through with it. Just couldn't do it in the end."

"Do you regret it?"

"About killing or not killing?" Benny chuckled joylessly. "No regrets about not going through with the poisoning. As for the ones we did kill ... mixed feelings. Back then, I just wanted to kill all of them. Wipe the Germans off the face of the earth, as they tried to do to us."

"Well, why didn't you?" I shouted.

"Back in 1947, just before the U.N. vote on whether we were to have a country, we'd been told by a certain high-level American: 'You can have your vengeance, or you can have a country, but you can't have both.' We needed the votes, we chose a country."

"I don't understand." Avi spread his arms helplessly. "Why one or the other?"

"Avi, do you know why your people didn't receive the legal justice or their own country that they were promised?"

"Well, the Bolsheviks took over what was left of the Armenian land," Avi said uncertainly.

"No," Benny cackled weakly. "It was about oil. The British and the Americans wanted the Mosul oil fields that were Turkish before the war. While most Americans condemned the genocide and wanted to punish the Turkish leaders, the State Department and the business honchos were much more concerned with the oil. The Turks agreed to hand over the oil fields, and all the promises to the inconvenient Armenians had been forgotten."

"Oil? They betrayed us over oil?"

"Yes. And they would have betrayed us too. Hitler remembered the Armenians, so did we: we knew that the Armenians were sold for oil, and that we were expendable. Moses had to find the one place in the Middle East where there is not a drop of oil. They would have done it to us, the British especially. We did not have the luxury of revenge. We had to play the few cards that we had."

"Like what?"

"It's a dirty game with dirty secrets. Some high-level American and British people could have been implicated in improper dealing with the Nazis. After all, business people had their interests to protect. So many participated in the plunder and murder. And with the Russians being the new enemy, scores of Nazi war criminals went to work for the CIA and the MI6. Embarrassing secrets are valuable for blackmail, as long as they remain secret. For thirteen years, we kept quiet. Until Eichmann. They rewrote the history of what was done to the Armenians. They would have rewritten ours, but we kidnapped Eichmann and put him on trial. Do you think that the CIA or the German BND didn't know where he was hiding? Pffttt... They just wanted it all to quietly go away."

Benny stopped, took a few painful, rattling breaths.

"Did you try to find out what happened to my father?"

"No. I wondered about David. But we were busy preparing for war. And my good friend Eli Cohen was hung in Damascus in 1965. It was a hard year."

"You know, Mr. Hadan," I said, "I think you all betrayed him. My father."

"I don't blame you for thinking that. You can point a finger at me for getting him involved." He shrugged helplessly. "Your father had been betrayed by many people before, during and after the war: the nations that closed their doors to desperate refugees; the British that let Hitler take Czechoslovakia and didn't want to allow Jews into Palestine; the Vatican that kept silent; the ones that didn't punish the criminals … It's a very long list. He didn't know the full extent of the betrayal. But I know he wanted a chance at revenge. And I'd like to think that I gave it to him."

"Mr. Levy was angry over the lack of justice," Avi interrupted. "Just like my grandfather was. And it burns me that so many of these people got away."

"Yes." Benny nodded. "David was in Auschwitz and nine out of ten of Auschwitz SS personnel escaped any prosecution. The Austrian jury acquitted Walter Dejaco, the SS officer that designed the Auschwitz gas chambers and ovens: they found that Dejaco did not bear a "remote" guilt for the deaths. Really? Or take Britain—they took in hundreds of Nazis. They just passed the War Crimes Bill this year. Forty-six years after the war and they finally did it, thanks to Mrs. Thatcher. Over objections from the House of the Lords. The Lords never liked us, we are not their country club crowd."

"But why? Why? I don't get it!" Avi's face contorted in puzzlement.

"Because so many were implicated and where do you draw the line? The Americans, the British —they all have their own elites, and elites help each other. Why do you think Nazis were able to run occupied France and other occupied countries with a few thousand people? There was no shortage of collaborators. People that were strong on connections, but weak on principles. On the balance sheet of money and power, things like empathy and morality don't carry much weight. Remember what I said about a rabbit hole? It's dark in there, and some important people don't want you to shine the light in. They know that regular people want justice to be done. The more truth comes out, the less shadow left to hide. There would have been no Nuremberg, if not for the videos of Nazi camps. Once people saw that, the top few dozen Nazis were doomed. But the other ones, those that ran the weapons factories on slave labor, wrote racist laws, laundered stolen gold, they went free. Short-term, *realpolitik*. Long-term, more bloodshed."

"Then what do you do?"

"For the most part, you can't put them on trial. You can embarrass them, as we did with Kurt Waldheim, the Austrian head of state that's a *persona non grata* in most countries. You can hit them in the pocket for what they stole. And you can expose them. People care about their legacy. I know, I'm standing at the edge of my grave, I care about mine. There is much about the war that's yet to come to light, even at this time. And it will, it will … The truth will come out. You just have to keep at it, shine the light into their shadows …"

Benny suddenly raised his right hand and curled it into a fist. "There are things I kind of understand. About protecting the scientists, the bankers, the captains of industry, building a 'bulwark against communism', all that. But hiring the ones that personally murdered, that I don't get. Dr. Friedrich Burchardt, commander of *Einsatzkommando* that killed tens of thousands, his elbows deep in blood. Employed by MI6, then by CIA. Lived openly, never tried, died peacefully. Why? What was so valuable about his service to overlook that he was a murderer? How did they shake hands with him? Did they wash after? Check for blood? No, I don't get it."

Benny's breathing became even more labored. "I apologize, I'm running out of steam here. Now you see why I don't want visitors. Don't like people looking at me like that."

"Like what?"

"With pity."

I got up to leave, but not before I got one more thing off my chest. "You never said that you feel sorry for what you did to my father. You dragged him into this business. I know he's dead."

"Oh, child." Benny slowly shook his head. "I'm sorry about so many things. I'm sorry about sending Eli Cohen to Damascus. There are many other friends that I sent onto dangerous missions and quite a few didn't return. I'd like to think that I did what I had to do. We were two million people surrounded by a hundred and twenty million Arabs that wanted to destroy us. As for David … if he decided to seek justice for his friend, that's the road he chose. I didn't push him into it, but I wouldn't blame him either. Justice was a precious commodity in those days. It still is."

4

I was nervous about meeting Erika Jager the next morning, so I went to the hotel bar. Avi, ever a gentleman, accompanied me. Again, I wished that Max was here. He wanted to come, but I was afraid he wouldn't get along with my relatives. He was not like them; mother pretty much hated him. I should have let him come.

"Are you doing OK? Not sorry that you came?" Avi asked.

"I'm OK. I just feel strange being here. I never even wanted to set a foot in Germany and now ... second time in a month. I know about Gerhardt, but every other elderly man I see, I wonder whether he was a guard in Auschwitz. And meeting that woman, Erika. It's been mostly about your grandfather so far, but this is the woman that my father lived with."

I wanted to say: 'the woman he left my mother for,' but now I knew that was not true.

"Not true, not true ..."

A twenty-year-old memory intruded. We were in the pool of the Aunt Becky's house. My cousin Ella and I raced two lengths of the pool and I won.

She looked at me angrily and said, "Uncle Jonathan is not your real father."

"That's not true!"

"Yes, it is. My mother said that your real father's got himself a Nazi girlfriend."

"Not true, not true! Why are you saying this?" I cried.

"It's true," my other cousin Nina confirmed. "You're a bastard. And your mother is a tramp and a gold digger."

The other kids laughed and started to chant: "Iris is a bastard, Iris is a bastard!"

I burst into tears and ran into the house. "Mommy, Ella and Nina said that I'm a bastard and you're a gold digger!"

There was a lot of screaming over the next few minutes between my mother, my father (I thought) Jonathan, his sister Becky, his mother, and more. If only Jonathan had the guts to tell them all to go to hell and slam the door in their faces! But he was always a peacemaker, under the foot of his queen mother. Ella and Nina haughtily apologized to me and I was told to forget the whole episode. How could I? Ella and Nina gleefully whispered, 'Bastard!' whenever adults were out of the earshot. My innocence over, I had learned to listen to adults' murmurs. By the time Mother confirmed that Jonathan was indeed not my biological father, I already knew it well.

Jonathan Goldfarb's family believed that he married a damaged woman beneath himself. He tried to keep peace instead of confronting them. And my mother quietly accepted it. Later, much later, I understood that she didn't have much choice: without her husband's support, she couldn't stand up to her domineering mother- and sister-in-law. And I forgave Jonathan: he was what he was; although he didn't have the strength to become my real father, he was kind and generous to my mother. And to me—after he died, I found out that he left me a trust fund. A small one, yet enough to give me the freedom to do what I wanted. Or, at least, not to do what I hated: I cut down my expenses and quit the law firm. But at the time, I lay in bed fantasizing of my real father coming to reclaim me. Under my pillow, I kept the picture that my mother shared with me: she and my father, David Levy, in the spring of 1962. Both so young and beautiful and happy. Even in that old black-and-white photo one could clearly see that I looked like him.

"You know, Iris, whatever happened here in '65, your father, my grandfather, it's all intertwined. And then it cascaded to your mother and my father and my uncle and my brother. And now, you and me."

"I wish he came looking for me." I twirled the olive pick in my martini. I knew it was not fair.

"He didn't know you existed."

"I know, I know. It's not logical, but I wish he sensed my presence. I never felt quite right. I thought if I had my real father … I realize it makes no sense. Still, I want to understand who he was. Maybe I'll understand myself better."

"Iris, I practically ran away from my dad once I graduated from high school. I blamed him for my brother's death. We just expect so much from parents. Three years ago, Mom called me about Dad being in a hospital. I was having all these problems with Amy and did not leave the same day. By the time I got there ... it was too late."

"Oh shit, I'm sorry, Avi. I now have this tiny hope that perhaps my father is alive, and I'll get to see him." I ate the olive. "Who's Amy?"

"My ex-girlfriend."

"Ex?"

"Very much so." I heard a sense of loss in his voice.

"Good. You like Rivka?"

"Yeah."

"She just might like you a little bit."

Rivka did, she told me. The two of them were like two nervous creatures, cautiously circling each other. Both burned by the fire of the previous love.

I knew that my mother loved me more than anything. I knew she was terrified of what these notebooks brought out, scared that I would blame her. Yes, I did blame her. But I'd have to forgive her. She was a young girl caught in difficult circumstances, unable to withstand the pressure from others. This trip, this search for my father was not about her—it was all about me, about the blood and passion that flowed through my veins.

5

"Erika, don't you think you need a bigger place?" Gerhardt asked with a smile. The four of us were sitting around a small table, sipping coffee from tiny cups. The room had a large dining table, but it was piled up a foot high with layers of books and papers. More books were on the shelves, and even in carefully arranged stacks on the floor.

"No, I like it here." Erika laughed. I noticed her looking at me nervously. When we walked in and I extended my hand in a greeting, she took it carefully, studied my face, then stood up on her toes, hugged me and whispered, "You do look like him." She still fit my father's description from years ago: slender, short wavy hair, pronounced cheekbones, narrow nose. But the hair was more white than blond now, the skin not as silky or smooth, deep crow's feet around large blue eyes. Reading glasses hang on a chain off her neck. "If you think this room is cluttered, you haven't seen my bedroom. But I've grown attached to the place over thirty years. Most of the neighbors know me, my daughter grew up here. And I travel a lot anyway. I'm glad to be back in Frankfurt. I'm sorry I had to stay in Cambodia longer than I planned."

"What did you find there?"

"Sadly, a desperate situation even twelve years after the fall of Khmer Rouge. My daughter, Ingrid, is a doctor, and they are trying to install just basic medical facilities that Khmer Rouge destroyed. It's shameful that some of the Western governments continue to support the Khmer Rouge, even after they exterminated two million people."

"Why?"

"Oh, the same old 'lesser evil' thinking. The US and China are more afraid of the Vietnamese communists than of Pol Pot's band of murderers. So they just stood by. The Holocaust, the Armenian

Genocide, the killing fields of Cambodia—they spring from the same source of evil."

Erika got up, rummaged in the papers on the dining table, came back with two large photos of an elderly Asian man that she offered to us. "He doesn't look unusual in any way, does he? That's Comrade Sary, the former head of the largest Khmer Rouge prison. Responsible for the torture and murder of tens of thousands."

"You're still trying to understand what makes people like him tick?" Gerhardt asked quietly.

"Yes. Twenty years ago, I interviewed a commandant of one of the Nazi extermination camps. On the surface, two completely different people, but it's amazing how similar their characters and their self-justifications were: I was not involved, not in the operational sense of actual killings; I only cared about the place running well; I had no alternative, my career would have been ruined. And the kicker: 'My conscience is clear about what I did myself.' This is the worst thing about it—they were proud of themselves over a job well done. The nature of the job didn't matter."

"The banality of evil?"

"Yes, but it's more complicated than that. It's like a pyramid. At the top is a leader with a recipe for improving the world—as soon as we get rid of some enemies. In the middle, the ideological warriors, like Comrade Sary and Adolf Eichmann. And at the bottom layer, there are multitudes of those that follow orders. These are the people that torture and shoot and pour Zyklon-B. It's the chasm between what they did and the banality of their motivations that blows the mind: desire to conform, make a profit, gain a promotion."

"Yours is a depressing job," Avi said.

"Not necessarily. I interviewed many of those that David would have called 'righteous.' You know"—Erika fingered her glasses—"there is something I observed. They tended to be the irresponsible ones. Those that refused to participate in persecuting their neighbors, profit from plunder, take advantage of the opportunities. Many of them came across as doubters, skeptics, even cynics … not always pleasant, not feeling the need to belong, but making up their own mind ..."

"Ms. Jager, the letters and notebooks we have are only half of the correspondence," I interrupted. I knew I was being rude, but I'd waited for weeks to ask this. "Have you ever seen any letters from

Avi's grandfather to my father?"

"I'm sorry, Iris. I'm blabbering on and on," Erika apologized. "No, I'm afraid not. David was a very private person. Have you checked in Israel?"

"We did. There was nothing in the moshav, and the place where he stayed in Tel Aviv is no longer there. Did my father talk about his plans before he disappeared?"

"David was shaken up by the death of a friend. Now I know who the friend was. And David was angry over the verdicts in the Auschwitz trial. The majority of the accused were either released or received relatively short terms. Herbert Scherpe killed thousands of children with phenol injections and walked out a free man. I think it was the Stark's decision that drove David to the edge. I remember David saying: 'Time after time, the man poured Zyklon B into gas chambers. He enjoyed taking women aside, torturing and killing them—and they gave him ten years. He'll be out in five'."

"Was Stark out in five years?" Avi asked.

"Stark was out in three. David went to Israel right after that, returned, then left again. I was used to his absences. He needed time alone. In September, when I hadn't heard from him in two weeks, I began to worry. Called people in Israel, went to the police. But David disappeared without a trace."

"I think of all the people, you knew him the best. My mom, she'd been with him for less than a year. What was he like?"

"He kept a lot inside, he bottled it all up. It's like there were multiple David's. There was a bitter one, and there was one overcome with fury, and at times he was gentle and loving. I believe that the last one was the real David, but he'd been too broken to allow himself to be this way. He loved your mother; she was the one true love of his life. As hard as I tried, I couldn't take her place. My being German was too much of a barrier to overcome. I really wanted him to be happy." Erika stared at her hands.

"I'm sorry." I tried to hate her, but I couldn't. She didn't steal my father. She couldn't have known that my mother wanted to reconcile.

"Don't be. It's to be expected, after all that was done to him."

"My mother loved him too. Do you think their breakup was the last straw for him?"

"Oh, he had more last straws than the population of a small

village." Erika shook her head. "He blocked a lot of what happened. I think he was hiding his time in *Sonderkommando* even from himself. He interviewed others, he wrote about it—but he blocked the personal experience. I dragged him right back into it with the Auschwitz trial."

"It was Itzhak who forced it, not you!" I said.

"I don't know. Here." Erika got up and brought us some papers. "This is from his preparation for the trial. I kept them in my files. We had him read the Broad report, confirm it, describe his experience. That's what I eventually understood in my years of being a journalist: you can write down the words, but there are things where the language is utterly helpless. People that saw it, they can never un-see and they can never describe. It's just not possible. I'll give you a few minutes."

Interview with David Levy (DL), Thursday, 15 November 1962, Frankfurt am Main. Conducted by Karl Sassen (KS).

KS: Mr. Levy, have you reviewed the Pery Broad report about gassing operations in Auschwitz?
DL: Yes. It is essentially correct.
KS: Can you tell us about your experience?
DL: I was assigned to *Sonderkommando* in October of 1943, one year after we arrived in Auschwitz.
KS: We?
DL: My parents, my sister Leah and I. We were lined up and made to walk past some officers. One of them was pointing left or right. I was sent to the right, my parents to the left. The officer sent Leah to the right, but she held on to our mother and the officer said, "Fine, go with her." He was very friendly. Someone asked where they were going, and he said, "To the showers, you'll meet soon." Leah waved back at me and they walked away.
KS: What did you do in *Sonderkommando*?
DL: First, I was loading corpses into the ovens. Then, I was also assigned to clean the gas chambers.
KS: Were people killed with gas only?
DL: No, when there was a small convoy, a hundred people or so, the SS killed them with bullets in the nape of the neck. But most people were

killed with gas. I worked first in Crematorium 3, later in Crematorium 5.

KS: Can you tell us how Crematorium 3 was laid out?

DL: [makes a drawing on a piece of paper] Here. People would come down these stairs into the changing room where they would undress and hang their clothes. And then they would go into the showers. Except that these were gas chambers with hermetically sealed doors.

KS: And how was the poison gas injected?

DL: There were openings in the roof through which gas mask-wearing SS officers would throw in Zyklon B pellets.

KS: Who would throw in the poison?

DL: I saw Stark and Teuer carrying the canisters, others too. There were always quite a few SS present: Grabner, Voss, Boger, Kaduk, Gorges, Hössler, Shlage, many of them.

KS: What would happen then?

DL: The SS would start up engines of the trucks that they parked nearby to drown the screams. But we could hear it all. The guards laughed: "The water in the showers must be really hot!" This would last a few minutes, then all noises subsided and a doctor overseeing the gassing would motion to start the fans. Once the gas dissipated, we opened the door and corpses tumbled out.

KS: Tumbled out?

DL: Yes. Zyklon B gas would start on the bottom and rise up. People inside would rush away, try to get to the door, the only way out. Because of that, the door was always blocked by a pile of dead bodies that we had to pull apart. Bodies were covered with blood and excrement. Pregnant women would partially eject their fetuses. We would rinse the bodies, load them onto lifts and take them up to the incineration room. Then wash and scrub the room clean, making it ready for the next convoy.

KS: Did people resist going into gas chambers?

DL: Very rarely. Every little detail was designed to fool people into thinking they were safe. The SS would give them a friendly speech

331

promising food and water and assignment to work detail after disinfection. They were given towels and soap. There were signs "To the showers", "Lice will kill you," "Cleanliness required." The SS would tell them to memorize the hook number, so they could retrieve their things. They took pride in their role-playing. Once Hössler pretended to be a representative of the Foreign Ministry, in order to deceive the Jews that thought they bought a passage to Paraguay. Only a few times people would suspect that something was wrong.

KS: And what happened in these cases?

DL: If the SS could not talk people into going peacefully, they would use brute force. Once I saw them simply machine gun everybody. But they preferred not to do that. They wanted to squeeze every utility out of these people. Clothes and luggage were collected. After the gassing, gold teeth were pulled from corpses' mouths and thrown into acid to clean off any flesh and bone. I've heard five to ten kilos of gold was "mined" daily and sent to Reichsbank. Women's hair was cut off, dried out and shipped to Germany. Nothing would be allowed to go to waste.

KS: What was the capacity of the operation?

DL: In Crematorium 3 they could kill over a thousand people at a time. And then there were Crematoriums 2, 4 and 5. But the real difficulty was not in gassing but in getting rid of the corpses. There were fifteen ovens in Crematorium 3. Specialists from the Topf crematorium company came in 1943 and experimented how best to burn corpses.

KS: What do you mean?

DL: You know, the fastest incineration with the least amount of fuel. We divided the bodies into four groups: well-nourished adults, skinny adults, adults, children and *Mussulmen*. That was the name of the prisoners that starved in Auschwitz, they were skin and bones. The Topf company specialists decided that the optimum temperature was 1470 degrees Fahrenheit and that it's best to combine a well-nourished

adult with a child and a *Mussulman*. They
improved the design, making it easier to load
the corpses. It was all very scientific. They
calculated we could burn three bodies in an
oven in about twenty minutes.

KS: So with fifteen ovens?

DL: We were capable of cremating three thousand a
day. And there were three other crematoriums,
with thirty-one ovens. We were a factory
designed to eliminate nine thousand people
daily. But that was not enough.

KS: Not enough?

DL: In May of 1944 *Hauptscharführer* Möll took over
the process. He was a real extermination
expert. You see, Auschwitz was preparing to
exterminate the Hungarian Jews. They were
expecting over a hundred thousand to arrive
weekly. He had us dig five pits, each about 150
feet long, 25-30 feet wide, and seven feet
deep. And in the middle of each pit he made us
dig a foot-wide sloping channel to collect
human fat from burning bodies and use it as a
fuel. We would load twelve hundred corpses into
each pit in three layers and burn them. Möll so
enjoyed the scene, he would drag naked young
women from the changing room to see it and
revel in their terror. Then he would put a
bullet in the back of their head.

KS: How long did these operations continue?

DL: Until October of 1944, when *Sonderkommandos*
staged a rebellion. I did not take part. As the
Red Army came closer, Nazis evacuated the camp
and led all the prisoners on a forced march. I
survived and ended up at Bergen-Belsen in
Germany.

David Levy was unable to continue the interview.

"David blacked out," Erika said after we put down the type-written
pages. "He was there, and he was not there. That was the first time I
saw him black out."

"Did he do it often?"

"No, not often. It happened at my grandparents, it happened in court a couple of times. It was scary, but he would come out of it."

"And after the interview?" I didn't recognize my own voice, it came out so hoarse.

"I took him home. He said in his writings that that was the first time we had sex. It's true, but he does not tell it how it happened. Iris, I'm sorry to be explicit; I know we are talking about your father. I hugged and kissed him. He threw me down, face down, and took me in anger, in such anger. I cried afterwards. I kept saying 'I am sorry, I am sorry, it was not my fault.' When he came out of his blackout, he apologized. He was protecting me in the notebooks."

Erika swallowed hard, closed her eyes but continued. "He tried to hide the pain, but it came out in his sleep. The dreams he had ... they were usually about fire. He called out Möll, Yael, Ezra, Leah, Father. In the beginning, I would get up and leave the bed, but then he would wake up. I had learned to stay and to let him hold my hand. I thought he was getting better. In the sense of being able to—for lack of a better word—control the anger and the pain. Now, from the notebooks, I realize that he was channeling them in a different direction. I knew that he became obsessed with trying to understand."

"What do you mean?"

"Understand who these people were. He would go to court and watch the defendants, trying to get inside their minds. And he was obsessing on Eichmann, especially after Arendt's book."

Gerhardt broke his silence. "He became despondent over what he saw as the lack of justice in that courtroom."

"Yes," Erika agreed. "He was looking for something to help stop this from repeating. I wish he were alive to see Germany now. It took us a whole generation, but I think we are getting there. The Nazis are despised, dark and shameful chapters are being aired out. We have more to do, of course. Much more ..."

"And the Auschwitz trial?"

"I didn't agree with the verdicts, but at least the trial brought it out into the open."

"What 'it'?"

"What happened. My late brother, Fritz, was right. We got through to the people here in Germany. It took a long time, but we did. The trial was the first blow to shatter the wall of silence. The next blow came fifteen years later, when the Holocaust TV series shocked the country."

She got up, went to the table, picked up what looked like a thin notebook. "I've had this since 1965, but it properly belongs to you, Iris."

"What is this?"

"A notebook I found amongst his things. I'm afraid I hid it from the police. It was too personal. I think it's the last part of his diary. I didn't quite understand it until now. It'll tell you more about your father. I'm sorry I didn't offer it to you immediately. It's a difficult read. But you seem to be strong enough."

PART 8:
DAVID

1

The train was taking me to Bremerhaven, where a car would pick me up. I avoided looking out the window, until we crossed into Lower Saxony. I grew up in a small town in Westphalia—now a much larger North Rhine-Westphalia courtesy of the British occupation—and didn't want to engage in memories. I had to keep my head clear for a meeting with Kurt Becker.

On my lap there was Erika's file with handwritten notes on Herr Becker, but I knew them by heart. Kurt Becker, member of the SS since 1932. During the war, served as an SS Major in Poland and Russia, as part of the *SS-Deathhead* organization. Commissar of all concentration camps, and Chief of the Economic Department of the SS Command in Hungary. The Nazis were masters of bureaucratic language—the "Economic Department" was created largely to extract maximal economic value from the Jews. This included not only confiscating goods and property, but also using clothing, shorn hair, and gold extracted from teeth of the people that no longer needed them. In 1944, he arrived in Hungary with Adolf Eichmann and extorted much wealth from Hungary's doomed Jews. He was arrested in 1945, but not prosecuted because of a statement provided on his behalf by Kasztner. The Israeli court later found that Kasztner perjured himself to save a war criminal. Kurt Becker was a free man in 1948. He went to Hamburg, seemingly penniless, but before the end of that year he suddenly gained access to a substantial sum of money and quietly became one of the wealthiest men in West Germany. His name hit the papers in 1961 when he served as a witness during the Eichmann trial. He provided his testimony from his home in Germany, because he was—wisely—unwilling to travel to Israel. Last year, he testified at the trial of another SS cavalry officer, where he claimed, rather fantastically, that he now heard for the first time about the massacres of Jews in Ukraine and Russia. I must admit that I was quite curious to speak with him, not only for information, but also out of a genuine wish to understand these people.

I opened the window after we passed Bremen. Cool air felt like a pleasant change from the hot Mediterranean winds. I was now in a different state: Free Hanseatic City of Bremen which was basically two cities, Bremen and Bremerhaven. They had a love-hate relationship because the city of Bremen owned the "overseas port" within Bremerhaven but Bremerhaven was responsible for its administration. Complicated politics of German cities.

There was a shiny new Mercedes Benz 600 waiting for me at the station. The chauffer seemed surprised that I had no luggage, but I didn't plan to stay with Mr. Becker. The residence was about half an hour drive northeast of the town, on the eastern shore of Flogelner Lake. The automated gate opened, and we drove past solid stone gateposts along a tree-lined paved road before arriving at a wide courtyard blocked on three sides by a building with two wings. From the outside, the house could have easily accommodated all four hundred-plus inhabitants of Kfar Tahpooz moshav. Halfway up the steps to the front door, a man awaited us. He appeared to be about sixty and yet I had no doubt that, despite my age advantage, he could easily break me in half with his bare hands. I wondered what he did during the war.

"Mr. Becker," I started.

"Oh, no, my name is Helmut. I work for Mr. Becker," he politely corrected me. "I apologize, but I must pat you down."

It was a choice between letting some Nazi manhandle me or going back to Frankfurt empty-handed. Since I just traveled seven hours into the middle of nowhere, I decided not to argue. To Helmut's credit, the search was quick and masterful. Afterwards, he led me through the front door, down a hallway and into what would have been a library except it had no books.

"Mr. Becker, Mr. Levy is here," Helmut announced.

I knew from the notes that Becker was pushing fifty-five, but the handsome, slightly built man in front of me looked ten years younger. If I passed him on the street and someone told me that twenty years ago this man was appointed a Special Reich Commissioner for all the

Lagers, I would have laughed. Then he spoke, and his smooth voice told me why he was so successful at climbing the Nazi's hierarchy. Come to think of it, save for the total lack of conscience, the SS corporate ladder was no different from that of "normal" bureaucracies. I had to admit at that moment that Ms. Arendt had a very valid point.

"Mr. Levy, I apologize for the little security precaution. I'm afraid I've been getting too much attention lately and with you being ... I trust Helmut was not too rough."

"Not at all, he was entirely professional," I ensured Becker. "He must have had a lot of experience."

"Yes, during the war he was a bodyguard for ..." Becker caught himself, smiled, pointed to a small table with an assortment of bottles. "Well, it's not important. What would you like to drink: whisky, scotch, schnapps, vodka, wine?"

"Whisky, please."

"I will take scotch." Becker poured two glasses. After we situated ourselves in two deep chairs around the drinks table, he said, "It was a long trip for you. Would you care to stay over?"

"No, thank you. I must be in Frankfurt tomorrow morning," I lied.

"Well, in such case we better get started." He looked at me expectantly.

"I'm curious: why have you agreed to see me?"

"That's an interesting gambit." Becker showed his very white teeth. "If you must know, it's because you mentioned someone I knew in the past. Ekrem Celik. It just so happens that not long ago I received a message from him. Someone I had not heard from or about for a long time. Then he runs off into Spain, into a highly fortified compound, just to disappear for good. This worries me. And that's why I agreed to meet you."

"You seem to be well-informed, but I'm not sure I follow."

"Ah, Mr. Levy." Becker's smooth voice was full of reproach. "I know who you are. You are working for Mossad."

He paused and looked at me; I just sipped my whiskey.

"Look." Becker appeared slightly flustered, his master-of-the-universe smile not so confident. "I want to be open with you people. All these German courts, they are a joke. My lawyers eat them for lunch. The Americans, the British, whatever, they don't give a damn anymore. But you, you are different. Adenauer's been trying to buy you off, but there are always some that just want blood, whether it's pragmatic or not. Like with Wilhelm Stuckart. You people just off'd him even though he was no danger to you."

"He was at the Wannsee conference," I offered. I had no idea whether Benny—or someone else—had actually killed Stuckart, but I was willing to play along.

"And Celik?"

"His real name was Ahmet Yavuz. In 1915, he commanded a Hamidiye regiment that killed tens of thousands of Armenians."

"Oh, the Armenians." Becker fell back, his body relaxed. "But why did you bring up his name?"

"Because he brought up yours." I enjoyed watching Becker's eyes grow scared again.

"Why?"

"Yavuz told us that you have some information that we want."

Becker stared at me appraisingly. I thought I could read his thoughts: *if this is an Armenian-Turkish thing, how come he is involved? But do I want to risk telling him to go to hell? He's Mossad for sure and they don't care about the legalities. I'll be looking over my shoulder every day.*

He exhaled, made a decision. "What information?"

"You were friends with the Klopher family, right?"

"Let's just say I knew them." A smile spread over Becker's face. Relief of *they are after the Klophers, not me.* But there was something else. "Are you interested in Otto or Peter?"

"Both. And their sons."

"I met them around 1934, I think. I was buying horses for the SS. We needed a loan from the Deutsche Bank, and that's where Otto was. We hit it off and Otto invited me to a family event. I think he was looking to marry off his daughter. They were wealthy then, but not old money. Peter made his fortune by running guns for the Kurds in the war."

"What do you mean?"

"He was stationed in Turkey in the first World War. The Kurds loved our Luger pistols. Peter shipped them through the diplomatic post and traded for gold and diamonds that Kurds robbed from the Armenians. Everyone knew that. It was a good business. A refill?"

"Please."

Becker poured me a couple more fingers of whisky.

"Gold proved to be a valuable asset after the war, when the paper money became worthless in the hyper-inflation of the Weimar Republic. In 1922, Peter bought a chemical dye company. In 1925, it became one of the six companies that merged to form the IG Farben conglomerate. But you already know all that?"

"Yes. Please continue." I knew some from Erika's and Gerhardt's research, but didn't want to interrupt.

"Peter's older brother, Otto, went into banking. He joined the Nazi party early and when the Nazis grabbed power, his career took off. When I met him, he was a vice president of Deutsche Bank, and soon thereafter he was elected to the board of directors. By wartime, Otto was the Minister of Economics and President of the Reichsbank."

Becker took a sip of the whisky.

"See, I am being vilified now. But I was just an SS cavalry officer; they sent me to Hungary to buy horses. These guys, they were the lynchpins of the Nazis. Deutsche Bank funded construction of Auschwitz. IG Farben licensed out Zyklon-B and tested their drugs in Auschwitz. They were buying from us, the SS, prisoners for experimentation. The prisoners would die from the injection, and they would order another batch. The gold from the camps—we delivered it to Degussa, the other company that Peter was on the board of. Both Otto and Peter were arrested by the Allies after the war. Otto was released, Peter served a year and got pardoned. Now they are back to where they were. Otto is a chairman of the Deutsche Bank. Nobody drags their names through the mud. As if they had no responsibility for what their companies did during the war. Different rules for well-connected folks."

My hand tightened around the heavy whiskey glass. I had to restrain myself from throwing it into his face. A murderer and a thief that got away scot-free, complaining that other murderers and thieves got away even better.

"What about their sons?" I asked.

"Artur, Peter's son, there was a dyed-in-the-wool Nazi if I've ever met one. He was in the SS on the Eastern Front, working for Otto Ohlendorf."

"Ohlendorf?"

"Yes, the head of the *Einsatzgruppe D*. I met him at Klophers' parties, he was friends with them. In 1943, Ohlendorf was brought back as a deputy director general in the Reich Ministry of Economic Affairs, working for Otto Klopher. Otto and Otto. They tried hard to save Ohlendorf after Nuremberg. Even got Pope Pius XII to seek clemency. If they tried Ohlendorf now, he would have said he just followed orders and got away with perhaps ten years, released after four for good behavior. But back then murdering ninety thousand men, women, and children proved to be too much to overcome, and the Allies executed him."

Becker leaned back, smiling thinly. He clearly had no sympathy for Ohlendorf. "Mr. Levy, you have no idea how tightly all these things were interconnected. The Wehrmacht would have not lasted more than a few months without the economic and financial operations. Murdering your Jewish kin was not just the ideology, it was business. Just like Turks murdering Armenians was business. The Nazis were actually quite scientific about it. They had statisticians calculating the value of people for them. The assets got recycled into the war machine. Of course, now we all work for the cause of Western defense. As long as you are against the communists, it does not matter what you did back in the 1940s."

"Had Artur been tried? I haven't heard of that."

"No. In 1942, before the Stalingrad's disaster, Artur got transferred to Germany and placed into a low-profile diplomatic post. There were rumors within the SS of some funky stuff."

"What kind of stuff?"

"I don't know. Perhaps he pissed off someone he was not supposed to. His powerful uncle covered it up. In the end, it worked out well for Artur. Had he stayed in the SS, he probably would have been hung with Ohlendorf. As it was, he became a lawyer and now works for his uncle, in the Deutche Bank in Frankfurt. He's done well, but not as well as Otto's son."

"Henrick? The one in Switzerland?"

"Yes. Henrick never even dirtied his hands in the war. In 1937, he married a daughter of the president of the Swiss National Bank, the SNB, moved to Switzerland, and became the Reichsbank's representative in the BIS."

"What's BIS?"

Becker rolled his eyes to the ceiling. "You people in the Mossad have a lot to learn. The Bank of International Settlements, created in 1930. It's beyond the reach of either national or international law. They were such cozy buddies of ours. We called them a 'foreign branch of Reichsbank.' Remember, we had to buy raw materials and pay in hard currency. Degussa melted down the looted gold and stamped it with false identification numbers. Nobody else would take Reichsbank's gold, so the BIS would swap it for Swiss gold and pay on our behalf."

"Is that how, for example, Turkey was paid for chromium?"

"Sure. The BIS swapped nine tons of gold to Turkey."

"They, the BIS, didn't care where the Reichsbank's gold came from? They must have known about the Holocaust."

"Of course, they knew. The last truckload of Reichsbank's gold was delivered to Bern on April 6, 1945. Everyone knew. Gold is gold, the Swiss didn't ask questions." Becker paused. "Well, I think that covers both fathers and sons."

"Wait, what about Arno?"

"Arno?" Becker looked puzzled. "Neither of them had a son named Arno."

"A nephew? He may have had a nickname Prinz."

"There were other young people at their parties. I'm not sure which one you're talking about. What did he look like?"

"Blond, tall, a typical Aryan."

"Hmmm ... I recall there was a scientist friend of the Klophers, Zachary ... Zachary Lorens, that's it. He was talking about Aryan characteristics and showing his son, whose name I don't remember, as an example of a perfect Aryan. That's all I can think of." Becker got up. "It's getting late for your train back."

"Please, Mr. Becker. One more question."

"Yes."

"Did Kasztner know where the trains were going?"

"Ohhh." Becker sat back down, poured himself another helping. "Poor Rudy, your people killed him as a traitor. In a way, for saving my life. I think he knew ... It was the summer of 1944, he was in touch with the people abroad. And Eichmann told him what would happen."

"But Kasztner did not say anything to the people."

"If he did, he would have been shot. Eichmann's whole strategy was to avoid another Warsaw Ghetto uprising by keeping people in the dark."

"And Kasztner played along."

"People value their lives … and the lives of their relatives and friends. He did get sixteen hundred out." Becker lifted the glass to admire the color of the scotch. "I swear, you can tell the difference between a single malt and blended by just looking."

"But half a million were shipped to Auschwitz."

"Who's to say how many would have survived in an uprising or attempt to escape?"

"And this way you were able to charge people for a chance to escape, to get on the train or be smuggled out of the country. How much did you charge for extra seats on the Kasztner train—I heard it was twenty-five thousand dollars?"

Becker tilted his head, smiled at me in a mock amusement. "Mr. Levy, we—you, me, Kasztner—are all in a kind of a moral netherworld. From what I understand, you may have escorted more people to their deaths than any of us. I'm not saying this to make you feel guilty; there was not much you could have done. And people that could do something, they did not care. Eichmann sent Joel Brand to the Jewish Agency in Palestine to negotiate the release of Hungarian Jews. And nothing happened. They left Kasztner and Brand with nothing."

"Eichmann was asking for war materials; you know they could not give it to him."

"They could have given money, real money, not the pittance that the Jewish Agency offered. The British could have opened up Palestine, but they didn't want to upset the Arabs. The Americans could have bombed Auschwitz and the railroads, but there were too busy fire-bombing German cities. They all watched the tragedy unfold, made pronouncements, and turned away. Don't put it all on me or poor late Rudy Kasztner."

2

Elam Fishel greeted me with, "The US Congress passed the Tonkin Gulf resolution. There is a war brewing in Vietnam."

"It's good to see you, Elam." I smiled.

And it was good to visit the moshav. The place felt like a refuge, a safe harbor. By now, I was spending close to half of my time in Europe, the rest in Tel Aviv. Sales were going well, the *moshavniks* were happy.

When I was in Jerusalem, I went to the Avenue of the Righteous in Yad Vashem. Heinrich Gruber was recognized as Righteous just a couple of weeks prior, and I wanted to pay my respects. I sat on a bench, looking at a few dozen young trees and wondering how many would eventually be planted here. For each Righteous that we would celebrate, there would be many whose deeds would remain anonymous.

"David!"

I turned to find Dov Cohen, my former boss.

"I'm about to leave, Dov. No need to make a scene."

"Ahhh, David, I'm not here to make a scene," Dov said, flustered. "I saw you and came out to say hello. Look, I'm sorry for how I behaved two years ago."

He offered his hand and, after a pause, I shook it.

"You no longer think I'm a collaborator?"

"We didn't even think that anyone from *Sonderkommandos* survived. But now, more people came out. And I spoke with some of them and …" He hesitated.

"And?"

"And I no longer think it's black-and-white. It's awful what you went through."

"Thank you, Dov. I'm sorry I haven't done much with that list of the righteous Germans. There were quite a few."

"We recognized Ludwig Wörl and Oscar Schindler already, soon we'll recognize Anton Schmid, Armin Wegner, Hermann Graebe, and others. David, do you want to come back?"

"Come back?"

"To work for us. Since Eichmann's trial, we've been getting a lot more material. You can continue your work about the righteous. You were right, we must acknowledge as many of them as possible."

"I don't think so, Dov. Yes, we must acknowledge them, but I'm not coming back."

"Do you really want to sell oranges?"

"They are good oranges. And I have other things to do."

"OK, David. Let me know if you reconsider. You know, people are beginning to recognize the importance of our work. Even the Russians asked for our help. They are going to try some of the Ukrainian guards from Sobibor and Belzec. It was your research."

He was still within the earshot when I had an idea. "Hey, Dov, did you give the Russians that research?"

"Not yet. Your former assistant, Chaia, is putting the report together. It's slow going; she doesn't speak German. Please, come help with that for a few days. I can pay you. You don't even have to go to Russia. You can give them the report in Germany. I'm sure they won't be as lenient with the guards as the West Germans."

"All right, but just for two days."

It was not the Ukrainian guards that I was interested in.

3

From my notes at the Frankfurt Auschwitz trial:

I watched the defendants closely. With some of them—like Schawik or Stark—I had a sickening bond. For months, we had worked on the same task: obliteration of human beings. A transport of three thousand would come in, and in a few hours they would turn into ashes, gold teeth, jewelry, hair. We connected over work well done, partners in the business of oblivion.

Hannah came to testify:

"I worked in the Political Division. Typist and interpreter. I worked for Mr. Boger. Yes, he is sitting there."

Boger smiled at Hannah.

"We were treated differently from other prisoners. We wore normal clothes, normal hair. There were flowers and pictures in the Political Division. Mr. Boger always treated me well. He saved my life when I made a mistake and was going to be transferred to a penal company. People sent to penal company did not survive. We kept the death lists. Causes of death were made up: heart failure, a disease of some kind. We only recorded deaths of people admitted into the camp. Most arrivals were sent directly to gas chambers, and their bodies burned. They were not recorded in any lists."

Defense attorney Laternser attacked her testimony. He attacked each and every witness.

A witness: "If I knew of the kind of interrogation I would have to endure, I would have not come. In fact, I did not want to come. I was finally forgetting. But then I felt I owed it to my dead comrades. If we don't speak now, all that suffering will have been in vain."

Defendants claimed to know nothing of even the most basic functioning of the camp.

Defendant S, who worked in Block 11, adjacent to the Black Wall where systemic executions were conducted, claimed merely to have heard rumors about these.

Defendant B: "I knew nothing about people being gassed. I heard nothing about selections. I never heard of liquidations."

Defendant M, adjutant to the camp commandant: "Personally, I never heard anything about executions in the camp. I never heard shots. I never saw the gas chambers. I was never in the camp. Gassing was murder and I am deeply incensed about it."

The prosecution to Defendant M: "You didn't know about gassing? Here are Zyklon B purchase orders to I.G. Farben, signed by you."

Witness: "These gentlemen claim they did not know what was happening in Auschwitz. The prisoners, even the children, knew it after only two days there."

Judge Hofmeyer: "No one did anything ... The commandant was not there, the officer in charge only happened to be present, the representative of the Political Section only carried lists, and still another one only came with the keys."

Somehow over a million of innocent people were murdered in the place where nobody did or knew anything. Was Auschwitz a natural catastrophe?

Witness: "We were sent out to dig graves. We worked up to our hips in water. One of the women turned to the captain and said, 'I can't work this hard, I am pregnant.' The guards laughed and one of them pushed her down with a shovel and kept her under water until she drowned."

Defendant K: "I personally did not have anything against those people. After all, they are human too. The transports rolled in, and we had to make sure that the operation ran smoothly. It was a regular place, except for the gassings, which naturally were terrible. Orders are orders. They did not resist, resistance would have been pointless."

Defendant F: "I did not have anything against these people. Orders are orders."

Witness: "Defendant S was twenty years old then. He studied for a law degree. He was discussing aspects of humanism in Goethe with us, when a woman with two children was brought in. Their crime was that one of the children played with a pet rabbit of a camp official. He shot them and came back to discuss Goethe. He also regularly dropped Zyklon B into gas chambers."

Defendant S: "Your Honor, we weren't supposed to think for ourselves. There were others around to do our thinking for us."

State's Attorney Kurt Hinrichsen: "I have been unable to find a single SS case in which the failure to carry out an order resulted in physical punishment."

Defense: "We cannot allow these insults to our clients to pass unchallenged."

Erika observing the defendants: "There is no remorse, no guilt, no shame, no outrage, no taking responsibility. They are fine with the collective guilt, just not their personal one. As if they are not individuals."

Follow orders, follow orders, follow orders. Do your duty, be obedient to the authorities and nobody's guilty. If only they were forced, against their ongoing opposition, to do the things they did. Like a slave doing a master's bidding unwillingly. But they were conscientious and creative. They did their job well. Consciousness instead of conscience. All the *Lager* survivors I knew carried guilt of knowing that our lives were preserved at the expense of others' deaths, and we were helpless to change that. But these defendants showed no signs of guilt. Like Eichmann, they would have felt bad if they didn't follow their orders to kill.

Defense: "One can't be convicted of a crime if the action was not illegal at the time."

Mass murder wasn't illegal. The law itself became a shield from culpability. You can call your proceedings legal. But can you call them just?

The witness interrupted his testimony, as joyful cries of children playing at a nearby school suddenly intruded. For several seconds, dead silence in the courtroom. The witness continued: "As Scherpe stopped and went drinking, Hantl took over and killed the remaining thirty children with phenol injections."

Witness: "The dead and the luggage were thrown out of the cars. A Red Cross car was parked on the side of the road. We didn't know it carried poison gas. The officer who divided us was very friendly. I asked him where the others were going, and he said: 'to the showers, you'll see them in an hour.' We did not suspect anything. That's him, Dr. Capesius."

Attorney Laternser replied, "Selection was an act of mercy."

Filip Muller on the witness stand. I knew him in *Sonderkommando*; he survived since the summer of 1942: "One day in 1944, twenty-five thousand Hungarian Jews were gassed. The dental gold was melted down in Crematorium 2. I saw Möll throw a child into the seething human fat. Members of the *Sonderkommando* who warned people about gassing were burned alive."

Witness: "I saw seventy dead young women after medical experiments. Their breasts were cut off. Seventeen- or eighteen-year-olds from the healthiest prisoners were used for X-ray experiments. The girls were placed in front of the X-ray machines. Their ovaries were burned out. Then they were operated on, and their ovaries and gonads were removed. After a few weeks they looked like old women. They all died. Syringes were used to inject a fluid into the womb. It was a cement paste to glue together the fallopian tubes. The women were in terrible pain. There were hundreds of these experiments."

Witness: "We carried out research for pharmaceutical concerns. The camp was a large industrial complex that employed prisoners. We were a subdivision of the Buna Works of I.G. Farben. We paid the SS for the workers. How much? A dollar a day for a skilled worker, 75 cents for an unskilled one. The work day was 11 hours."

Prosecution presented a communication from the Bayer company to the Auschwitz authorities: "The first group of 150 women died. We would kindly request that you send us another group of women to the same number and at the same price of 170 Reichsmarks."

At the 1945 exchange rate of RM10 to US$1, a human life for experiments was worth $17.

Zyklon B's price was 50 cents a pound. Sixteen pounds were needed to gas 2000 people. That's $8. Less than half a penny to kill a person. Very cost-effective. Transportation cost money: Deutsche Reichsbahn charged transportation expert Eichmann four pfennigs per track kilometer (children under four went free), but the Jews had to pay the SS for their resettlement tickets to Auschwitz. Incineration cost two Reichsmarks per corpse, even with free *Sonderkommando* labor. But the possessions of the victims, their hair, their gold teeth. Just gold crowns and jewelry averaged sixty to seventy Reichsmarks per corpse. … the business of genocide was highly profitable.

I remembered something from the official record of the Nuremberg trials:

"Witness, an Auschwitz guard: "When the extermination was at its height, orders were issued that children were to be thrown straight into the furnaces, or into a burning pit without being gassed first."

Smirnov, Russian prosecutor: "How am I to understand this? Did they throw them into the fire alive, or did they kill them first?"

Witness: "They threw them in alive."

Smirnov: "Why did they do this?"

Witness: "We don't know whether they wanted to economize on gas, or if it was because there was not enough room in the gas chambers.""

Planet Auschwitz was created by humans. While from the outside it may seem incomprehensible, within it everything was orderly and cost-effective, everything made sense. That's what Prosecutor Smirnov did not understand: burning two-dozen children alive saved a Reichsmark in Zyklon B. It's perfectly logical: a Reichsmark is an asset, and children didn't have gold crowns to extract.

4

A bit earlier today, I sat in a waterfront restaurant on Carrer Fenix, just south of Denia in Spain. The place smelled of the sea and paella. I was not there for the food. It was my second trip in as many months. Thankfully, I collected good orders for Jaffa oranges. Probably Ruben's people were helping in the background. I'd heard a lot of German language and came across quite a few German men in their fifties and sixties. I didn't think they were vacationing on Spanish beaches; they looked like they lived here. I could understand why, I would haven't minded living here myself. Surely some of them had blood on their hands. But I was here for just one man. I was looking for Erich Rolff on the hundred-and-eighty kilometers of coastline between Valencia and Alicante. I'd never met him. I only had two photos, one from 1944, the other from 1952. He was older now. I hoped I would recognize him.

Without outright staring, I was trying to get a better look at two people three tables away. One of them bore a similarity. The wind carried a few German words across. Finally, they got up to leave. As they passed by my table, my heart pounded because the profile seemed to be just right. The man must have felt my gaze because he looked back with curiosity. He was well lit by the sun and I saw that it was not Rolff. I smiled at him and he smiled back.

I waved to the waiter. I wanted to drive a few kilometers farther, to Xabia. To sit in another restaurant, to strike up a conversation or two. Looking for my German compatriots. Sometimes people would tell me about residential areas where they clustered, seeking safety in numbers.

But one must be careful when asking questions. I might have been too inquisitive in La Villa, where two robust men accosted me at night as I was coming back to the hotel. Thanks to my native mastery of

354

German, I talked my way out of it. They even invited me to a dinner the next night. When I got to my room, I found it ransacked. I mentally thanked "Anton" for his advice to be careful and not use the same passport.

5

"Mozart was born here," Erika said as we pulled into Salzburg.

"So was Hitler. A few kilometers away."

"Come on, David. It's a beautiful city. The Americans just filmed a big movie here, *The Sound of Music.*"

"You are right. Just irks me how the Austrians now portray themselves as victims of Nazis. They were very enthusiastic fans, until Hitler started losing the war."

The recently reopened University of Salzburg was smack in the center of the city. We found the Faculty of Sciences in a large building next to Frohnburg Castle. Zachary Lorens's office was on the third floor, and he began by guiding us to the window to admire the view. Which was something to behold, especially after the rain had cleared the already pure air.

We were here under somewhat false pretenses. Just recently, Dr. Lorens had been decorated by the Republic of Austria for his science achievements, and Erika offered to write a newspaper article about him. Thus, we patiently listened to him explaining the intricacies of animal behavior, especially that of the Greylag goose. Erika feigned writing in her notebook.

After about twenty minutes, she saw an opening and politely enquired, "We want to make sure that the article will cover the total body of your work. Let me see if I quote this correctly. Didn't you say in 1940 that 'preservation of a race would have to be concerned with an even more rigorous eradication of those who are ethnically inferior'? What exactly did you mean by that?"

Dr. Lorens turned pale and stammered, "I don't recall exactly … My words must have been edited for publication …"

"But didn't you state even earlier, in 1938, that 'my whole scientific work is devoted to the ideas of the National Socialists'? Did not you write about the dangers of inferior races?"

"Well, you are taking it out of context ..."

"And what context should I use?" Erika remained icily polite. "That of you being a member of the Nazi party since 1938 and promoting ideas of 'racial hygiene' as a university chair in Königsberg? Or that of your position as a psychologist in the Office of Racial Policy?"

"What is this? You said you were going to write about my science achievements ..."

"A newspaper article won't be complete without research. And it seems that your view of science was quite different twenty-some years ago. Had a very strong National Socialist flavor. People don't just cross the threshold into genocide; the Nazis needed a scientific and ideological framework. If not for people like you, how would they have come up with justification for their racial superiority?"

"But none of this has to go into the article." I was going to play the good cop, as Erika and I had agreed. "We just want some information."

"What kind of information?"

"I understand you were friends with Otto and Peter Klopher?"

"Friends? I would not say we were friends." Dr. Lorens sounded bitter and defeated.

"Well, how would you characterize your relationship with them?"

"I was married to a friend of their family. For a few years."

"Who was that?"

"Rose Haufmann. Her father was friends with Waldemar Klopher, Otto and Peter's father. I married Rose in 1935. She was a widow. We divorced in 1941, when I was called into the army and sent to the Eastern Front. I asked Klophers to help, to get me out of this conscription, but they didn't even bother to reply. And Rose said to me: 'you reap what you sew.' I was captured by the Russians and served four years in the Gulag. But you must know that if you've done your 'research'."

"Did you have children?"

"Not of my own, but Rose had a son from a previous marriage. Hans."

"Did he have a nickname Prinz?"

"How did you know?" Lorens's mouth dropped open. "Yes. He was a very good-looking kid, tall, blond, blue-eyed."

"Very Aryan?"

"You could say that, yes. That's why Otto called him 'my Prinz.' Otto really loved the kid."

"Did he have a scar on the left cheek?"

"Yes, from a riding accident."

"And what happened to him?"

"He signed up with the SS, together with Artur, Peter's son. I heard he was killed somewhere near Stalingrad. His mother and I had no contact by then."

"What about Rose?"

"We lived in Königsberg after I took the university position there. She stayed there with her daughter-in-law, Hans's wife—they got married just before the Russian campaign. Most of Königsberg's civilians didn't make it out alive. I've never heard about them again."

Erika and I looked at each other.

"Thank you, I think that's what we wanted to find out. We'll see ourselves out."

We got up to leave.

"I've made mistakes, but I deserve the recognition," Lorens whispered. "I wanted to be a spiritual agent of change. I didn't know it would lead where it did."

"But you gave a scientific foundation to a primitive barbaric ethos, a collective paranoia. Social Darwinism as freedom from all restraint, removal of moral law."

"I'm a good scientist!"

"I believe you. You are a good scientist. But a moral barbarian." Erika slammed the door as we left.

"Well, I've got my newspaper article, thank you. Are you going to tell Yosef?" Erika asked in the train on the way back.

"Not yet. I want to talk to the Klophers, perhaps get a photo. See what we can find out about Rose Haufmann."

358

6

It was an unusually warm October day in Frankfurt. Shimon, Gerhardt and I relaxed on a bench in *PalmenGarten*, a botanical garden on *Siesmayerstraße*. Gerhardt was looking at the roses, Shimon at two women in a row boat, I was doing both.

"I came to say good-bye," Shimon announced. "Going back to Israel, at least for a while."

"Is this because of the arms deal?"

Newspapers were splashed with headlines about a secret deal between Bonn and Jerusalem, with Israel buying surplus NATO tanks, cannons, missile boats, and even submarines.

"Yes, I am being recalled for consultations."

"Is that what von Eckner referred to as a 'profitable arrangement'?" I asked.

"You have a good memory, David." Shimon smiled. "That conversation was—what—three years ago?"

"Yes, three years. I never believed you were here only to support medical compensations."

"The deal was put in place because of Adenauer and Kennedy. The West German Foreign Ministry, with its nest of Nazis, was always opposed. Now, with Ludwig Erhard in power and Kennedy dead, the vultures came out and they are trying to kill the arrangement. But we need those weapons."

"Why do you need them so badly?" Gerhardt asked.

"Because another war with the Arabs is coming."

"The ancients saw the history as a circle. The Enlightenment, as a line of progress." Gerhardt shook his head. "What kind of progress is that, stumbling from one war to the next?"

"After Auschwitz, what's the point of talking of Enlightenment?"

"But then—how do we break the circle?"

"You know, Gerhardt, three hundred years ago civilized nations started adopting new rules of war. That a war should be fought between armies, not civilians. But then you, our German friends, came up with a nasty concept of 'total war.' Credit famed Carl von Clausewitz. Hundreds of years of civilizing process thrown away in favor of victory at any cost."

"It was not a German who piloted Enola Gay, pushed a button and incinerated a hundred thousand human beings below," Gerhardt retorted. "I agree, 'win at all cost' plants the seed of our common destruction. But this mentality is not reserved to us Germans."

"Well, big philosophical issues aside, we need the weapons." Shimon's jaw stuck out angrily.

"I understand. I wish I could help, but I am handling much smaller matters." Gerhardt passed me an envelope. "I looked into Hans Krentz, as you asked. Born to Rose Haufmann and Rudi Krentz in 1919. Must have been a shotgun wedding since they got married just a couple of months prior. Rudi was killed in 1929, in a street fight between the Nazis and the communists. He was obviously on the Nazi side. The kid's full name was Hans Werner Arno Krentz. We Germans like multiple names. I guess later in life he preferred to be called Arno. Rose remarried to Zachary Lorens in 1935, they moved to Königsberg in 1938, and divorced in 1941. Arno married Lilly Weber, also in 1941. They had a daughter, Anna, born in 1943. Although Arno did not know about it. According to the official records, he was killed by a Russian sniper in August of 1942."

"Was he in the SS?"

"There is actually nothing about his service. It's not unheard of, with many files being fully or partially destroyed at the end of the war. Still, a bit unusual. I can tell that he was a Nazi through-and-through: I found his wedding papers. Arno required from his future wife, besides other documents, the testimony of Aryan descent certified by a notary. Kind of like the Klophers, who had the Aryan paragraph written into the family's constitution."

"What's that?"

"Proof of racial purity. A member that marries a non-Aryan is ejected from the family."

"And what about Rose and Lilly?"

"It appears that they were trapped in Königsberg when it was surrounded by the Red Army in January of 1945. It's now in Russian hands. I was there before the war, a quaint medieval town of brightly colored towers and attractive churches. Probably not many were left standing after the battle. The garrison surrendered, but the terms didn't apply to the German civilians. Some were killed during the siege. The majority of those that made it through, died later from disease or starvation. Only about twenty thousand returned to Germany. Rose and Lilly Krenz were not amongst them."

"Would it make sense to inquire with the Russians?" Shimon wondered.

"It's not likely you'll get anything."

"I can ask von Eckner to check through diplomatic channels. He's been pretty helpful to us before. It won't hurt."

"No, it won't," Gerhardt agreed.

361

7

The Deutsche Bank's building on *Junghofstraße* was an example of efficient and ugly simplicity, like military barracks or a prison. Artur Klopher had a corner office on the third floor. The secretary that showed Erika, Gerhardt and me in, seemed quite flustered. The reason became obvious when we heard excited whispers of "the Chairman is here" in the corridor.

Three men waited for us in the office: a tall, handsome elderly man with a mane of white hair stood very erect by the window; another elderly man, this one portly, red-faced and bald, sat in the chair facing the door; lastly, a very angry-looking man around fifty was positioned behind the desk.

"Would you like ..."

The secretary was cut off midsentence by the younger man. "No, we don't want anything. You can go." He then turned to us and pointed at Gerhardt. "Who are you? I agreed to meet with this so-called journalist and this ... this ..."

I tried to help. "I think that 'Jew' is the word you're looking for."

"Don't put words in my mouth, you ..."

"Artur, stop!"

The tall man by the window wielded his words like a whip. The man behind the desk shrank into his shoulders.

"I apologize for my nephew's rudeness," the tall man continued. "I am Otto Klopher. This"—he pointed to the others—"is my brother Peter, and my nephew Artur. I presume you are Gerhardt Schrumpf. While we only expected Mr. Levy and Ms. Jager, you are welcome. Please make yourself at home." He gestured towards a leather couch facing the desk.

Shimon told me once about his encounter with a Jewish man who was trying to get compensation from the German government for mental damage during the war. The man was a *greifer*, a "catcher" working for the Gestapo to hunt down "U-Boats," Jews hiding in Berlin. "Here was a man that I knew betrayed dozens of others to their deaths. And yet, he was so charismatic that for a moment I had forgotten all about the blackness of his soul and empathized with his plight," Shimon shook his head in wonder. "He put his spell on me. He was a textbook definition of a brilliant charming sociopath." There was something about Otto Klopher that reminded me of that conversation, sending a tingling sensation down my spine.

"I understand you have some questions, and we'll be happy to discuss them with you." Otto Klopher remained smiling and standing as we sank into the couch.

The sentence broke the spell with its outright falseness. We'd been trying to talk to the Klophers for months and had been ignored until the name of Hans Werner Arno Krentz was mentioned, together with an implication of an exposé in the paper.

"For starters, what was your connection to Arno Krentz?"

"Arno, yes." Klopher picked up a photo from the desk. "Our apologies, we at first misunderstood you. The boy's official name was Hans, after his grandfather on his father's side. When he was in his teens, he found out that Hans Krentz was a petty criminal who died in jail. After that, he preferred to use Arno. As you asked, we found you a picture of his. With our boys. It's yours to keep."

No doubt, the picture was carefully selected. Three boys in their late teens, laughing on a sunny day. One of them, a very good-looking blond kid, had a visible scar on his left cheek.

"Our father, Waldemar Klopher, was friends and neighbors with Eberhard Hauttmann. Eberhard had two children, son, Gustav, and daughter, Rose. Gustav was born the same year as I, and we were dear friends. Gustav was killed on the Western Front in 1914. Rose was like a sister to me."

"Is that why you called Arno a nephew?"

"Yes. It was not a blood connection, but a very strong one nonetheless. Artur and Arno were especially close."

"Close enough to work together for Otto Ohlendorf in the *Einsatzgruppen D*?" Gerhardt asked.

"Hey!" Artur started, but Otto Klopher raised his palm to shut him down.

"Artur and Arno both served on the Eastern Front for a time. That's all."

"So, when Arno killed another German soldier and ran off with a Jewish boy, that did not reflect well on you," Gerhardt pressed on.

"Arno was killed by a Russian sniper." Otto Klopher remained calm, but his lips twisted into a grimace.

"That's the official story. I wonder what it cost you to change Arno's file. Although, Otto Ohlendorf was your good friend, so perhaps not much." Gerhardt's voice was full of sarcastic venom.

"Don't you dare to speak of Ohlendorf! He was a great, brilliant man! You are a pigmy compared to him!" Artur slammed his palm on the desk. Otto Klopher turned to Artur and raised his arm to hit him, then pulled back.

"Yes, if you measure greatness by the number of women and children one has killed, he was a great man and I am a pigmy," Gerhardt agreed.

By now I understood that Gerhardt was deliberately provoking them. I could see Otto Klopher understood it as well.

"You see, that's why I was not going to let you meet with my hot-headed nephew without me." He smiled. "The official version is the version; you can't prove otherwise."

"Actually, we can," I chimed in. "The Jewish boy that Arno saved, he made it. Thank you for the picture. I'm sure he'll recognize Arno. Now that we know who his savior was, I will submit an application to the Yad Vashem museum to recognize Arno Krentz as a Righteous. I doubt they would agree, given his background, but the publicity …"

"We'll definitely cover it in our newspaper," Erika added.

This blow knocked Klopher's mask off. He squeezed out, "Why would we care?" through clenched teeth.

"Oh, for the same reason that you staged the cover-up surrounding Arno's disappearance … embarrassment. Murdering Jewish kids was perfectly acceptable, but to kill one of your Aryan own, well, that's another story. And once Artur's war background is questioned … the Ludwigsburg office might get interested as well."

"Look, if you already know all that, what do you really want?" Peter

Klopher finally broke his silence. "Why would you go after my son? Do you want money?"

"Peter, I don't think they want money," Otto said, cutting him off. "And there will be no public submissions to Yad Vashem. The Israeli government wants the weapons we are supplying, and they need all the support they can get. They want my vote. And as for our visitors, they are idealists. They want the truth. Until today, they only suspected it. Is that so?"

"Yes." I nodded. "But we still don't know why Arno did it."

"Unfortunately, we don't know either." Otto Klopher shrugged. "I was never able to figure it out. Drives me crazy to this day. If you find out, please let me know."

"Was that it?" Peter sounded surprised. "I thought you'd have more."

"You mean about the looted gold? The role of Degussa, Deutsche Bank, I.G. Farben, Swiss bankers?" Erika shook her head. "The truth will keep coming out."

"I never personally killed anyone," Peter protested. "Unlike your friend here, who helped his own into gas chambers. He is guiltier than I am."

"No," Erika disagreed. "You had choices. His only other choice was death."

There was a pause, then Gerhardt asked, "Do you know what happened to Rose and to Arno's wife and daughter?"

"No, I presume they died in the war or the aftermath."

"And Hans Vogel—he served with Arno, he was a part of the cover-up, right?"

"Yes." Otto Klopher nodded. "Ohlendorf ordered him to keep quiet. After the war, he rightfully should have been hung, but we helped to secure his release. Good deeds don't go unpunished. When you showed up he tried to blackmail us. I apologize, the things that happened three years ago were not necessary." He glared at Artur. "Some people just don't know how to get good help."

After another pause, Otto added, "Let the sleeping dogs lie and I will use my influence to help your country. We'll continue to supply the weapons and even loan you the money to pay for it and won't ask for repayment. But if you press on … remember that my vote on this matter counts."

"You bluffed about covering it in your newspaper, didn't you?" Gerhardt asked after we were escorted out.

"Of course." Erika nodded. "They won't do it. And he knows that. He thinks he's untouchable."

"So did Globke," I offered.

"You mean the show trial in East Germany that cost Globke his job?"

I smiled and said nothing.

"Fine, keep your secrets." Gerhardt shrugged. "That boy, Hans Krentz, he's still a mystery."

"Yes, we know he existed, we know he saved Yosef, but we don't know why."

"Still," Erika said, "in the midst of all that horror just knowing he was real gives me a glimmer of hope."

Afterwards, I compiled a report about Becker and the Klophers and mailed it to Benny. Nothing regarding Arno or Rose, only about the BIS, the gold, and the Klopher's offer. At some point, all debts would be called.

8

A few days later, Erika called me with incredible news: the Frankfurt Auschwitz trial was going to Auschwitz.

"There were talks underway for weeks and it was decided: the court would go there. The Polish government gave its permission and agreed to cooperate with the visas and travel arrangements."

"Why?"

"They want to examine the grounds, verify eyewitnesses' accounts. To make it real. I will go."

Erika paused and then asked carefully, "Do you want to come with? I can get you journalistic credentials for the trip. You don't have to answer now. Think about it."

Why did I agree? I can't say that I had a good explanation. I certainly didn't need to verify the accounts. Most of all, I wanted to see the faces of the Germans. A *German* court in Auschwitz. Witness testimonies, diagrams, photos were an abstraction—how would they react to the real place?

We arrived at Auschwitz on December 14th for a three day visit. one of the judges, three prosecutors, eleven defense attorneys. About a hundred journalists trailed the court.

The room, fifteen feet wide and sixty feet long, was whitewashed. Heavy concrete beams supporting the ceiling. The gas chamber of the old crematorium.

The gallows where Höss was hanged.

Block 11 and the Black Wall a few steps away. Thousands of executions had been carried out here. A page from the bunker book with names of thirty-five prisoners shot on a particular day.

Grass covered the ditches where Möll's pyres burned.

In the summer of 1944, we'd let the fire billow up, hoping that the American and British pilots would see them and bomb us. They flew by. They had more important targets.

The woods where children played, before they were taken to be gassed. A woman guard would come and say nicely, "Let's go take our showers."

Silently, I recited the opening of Yevtushenko's poem that Hannah brought to me:

> No monument stands over Babiy Yar.
> The steep precipice is an unhewn headstone.
> I am terrified.

And so was I.

How could you work here and claim you did not know what was going on?

Everyone was watching the forensic investigation:

"How far was it from the pits where bodies were burned to the train tracks?"

"We measured it at 5.4 meters."

"Could you see the execution wall from the first floor of Block 28?"

"Could you hear inmates from the cells of Block 11?"

"These yellow-gray lumps at the bottom of the ditch—are these the ashes of burnt people?"

Amongst the ashes, a fragment of a charred bone.

A defense attorney protested, "Allegedly burned people!"

I wanted to scream but whispered instead, "These were people. Not alleged, real people."

The defense attorney insisted, "We don't know if these are ashes, unless they are sent for analysis."

Erika rushed to me, but she was too late, I snapped. "You don't know that people were killed and burned here by the thousands every day, in ovens and pyres? You need a lab test???"

A polite Polish host gently guided me aside, away from angry looks. "I'm sorry, were you here during the war?"

"I was in *Sonderkommando*."

He took my hand, shocked. "Did you know Zalman Gradowski? Leib Langfus?"

"Yes, I worked with them."

"We found their notes buried by the crematoria. Would you like to see them?"

Ezra had pushed me out, but I never truly left. I didn't want to be here—but where did I belong?

Erika inserted herself between us. "It's not a good idea right now."

Poor Erika, I had ruined her trip. *Am I getting unhinged?* I increasingly asked the question of myself. Probably. She deserved so much better.

How could you visit and not realize how the death machine ran? Hitler was never in Auschwitz. Himmler and Eichmann visited, but they did not run the place. The defendants did. I thought that being here would drive that home.

And then we returned to the courtroom, and it was back to legal maneuvering as if they saw nothing. Grandstanding defense attorney Laternser continued to insist that the sole agent of murder was Hitler, while the defendants were saving lives by selecting some people to not go immediately to gas chambers. And most seemed to share this wishful fantasy that there were only a few people with responsibility ... and the rest were merely terrorized, violated hangers-on, compelled to do things completely contrary to their true nature. The accused—all of them in all trials—had a point. They were a small tip of the iceberg. It took lawyers, scientists, bureaucrats, statisticians, secretaries like the one in Von Eckner's office—it took all of them just doing their jobs.

Were people uneasy at the effortlessness with which the defendants turned into law-abiding citizens? In the press, the defendants were repeatedly referred to as "monsters," "beasts," or "barbarians." Pure, metaphysical evil. Here, they were strikingly ordinary, harmless men. If I met them on the street, I would have not thought "here goes a mass murderer." But then I would have taken Eichmann for a shipping clerk. Eichmann tried to paint the same picture, of a simple law-abiding person. But when the rules were lifted, they murdered without remorse. I thought that in '61, in the Jerusalem courtroom, I'd figured out who Eichmann was. Here, in Frankfurt, I realized that I'd just peeled off a layer or two. The core of the darkness was still there, hidden from sight.

At the Jerusalem trial, defense attorney Servatius had said about Eichmann: "Since the killing was done by gas, it was a medical matter." I'd thought he misspoke. Now I understood him. In *Lager*, I kept my sanity by blocking the true meaning of what was taking place. Just like the SS doctors and guards that divorced themselves from the actuality of what they were doing, so did the attorney Servatius. He divorced himself from the reality of his client's work. That was why he could call it a "medical matter." That was why they could be evil murderers on planet Auschwitz and perfectly normal on planet Earth. Calling them "beasts" and "monsters" was a dangerous oversimplification. The Milgram experiments showed that Auschwitz was within the potential capability of many of us. But potential is not the same as action.

We need to place barriers. Conscience is not enough of a barrier: there must be fear. They must know that no matter where in the hierarchy they are, from giving orders to informing on a neighbor in hiding, there may be a heavy price to pay.

9

On January 20th, the Baden-Württemberg authorities officially declared Kurt Gerstein to be not guilty. Erika, Fritz and I decided to go out and celebrate on Friday, the 22nd. Unfortunately, it didn't turn out to be a celebration, as on Thursday the 21st the last of the Belzec trials ended. After three years, the courts produced one conviction for 4.5 years for being an accessory to 300,000 murders. Everyone else was acquitted.

It was completely unfair, but I took it out on poor Fritz. "Remember our conversation from a year ago? So, this is your famed German justice? Eight defendants, four-and-a-half-years between all of them. That's less than a minute for each murder."

"I'm sorry, David." Fritz turned red-faced. "This is not right. But we are obligated to follow the law, wrong as it might be. To do otherwise would be an even greater wrong."

"It's hard to imagine a greater wrong. There was no law in Belzec."

"Precisely. That's why it happened."

"There are other laws, Fritz."

"What are you saying?"

"Forty-three years ago, a man named Soghomon Tehlirian executed Talat Pasha, the former Grand Vizier of the Ottoman Empire, one of the architects of the Armenian genocide. And the German jury acquitted him. These German jurors had no legal training, but they knew a hell of a lot more about justice than the judges in the Belzec trials. Or the Chelmno or Ulm trials."

"I won't hear of that, David. Extra-judicial vengeance is not the way. These prosecutors, they are good people. They risked their careers for these trials. Most of the German population opposes any further Nazi trials. They believe it damages our reputation abroad, wastes money, it's time to finally be done with all this."

"Do you understand how sad this is? Prosecutors must risk their careers to try murderers, and nobody wants them to succeed."

"People are uncertain about how they might have behaved in Belzec and Auschwitz. David, it's not only about the punishment. Two years ago, nobody knew about Auschwitz. Now, everyone does. They may not like it, but at least they know. We may yet succeed with the Auschwitz trial."

"Why would I believe that? Your justice system already failed with Belzec and Chelmno. It's almost amusing how you pray on the altar of the law. Must be a German thing. In 1933, you passed the Enabling Law, which permitted Hitler to ignore the law. The law as a shield for amorality. There were hundreds of thousands in the SS alone. Over nine million in the Nazi party. How many can you possibly try?"

"Don't you understand that I want to put them all away for life?" the usually calm Fritz shouted. "I want to strangle Laternser with my own hands, but we must let him do his job. The truth is coming out."

"You want truth, but no justice?"

"We put some of the defendants away. Even if it's only for seven or ten years."

"And they'll be out for good behavior in three or four. Oh, Fritz, there is justice and then there is Justice with a capital 'J'. Fritz, Fritz … besides a few dozen defendants that will likely get away with a slap on the wrist, there are much bigger criminals that not only eluded justice but now enjoy high positions in the country. I've met with a few of them recently and found no remorse."

Erika started to cry.

"What's the matter?" I put my arm around her.

"We came here to remember Kurt Gerstein. A man with a conscience. Instead, we argue about murderers."

I felt bad afterwards. Fritz was one of the good guys. There were just too few of them here.

I didn't tell Fritz the real reason for my outburst. Earlier that week, in the Frankfurt courtroom, I was studying a photo from the Auschwitz album that was submitted as a part of the evidence. A picture of a young girl in a beret, waiting in the woods near the gas chambers. She was looking at the photographer with a questioning innocence: "Why are you taking my picture?" I may have seen her. The summer of '44. I couldn't be sure because we were "processing" thousands daily. But it kept coming back to me: a little girl under a pile of bodies, the ones that rushed to the door in their mortal terror. Her small naked body twisted, with feet pointing down but wide-open brown eyes staring at the ceiling. I froze for a moment and received a blow from our foreman. "Hurry up!" Perhaps it was her. Logically, I knew it was unlikely: thousands of girls her age had been gassed or shot or worse in Auschwitz that summer. And yet, I kept thinking it was her in the picture.

Who was that girl? Nobody at the trial spoke for her. The defendants were only being tried for exceeding their orders. Her murder was not really a crime in this courtroom. What would they have said if she was a German girl? What kind of justice would they have demanded? Would defense attorneys argue that no one was responsible for her death? Would church fathers tell them to love and forgive the perpetrators? No, I imagine there would be torches and pitchforks. If I were the accused, would I even make it to a trial? Or would I be lynched like dozens of others during the *Kristallnacht*? That was still well before Auschwitz, before the war, when the vaunted German law that was being upheld here was still very much in force.

I thought of the girl as Leah. My sister's name. Someone—perhaps Hans Stark sitting but a fifty-feet from me—poured in Zyklon-B crystals that killed her. Forget the past? Why was I being asked to put it all behind, while that man was walking amongst us? Or Ezra's daughter Lia. Was it Wilhelm Boger who put a bullet into her brain? He was laughing now, amused by the latest testimony.

I did something unthinkable: I secretly took documents from the museum and gave them to the East Germans. Documents that implicated some of the senior government and industry officials. I wanted show trials, like the one that they put Hans Globke on. I wanted to embarrass the government into at least firing these people. But I found out that the information I gave would be used for blackmail, not justice.

The people that killed that girl must be held fully accountable. This court wouldn't do that. As Fritz Jager explained to me, it's so vitally important for the German people to "get back" to the rule of the law. But nobody speaks for the little girl. I know that my friend Fritz is right about the limits of the law. But I know I'm right too. The law failed her. She's a non-person in this courtroom. She's being murdered again, written out of humanity. How do you burn hearts with words, when words can be twisted into anything? There is a lawyer in this courtroom that says that the act of "selection" was an act of mercy. What good are words?

10

I had to make sure it was him. One does not want to make a mistake in such matters. It was my eighth trip to the town that Anton pointed me to. I was doing my Jaffa oranges pitch in a local supermarket, when I heard people speaking German. I turned around just in time to get a good look at three men in their fifties, laughing at some joke. The one nearest to me had a slightly hooked, bird-of-prey nose, similar to what Rolff's was in the photo. The men disappeared down one of the aisles.

I turned back to the manager and interrupted him with, "*Estoy de acuerdo.* I agree."

The manager looked at me in surprise and slight disappointment. I robbed him of the excitement of haggling. But he couldn't pass up the deal. "*Muy bien!*"

I told him I'd be back with the contract and left abruptly. For a moment I was terrified that I lost them, but then I heard German speech again. They were in the wine section, trying to choose between Garnacha and Rioja. I hung around within a listening distance, then shadowed them into the parking where they got into a late-model Mercedes and drove off. My rented Barreiros Dart took its time to start, but I managed to catch up with them, through a roundabout and down to the beach. The Mercedes stopped by a seafood restaurant, where they got out. I looked at Rolff's pictures one more time and went into the restaurant. The men were at one of the beach-fronting tables, the bottle already uncorked. I could not get close enough to hear what they were saying, so I sat in the back where I could see them. The more I looked, the more I was convinced that one of them was indeed Erich Rolff. After lunch, I discreetly followed them about ten kilometers north, to a residential area. They all lived on the same small, palm tree-lined street, a few short steps from the beach.

I extended my stay in the area by three days. The next morning, I had returned to the supermarket with a contract and invited the manager to have a dinner that night to celebrate. Then I found a real estate agency and pretended to be a well-to-do West German salesman looking for a vacation place near the beach, preferably where I would have some German compatriots. Between the manager, whose tongue was loosened by strong Spanish wine, and the enthusiastic real estate agent, I found out that a little German colony there began in the late 1940s and grew in the 1950s. Amongst others, a man called Ernst Wolen came in 1952. His wife, Sylvia, joined him two years later. I knew that Rolff's wife, Gretel, left Germany in 1954. I had her photo as well. The agent told me about wonderful parties that took place in the tightly knit community. "What a great place it is to be a German!" he said.

I purchased swimming trunks and each day I went to the beach. On the third day, they showed up, with beach chairs and towels. A tall, lanky man who looked to be in his late fifties and his short, plump wife, early fifties. Ernst and Sylvia Wolen. Also, Erich and Gretel Rolff. There was no doubt at that point.

11

It's been four months since I touched this notebook. A friend died in April, and there was no point in writing. But it was a part of my nature to strive for a proper logical conclusion, and for that sake I had to make one last entry. I waited for the verdict in the trial, and the verdict was in. I don't know why I hoped for anything different than in the Belzec trial, or the Chelmno trial, or so many of those judicial farces they'd been staging. But my verdict was in too. I'd been thinking of them all: the righteous, the collaborators, the murderers.

In the Bible, God was willing to spare Sodom if ten righteous people could be found there. How low are our expectations for righteousness! When Grüber testified in Jerusalem, there was a headline about one righteous man redeeming a nation. It's not possible. Like guilt, the righteousness is individual, not collective. The righteous are not there to redeem or assuage our sins. Many of them perished in anonymity, and the ones that survived are, more often than not, still ostracized by their countrymen. We don't like those that made us look bad by their courage, or by even a simple refusal to conform. They are to be celebrated for what they are, for knowing in their hearts that a murder is a murder, even if sanctioned by the authority. For them, we must be eternally grateful. They deserve to be honored, but let's not think of them as our redeemers. The only redemption there is, must be our own.

The collaborators, and those that stood by, are a painful topic for me. When Aram asked me to write, I was tempted to begin with the 1954 trial of Rudolf Kasztner for collaborating with the Nazis in Hungary. Did he "sell his soul to the devil" as Judge Halevi found?

377

What to do about those that saved a few and betrayed others? To some, Kasztner is a hero for saving sixteen hundred people. To others, he is a villain for not warning thousands of others. I think he was neither, for he was in an impossible situation. He probably thought that he could outsmart Eichmann and find a "lesser evil" alternative.

But the "lesser evil" road is often a very slippery one. Much more important personas than Kasztner failed at playing diplomacy with the devil. Such as Pope Pius XII, who knew and yet spoke nothing but generalities. Do I point an accusatory finger at the US War Department for refusing to bomb Auschwitz? Had they done so in July of 1944, perhaps one or two hundred thousand living beings could have been saved. Or do I point it at Lord Moyne, the British High Commissioner in Egypt: after receiving a message that the Nazis might be willing to spare the Hungarian Jews in return for supplies, he replied: "What shall I do with those million Jews? Where shall I put them?" Perhaps he was not too adverse to the 'final solution' as long as the Germans did the work.

We can't equate them with deliberate malevolence, but we can pass a judgment on indifference, selfishness, even heartlessness—what happened would not have been possible if not for them. There are shades of darkness here. And that's the twilight that I dwell in: for the people I escorted to Auschwitz's gas chambers there was no escape, their fates had been sealed the moment that the doors of cattle cars closed behind them. But I know it's a self-serving argument.

At last, I get to the murderers. In the final analysis, I must admit that these people are beyond my comprehension. There was no giant impersonal machine. There were individuals that chose— not on the pain of death—to murder. They can't be judged by a court based on morality, because they are beyond it. We don't want to undermine our view of ourselves, so we have this belief that certain values and ideals are given, not up for discussion. These people are the evidence that this is not the case, that there exists some fundamental darkness in the human psyche. The only way to judge them is to accept that our idealistic belief is false, and to invoke and enforce an absolute and universal moral standard: that rights to life and liberty are not negotiable, and the consequences of our actions can't be left to God or a supreme leader but belong to us personally. We must insist on individual responsibility, that's why we've been given free will. I owed it to my brothers and sisters, whose ashes remained in Poland, to tell the truth, to bear witness. But with all the witnesses, the little girl's murder was not a crime in the Frankfurt's courtroom. Like millions of others, she's been forgotten, erased, blotted out of memory – but not by me. Justice for her requires another judgment—which I'm now willing to pass. Sometimes retribution is the only way to serve justice, in hope that it will deter others.

For years, I wondered whether my survival on that October day had been an accident. And it was, but not in the way I imagined. Ezra's life was about protecting Lia. Unable to save her, he saved me. And so my body—tissue and bones and blood—is here. But I, David Levy, I'm not here. Too many voices inside of me, too many memories. I didn't really go to see Schawik that morning of October 7, 1944. I went to work in the crematorium as usual, and someone grabbed a Nazi guard and threw him into the burning furnace, and Ezra and I hammered another furnace until the bricks came loose inside, and then we ran out into the hail of machine gun fire. That's how it was supposed to end. But I was allowed to—forced to—go on a bit longer. There is nothing like the despair of the *Lager*, of the inability to change anything. And ultimately dying for naught.

But I've been given the privilege of fighting back. Even if it's a small measure compared to what's been lost, it's not nothing.

My family returned. I saw them: my mother cooking dinner; my father looking through his papers, books-books-books all over the place, Leah practicing her violin, swaying with the music. Mendelsohn's violin concerto was her favorite. When the haunting melody of the first movement would begin to flow from under her bow, we would all stop whatever we were doing and let the music take us. Afterwards, she would let me touch the violin and I gently traced my index finger along the exquisite curves. Ever since, I thought the violin's shape to be the most graceful, the most beautiful. I had no gift to extract the music from its slender body; to me it was magic. Leah had to stop playing Mendelssohn after the *Reichsmusikkammer* declared it to be a degenerate Jewish music. My poor sister couldn't understand why cultured German people would do something like that. She didn't know how much higher the wall of hatred and cruelty would rise. She didn't know what a powerful, evil, metaphysical force our little family represented to them.

Once they came back—my family—they did so with disturbing frequency. My mother patiently conjugating English verbs, she was the one with the true genius for languages. My father discussing Socrates with me. "Always ask questions; the really important thing is not to live, but to live honorably." There was always a touch of sadness within him, like a premonition that he carried inside. Perhaps that's why he was one of the few to not despair when the cattle car's door closed. Instead, throughout the whole miserable journey he told us stories.

What did they think about in their last moments? After being forced to undress and go in naked —did they know that it was the end, or did they believe the deception about a warm shower and a hot coffee waiting? Were they together? I'm sure they were. Holding on to each other as the poison gas rose up and there were no more lies or hopes.

I made it out, Ezra. You pushed me out of there. Right now, I'm drinking *slivovka* in your memory. You gave me this gift for a reason. Your daughter Lia and my sister Leah, their names were the same. In another universe, they might have been giving a concert together: Lia's voice, Leah's violin. What was it like for you, knowing that your daughter had to daily endure German soldiers and criminal *kapos* that got passes to the bordello for being sufficiently vicious? You just wanted to keep her alive, to protect your precious baby whatever it took. Kindness is compassion. Justice is also compassion. I could not save my Leah or your Lia. I can't bring them back, just like I can't bring back the little unnamed girl in the Auschwitz Album. But there might be another girl that I can still save. She might have been born already, a happy girl playing violin or singing or dancing or writing. Justice is compassion for future generations.

Yael, my love, you were right too—you couldn't be my salvation. I had another purpose.

I wonder where Itzhak is now. My enemy, my duty-bound brother. No, Itzhak, my life is mine, my own. And so is my justice to dispense and my freedom to choose how to leave.

My brave, strong, generous, beautiful Erika—you deserved so much better. In another life, you would have been my soulmate.

Benny—finally, I'm ready to accept that needle that I refused in Grottaferrata. I have no illusions, I can't fix the world, but I can do what's right.

PART 9:
AVI

1

The exchange took place near Sidon. As arranged, Aron Milman drove me to a checkpoint controlled by the South Lebanese Army. I walked about a hundred yards and was ushered into a large black Mercedes with tinted windows and a small red, blue and orange Armenian flag. Just a month ago I was playing volleyball in Hermosa Beach and the difference in the surroundings, with burned out cars and military vehicles on the roadside, was jarring. I kept thinking of my brother Tigran, who lived and died here. How much anger must have burned inside of him to trade peaceful and free-wheeling California for this.

The man that held the door open for me got in, and I found myself in the middle of the back seat, next to a smallish man around sixty. Whatever hair he lacked on the crown of his head, he had in abundance elsewhere. His fingers gently stroked his grey and bushy beard. He did this pretty much throughout the time I'd had with him.

"Hello, Avi." His voice was surprisingly deep for his size. "We spoke on the phone. I'm Van Matusian."

"You were in Levy's notebooks," I said, "He saw you in Beirut in 1962, and then again in Italy and in Carcassonne in 1964."

"Of course, I remember. A nice man. What happened to him?"

"He disappeared in 1965."

"Oh … the same year as your grandfather …"

We drove by many signs of war: bomb craters, destroyed buildings, burned out tanks and military vehicles on the side of the road. I must have appeared anxious, because he added, "I know it's scary for an American to be in Lebanon, but the war died down, at least for now. My bodyguards are here in case we get stopped, but that's rare. Most checkpoints know my car. Just in case, we have a Canadian passport in your name. We, the Armenians, remained neutral in the conflict so we enjoy a safe passage through multiple zones of influence. Not in Southern Lebanon, that's General Lahad's territory. But they are allied with the Israelis. Your friend, Aron Milman, was very nice to personally take you here. How do you know him? I'd like to reciprocate for his kindness."

"He's a son of Yosef Milman, David Levy's friend. It's a long story, but that's how the notebooks to my grandfather came about. Mr. Matusian, I know from the correspondence that you knew my grandfather, my father and my uncle. Have you also met my brother?"

"Call me Van, please. Yes, I met Tigran. He came here with your uncle—I think it was in 1977? —but they didn't stay or spend time with us. Sadly, they saw us as collaborators. My father died in 1978, and they came to the funeral. That was the last time I saw them.

"Why was there a disagreement?"

"You know, way back in the 1960s, as the catastrophe of the Jewish people was coming to the world's attention, your grandfather wanted to force the world to confront our catastrophe as well, by violent means if necessary. My father didn't agree with him. It was ten years later, after an Armenian killed two Turkish diplomats in California, that your grandfather's ideas found enough followers. And the civil war here in Lebanon provided an opportunity."

We came to a sudden stop, the driver said something sharply, and Van Matusian replied in a raised voice. I understood "Hezbollah." There were stopped cars ahead of us, a truck with a mounted machine gun on the left side of the road. On the right, a car was pulled over and the occupants stood next to it, hands up in the air, surrounded by people in olive drab uniforms with AK-47's. The driver lowered his window, but we were waved through without further delay. The driver exhaled, visibly relieved.

Van Matusian turned to me. "Apologies. This checkpoint caught us by surprise. It was not there in the morning. Thankfully, it was Hezbollah."

"Thankfully?"

"There is no love lost between us and them, but they are disciplined, unlike some of the others. I'm sorry, I didn't ask if you speak Armenian?"

"Only a few words, I'm afraid."

"If there is another checkpoint, I'll make sure to explain to you what's going on."

There was a question on the tip of my tongue ever since Aron told me about the arrangement. I blurted it out. "Van—are we related?"

He stroked his beard thoughtfully. "Yes, we are. But if you don't mind, I'll let my mother speak to that. She's been so looking forward to meeting you. We'll be there soon. Now, please tell me more about the Milmans."

I recognized the house from the Levy's description.

As I was following Van up the stairs, I asked, "Do you still have the Nemesis room, the one with the pictures on the wall?"

"How do you …" Van stumbled, then smiled. "Of course, these notebooks that you have. Yes, we do."

"Can I see it?"

Just as described by Levy, the room was circular with a round table and chairs in the middle. Pretty much all of the photos on the walls had a black ribbon around them.

"It's been seventy-five years. They are all dead now," Van stated matter-of-factly.

I walked to one photo without a ribbon, a picture of six men surrounded by human skulls.

"This is the one with the German officers."

"You are well-informed." Van bowed. "Why don't you stay here, and I'll bring mother over. She doesn't care where we meet."

I understood why in a minute, when Van rolled in a wheelchair with an old woman in it. She looked small, almost shriveled, her face a collection of lines, thinned-out gray hair settled on her shoulders. Her eyes looked at the room, unseeing.

"Mother, this is Avi Arutiyan," Van said as he motioned to me to approach.

"Mrs. Matusian," I offered.

"Avi, come here," she said. "Where I can reach you. I'm afraid I can only see with my hands now."

Her voice was still that of a younger woman. I bent towards her and she lifted her hands and gently explored my face. Her hands and arms were just bones with skin stretched over them.

"You are a handsome boy, Gori's grandson."

"So my grandfather's real name was Gor, Gor Gregorian?"

"Yes. My brother, Gor. I called him Gori. I'm your great-aunt."

"Would you tell me about him?"

"Of course. I was waiting for you, Avi. You are his last direct descendant, and I wanted to tell you directly, so the knowledge of your grandfather does not get lost with me. Van, give us some water and leave us. I'll ring the bell when I'm ready for you to return."

And so Nouvart told me the story of the old country. How she grew up in Erzerum with three sisters and two brothers. Her older brother, Gor, left in 1914 to study abroad. How in 1915, when the *Hamidiye* detachment came to their town, they hid with a friendly Turkish family, but an Armenian collaborator gave them away. How the rest of the family was killed, but Ahmet Yavuz took a liking to her and took her as his servant. How he repeatedly raped her, while the *Hamidiye* regiment moved through Anatolia, laying waste to Armenian settlements.

Nouvart spoke of death marches into the Syrian desert, sides of the road lined up with bodies of those that no longer had strength to walk. Further along, away from the path, there were small hills. When one looked carefully, each hill was made of a few hundred corpses. In the killing field of Deir ez-Zor starving children picked out bits of food out of horses' excrement.

Then Yavuz left for Ankara and could not take Nouvart, so he gave her to a Kurd tribal chief. The chief also enslaved Nouvart and made her his concubine. She forced herself to live, so she could seek vengeance later. Gor returned as an Armenian volunteer with the Russian Army, crossed the lines and mountains in the winter of 1917, and found her near the village of Hakkari. Gor killed the Kurdish chief, and they escaped to Iraq and then Syria, the part that in 1920 became Lebanon. Gor went back, found and killed the Armenian collaborator. And then he found and killed three Turks that served in the unit that massacred Armenians in Erzerum.

She paused to catch her breath and drink some water. I decided to wait with my questions, let her talk.

"The war finally came to an end," Nouvart said. "Turks lost. The

British and French forces occupied parts of the country. We expected justice, we were promised it. One couldn't put all who participated and profited on trial, but at least the leaders. We expected too much. Suddenly, we no longer had friends. All was forgiven with the Turks. And that's when Gor went hunting for the leaders in Europe, until the Dashnaks ordered him to stop. Turks had a big price on his head, and their agents were looking for him. So, he went across the world to California and took the name of Aram Arutiyan. That's why his real name had to be buried as deep as possible. But he swore not to rest until he took revenge on Ahmed Yavuz. And he did."

My Great-Aunt Nouvart stopped again, tired.

"Then revenge on Yavuz was personal for you?"

"Yes, it was."

"Can you tell me what happened in 1965?" I asked.

"Let me call my son back," she said and rang the bell that was hanging off the armrest of her wheelchair. "These recent things, he knows them better. And that's not an easy story."

Van appeared quickly; he must have been waiting nearby. "Yes, Mother?"

"Van, we made it to 1965. Avi deserves to know the truth."

Van swallowed hard, went to one of the file cabinets, pulled out a bottle of whiskey and two small glasses with, "I keep this here just in case." After downing a drink, he said, "You know about the trial?"

"The one in Carcassonne?"

"Yes. We had a disagreement there. My father wanted revenge on Yavuz, but he wanted to stay as close to the letter and spirit of the law as possible."

"Ruben was a man of the law," Nouvart added. "He believed that taking shortcuts from the law would damage the cause."

"Is that why he organized the trial?" I asked.

"Yes. My father organized a kind-of-a-proper court, as proper as we could do without having our own country, so we, the younger generation, would not forget history but would also remember to follow the rule of the law. We were promised a state and he wanted to act as if we had one. An Eichmann trial of our own. And he wanted to release some of the anger that was building in the *spyurk*, our diaspora. The fiftieth anniversary of the massacre was coming and none of the pledges made to our people had been kept. Fifty years is a long time to wait. He was afraid that the anger would spill out in other ways. And that's what eventually happened."

Van poured himself another glass.

"Aram … errr, Gor, he thought differently. He thought that these crimes were so far beyond the law, only a merciless retribution would serve as a warning to others. At the very least, he wanted the fact of Yavuz's proceedings to be publicized. Back in the 1930s, he warned that what happened to the Armenians would happen to the Jews, because without punishment there was no deterrent. And the Holocaust had proven him right, or so he felt. He and my father had a big argument. Most Dashnaks agreed with my father. We had a proper hearing and we kept it secret."

Van poured himself another drink.

"Since he did not get his wish of the trial being made public even after the fact, your grandfather decided on his own reprisal. On the morning of April 24, 1965, he was going to blow up the Turkish embassy in Bonn. It was a deliberate choice, because in his mind the Germans shouldered a part of the blame for the Armenian genocide and were guilty of the Holocaust. I remember talking to him in Carcassonne and he was very angry at how lenient Germany was with their war criminals."

"Why? I understand what he did in the 1920s—but why would he get into this forty years later? He was well in his sixties!"

"He believed that his work had not been finished yet. At the trial, he met Levon Bogosian, a fiery French Armenian in his forties, who had experience with explosives. Your grandfather was a hero figure to him. We don't know the exact dynamic between the two of them. The more that younger generation learned about the genocide, the more they—Levon in this case—wanted revenge. Later, we found out that Levon was unstable; he was in a psychiatric treatment previously. They were not villains that did not care about the victims. They planned to set off the explosion early, before employees came to work."

"So, what happened?" I was surprised at how hoarse my voice sounded.

"Your grandfather kept it quiet. Very few people knew the exact plan: himself, your uncle, and Levon. Somehow, they arranged to smuggle the explosives from the Red Army in East Germany."

"It was David Levy who helped them. He had a friend that dealt in black market arms. It was in the letters."

"I see." Van looked at me with interest. "I would very much like to see those letters. The party —Dashnaks—got the wind of the plan just a few days before April 24th. My father was petrified. He thought the Armenian reputation would be sullied by such as act. There would have been victims. There are always people in an embassy, even in the early morning hours. He and two others flew into Germany and arranged to meet your grandfather in the place your grandfather chose. They wanted to attempt to talk them out of it. But Levon pulled out a gun and opened fire. And … and that's how your grandfather died."

"It was not meant to be this way." Nouvart broke her silence. "My husband didn't mean for my brother to get killed. He told me that Gor wanted to stop the shooting, tried to step in the middle and got caught in the crossfire."

"It was Bogosian who accidentally shot him," I said.

"How do you know?"

"The police detective in Bonn said that grandfather was shot in the back. From a Makarov pistol. Bogosian was killed by different caliber bullets."

"I wish my husband knew that. It might have made it a bit easier," Nouvart said.

"And what about my uncle?"

"He was not at the meeting." Van shook his head. "He agreed to not take revenge, but he never spoke with my father again, only with me and my mother."

"And my father?"

"Your father did not follow their way," Nouvart said. "Perhaps because he was in the real war and had seen a lot of deaths, he didn't agree with your grandfather. It was your father who alerted Dashnaks to the plan to blow up the Turkish embassy."

"So that's why my uncle and my brother broke up with him."

"Yes. Of course, he never meant for any of that to happen."

After a silence, she continued. "Now you know. That year of 1965 was cursed. I had to tell you, so you could choose your path in the full knowledge of how you got here. Know your past but make your own way."

391

"The path of my grandfather or the path of my father?"

"I think of it as the path of my husband vs. a path of my brother. I don't like violence, I know that Ruben was right about the rule of the law. And yet I also see it through my brother's eyes: some crimes cry to heaven and must be avenged. Justice is a luxury reserved for the powerful; retribution is sometimes the only choice left to the weak. But we are no longer weak; we'll have our own country soon. I wish Ruben and Gori had lived to see it."

PART 10:
IRIS

Comisaría de Policía Nacional de Gandía was surrounded by residential buildings on Carrer Ciutat de Laval, its location given away by a half-dozen blue-and-white police cars parked in front. Inspector Antonia Serrano, a petite, very serious-looking mid-thirties athletic woman with short jet-black hair, was somewhat surprised by the four of us: Avi, Erika, Gerhardt and I, piling into her small office over an old case. She must have been assigned to us only because of her good English. She was way too young to have handled the case back in 1965. Being a good sport, she personally brought in two extra chairs, and situated us all around a timeworn metal desk. I was uncomfortably squeezed between Erika and Avi.

"It took us some time to find the file after we received an inquiry from Germany," Inspector Serrano apologized. "The files for cases that were closed more than twenty years ago are kept in a different location, and this one"—she checked—"was almost twenty-six years ago. On October 7, 1965, a man by the name of Stefan Lux, 41, walked into a party at 37 Carrer de Formentera at Platja de Gandia and opened fire, killing Ernst Wolen, 58. He didn't try to escape or shoot anyone else. The guards at the party shot Mr. Lux, who expired on the spot. Nobody else was injured."

"Do you have a picture of Mr. Lux?" Gerhardt asked.

"Yes, of course." Ms. Serrano offered him a photo. Gerhardt looked at it, nodded, passed the photo to Erika, who was sitting next to him.

"Stefan Lux was the name on the passport that he left at the hotel. Supposedly from Munich, Germany. But when we inquired with the Munich police, we were told that there was no such man there. A detailed examination proved that the passport was a forgery. A very good forgery," she added apologetically.

Erika quickly studied the picture and respectfully handed it over to me with, "Iris, I'm sorry. This is your father."

I took it gingerly. I'd only seen two photos of him so far: the one with my mom taken in Jerusalem in the spring of 1962, and the other with Erika from the summer of 1964. Both had been taken from a distance, but I could immediately see the resemblance: the same wavy hair, small and slightly button-ish nose, slightly crooked, dimpled, almost guilty smile. He was a good-looking man. I could see why women fell for him.

When this guy, Avi, came out of nowhere with my Dad's notebooks, I had that insane hope that perhaps he was alive, that I would be able to meet him. I don't know if I would have gone through this whole crazy trip to Europe and Israel otherwise. But it was over, all over: there was no smile, no dimples, his expression was calm. An absurd thought went through my mind: *he finally was at peace.* My hand, the one holding the photo, started to shake and I steadied it against the edge of the desk. Erika took my other hand, and that helped to stop the shaking.

"Your father?" Inspector Serrano looked at me with a mixture of sympathy and curiosity. "I'm so sorry."

"Štefan Lux was a Slovak Jewish journalist, who committed suicide in the general assembly of the League of Nations in 1936, to protest the rising Nazism," Erika explained. "This man's real name was David Levy. He was a survivor of Auschwitz. The man he killed was Erich Rolff, SS-*Standartenführer* that was responsible for the deportation and death of Italian Jews, amongst other things. David avenged his friend. Some new documents have been discovered recently, about David Levy finding Rolff in Gandia in 1965. That's how we knew where to look."

I had these very mixed feelings towards Erika. It was obvious that she loved my father, and I was grateful for that. But in the back of my mind I kept thinking that if not for her, it's possible that my parents would have gotten back together.

On the drive here, I had asked her, "Are you angry over the bombings that killed your mother?"

"Of course. I know what we Germans did. I don't blame the Allies for bombing our cities. And yet ..." She'd paused, looking out the car's window. "I wish they did not, I wish they'd found a slice of empathy for the civilians below."

I had almost replied that after Auschwitz it was not their place to speak of empathy, but I bit my tongue. Now, I was glad I did. Through the touch of her hand on mine, I felt a warmth of compassion.

"It's noted in the file that there were swastika flags at the party, and some of the guests were wearing black uniforms," Inspector Serrano confirmed.

"They were celebrating the sixty-fifth birthday of Heinrich

Himmler, head of the SS," Erika explained. "And October 7th was the anniversary of the *Sonderkommando* uprising in Auschwitz when his friend Ezra was killed. It probably was symbolic to David. How did he get into the party?"

"There was an extension ladder by the back wall. He even wrapped it in rags, so it didn't make sounds. He planned it in advance."

"Did he leave anything? Like a note?" Gerhardt asked.

"Well ..." The inspector looked uncomfortable. "As I went through the file, there seemed to be a slight discrepancy: the officers that searched the hotel room listed a sealed envelope addressed to the police, but the envelope must have been lost."

"What do you mean?"

"It's not in the file. I spoke with one of the officers and he thought that the head of the police department took the still-sealed envelope."

"I see." Gerhardt nodded. "And may I ask who... was the head of the police department then?"

"Senior Commissar Carlos Robledo. But he retired in 1976. Would you like to talk to the current head?"

"Hmmm, 1976 ... No, thank you. It won't be necessary."

"Can I see the place?" I was still holding the photo, my hand no longer shaking.

"No, I'm sorry. From what I understand, it was a small German colony on that street. But after the shooting, most of them packed up and left. A hotel was built on that block, I think about fifteen years ago. I know we had a bit of a ... how to put it? ... a Nazi problem," Serrano said. "But I think it's in the past."

"I'm afraid not. Aribert Heim, 'Dr. Death' of the Mauthausen camp, is still here. Two years ago, you had dozens of Nazis in fully regalia celebrating Hitler's one hundredth birthday in Madrid," Erika replied sharply. Then apologized with, "I'm sorry. None of this has anything to do with you, of course."

I interrupted her. "I meant the place where my father was buried?"

"Yes, it is in the file." Inspector Serrano leafed to one of the last pages. "There is a municipal cemetery just northwest of Grau i Platja." She looked at her watch and offered, "I'll escort you."

"Thank you, it's very kind of you but not necessary," Gerhardt said. "If you can just write the address for us ..."

Inspector Serrano stood up. She was petite, but forceful. "It's not easy to find, and you've come a long way."

"Any significance to the head of the police department retiring in 1976?" Avi asked in the car.

"Possibly," Erika nodded. "General Franco died in late 1975. Many of his Spanish fascist supporters retired or were retired soon thereafter. It's not by accident that so many Nazis found safety in this country, they had many sympathisers here."

Inspector Serrano was right, the cemetery was not easy to find. It seemed largely abandoned, on a dusty hill with a few trees, about a mile from the ocean. The side gate was rusted by the salty air and Avi had to hit it a few times with his foot to get it to open. We spread out and wandered for about twenty minutes until Avi called out, "Here!"

The grave was barely marked with a small roughly made cross, with hard-to-read lettering: "S Lux."

"I'm sorry it's in such poor shape," Serrano said. "He was a criminal ..."

"He avenged his friend," Erika disagreed.

"Still a criminal act ..."

"He was in a grey zone."

"What do you mean?"

"I read this in *The Drowned and The Saved*, a recent book by Primo Levi, another Auschwitz survivor. A 'grey zone' is the moral compromise that prisoners were forced to make in order to survive another day."

"How does it apply here, Ms. Jager? Mr. Lux—sorry, Mr. Levy killed a man. I understand that the person he killed was a bad man, but that's still very wrong."

"Of course, as a matter of the law, Mr. Levy is guilty. But, Ms. Serrano, if by killing a bad man you'd be able to save the life of a child ... a hundred children ... would you do it?"

"It's a hard question." Serrano shook her head.

"Yes, it is. That's why it's a grey zone."

I stood in front of the grave and barely listened to that exchange. It was a hot day with a pure azure sky. A delicate breeze from the ocean played with the leaves of a poplar tree nearby. There is a certain emptiness that comes with the closure: you know, but there is no longer anything to look for.

"This doesn't feel right." I didn't realize I said it out loud.

"What?"

"This place. Why would he be in Spain?"

"Where should he be?" Gerhardt said. "Israel, Germany, Poland—none of these would be right either. He chose this place."

"How?"

"By other choices he made. Iris, your father was a very intelligent man. The way that he executed Rolff ... He knew that he'd die and be buried here. He made this choice, the place of his sacrifice. I think we must respect it."

Erika took my hand. "Please try to understand. Try to feel what he felt. The rage, the hurt, the despair. These men did unthinkable horrors and walked away. He could not abide. He just could not. Your father wanted justice. He waited for it for twenty years, before he took it into his hands. How much can you ask of someone?"

"Thank you. But I wish he'd chosen to live."

I looked at Erika and thought, *She and Hannah were the only ones who stood by my father, who accepted him as he was.* Benny, Shimon, Itzhak, Gerhardt, my uncle, my mother—they all used him, wanted something from him. Erika just loved him. I let go of her hand and hugged her. Not out of politeness, at a distance, like the first time we'd met, but really hugged her. Erika's body went rigid for a moment, and then she just folded into me and cried.

We placed a small pile of rocks above my father. Serrano, Gerhardt and Avi moved to the side, while Erika and I stood together, hand in hand, heads bowed in our own prayers.

"Goodbye, sweet prince. We'll be back," Erika said. "Now that we know where it is. You found a good spot. One can feel the sea breeze here."

PART 11:
ROSE

From: Rivka Milman
To: Avi Arutiyan

Dear Avi,

I apologize for the long silence. Some interesting things happened since we last spoke. I'm sure you remember Van Matusian, your relative from Beirut. We heard from him in July. He used his contacts to see what he could find out about the family of that man, Arno Krentz, that saved my dad. It turned out that Arno's mother and wife survived the Königsberg siege because the wife remarried a high-level Russian officer. The wife, Lilly, is still alive in Leningrad, and my dad and I went to meet her and her daughter Anna.

After the Königsberg city garrison surrendered, Russian soldiers drove the civilians out of the city. An officer noticed Lilly, who's still quite beautiful even now, and told his adjutant to pull her out of the refugees' column. That officer was Colonel Sergei Burkov. Next year, in 1946, he married Lilly and brought them all to Leningrad. A few years after the war he became a general. He died in 1976.

Lilly told us that Arno came to Königsberg for a short leave in May of 1942. That's when Anna was conceived. He was in training in Poland. On the third day he told his mother, Rose Haufmann, that he was transferred to the same unit as his friend, Artur Klopher. Rose knew what Artur did in the SS. She told Arno that he couldn't be involved in it. Lilly heard everything. You see, Arno was a committed Nazi and they had a terrible argument. Then Rose showed Arno her diary from World War I. He read it, grabbed his things and left. That was the last time Lilly saw him. Three months later the Gestapo knocked on their door. They called Arno a traitor.

Lilly and Anna showed us Rose's diary from World War I. Rose was a nurse. In 1917, she was sent to the Eastern Front, just as Russia was convulsing in a revolution. I am attaching translated portions of the diary, beginning with March of 1918 when they arrived in Kiev. I think you will find them interesting.

From Rose Haufmann's Diary

<u>27 March</u>

```
    What a crazy two weeks it was! We came to Kiev
by train, with two cars equipped as a hospital,
```

403

and have been busy since setting up on the top floor of a three-story building just off their main street, Kreshchatik. A beautiful street with a strange name.

Earlier this month, our soldiers took Kiev without any resistance. I like being in a big city after staying in smaller places like Chernivtsi and Vinnytsa. The place is overflowing with those that came from Moscow and St. Petersburg to escape Bolsheviks. Lieutenant Scholz said that Kiev is the size of Frankfurt and about a third as large as Berlin. He's funny, always showing off his knowledge because he likes Emma.

From our building we can see a statue of a man holding a giant cross. Lieutenant Scholz explained that this is St. Vladimir, the prince that Christianized Russia almost a thousand years ago. "Kiev is the mother of all Russian cities," he said.

There are only six of us in the hospital: two doctors, Bruntz and Stein; four nurses, Lilly, Marie, Emma and I. Lilly and Marie are older in their forties; I'm the youngest at twenty-one, Emma is a year older. We have the whole floor in the building. We sleep here as well, each of us has our own room. There is always a sentry posted at the entrance, plus Lieutenant Scholz is around a lot, so we feel quite safe.

19 April

We have not been busy at all. At night we hear shootings, but during the day it's quiet. Nominally, the city is governed by the *Central Rada*, but they have no real power. Sometimes a regiment of our hussars would march down Kreshchatik to remind people that there are 400,000 German soldiers keeping peace here.

Lieutenant Scholz keeps Emma and me company. Well, he is really only interested in Emma, so I'm sort of a chaperone. But I don't mind it at all: he has access to the car from the army headquarters, he is knowledgeable, and he speaks Russian a bit. We are in the middle of Ukraine, but in Kiev everyone speaks Russian.

You can get pretty much anything in this crazy bustling city of trees and river and churches and squares and broad boulevards. Doctor Stein lost his music: when our train came under fire in February just west of Vinnytsa, his gramophone and record collection were the only casualties. With the help of Lieutenant Scholz, not only a gramophone was acquired, but also records of Russian composers. On warm days, we gather together after dinner to listen to the music in the spring air.

8 May

There was a coup in the city: General Pavlo Skoropadsky overthrew *Rada* and proclaimed himself a Hetman. What a funny title, Hetman— it's like a King in Ukrainian. To make this even more ridiculous, Skoropadsky's election literally took place in a circus. Now some of Herman's troops parade around in their *sharovary* — strange wide pants collected at the ankles. None of this matters much to the people: everyone knows that the German Army is the only thing that stands between order and anarchy.

The world has gone mad. Four years ago, my brother Gustav told me we'd win the war in weeks. He marched off and was wounded on the Marne a month later. He didn't get treated in time, the wound got infected and he died. That's why I became a nurse: so that the boys like Gustav don't die needlessly. Fighting on the Western Front continues, but when I graduated, they sent me east, to this strange country. Russia collapsed into a civil war, with that new party of Bolsheviks taking power in St. Petersburg and Moscow. Here, in Kiev, it's quiet. Quiet as in the eye of the hurricane. Why am I here? Sometimes I think I'm in the middle of a giant maelstrom hurling us all through time and space to an unknown destination.

30 May

A giant explosion rattled the windows a few days ago. Someone blew up stores of ammunition on

Lysa Hora, a large wooded hill two kilometers south of us. Its name means Bald Mountain. Earlier, Doctor Stein played us Mussorgsky's *Night on Bald Mountain*, a fantasy of a witches' sabbath on that very place. I'm sure the composer couldn't imagine the bloody affair that was going to take place there fifty years later.

Nights feel more dangerous, more shootings on dark streets. We can hear distant guns, nobody knows who is attacking whom. This city is like a beleaguered island, surrounded by a sea of thirty million angry peasants.

25 June

Lieutenant Scholz came in very excited, with good news from the Western Front: the Ludendorff Offensive that started three months ago had been steadily pushing the French and British forces back. Reportedly, our troops are only a hundred kilometers from Paris. After almost four long years, victory is in sight. Hopefully, they'll send us back to Germany soon. I just wish Gustav was there to greet me.

There is much excitement in our small hospital as well: Lieutenant Scholz proposed to Emma and she accepted. They will get married upon return home.

One of our patrol had been attacked, supposedly by Petlura's nationalists. Two soldiers received minor wounds. I've been taking care of one of them for a week. After discharge, he came back with a bouquet of flowers and asked me out. I was flattered, but I was not attracted to him in this way and didn't think it was fair to accept.

30 July

Horrible, horrible events today! Field Marshal Hermann von Eichhorn, our military governor, was assassinated by a bomb just a few short blocks from here. They brought him and two of his aides to us. Unfortunately, we couldn't save him or one of the aides. The third man is barely hanging on to life. He lost a lot of blood, his body is burned, the left leg is mangled badly.

406

31 July

There was a mistake made last night: the man
that they brought in, the one that's still alive,
is not Eichhorn's aide, but an innocent bystander.
Lieutenant Scholz explained that assassins threw
two bombs, one hit Eichhorn's car, the other a
taxicab next to it. There were three people in the
taxicab, two men and a woman. Two of them had
died. In the confusion, they brought the lone
survivor to our small military hospital.

Lieutenant Scholz wanted to have the man
transferred to a civilian hospital, but Doctor
Bruntz refused.

"We have room, and this man will die if you try
moving him. I don't care if he's a soldier or
not."

Scholz tried to protest, but Emma gave him a
stern look and he stopped.

Doctor Bruntz, Lilly and I are taking care of
the patient today. We keep him sedated with
morphine. Doctor gave me a tube of morphia tablets
as well and said, "I now carry a tube with me. To
take in case of emergency."

I looked at him carefully to make sure I
understood.

The doctor shrugged. "They just killed the
senior military commander in broad daylight. They
hate us."

"But we're protecting them from Bolsheviks!"

"Some of them hate Bolsheviks more than us, but
they hate us nevertheless. If someone came to
occupy Germany, you would hate them too."

Lieutenant Scholz returned with more
information: the other man killed in that cab was
identified as the driver. As for the woman and the
man that we had, their identities were unknown:

"If we were dealing with the Germans, we would
have had the documents and all," he complained.
"But these people don't understand the simplest
things about keeping order."

"But weren't there German soldiers on the
scene?" Doctor Bruntz wondered.

"Yes, but they were focused on the late Field
Marshall and on pursuing the assassins. In the

407

commotion, I suspect that the wallets, purses and anything of value had been stolen."

7 August

I sit by the open balcony, taking in warm and humid wind from the river. Chestnuts fall outside making crisp, bouncy sounds. I've never seen so many beautiful chestnut trees. Kiev is famous for them.

My patient moans in his sleep. I get up to check, gently move damp blond hair and dab a wet cloth over his burning forehead, then carefully lift the sheet that covers him. Blood and pus seeped through fresh bandages of his badly mangled leg. Dr. Bruntz said that if it's not better by tomorrow he'll have to amputate. I tried to protest, but the doctor just shrugged. "Would 'he' rather die from gangrene than live with one leg? I don't know, and 'he' can't answer."

The patient is calling for his mother again. I washed him in the afternoon. Sinewy, long-limbed body, delicate fingers, cleaved chin. He is circumcised. I stared, surprised. I have washed dozens of naked men in the past year but have not seen this. Lilly, the older nurse, laughed: he is Jewish. That's what they do to their boys. Part of the covenant. But he's been calling for his mother in German, I protested. "Mutter" is the same in German and Yiddish, she said. I traded with Lilly for tonight. She smiled and agreed. I don't want him to lose his leg. I foolishly hope that my presence will stop the infection.

The wind picks up and the air charges with electricity. I close balcony doors as rain lashes out against them. The patient quietly murmurs. I touch his chest reassuringly. Suddenly, he reaches out and grabs my hand. His fingers are strong and cool, the fever is breaking.

12 August

The man regained consciousness yesterday. He speaks good German; he is a physician, studied in

Germany for two years. His name is Aron Milman, and he's thirty years old. He and his wife just arrived in Kiev from Baku by train the day of the attack and were taking a cab to the apartment they rented by mail.

He took the news of his wife's death hard. They were married in 1914 and didn't have children yet. He served as a physician in the Russian Caucasus Army, until it disintegrated a year ago. Things in Baku had turned very dangerous, with rival factions fighting non-stop. They barely escaped and came to Kiev because they thought it safe.

His remaining family is in Rostov-on-Don, cut off. He doesn't have anyone here. He remembered the address of the apartment they rented, and Lieutenant Scholz kindly went there. The landlord was very solicitous and apologetic, but he had no information and since the Milmans didn't show up, he rented to someone else. He would have pocketed the deposit money but was afraid to upset a German officer.

23 August

Aron Milman began moving around on crutches. Physically, he needs much therapy, but he's recovering nicely. Emotionally, he's very sad over his late wife. We talk a lot about what's going on in his country. He's excited over the revolution. We both like literature and talk about Leo Tolstoy, Victor Hugo, even the new German writer Thomas Mann.

Lieutenant Scholz came to tell us that the news from the Western Front is suddenly not so good. It seems that our offensive has stalled, and we are now being pushed back. Everyone is awfully sad.

6 September

Aron is now strong enough to walk around with a cane. Doctor Bruntz instructed him to exercise by taking excursions around the city. I'm pretty much always the one to accompany him. Two days ago we walked up Nikolaevskaya Street to the spot of the attack. I didn't want to, but he insisted.

Afterwards, he said it gave him a touch of closure.

Emma came into my room at night to talk.

"Rose, please be careful."

"What do you mean?"

"I see how you look at him. Your face lights up."

I won't deny that I find him interesting and attractive. I don't know where this might lead. At some point soon, they'll probably call us back to Germany anyway.

22 September

Yesterday Aron took me to Mariyinsky Palace. It's about two kilometers' walk each way, some of it uphill. A good exercise for him. For me, too.

We walked around the palace and the Imperial Garden that surrounds it, it's as beautiful as any place at home. We stood by a crumbling parapet over a dizzying drop to the river Dnieper, surrounded by lush greenery and blooming white flowers. Aron told me how the palace was built in the eighteenth century by Bartolomeo Rastrelli, the same architect that built the Winter Palace in St. Petersburg. That's where the tzars stayed when they came to Kiev.

"This place has an identity crisis," he joked. "Are we in Europe? Are we in Asia? The answer is 'yes'."

I was looking at his mouth as he spoke, and I wanted him to shut up and kiss me.

4 October

I had a night shift. Aron couldn't sleep. He came into the nurses' office and we talked about Guy de Maupassant and his stories. We were sitting on the bench close to each other. I got tired of waiting for him to kiss me and I leaned over. When he put his lips on mine, I pressed myself against him and felt his excitement. And then we lost control. His leg is still painful, so I climbed on top of him, and we made love this way. My blood ruined his trousers.

29 October

I didn't write in weeks. Aron and I grab any private moment we can find. Our secret is out. Other nurses make good-humored fun of me. Except for Emma, who's worried sick. I told her that I'm being careful.

I'm so happy. Aron's leg improved greatly, and we continue our daily walks. Of course, I'm always the one escorting him. Yesterday we stopped by a photographer and took a picture together.

But Aron will be checked out of the hospital soon. Doctor Bruntz kept him longer than necessary. Then what? I know Doctor Bruntz would like for Aron to work with us, but it would be difficult to arrange. Nevertheless, our faithful Lieutenant Scholz is trying.

12 November

Everyone is in shock. The Kaiser abdicated. The armistice announced in the West: we lost the war. Some of the German soldiers are wearing the Bolshevik's red armbands now. The great city is cowering in fear and uncertainty. Gunfire and explosions every night.

I missed my period. Do I tell him? I don't want to pressure him. But he has the right to know. I don't know what to do. Aron likes Germany, he told me himself before. This place is too dangerous for him—for us?—to stay in.

14 November

With the deposit money that Lieutenant Scholz recovered, Aron took me to Maxim's restaurant. I only had my nurse's uniform, so I borrowed Emma's dress. Emma is thinner than I and the dress fit very snugly. I didn't like how some of the men looked at me.

In the darkened and busy room, a gypsy woman sang a passionate and sorrowful tune. I'd heard the song before; it talked about beautiful dark eyes that broke the lover's heart. Aron wanted to pour champagne, but I had placed a hand over my

411

glass. "Not today. I'll just have water." I was going to tell him tonight.

Suddenly, a man appeared by our table and excitedly shouted, "Aron!"

Aron got up. They embraced and spoke quickly in Russian. Then they both turned to me and switched to German.

"Rose, this is my brother-in-law, Lev. He recently came here from Baku."

"Nice to meet you," Lev said in broken German.

"Nice to meet you too," I said. "I'm very sorry about your sister's death."

"But she's not dead!" Lev said. "She was told that Aron was dead."

I dropped my glass. Aron looked at me, then at Lev, stunned.

"Yes." Lev nodded. "Sarah was badly injured and in a hospital for a long time. She's still not well. She'd been told that she was the only survivor. My wife has a cousin here and that's where Sarah's been staying. I actually traveled to Kiev so I could bring her back with me. I came here for a dinner with an old friend and I saw you and you're not dead!"

Then Lev stopped and looked from Aron to me and back.

20 November

We are leaving today. The order is for all troops to return to Germany. I didn't tell Aron, I didn't say goodbye to him—it would have been too painful. Yes, his wife is alive. I saw his face in the restaurant, torn between love and duty. He must stay and help his wife recover. There is no other way. I must not force him to choose: if he were to go with me, he would always live with the guilt and I would always wonder when he would abandon me. I will write to him.

412

Rose returned from the war pregnant. For propriety, the family forced her to marry a drunkard Rudi Krentz. Rudi insisted that the boy be named after his late father, Hans. Rose got to choose the third name, and she chose Arno. That's what she called her son, and eventually he began to use it as his main name. She secretly wrote to my grandfather until 1936, then it became too dangerous. Rose never told him about Arno. She died in 1971.

In the pocket in the end of the diary, there was an old black-and-white photograph of a man in a dark suite and a woman in a grey dress and a white apron with a medical cross. Both were smiling happily. For a second, I thought that the man was my father. You know, my father always said that he was a carbon copy of his dad – whose pictures I never saw.

I'm very glad that I returned your call six months ago. Thanks to you, I now have a new cousin, Anna. And her two sons are my nephews, although they are close to my age, so I will call them cousins.

I will be coming to LA soon and I look forward to seeing you!

Hugs and kisses,

Rivka

P.S. Iris told me what Erika said about her father living in a grey zone. My uncle Arno—it feels strange to say this about an SS officer, but that's who he was—must have done terrible things, but I exist only thanks to him. I often think of the terrible grey zone hell he was in after he found out that he himself was precisely what he'd been taught to hate.

EPILOGUE

AVI

The long trip to Europe and the Middle East exhausted my savings, so by the time we returned I needed a job badly. I called Paul Collins. He seemed happy to hear from me.

"Avi! The computer I bought is still waiting for you!"

I set up for him a PC with an email and a simple file system. Then his dad wanted a computer, then a network had to be set up, the file system expanded, help was needed on some of their projects—by mid-July, I was working with them full-time. And while the pay was not quite what I made at Boeing, I actually liked the work, I had time flexibility and the bills were being paid.

In September, Armenia declared independence. I celebrated it with Elena's family. Evidently, they received a call from Beirut that reminded them about properly acknowledging relatives.

Rivka spent her summer in Israel. We exchanged a few emails and I still remembered the enchantment of her voice, but distance has a way of slowing things down. It was late September when I received a long letter from her, with Rose Haufmann's diary. I look forward to seeing her again, to see if the attraction is real.

I had dinner with Iris and her boyfriend, Max. I can see why they are together: both are fiercely intense. Traveling with Iris felt intimidating at times. During meetings I came to expect her intensity to spill over into a confrontation. But when she hugged Erika in Spain, I thought she reconciled with the past and found peace.

After learning about my grandfather's background, I debated whether to change my name to Grigorian, but decided to leave it as Arutiyan. After all, my family carried this name for seventy years. That's how people knew my grandfather, and my father, and my uncle,

417

and my brother. As my mom put it: "It's a good name." Sometimes I take out that photo from my third birthday, back in 1964: my grandfather Aram, my dad, Tigran and I on the bluffs in Santa Monica. Except for me, everyone was smiling. No one knew of the storm cloud on the horizon.

If Arno hadn't saved Yosef, Yosef would have not come to David. If not for David, there would have been no trial in Carcassonne. My grandfather would have not met Levon. Would my brother have been alive? I can imagine that. But things happened the way they did. Some years ago, back in college, I had a professor of statistics who claimed that studying probabilities inevitably makes one a philosopher. You trace into the past a chain of events, and it's infinitesimally improbable. But something always must happen, and if not you then someone else would be wondering about the impossible. A billion monkeys in front of a typewriter may not create *Hamlet*, but it's possible that one of them will produce: "*What's past is prologue …*"

I'm now almost as old as Tigran was when he left. There was a hole inside of me, that's how badly I missed him. And I missed my father—whom I had blamed for losing Tigran, but no longer. They all had horrible choices to make in the grey zone of justice, compassion and revenge that went back to 1915. Are we really "borne back ceaselessly into the past"? Is it impossible to break its pull? I know a niece of a genocidal murderer who's saving children of another genocide. Nothing is impossible.

The past is the context, but we get to write our own story.

418

IRIS

I had a visit from Ingrid, Erika's daughter. Ingrid completed her work in Cambodia and decided to fly back to Germany via LA. Ingrid looked like a younger version of Erika, matching my father's description from 1961. We were strangely connected by our mothers being in love with the same man many years ago.

"I remember your father well," she said. "The last time I saw him, I was eight. He was nice to me. Very gentle."

I felt a pang of jealousy that she spent time with my father, while I never had a chance. But it was not her fault. She didn't mean to take my father away from me, just like her mother didn't mean to take him away from mine. That's what is so ironic: for years I hated Erika Jager without even knowing her name, but she turned out to be the one who cared the most about my father.

"Now that I know more, I wish my father had married your mother," I told her.

"I wished so too," Ingrid agreed. "But for him, it just was not possible. My mother never blamed him for that. And neither do I."

For years, I wanted to know my biological father. Now, I feel like I know him a bit. He's no longer an abstract father-I-wish-I-knew. I think in life there are those that travel on paved roads and those that go their own way through the wilderness. I wish my father had chosen to live—I know he would have if he'd known about me—but I understand why he did what he did. I felt his anger and his passion. I inherited them, they flowed into me through his genes. He saw into the heart of darkness. As did Aram, Avi's grandfather. They both knew that one can't excise it by high-minded words and a slap on the wrist. They knew that some debts must be settled fully, in blood.

I'd been playing with images because numbers lose their meaning; they were just numbers. Six million names, one name per line, thirty lines on a page: that's two hundred thousand pages. A hundred and sixty-six volumes of *War and Peace*, stacked up three stories high. Line up the bodies shoulder-to-shoulder and they'd stretch from Los Angeles to Chicago. You could drive non-stop for thirty hours and that would be all you'd see. But you shouldn't drive. You should walk, and you should take at least five seconds to look at each face. Because it's not the story of six million, but of a person times six million. You'd walk twelve hours a day and you'd get to the end in three years. And somewhere along the way you would see my father. Because he was a part of it. He was sent back to exact a small measure of justice for his friend, but his soul never left that place.

I have two pictures in front of me. One is of a young girl in a beret, waiting in the woods before the gas chambers. The girl whose murder was not a crime in that Frankfurt courtroom. Sometimes I talk to her and tell her that she's not been forgotten. The other picture is that of my father and Erika, the last picture of him alive. Father took a measure of justice for Ezra's family. I will seek justice for him. I've been making a list. And I don't need anyone's permission to pursue it. I've been told that it's too late, it's been forty-six years since the war and many of the perpetrators are dead. But that's precisely the point: we must hurry while some are still alive. Benny's warning aside, I want to go down the rabbit hole. My father was handicapped by his guilt and his knowledge. I'm not. What about the Starks of the world? The Beckers? The ones that stole and got away with "what choice did we have?" And the ones that helped them. Soon, it'll be time to visit the retired police commissar, Carlos Robledo, in Spain. Former lieutenant in the Falangist forces, a German sympathizer. I have questions about the letter my father left behind.

Only the truth will set us free.

420

COMMENTARY

We've come to the end. It's just fiction, after all. Except that it's not. While the main characters are fictional, most of the events described here, the Carcassonne trial being a notable exception, took place. And many of the characters are fictionalized versions of real people, as explained below.

I started this book from the personal desire to understand who people like Adolf Eichmann were, to get a glimpse into their mentality. How could these events have been possible? With two-thirds of young Americans not knowing what Auschwitz was, the majority believe that this can happen again. As I was working on this book, I was dismayed to find how inadequately the murder of the Armenians had been recorded in literature and film, how the killing fields of Cambodia had been forgotten. To quote the late Elie Wiesel: "tragedies do not cancel each other out as they succeed each other."

This commentary is to provide a context, not present a complete picture of complex issues (that would take volumes). To help the reader separate fact from fiction, here are some of the events and personas listed alphabetically.

Armenian Genocide

Each year, on April 24, Armenians all over the world honor the victims of the Armenian genocide—the day when Ottoman authorities arrested more than 200 prominent ethnic Armenians living in Constantinople in 1915. What followed was a systematic extermination and mass deportation of ethnic Armenians under the cover of World War I. Ultimately, more than 1.5 million were killed.

An attempt to try the men who orchestrated the genocide by an international tribunal was not successful. For Armenians, there was no equivalent of the Eichmann or Frankfurt Auschwitz trials—the fictional tribunal in Carcassonne is the trial that should have happened but never did. While during the war the Allies promised that the criminals would be punished, and that Armenians would get their own country, these promises had been left unfulfilled. Britain occupied the oil-rich Mosul and the Turks conceded it. Mark Bristol, the post-war United States' High Commissioner in Turkey, was opposed to Armenian aspirations. Allen Dulles, a future chief of CIA but then a

State Department employee, worked for Bristol and was assigned to cover up the Armenian massacre. In 1920 he wrote to Bristol that "Our task would be simple if the reports of the atrocities could be declared untrue or even exaggerated, but the evidence, always, is irrefutable ... I've been busy trying to ward off congressional resolutions of sympathy for these groups." True to form, twenty-five years later he was short on sympathy for the victims of the Holocaust.

This moral failure led to an even greater tragedy down the road. There is little doubt that there is a connection between the Armenian Genocide and the Holocaust. It's not only epitomized by the sentence attributed to Hitler: "Who, after all, speaks today of the annihilation of the Armenians?" Many of the future Nazi leaders were in Turkey during World War I and witnessed the events first hand. There exists photographic evidence that the officers of the Imperial German Army were present at some of the atrocities. The genocide was extensively covered in the German press in the 1920s, especially following the trial of Soghomon Tehlirian, an Armenian that assassinated Talaat Pasha in Berlin in 1921. The Nazis were discussing the Turkish model already during those years: to them, the New Turkey was something of a post-genocidal utopia. The Nazis learned that nations at war can commit horrible atrocities and get away with it.

The Republic of Turkey is yet to fully acknowledge the facts and consequences of the Armenian Genocide. The leaders of the genocide are still heroes in Turkey. They were buried in Istanbul with full military honors. There are numerous neighborhoods, streets, public schools, buildings, and mosques named after them.

In this year of 2018, governments of 28 nations, including Canada, Sweden, Italy, France, Argentina, Germany, Poland, Brazil and Russia, recognize the Armenian Genocide (in six of these countries denial of this genocide has been criminalized). It's been recognized by the European Parliament and by the Catholic Church. All but two US states formally recognize the genocide. The government of the United States of America does not. Turkey is an ally with important NATO military bases, and evidently the US government doesn't want to harm Turkish-American ties. In this case, "never again" is more of a "never again unless it's politically inconvenient."

Armenian Terror Groups

In 1965, Armenians around the world publicly marked the 50th anniversary of the Armenian Genocide and began to campaign for world recognition. As peaceful marches and demonstrations failed to achieve it, the younger generation of Armenians turned to violence. In 1973, two Turkish diplomats were assassinated in Santa Barbara by Kourken Yanigian, a genocide survivor. This event initiated a chain of events which turned it, and its perpetrator, into a symbol representing the end of the conspiracy of silence. The Armenian Secret Army for the Liberation of Armenia (ASALA) was founded in 1975 in Beirut. At least three other terrorist organizations had been known to operate and conducted multiple bombings and shootings in the 1970s and 1980s. Terror actions largely ceased by the end of 1980s.

Arms Deal Between West Germany and Israel

In the early 1960s, Israel began buying arms from West Germany in order to renew the IDF's military arsenal. The deal was kept secret. But in late October 1964, word of the deal leaked to the German press. In response to the media reports, the German government revealed the scope of the deal, saying it was worth 200 million deutsche marks a year and included arms, planes and boats. Domestic opposition resulted in a decision to cancel the deal. Israel insisted on the agreement being fulfilled. The West Germans responded by sending a special envoy to Israel to discuss the entire bilateral relationship, including the issue of arms sales. In the end, following substantive discussions, the two countries announced the establishment of formal diplomatic relations, as well as the completion of the arms deal.

Auschwitz

According to a new 2018 survey, fully 41 percent of Americans don't know what Auschwitz was, including two-thirds of millennials (18-34-year-olds).

It's not feasible—nor is it my intent—to try to describe Auschwitz here. I believe that what took place there is fairly represented in the story. I will only offer the report of Pery Broad, *SS-Unterscharführer* in Auschwitz. It had been submitted as evidence in the Frankfurt Auschwitz trial and is slightly edited here for brevity:

"There at the ramp, cattle vans were being unloaded. The SS men of the camp garrison had meanwhile made the newcomers get off the train. The SS doctor then began to segregate those fit for work from those he considered unfit. Mothers with babies were unfit as a rule. Just as those who had impressed him as being weak or sickly.

Suspecting nothing, the column marched in. The SS guard at the entrance waited for the last man to enter the yard. Quickly he shut the gate and bolted it. Grabner and Hossler were standing on the roof of the crematorium. Grabner spoke: "You will now bathe and be disinfected, we don't want any epidemics in the camp. Then you will be brought to your barracks, where you'll get some hot soup. You will be employed in accordance with your professional qualifications. Now undress and put your clothes in front of you."

They willingly followed these instructions, given them in a friendly, warm-hearted voice. All felt relieved after their days full of anxiety. Grabner and Hossler continued from the roof to give friendly advice, which had a calming effect upon the people.

"Put your shoes close to your clothes bundle, so that you can find them after the bath."

"Is the water warm?"

"Of course, warm showers—what is your trade? A shoemaker? We need them urgently, report to me immediately after."

Such words dispelled any last doubts or lingering suspicions. The inscriptions pointing to "disinfection" the talk of the SS men and, above all, the pleasant look of the little farmhouses had many times made those who were about to die feel hopeful. Suddenly the door was closed. It had been made tight with rubber and secured with iron fittings. Those inside heard the heavy bolts being secured. A terror spread among the victims. They started to beat upon the door. Derisive laughter was the only reply. Somebody shouted through the door, "Don't get burnt, while you make your bath."

The "disinfectors" were at work. They opened tins which bore the inscription "Zyklon. Attention, poison." Immediately after opening the tins, their contents were thrown into the holes which were quickly covered. Meanwhile, Grabner gave a sign to the driver of a lorry which had stopped close to the crematorium. The driver started the motor and its deafening noise was louder than the death cries of the hundreds of people inside, being gassed to death.

Sometime later, when the ventilators had extracted the gas, the prisoners working in the crematorium opened the door to the mortuary. The corpses, their mouths wide open, were leaning on one another. They were especially closely packed near to the door, where in their deadly fright they had crowded to force it. The prisoners of the crematorium squad worked like robots, apathetically and without a trace of emotion. Then one of the SS criminals detailed to the gruesome task began to extract gold teeth from the jaws of the corpses, using a special tool. He collected them in a pot. Even the hair, shorn in the sauna from the heads of the new arrivals, was converted into money. If one asked an SS man, pointing to the corpses of men and women lying on the ground together with the children who lay as if asleep, why these people had to be exterminated? Then as a rule one got the answer, "It must be so." And that answer seemed, in his opinion, to be quite conclusive."

Bank of International Settlements (BIS)

The BIS was created in 1930, beyond the reach of either national or international law. It was headquartered in Basel and had a close relationship with the Swiss National Bank (SNB). Ernst Weber, the chairman of the BIS board from 1942 to 1947, was also the president of the SNB. BIS was also quite close with the Reichsbank, a Nazi bank engaged in state-sponsored theft. Hermann Schmitz, the CEO of IG Farben, was a member of the BIS board. Emil Puhl, director and vice-president of Reichsbank (and a war criminal convicted in Nuremberg), also served as a director for the BIS. In 1942, Germany and its allies controlled more than 75% of the votes on the BIS board. Even while technically the wartime president of the BIS was Thomas McKittrick, an American, the BIS served largely German interests. Puhl even described the BIS as a "foreign branch of Reichsbank."

The Nazis robbed the countries they occupied, and the BIS was essential to "legalizing" the theft. The BIS illegally transferred Czechoslovakian gold into Reichsbank's account. It accepted looted gold until the final days of the war. Nazi Germany had to buy raw materials and pay in hard currency. It paid the BIS in gold, most of it plundered. The gold had been melted down and stamped with false identification numbers. As an example, the BIS carried out thirteen gold swaps with Turkey, a total of 8.6 metric tons so Germany could pay for chromium.

After the war, Thomas McKittrick helped to prepare a white list of "good" German bankers, many of whom in actuality had enthusiastically worked with the Nazis, such as Karl Blessing.

Becker, Kurt

The character of Kurt Becker in the book is partially based on the actual person by the name of Kurt Becher.

Kurt Becher was an SS commander who was Commissar of all German concentration camps, and Chief of the Economic Department of the SS Command in Hungary during the German occupation in 1944. The "Economic Department" was tasked with extracting maximal economic value from Jews, which included confiscating goods and property, and selling or using belongings and body parts, including shorn hair and gold extracted from teeth.

From 1944-45, he collected large sums of money, jewelry, and precious metals from Hungarian Jews. He placed the fifty extra passengers on the Kasztner train at an average fee of $25,000 each. In January 1945, he was appointed as Special Reich Commissioner for all the concentration camps by Himmler. He was arrested in May 1945 by the Allies and imprisoned at Nuremberg but was not prosecuted as a war criminal as a result of a statement provided on his behalf by Rudolf Kasztner, a leading member of the Jewish Aid and Rescue

Committee in Hungary. It was suggested that Becher had hidden most of his loot before he was captured. On 24 May 1945, Subsection B of the 215th American Counter Intelligence Corps (CIC) detachment found 18.7 pounds of gold, 4.4 pounds of platinum, and some jewelry hidden under beds in a house Becher had been living in.

Kurt Becher was a free man in 1948. He went back to Hamburg, seemingly penniless, but before the end of that year he suddenly gained access to a substantial sum of money. Where it came from remains unclear. He bought out a fodder and agricultural products wholesaler in Bremen. By 1960 he was one of the wealthiest men in West Germany.

(Operation) Bernhard

Operation Bernhard, mentioned as a source of payments to Yavuz, was an exercise by Nazi Germany to forge British bank notes. Prisoners from Nazi concentration camps were selected and sent to Sachsenhausen concentration camp to work under SS Major Bernhard Krüger. The unit produced British notes until mid-1945; estimates vary of the number and value of notes printed, from £132.6 million up to £300 million. The counterfeit money was laundered in exchange for money and other assets. Counterfeit notes from the operation were used to pay the Turkish agent Elyesa Bazna—code named Cicero—for his work in obtaining British secrets from the British ambassador in Ankara, and £100,000 from Operation Bernhard was used to obtain information that helped to free the Italian leader Benito Mussolini in the Gran Sasso raid in September 1943.

Jaac Van Harten was a Dutch-Jewish businessman that was involved in laundering the counterfeit money. Some people considered him to be a Jewish agent, some a Nazi agent. He likely played both sides. After the war, he lived in Israel until his death in 1973. His activities were never investigated.

Bishop Hulda

The character of Bishop Hulda is based on Alois Hudal, an Austrian titular bishop in the Roman Catholic Church. In his 1937 book, *The Foundations of National Socialism*, Hudal praised Adolf Hitler.

After 1945, Hudal gained notoriety for working on the ratlines. He viewed it as a charity. He used the services of the Austrian Office in Rome, which had the necessary cards for migration mainly to Arab and South American countries. He is credited with organizing the escape of war criminals such as Franz Stangl, commanding officer of Treblinka; SS Captain Eduard Roschmann, known as the "Butcher of Riga"; Josef Mengele, the "Angel of Death" at Auschwitz; Gustav Wagner, commanding officer of Sobibor; Alois Brunner, organizer of deportations from France and Slovakia to German concentration camps; and Adolf Eichmann.

He resided afterwards in Grottaferrata, near the city of Rome. To the end, Hudal was convinced he had done the right thing, and said that he considered saving German and other fascist officers and politicians from the hands of Allied prosecution a "just thing" and "what should have been expected of a true Christian," adding: "We do not believe in the eye for an eye of the Jew."

Until his death in 1963, he never gave up in trying to obtain an amnesty for Nazis.

(The) Carcassonne Trial

This event is fictional. However, the testimonies of witnesses were based on actual materials. In particular, Faiz El-Ghusein was a real person. Faiz El-Ghusein was exiled to Diyarbakir under the suspicion of being a revolutionary. While in Diyarbakir, El-Ghusein witnessed the massacres of Armenians in and around the area. El-Ghusein wrote much of what he witnessed in his book *Martyred Armenia*, which provides an eyewitness account of the massacres and exposes its systematic nature. The account was originally published in Arabic in 1916 under the title "Massacres in Armenia." In the foreword of the book, El-Ghusein states, "The war must needs come to an end after a while, and it will then be plain to readers of this book that all I have written is the truth, and that it contains only a small part of the atrocities committed by the Turks against the hapless Armenian people."

Comrade Deuch

The character of Comrade Sary that Erika references towards the end of the book is based on Comrade Deuch, the head of the government's internal security branch of the Khmer Rouge. He oversaw the S-21 prison camp where tens of thousands of Cambodians were brutally tortured and executed. The Khmer Rouge regime perpetrated an ideologically driven genocide that killed an estimated 1.7 to 2 million people during its four-year reign in 1970s. After the Khmer Rouge regime was largely driven out of power by the Vietnamese army in 1979, for another twelve years the government that they controlled was still recognized and supported by major powers opposed to Vietnam (including the US and China).

Chrome Ore

Chrome is an essential constituent of all stainless steels and chrome-nickel and chrome-molybdenum alloys are required for armor plating, gun barrels and many types of shell. Turkey is one of the leading chrome exporter countries, while Germany was entirely dependent on imports of chrome ore. Without it, the German military production was virtually impossible. Knowing that, the US and Britain made an agreement to buy all the Turkish chromium. Officially, Turkey complied with the agreement until January 1943, when formal deliveries of chrome from Turkey to Germany resumed until April of 1944. There were rumors that clandestine chrome ore shipments from Turkey continued both prior to January of 1943 and after April of 1944. For example, Italian sources were reporting that in May and June of 1944, Turkish chrome was passing through Soutli (Sicily) en route to Germany and that 150 wagons of ore a week were arriving in Salonica from Turkey. There were also reports of smuggling of chrome from the Turkish ports of Alexandroupolis. It is also possible that the Germans might have made a clandestine arrangement with the masters of the vessels to off-load some of the ore at one of the German occupied islands on the route.

Deutsche Bank

After Hitler came to power, Deutsche Bank promptly dismissed its Jewish board members and took an active part in the *Aryanization* of Jewish-owned businesses; according to its own historians, the bank was involved in 363 such confiscations by November 1938.

In 1999, Deutsche Bank confirmed officially that it helped finance construction of the Auschwitz death camp. The bank serviced accounts for the Gestapo, the Nazi secret police, which deposited proceeds from auctions of property confiscated from deported Jews.

(The) Eichmann Trial

In May 1960 Adolf Eichmann was kidnapped in Argentina by Mossad agents and taken to Israel. The trial of Adolf Eichmann took place in Jerusalem in 1961. This was the first time that the Holocaust was presented to a judicial body in full detail, in all its stages and from all its aspects. Journalists from many countries covered the trial.

The indictment against Eichmann consisted of fifteen counts of "crimes against the Jewish people," "crimes against humanity," "war crimes," and "membership in a hostile organization"—that is, the SS, SD (Sicherheitsdienst; Security Service), and Gestapo, all three of which had been declared "criminal organizations" by the International Military Tribunal at the Nuremberg Trial. The charges were not confined to Eichmann's participation in crimes against the Jewish people; they also included crimes against other peoples.

The trial began on April 10, 1961. The court consisted of Supreme Court Justice Moshe Landau (who presided), Jerusalem District Court President Benjamin Halevi, and Tel Aviv District Court Judge Yitzhak Raveh. The public prosecution was represented by a team headed by Attorney General Hausner, and the defense team was headed by Dr. Robert Servatius, a German lawyer.

Eichmann's answer, on each count of the indictment, was: "In the sense of the indictment, not guilty." The prosecution presented to the court over one hundred witnesses and some sixteen hundred documents, many of them bearing Eichmann's own signature. The prosecution demonstrated what had happened country by country and camp by camp; it proved the personal involvement of Eichmann, as the head of section IV B 4 (the Gestapo section for Jewish affairs), in every stage of the "Final Solution."

The defense played down Eichmann's role in the whole process by depicting him as a small cog in the machinery of murder, an underling who had no choice but to carry out the orders he was given by his superiors. Servatius did argue in the court that killing by gas was a "medical matter," leaving even the judges stunned. The court rejected this claim and determined that Eichmann fully identified with his task; this was particularly demonstrated in Hungary, where Eichmann took personal charge of the deportation of that country's Jews to Auschwitz. The court found Eichmann guilty on all counts (with some unimportant changes) and, on December 15, 1961, sentenced him to death.

Eichmann lodged an appeal against the verdict that was heard by the Supreme Court. On May 29, 1962, the Supreme Court rejected the appeal. Eichmann was executed by hanging at midnight between May 31 and June 1, 1962. It was the only instance in the annals of the state of Israel of a death sentence being carried out. Eichmann's body was cremated and the ashes scattered over the sea, beyond Israel's territorial waters.

The Eichmann trial led to increased interest in Holocaust research and to a chain reaction in the investigation and trial of Nazi war criminals. In Germany particularly, the investigation of charges of complicity in Nazi crimes was intensified.

Former Nazis in West German Government and Industry

Hitler's criminal empire could not have existed without bureaucrats, diplomats, industrialists and bankers that made it run. A few of them were put on trial in Nuremberg.

For example, in 1947, twenty-four IG Farben executives were tried. IG Farben was the only German company in the Third Reich that ran its own concentration camp in Auschwitz. At least 30,000 slave workers died in this camp; a lot more were deported to the gas chambers. The Zyklon B gas was produced by IG Farben's subsidiary. In the Auschwitz files, correspondence between the camp commander and IG Farben's Bayer group was discovered. It dealt with the sale of 150 female prisoners for experimental purposes:

> "With a view to the planned experiments with a new sleep-inducing drug we would appreciate it if you could place a number of prisoners at our disposal (...)" – "We confirm your response but consider the price of 200 RM per woman to be too high. We propose to pay no more than 170 RM per woman. If this is acceptable to you, the women will be placed in our possession. We need some 150 women (...)" – "We confirm your approval of the agreement. Please prepare for us 150 women in the best health possible (...)" – "Received the order for 150 women. Despite their macerated condition they were considered satisfactory. We will keep you informed of the developments regarding the experiments (...)" – "The experiments were performed. All test persons died. We will contact you shortly about a new shipment (...)"

Twelve IG Farben executives were found guilty. By February 1951, all of them were free and welcomed back into the German business community. Hitler's banker Hjalmar Schacht was cleared of all charges and started a lucrative second career as an investment adviser to countries in the developing world and set up his own bank, Schacht & Co. Hans Globke, one of the most powerful people in the West German government, wrote the infamous Nuremberg Laws. Theodor Oberlander, Minister for Refugees, was found to have participated in the liquidation of 7,000 Jews and Poles in Lvov.

This was repeated over and over as after the war Hitler's diplomats, bankers, industrialists and even SS members regrouped to serve a democratic government willing to overlook their pasts. They protected each other. The new mantra was that only a small Nazi clique was responsible while the rest either resisted or were threatened into submission. In the Foreign Ministry, the political division alone counted 13 former Nazi Party members among its top officials, while 11 of the 17 senior members of the legal department were former Nazis. The British press openly scoffed at the "Gestapo Boys" working for the organization headed by Reinhard Gehlen, the precursor of the

434

Federal Intelligence Service (BND). The situation was even worse at the Federal Criminal Police (BKA): at times, former members of the SS's *Totenkopf* division held more than two-thirds of all senior positions. Roughly 80 percent of the judges and prosecutors who had served Hitler's regime of terror were soon working for the Federal Republic of Germany. Half of all state secretaries, section heads and subsection heads in the 1950s were former members of the Nazi Party. The murderers of yesterday were afforded public support. Even church leaders put in a good word for Nazis who had been convicted by the Allied courts as principal perpetrators. The distinction between perpetrators and victims disappeared in a haze of self-pity.

It's certainly not the purpose of this commentary to provide any kind of detailed analysis of the re-integration of the Nazis into post-war West Germany and the moral price that the society paid for it. The intent here is to provide a proper context for the 1960s atmosphere in West Germany and the difficulty of prosecuting war criminals during that time. But it seems safe to say that most of those complicit in mass murders got away with it.

Frankfurt Auschwitz Trial

The Frankfurt Auschwitz trials ran from 20 December 1963 to 19 August 1965, charging 22 defendants under German criminal law for their roles in the Holocaust as mid- to lower-level officials in Auschwitz. Hans Hofmeyer led as Chief Judge the "criminal case against Mulka and others".

The trial in Frankfurt was not based on the legal definition of crimes against humanity as recognized by international law. This meant that an SS man who killed thousands while operating the gas chambers at Auschwitz could not be found guilty of being accomplice to murder because he had been following orders, while an SS man who had beaten one inmate to death on his initiative could be convicted of murder because he had not been following orders. The court heard testimony from 359 witnesses. The members of the court even traveled to Poland to see Auschwitz for themselves.

Defense attorney Laternser did argue that the selection on the platform was an act of mercy.

The trial attracted much publicity in Germany. It was considered by some to be a failure because of relatively lenient verdicts and because it allowed the German public to distance themselves from feeling any moral guilt about what had happened at Auschwitz, which was instead presented as the work of few sick people who were not at all like normal Germans. However, the broad coverage of the trial demolished the silence that largely surrounded the Holocaust after the end of the war. Overall, only 789 individuals of the approximately 6,500 surviving *SS* personnel who served at Auschwitz and its sub-camps were ever tried.

(The) German Scientists Affair

On the morning of July 21, 1962, Egypt's newspapers reported the successful test launch of four surface-to-surface missiles. The next day President Gamal Abdel Nasser proudly declared that the military was now capable of hitting any point "south of Beirut." A few days later, Israelis learned that a team of German scientists had played an integral role in developing these missiles. "Former German Nazis are now helping Nasser in his anti-Israeli genocide projects" was how the Israeli press described the news. The German scientists developing the Egyptian missiles were some of the Nazi regime's most senior engineers, men who'd worked during the war at the research base at Peenemünde, a peninsula on the Baltic coast where the Third Reich's most advanced weaponry was developed. Mossad intercepted documents that raised fears that the Egyptians' true aim was to arm the missiles with radioactive and chemical warheads.

Then chief of Mossad Isser Harel was convinced that the German scientists were Nazis, still determined to complete the Final Solution, and that the German authorities were aware of their activities but doing nothing to stop them. A decision was made to kidnap or eliminate the scientists that were critical to the program. One of the chief scientists, Heinz Krug, was kidnapped in Germany and taken to Israel. After debriefing, he was killed. Attempts were made on others. Mail letter bombs were sent to Egypt and wounded some of the workers. However, this didn't stop the project.

In 1963, Harel was forced to resign. His successor Meir Amit focused on gathering intelligence about the project. In order to do that,

Mossad successfully "turned" a famous former Nazi, Otto Skorzeny. In December of 1963, detailed information about the project was delivered to some of West Germany's senior politicians. Presented with the evidence and wary of the possible international fallout, the West Germans convinced the scientists to return to Germany. By mid-1965, most of them left Egypt.

Gerstein, Kurt

Kurt Gerstein was a German SS officer and head of technical disinfection services of the *Hygiene-Institut der Waffen-SS* (Institute for Hygiene of the Waffen-SS). As he witnessed mass murders in the Nazi extermination camps Belzec and Treblinka, Gerstein gave corresponding information to the Swedish diplomat Göran von Otter, as well as to members of the Roman Catholic Church with contacts to Pope Pius XII in an effort to inform the international public about the Holocaust. In 1945, following his surrender, he wrote the *Gerstein Report* covering his experience of the Holocaust. He died, an alleged suicide, while in French custody.

Rolf Hochhuth's play *The Deputy* and Costa-Gavras's film *Amen* were largely based on Gerstein's attempts to get the Pope to actively interfere against the Holocaust.

Globke, Hans

Hans Globke was a German lawyer, high-ranking civil servant and politician. During World War II, Globke played a big part in the perfidious Nuremberg Race Laws, setting the path to the Holocaust. Globke later had a career as Secretary of State and Chief of Staff of the German Chancellery in West Germany from 1953 to 1963. Globke's key position as chief of staff to Adenauer, responsible for matters of national security, made both the West German government and CIA officials wary of exposing his past, despite their full knowledge of it. CIA pressured *Life* magazine to delete references to Globke from Eichmann memoirs.

Globke was accused of being heavily responsible for the Holocaust in Greece, as he could have prevented the deaths of 20,000 Jews in Thessaloniki when Eichmann contacted the Reich Interior Ministry and asked for Globke's permission to kill them. In 1963 East Germany convicted Globke in a show trial *in absentia*; the trial was dismissed as communist propaganda. Nevertheless, Globke's political career ended that year. After retirement, Globke decided to move to Switzerland. However, the Swiss government declared him an unwanted foreigner and denied him entry.

Inaction of the Allies over the Holocaust

The Allies knew about the extermination campaign in 1942. With pressure building on the American and British governments to do something, they pushed through the war crimes declaration on December 17, 1942. As the pressure continued to mount, the British Foreign Office sent the proposal to the American State Department for a conference on saving refugees from the Nazis. Unfortunately, the proposal also stated that "there is a possibility that the Germans or their satellite may change over from the policy of extermination to one of extrusion, and aim at embarrassing other countries by flooding them with alien immigrants." Evidently, the policy of extermination was more acceptable than the prospect of taking in the otherwise doomed people.

The conference took place in April of 1943 in Bermuda. After five months, the conference issued a report that proposed no meaningful steps to save anyone from the Nazi extermination and specifically stated that "no approach be made to Hitler for the release of potential refugees." The actual report of the conference was kept secret. One conferee said to reporters "Suppose Hitler did let 2,000,000 or so Jews out of Europe, what would we do with them?" The minutes of the American delegation discussion show that the British delegation believed that if approaches to Germany to release Jews were "pressed too much that that is exactly what might happen."

Szmul Zygielbojm, a member of the Polish National Council in London, committed suicide after the conference. He wrote: "The responsibility for this crime of murdering the entire Jewish population of Poland falls in the first instance on the perpetrators, but indirectly it is also a burden on ... the governments of the Allied States which thus far have made no effort toward concrete action of curtailing this crime. They have become the criminals' accomplices."

In 1944, the Allies were approached about bombing Auschwitz and the railroads leading to it. The Allied planes bombed the IG Farben synthetic rubber plant (which didn't produce anything) but not a single bomb fell on the crematoria or the railroads.

In summary, the British and American governments never went beyond declarations. And the Soviets didn't care. In the big strategic picture, the Jews, like the Armenians before them, were expendable.

Jager, Karl

Based on the persona of Karl Jäger, who served as commander of the *SD Einsatzkommando 3a* that operated in Lithuania. The actions of this killing squad were tallied by Jäger himself. His report keeps an almost daily running total of the liquidations of 137,346 people, most of them women and children. Jäger escaped capture until his report was discovered in March 1959. Arrested and charged with his crimes, Jäger committed suicide while he was awaiting trial in June 1959.

(The) Kasztner Trial

The Kasztner (also Kastner) trial, was a libel case held in Jerusalem in 1954 before Judge Benjamin Halevi, who published his decision on 22 June 1955. The defendant, Malchiel Gruenwald, who lost fifty-two relatives in the Auschwitz concentration camp, had accused Rudolf Kasztner, a Hungarian lawyer, of collaborating with the Nazis in Hungary during the Holocaust, when 437,000 were sent to Auschwitz. The allegations were made in a self-published newsletter. The Israeli government sued on Kasztner's behalf. Gruenwald's lawyer turned the case into one that examined the actions of the governing Mapai party during the Holocaust, and what had been done to help Europe's Jews. One of the key issues was whether Kasztner had in effect collaborated with Adolf Eichmann and Kurt Becher, two SS officers, in his efforts to secure safe passage from Budapest to Switzerland of 1,684 Jews, on what became known as the Kasztner train. The judge agreed, accusing Kastner of having "sold his soul to the devil." Kastner was assassinated in 1957. Parts of the decision were overturned by the Supreme Court of Israel in 1958. The court upheld the charge that Kastner had helped

Kurt Becher escape punishment after the war by writing him a letter of recommendation.

When Eichmann arrived in Hungary in the spring of 1944, he was accompanied by 150 to 200 staff who were expected to deport 750,000 people. The Nazis wanted to avoid—at all cost—another Warsaw Ghetto Uprising. It is likely that in order to do that, Eichmann entered into negotiations with Kasztner and others: to dangle the hope of rescue and to drag them out while the deportations continued apace. If people knew that they were condemned to death, they would have likely fought or tried to escape. When Kasztner came to his hometown of Kluj, there were only twenty gendarmes and one SS officer guarding twenty thousand people. Romania was only three miles away. Kasztner knew about the upcoming deportations and he knew what happened to Jews in other Nazi-occupied countries, but he didn't say a word except to his select group of 380 that were saved.

Kasztner remains a hero to some (e.g., Anna Porter, *Kasztner Train: The True Story of an Unknown Hero of The Holocaust*), a criminal to others (Paul Bogdanor, *Kasztner's Crime*). After reviewing these and other sources, I veer to Bogdanor's side. His book is well-researched and troubling. But given the environment he operated in, defining Kasztner in absolute terms as either collaborator or a hero is impossible. Kasztner appears to have become entrapped in a delusion of self-importance and a belief that eventually his many compromises would pay off. He even wrote that the deported Jews were alive in "Waldsee"—a Nazi euphemism for the reality of Auschwitz. His is a tragic figure of a victim and a collaborator, who lived and died in a "grey zone" where some of the judgment should be suspended.

(Occupation of) Kiev in 1918

After the Bolshevik revolution in 1917, the Russian army collapsed, and the German army moved into the power vacuum. The German army occupied Kiev, Ukraine's capital, in March of 1918. Former Imperial Russian Army General Pavlo Skoropadsky led a successful German-backed coup in late April, making himself a dictator and declaring the "Hetmanate."

Field Marshal von Eichhorn was the supreme commander of the German army in Ukraine and the military governor. He was assassinated on July 30th. The story of Aron Milman as an injured bystander is fictional.

For a few months, Kiev was a safe haven for people fleeing Bolsheviks and/or conflicts in other parts of the disintegrating Russian empire. In November, Germany was defeated on the Western Front and withdrew from Ukraine.

Klopher, Otto

The character of Otto Klopher in the book is loosely based on German banker Hermann Josef Abs. He was a member of the board of directors of Deutsche Bank from 1938 to 1945, as well as of 44 other companies, including IG Farben. As the most powerful commercial banker of the Third Reich, he was, according to economic journalist Adam LeBor, "the lynchpin of the continent-wide plunder". The Allies arrested him as a suspected war criminal in 1946, however British intervention got him freed after three months despite a detailed report that would be published later. After World War II (1957–1967) he was chairman of Deutsche Bank.

Kolbe, Fritz

Fritz Kolbe was a German diplomat who became a spy against the Nazis in World War II. After the war, Kolbe was a despised and much-hated figure in Germany, where he was widely viewed as a traitor. *Der Stern* magazine commented that: "Kolbe's story demonstrates that ordinary Germans could do something to fight Hitler's madness—and post-war Germany treated him like a leper because of his actions." Kolbe's work was officially recognized by the Foreign Office of the German Federal Republic when a hall bearing his name was inaugurated in the ministry in 2004. He was listed at the Memorial to the German Resistance in 2005.

Lorens, Zachary

The character of Dr. Zachary Lorens in the book is loosely based on Konrad Zacharias Lorenz, an Austrian zoologist and ethologist. He shared the 1973 Nobel Prize in Physiology or Medicine and is often regarded as one of the founders of modern ethology, the study of animal behavior.

Konrad Lorenz joined the Nazi Party in 1938 and accepted a university chair under the Nazi regime. In his application for party membership he wrote, "I'm able to say that my whole scientific work is devoted to the ideas of the National Socialists." His publications during that time led in later years to allegations that his scientific work had been contaminated by Nazi sympathies. His published writing during the Nazi period included support for Nazi ideas of "racial hygiene" couched in pseudoscientific metaphors.

After the war, Lorenz denied having been a party member, until his membership application was made public; and he denied having known the extent of the genocide, despite his position in the Office of Racial Policy. He also denied having ever held anti-Semitic views, but was later shown to have used frequent anti-Semitic language. In 2015, the University of Salzburg posthumously rescinded an honorary doctorate awarded to Lorenz in 1983, citing his party membership and his assertions in his application that he was "always a National Socialist" and that his work "stands to serve National Socialist thought." The university also accused him of using his work to spread "basic elements of the racist ideology of National Socialism."

Möll, Otto

Otto Möll was an *SS-Hauptscharführer* and the chief of the crematoria at Auschwitz. A sadistic murderer, he is said to have personally killed thousands of innocent victims, in some cases throwing them alive into flaming pits. He was executed by the Americans on May 28, 1946.

He always said to his men: *"Befehl ist Befehl!"* ("An order is an order!").

Nazis in Los Angeles

Referred to during Avi's visit to see Paul Collins. It might be hard to believe, but there indeed was a $70 million (today's dollars) compound that Norman and Winona Stephens built in Pacific Palisades, intended to serve as Hitler's West Coast headquarters, halfway between Tokyo and Berlin. The ruins of the project are easy to

442

find: it's now known as Murphy Ranch, on the way to the Boy Scouts' Camp Josepho. There was a strong Nazi presence in pre-war Los Angeles. Leon Lewis was a lawyer that led an undercover campaign against them. As a part of this work, he recruited World War I veterans to join the Nazi organizations and report on their activities. A number of sabotage and murder plots had been prevented through these efforts.

Nazis in Spain

In 1989, dozens of high-ranking Nazis gathered in Madrid for the centenary of Hitler's birth. Spain was the only European country to allow such a tribute. Hundreds of high-ranking Nazis found refuge there, not counting the Nazis of lesser rank. Many fleeing Nazis chose Spain because of a high level of cooperation between Spain and Nazi Germany. During the war, any German resident of Spain suspected of not supporting the Nazi cause could be detained and repatriated immediately, without any preliminary extradition appeal or trial. Spain, although in theory a neutral country, supplied the Nazis with a large quantity of materials that were of vital importance to their war effort. In 1941, the Franco regime ordered provincial governors to draw up a list of Jews living in Spain. The census was, according to Spain's El País, "presumably given to Himmler."

After the war, scores of the Nazis found themselves at home on the beautiful Mediterranean coast of Spain. There are many stories about old German guys with either their SS tattoo or, more often, a mark where it had been removed. Reports came in of all-German communities that sheltered in surprising locations away from the coast.

Barranco Blanco (which means White Ravine in Spanish) mentioned in the story as a hiding place, is set in stunning woodland with a river that ends in a magical waterfall. During the war it was used as a secret meeting place for Franco, Hitler and Mussolini. An army barracks was built and used by the Germans for clandestine SS training. Following the war, it became a camp, the most secure of Spain's Nazi refuges. Visitors in the early 1970s describe German-style homes openly flying the swastika and a German themed bar, before being escorted clear by armed guards.

(Operation) Nemesis

In 1919, Great Britain seized some of the perpetrators of the Armenian Genocide and transported them to the British colony of Malta to be tried. However, after Mustafa Kemal Atatürk's incarceration of Lord Curzon's relative, they were acquitted and exchanged for British prisoners of war by the new Turkish government of Atatürk. The men who orchestrated the genocide went free.

The Armenian Revolutionary Federation met in Yerevan in October 1919. Over many objections, it was decided to mete out justice through armed force. A "black list" was created, containing the names of 200 persons deemed responsible for organizing the genocide. Operation Nemesis was named after the Greek goddess of divine retribution. A number of the Turkish perpetrators and Armenian collaborators had been assassinated in 1921-22 in Germany, Italy, Turkey, Georgia and Tajikistan.

Notably, in March of 1921, Talaat Pasha, former Ottoman Grand Vizier and Minister of the Interior as well as the widely perceived author of the genocide, was assassinated in a crowded Berlin shopping street. Three months later the assassin, Soghomon Tehlirian, stood trial in Berlin and was acquitted by a jury—the trial had been completely turned around and focused rather on the Armenian Genocide and Talaat Pasha's role in it than on the actual assassination.

The character of Aram Arutiyian is based on stories of some of the avengers.

Photo Albums

Three photo albums are mentioned in the story. These are actual albums that provide visual evidence of the events that took place. I believe that they tell us more than words ever could.

Armin T. Wegner was sent to the Middle East in 1915 as a member of the German Sanitary Corps. Against the strict orders of the Turkish and German authorities, Wegner collected documents and took photographs of the Armenian Genocide. With the help of foreign consulates, he was able to send some of this material to Germany and the United States. His activities were discovered, and Wegner was arrested and was put to serve in the cholera wards. Having fallen seriously ill, he left Baghdad for Constantinople in November 1916. Hidden in his belt were photographic plates that form the Wegner Album.

In 1933, Wegner denounced the persecution of Jews in Germany in an open letter to Adolf Hitler. Shortly after authoring the letter, Wegner was arrested by the Gestapo and thrown into concentration camps. Upon his release, he fled to Rome, where he lived under a false identity.

In 1967 he was accorded the title of Righteous Among the Nations by Yad Vashem.

He died at the age of 91 in Rome. Some of his ashes were later taken to Armenia to be honored at a posthumous state funeral. He had been virtually forgotten by the German people. The inscription on Wegner's gravestone reads: "I loved justice and hated iniquity. Therefore, I die in exile."

The Auschwitz Album is the only surviving visual evidence of the process leading to the mass murder at Auschwitz-Birkenau. The photos were taken at the end of May or beginning of June 1944, either by Ernst Hofmann or by Bernhard Walter, two SS men whose task was to take ID photos and fingerprints of the inmates (not of the Jews who were sent directly to the gas chambers). The photos show the arrival of Hungarian Jews. The album was presented as testimony at the Auschwitz trials in Frankfurt.

Kurt Hubert Franz was an SS officer and one of the commanders of the Treblinka extermination camp. He was arrested on December 2, 1959. A search of his home found a photo album of Treblinka with the title, "Beautiful Years." In 1965, he was found guilty of collective murder of at least 300,000 people. He was sentenced to life imprisonment, released in 1993 for health reasons. Kurt Franz died in 1998.

Pius XII

In 1963, Rolf Hochhuth's play *The Deputy* created a storm over the Pope's knowledge of and alleged inaction in response to the Holocaust. Hochhuth has not been alone in his criticism. Many others have passed a harsh judgment upon Pope Pius XII because of his silence on Nazi crimes. During the years of the Final Solution, numerous religious leaders and diplomats beseeched and implored the Pope to speak out clearly, specifically and forcefully against the Nazi effort to exterminate the Jews. But he never did. He feared that to do so would risk even worse atrocities. The farthest he went was to produce a vague exhortation in his Christmas message of 1942.

Pius XII's defenders point to the direct aid that the Pope accorded the persecuted Jews of Rome, included sheltering and protecting some Jews in the buildings and offices of the Vatican itself; also, to secret instructions urging the national churches to intervene on behalf of oppressed Jews in whatever ways they could. In other words, they argue that Pius XII did what realistically could have been done.

It's not possible to resolve this argument, nor is it my place to do so. The secrets are buried in the Vatican. Twenty years ago, the Vatican opened the Inquisition archives from the 16th century. We probably have only four hundred years to wait until the WWII archives are opened. But a few points seem to be difficult to dispute:
- Pius XII detested Hitler.
- One of his main goals was to save Christianity from Bolshevism. In that regard, he was highly engaged in diplomacy and was careful to not criticize Germany harshly. That's probably why he showed much empathy to the Nazi war criminals post-1945.
- As early as 1942, he knew about the Holocaust taking place. Too many witnesses, too many documents, many proven to be presented at the highest levels.
- Pius XII had tools available to use against Hitler: excommunication, revocation of the concordat between the Church and the Nazis, a powerful direct condemnation. These tools had been used by his predecessors. He opted to remain silent.

The picture is that of the Pope that was not driven by anti-Semitism or love of the Nazis (unlike Bishop Hudal), but simply had other priorities. To his defenders, I'd say that even taking into account very difficult conditions that Pius XII faced, this was still an astonishing moral failure. To quote Father John Morley that wrote *Vatican Diplomacy and the Jews During the Holocaust*: "It must be concluded that Vatican diplomacy failed the Jews during the Holocaust by not doing all that it was possible for it to do on their behalf. It also failed itself because in neglecting the needs of the Jews and pursuing a goal of reserve rather than humanitarian concern, it betrayed the ideals it had set for itself. The nuncios, the secretary of state, and, most of all, the Pope share the responsibility for this dual failure."

The Vatican elevated Pius XII to the "Venerable" status but is yet to canonize him. Out of the four popes that followed him, three had been canonized already and the one that hadn't had only been in the office for 33 days.

Prosecution of Nazi Crimes in West Germany

The Nuremberg trial of the twenty-one major German war criminals ended in October of 1946. Eighteen were convicted, eleven sentenced to death.

Following that, the Americans held twelve trials of Einsatzgruppen members, of doctors, lawyers, industrialists, etc., from December of 1946 to April of 1949. In all, 142 of the 185 defendants were found guilty. Twenty-four persons received death sentences, of which 11 were converted to life imprisonment, 20 were sentenced to life imprisonment, 98 were given prison sentences of varying lengths, and 35 were acquitted.

Between 1950 and 1962, the West Germans tried 5,426 former Nazis. The vast majority were acquitted, only 155 were convicted of murder.

At the end of 1958, the Central Office of the Land Judicial Authorities for the Investigation of National Socialist Crimes (ZS) was established in Ludwigsburg. Their work was unpopular, but this small group of courageous lawyers and investigators broke the semi-official policy of silence about the Nazi past.

Ratlines

Ratlines were a system of escape routes for Nazis fleeing Europe at the end of World War II. These escape routes mainly led toward havens in South America. There were two primary routes: the first went from Germany to Spain, then Argentina; the second from Germany to Rome to Genoa, then South America. Argentine diplomats and intelligence officers had, on Perón's instructions, vigorously encouraged Nazi and Fascist war criminals to make their home in Argentina.

Bishop Alois Hudal was rector of the *Pontificio Istituto Teutonico Santa Maria dell'Anima* in Rome, Hudal used this position to aid the escape of wanted Nazi war criminals. Hudal provided the objects of his charity with money to help them escape, and more importantly with false papers including identity documents issued by the *Vatican Refugee Organization*.

Another major Roman ratline was operated by a small, but influential network of Croatian priests led by Father Krunoslav Draganović, who organized a highly sophisticated chain with links to the final embarcation point in the port of Genoa. The ratline initially focused on aiding members of the genocidal Croatian Ustashe movement.

Ex-Nazis themselves, organized in secret networks, also ran the escape routes. The most famous such network is ODESSA (Organisation of former SS members), founded in 1946. ODESSA was supported by the Gehlen Org, which employed many former Nazi party members, and was headed by Reinhard Gehlen, a former German Army intelligence officer employed post-war by the CIA. The Gehlen Org became the nucleus of the BND German intelligence agency, directed by Reinhard Gehlen from its 1956 creation until 1968.

Some of the Nazis and war criminals who escaped using ratlines include:

- Adolf Eichmann, fled to Argentina in 1950, captured 1960, executed in Israel
- Franz Stangl, fled to Brazil in 1951, arrested in 1967 and extradited to West Germany, died in 1971
- Gustav Wagner, fled to Brazil in 1950, arrested in 1978, committed suicide in 1980

- Erich Priebke, fled to Argentina in 1949, arrested in 1994, eventually died in 2013
- Klaus Barbie, fled to Bolivia with help from the United States, captured in 1983, died in prison in France on 23 September 1991
- Eduard Roschmann, escaped to Argentina in 1948, fled to Paraguay to avoid extradition and died there in 1977
- Aribert Heim, disappeared in 1962, most likely died in Egypt in 1992
- Andrija Artuković, escaped to the United States, arrested in 1984 after decades of delay and extradited to Yugoslavia, where he died in 1988
- Ante Pavelić, escaped to Argentina in 1948, initially survived an assassination attempt in 1957, but died of his wounds in Spain in 1959
- Walter Rauff, escaped to Chile, never captured, died in 1984
- Alois Brunner, fled to Syria in 1954, died around 2010
- Josef Mengele, fled to Argentina in 1949, then to other countries, died in Brazil in 1979.

(The) Righteous Among Nations

A core goal of Yad Vashem's founders was to recognize Gentiles who, at personal risk and without a financial motive, chose to save their Jewish brethren during the Holocaust. Those recognized by Israel as Righteous Among the Nations are honored in Yad Vashem and have trees planted in their honor. The Avenue of the Righteous Among the Nations was dedicated on Holocaust Remembrance Day, May 1, 1962. The first eleven trees were planted that day.

Rolff, Erich

The character of Erich Rolff is loosely based on two SS officers, Walter Rauff and Karl Wolff.

Walter Rauff had been responsible for nearly 100,000 deaths in the Chelmno extermination camp. He was instrumental in the implementation of gas vans. In 1942, Rauff was transferred to Rommel's

Afrika Korps to set up an extermination unit. Rauff was responsible for the death of more than 2,500 Jews in Nazi-occupied Tunisia. After Rommel's defeat, Rauff took charge of all Gestapo and *SD* operations throughout northwest Italy. He was arrested after the war and held in a high security prison at San Vittore. When the Italians wanted to prosecute him, the U.S. authorities transferred him to a low security POW camp, from which Rauff walked out and went to Rome where the Catholic Church hid him until his family was able to come to Rome. After that, they left—with the help of Bishop Hudal-provided documents—to Syria and South America.

In Damascus he served as military adviser to President Hosni Zaim when they fought against Israel. He fell out of favor and escaped back to Italy, from there he went to Chile. From 1958 to 1962, Rauff was on the payroll of the Federal Intelligence Service of West Germany (BND). His contact was Wilhelm Beissner, a paymaster for BND and a war criminal. In 1960, he traveled to Germany in order to claim his pension for the time served in the *Reichsmarine*, and had no trouble with the German authorities. Rauff was dismissed from BND in October 1962. When Hans Strack, the German ambassador to Chile, was ordered to request his extradition, Strack, a supporter of exiled war criminals, forwarded the application for Rauff's extradition only 14 months later. The delay allowed Chile to refuse the extradition request because the time elapsed from his 100,000 murders overran the country's statute of limitations.

Karl Wolff, SS Obergruppenfuhrer and a war criminal, was protected by Allen Dulles, director of the Office of Strategic Services and later the head of the CIA. Wolff escaped meaningful prosecution for many years. He was re-arrested in Germany after the Eichmann trial. Allen Dulles could no longer protect him, having been fired by John F. Kennedy in 1961. In 1964, Wolff was convicted of the death of 300,000 people in Treblinka and served seven years.

Skorzeny, Otto

Otto Skorzeny, the self-proclaimed "most dangerous man in Europe," was a lieutenant colonel in the SS, who became famous for a string of daring operations, including freeing the deposed Italian dictator, Mussolini. After the war, he settled in Spain. In 1953 he became a military advisor to Egypt and recruited a staff of former SS and Wehrmacht officers to train the Egyptian Army. Around 1962, Skorzeny was recruited by the Mossad to obtain information on German scientists who were working on an Egyptian project to develop rockets to be used against Israel. His work for the Mossad included assassinating German rocket scientist Heinz Krug who was working with Egypt and mailing a letter bomb which killed five Egyptians at the Egyptian military rocket site. It is speculated that Skorzeny worked for the Mossad in order to avoid assassination.

Sonderkommando

Sonderkommandos (German: *special unit*) were work units made up of German Nazi death camp prisoners. They were composed of prisoners, usually Jews, who were forced, on threat of their own deaths, to aid in the killings. While this section describes Auschwitz, such units existed in multiple camps.

Sonderkommando members did not participate directly in killing; that responsibility was reserved for the guards, while the *Sonderkommandos'* primary responsibility was disposing of the corpses. In most cases they were inducted immediately upon arrival at the camp and forced into the position under threat of death. They were not given any advance notice of the tasks they would have to perform. They had no way to refuse or resign other than by committing suicide.

Because the Germans needed the *Sonderkommandos* to remain physically able, they were granted better living conditions than other inmates: they slept in their own barracks and were allowed to keep and use various goods such as food, alcohol and cigarettes brought into camp by those who were sent to the gas chambers. The Germans followed a policy of regularly killing almost all the *Sonderkommandos* and replacing them with new arrivals at intervals of approximately three months. Since the inception of the *Sonderkommando* through to the liquidation of the camp, there existed approximately 14 generations of *Sonderkommando* victims.

On October 7, 1944, the *Sonderkommando* attacked the SS and Kapos with two machine guns, axes, knives and grenades. Some of the

Sonderkommando escaped from the camp, but they were recaptured later. A total of 451 *Sonderkommandos* were killed on that day.

A few dozen out of several thousand members of the special squads survived until liberation and were able to testify to the events.

The *Sonderkommando* were always a subject of considerable controversy. Other prisoners often viewed them as collaborators. The horrors and moral dilemmas faced by the *Sonderkommando* have been the subject of many historians, authors, and cinematographers. Primo Levi, in *The Drowned and the Saved*, asked his readers to refrain from condemnation: "Therefore I ask that we meditate upon the story of 'the crematorium ravens' with pity and rigor, but that judgment of them be suspended."

Swiss Banks

None of the countries in which Hitler purchased strategic materials was willing to accept Reichsmarks or, in many cases, German gold because of its suspicious origin. But they were willing to accept Swiss gold or Swiss francs. The Swiss role in the financing of the war was in taking gold (mostly looted) and converting it into hard currency Swiss francs. The Reichsbank had a deposit account with the SNB and bars of looted gold traveled by trucks from Germany to Bern. The gold flow from Germany continued throughout the war, in spite of the Allies' warning against accepting the Nazi money because of its criminal origin. The last truckload of gold was delivered on April 6, 1945.

Hitler had specially arranged units that specialized in robbing banks, companies and individual possessions for gold and silver, jewelry and currency. He emptied the central banks of the countries he occupied and transferred gold and jewelry from the concentration camps to the German Reichsbank. According to the Swiss Bergier Report, the estimated value of the gold that went to Switzerland was about $4 billion — of which $2.7 to $2.8 billion was stolen. More than $2.6 billion in Nazi gold reached suppliers in Portugal, Spain, Sweden and Turkey during the war. Three-quarters of this amount was transferred from Germany through the Swiss National Bank.

Topf and Sons

Topf and Sons was the company that designed and built crematoria ovens for concentration camps and extermination camps during the Holocaust. The company not only made crematoria ovens, it also made ventilation systems for the gas chambers at Auschwitz-Birkenau. In 1951, Topf founded a new company, in Wiesbaden, to make crematoria and refuse incinerators. He used the old family firm's name, J.A. Topf & Sons, hoping to capitalize on its good reputation prior to World War II. However, in 1957 the book *Macht ohne Moral* (*Power without Morals*) was published, containing photographs of piles of bodies and crematoria at various concentration camps. It also includes transcripts of two documents from the original Topf company, making its collaboration with the SS clear. The company went bankrupt in May 1963.

In 1959 the state prosecutors in Frankfurt reopened investigations into Topf. Two further legal proceedings followed in 1962 but neither resulted in a formal charge. Ernst Topf died in 1979. He never made any apology for the company's involvement with the Nazi regime.

(The) Yad Vashem Museum and Early Israeli Attitude Towards Holocaust

In 1953, the Knesset, Israel's Parliament, established the Yad Vashem as the Martyrs' and Heroes' Remembrance Authority. The debate on the nature of Yad Vashem began immediately and provoked a sharply defined split between a group of researchers who were born in Israel, or had arrived here before the Holocaust, and a group of researchers who were Holocaust survivors. The survivor historians wanted research that dealt with the difficult questions that the Holocaust raised. The "establishment group" comprised of graduates of the Hebrew University and headed by the chairman of the Yad Vashem directorate, Prof. Ben-Zion Dinur, related to the Holocaust as an historical event that was a direct result of the Diaspora. The conflict between the two groups in effect paralyzed research: Yad Vashem only managed to publish two books by 1960, only one of which dealt with the Holocaust.

The conflict largely mirrored the attitudes of the society as a whole: many Israelis wanted to separate themselves from the "weak Jews" who died without a fight. They were supposed to be very different from Jews in the diaspora. To quote Tom Segev: "At the beginning, in the first years of Israel, the Holocaust was a taboo. Parents didn't tell their children about their experiences and their children wouldn't dare to ask. A great silence surrounded the Holocaust. That began to change in the 1960s with the trial of Adolf Eichmann. For the first time, people started to find an audience for the terrible things they had gone through. Until then, most Israelis refused to listen." Many survivors were viewed as likely collaborators. David mentions Hirsh Barenblatt, the conductor of the Israel National Opera who in 1964 was sentenced to five years imprisonment on charges of collaborating with the Nazis. He was later acquitted by the Israel Supreme Court.

The distribution of power within Yad Vashem tended in favor of the establishment. The survivors were for the most part employed in mid-level and junior positions, while most of the senior positions were in the hands of veteran Israelis. In 1959, Dinur was forced to resign and Yad Vashem's agenda slowly began to change.

(The) ZS Office

The Central Office of the State Justice Administrations for the Investigation of National Socialist Crimes (German: *Zentrale Stelle der Landesjustizverwaltungen zur Aufklärung nationalsozialistischer Verbrechen* or German: *Zentrale Stelle* or German: *Z Commission*) in Ludwigsburg is Germany's main agency responsible for investigating war crimes during Nazi rule. The commission possesses the largest collection of files, documentation and materials concerning criminal activities during Nazi rule. It was formed in December of 1958 and was instrumental in enabling the 1960s Nazi trials in West Germany, such as the Frankfurt Auschwitz trial.

Zmiyevskaya Balka

Referenced in Yosef Milman's story: Zmiyovskaya Balka, which means "the ravine of the snakes", is the site in Rostov-on-Don, Russia,

454

where which 27,000 Soviet civilians, predominantly Jews, were massacred by the SS Einsatzgruppe D on August 11-12, 1942.

LIST OF CHARACTERS

It can be difficult to navigate all the characters in a complex story. If you ever get "lost," here is a short guide listed alphabetically by first names.

(Bishop) Alfonse Hulda
The pro-Nazi priest who ran "ratlines." See the Commentary.

Anna Burkov (Krentz)
Arno's daughter. Born in 1943. Teacher in St. Petersburg.

Aram Arutiyan (real name: Gor Grigorian)
Avi's grandfather, David's friend; Nouvart's brother, Ruben's brother-in-law. Part of Nemesis (see Commentary). Editor, publisher.

Arno - Hans Werner "Arno" Krentz (Prinz)
The SS officer who saved Yosef. Son of Rose Haufmann.

Avi Arutiyan
Aram Arutiyan's grandson. Inherited the house that Aram purchased thirty years ago and discovered a valise with letters from David to Aram.

Benny Hadan
Hannah's friend. Worked for Mossad. Used David to obtain information about German rocket scientists.

Bruno Huber
In 1965 was a police detective in Bonn. Investigated the death of Aram, Avi's grandfather.

David Levy
The author of the letters to Aram Arutiyan. Auschwitz survivor. In 1961, David was a researcher in Yad Vashem. Yosef Milman came to him with the story of how Yosef was saved by the SS officer called Arno.

Dov Cohen
David's boss at Yad Vashem.

Ekrem Celik (Ahmet Yavuz)
The murderer of Erzurum, commanded the "butcher battalion." Escaped to Germany to avoid punishment. Was protected by the Klopher family. Went back to Turkey in 1937 as a German agent. Smuggled chromium ore to Germany. After the war used Nazi bank accounts to support escaping Nazis and terrorists.

Elam Fishel
News junky in the moshav.

Erich Rolff
SS officer who sent Ezra's family to Auschwitz. See the Commentary.

Erika Jager
West German journalist. David's lover.

Esther Arutiyan
Vrej's second wife, Avi's mother.

Ezra Klaudia
David's friend and protector. Died in Auschwitz.

Fritz Jager
West German lawyer. Erika's brother, David's friend.

Gerhardt Schrumpf
West German private investigator. Worked for Shimon, became David's friend.

Hannah
David's friend, Auschwitz' survivor. Worked for Israeli Foreign Ministry.

Dr. Hans Schawik
SS-Hauptsturmführer (captain) and medical officer in Auschwitz. Ezra was organizing gold for Schawik; in return, Schawik protected Ezra and David.

Dr. Hans Vogel
SS Officer. Served in the same *Einsatzgruppen* as Arno. Helped to hide the truth in 1942. Blackmailed the Klophers.

Hersh Pozner
David's friend, Auschwitz' survivor. Worked on a moshav near Jaffa, grew oranges. Convinced David to come work with him.

Iris Goldfarb
Daughter of Yael and David. Iris tries to find her father.

Itzhak
David's rival for Yael's attention.

Jacob Broder
David's friend, a survivor of Dachau where he was subjected to experiments with air altitude and freezing.

Karl Becker
West German industrialist, former SS officer. Modeled on Kurt Becher – see the Commentary.

Leon Chorsky
David's friend, Auschwitz' survivor. A black marketeer and an arms dealer.

Lilly Krentz
Arno's wife and Anna's mother. Saved in Konigsberg by Sergei Burkov, married him in 1946.

Maurice
David's friend, Auschwitz' survivor. Wife killed as a part of the skeleton collection.

Lia Klaudia
Ezra's daughter. In Auschwitz was selected for the whorehouse. Infected with syphilis, killed.

Nouvart Matusian nee Grigorian
Ruben's wife, Aram's sister. Survivor of the Armenian Genocide.

Otto Klopher
High-ranking German banker. A *de facto* guardian of Arno.

Peter Klopher
Otto's brother. Vice-Consul in Erzurum (Turkey) in 1915-16. Connected to Ekrem Celik.

Phil Baier
Senior attorney in Ludwigsburg. Investigated Nazi crimes. See Commentary.

Rose Haufmann
Arno's mother. A nurse with a German occupational force in 1918 Ukraine. Saved Aron Milman's life.

Rachel Milman, nee Isenberg
Yosef's wife, Yael's sister.

Rivka Milman
Yosef's and Rachel's daughter, Iris's cousin and a friend. Avi's love interest.

Ruben Matusian
Member of Lebanese parliament from ARF. Aram's brother. Seeks revenge on the perpetrators of the Armenian Genocide but wants to operate within the bounds of the law.

Sarkis Arutiyan
Aram's younger son. Was a member of ASALA. In jail in the 1980s, died in 1991, left the house to Avi.

Shimon Bezor
Officially in West Germany as a psychologist to help with compensation claims. Unofficially, buying weapons for the IDF.

Tigran Arutiyan
Vrej's older son, Avi's half-brother (different mother). Died in a bomb explosion in Lebanon in 1979.

Van Matusian
Ruben's son.

Vrej Arutiyan
Aram's older son. Avi's father. Did not agree with father's and brother's politics.

Wolfgang von Eckner
A bureaucrat in West German Foreign Office in the 1960's.

Yael Isenberg
Yosef's sister-in-law and David's love interest. Iris's mother. Moved to the US and married Jonathan Goldfarb.

Yosef Milman
In 1942, saved by a German officer and taken to Palestine. Approached David in 1961 in order to look for the officer.

Zakhary Lorens
Second husband of Rose (1935-42). Pro-Nazi scientist. See the Commentary.

I love to get feedback from my readers. Please consider leaving a review on Amazon and/or Goodreads. Thank you!

Made in the USA
Middletown, DE
28 September 2020